181 Days

Jasmine Cartwright

Dream Writer Publishing

Playlists

Apple Music

Spotify

Dedication

To you.

The person choosing everyone else, even when it hurts.

The person crying out for help, but no one is listening.

The person taking on more than they can handle.

The person stepping up to others' responsibilities.

The person who knows their path, but is afraid to walk it.

The person who knows that it's never too late.

FOREWARNING

Before you embark on Mischa and Jesse's journey through the pages of this novel, I feel it is my responsibility to provide a forewarning. Within these chapters lie themes that may evoke strong emotions, some of which might be distressing or triggering for certain individuals. The most prevalent among these triggering themes is the subject of suicidal ideation.

This novel also explores themes such as unmanaged mental health disorders, sexual assault, rape shaming, racism, and children who are forced into the position of head of household. The characters navigate difficult circumstances and adversity. Within this book, there are scenes depicting violence, abuse, and psychological distress. Through years of research, I have attempted to approach this story intending to portray such topics with honesty and sensitivity, aiming to illuminate the complexities of the human condition.

It is my sincerest hope that, while reading this story, you find moments of empathy, reflection, and understanding. However, if you find yourself feeling overwhelmed or distressed by the content, I encourage you to take a break and prioritize your well-being. Your mental and emotional health is paramount. Remember, as readers, we each bring our own experiences and sensitivities to the stories we encounter. I ask that you please proceed with mindfulness and self-awareness.

Thank you for choosing to explore this story with me. May it provoke thought, inspire introspection, and resonate with your spirit.

"Our lives are like the wind... or like sounds.

We come into being, resonate with each other...

Then fade away."

—Hayao Miyazaki

Chapter One

181

I'll start by warning you not to get too attached to me. I'm going to die.

I'm a lot luckier than most people. I already know my death date. Others aren't so fortunate. It kind of just... happens.

Like my father, Shannon Lawrence. He had no idea he would be traveling down the same two-lane highway as a truck driver who had been driving for ten hours straight with no rest. The short version? The driver fell asleep just as he was about to pass by my dad's car and hit him head-on. My dad was dead on impact.

I never met my paternal grandmother, but they say she was the sweetest woman you'd ever met. She died from breast cancer the year before I was born. I'm sure she was aware that she would eventually succumb to the disease, but the exact moment of her expiration was unknown to her. She did not know exactly *when* she would die.

I do.

I watched a news story once with my mom and siblings. Well, actually, the kids and I watched the TV in bed with my mom while she stared at the screen, completely disconnected from the world. It's how we bond, apparently. Anyway, some maniac stood up in the middle of a packed movie theater and began shooting. Forty people were injured and fourteen died. While watching the reporter interview survivors, I wondered if those fourteen people had a feeling that it was their final day. Did they wake up that morning sensing that it would be the last day of their lives? And if so, would they have spent it differently?

181 days.

That's how long I have to live. No cancer or terminal illness. No car wrecks or mass murderers. Just me.

"Mischa."

181 days.

I feel Fergal behind me, appearing seemingly out of nowhere, like always. Following me around and filling my head with nonsense. He's so annoying.

"Mischa."

That's one person I'll be glad to be away from when I'm gone. He's so snarky and a know-it-all. His cockney accent is like nails on a chalkboard. I wish he'd find someone else to attach himself to. I guess he's good company on lonely nights, though. Not that I have a lot of those.

"MISCHA LAWRENCE!" Fergal fades away when I turn around. He's replaced by Sheriff Freeman, dressed in full regalia. Tan shirt and a chocolate-brown tie that matches his creased pants. He's approaching me from his squad car, which is parked on the side of 120. I shrug at him and continue walking.

"Nope, uh-uh Mischa. Not today." He doesn't raise his voice this time, just chuckles. He's being patient with me. He's always overly patient with me. "It's your first day back, and you're already going to be late," he announces, as if I don't know that already. As if going to school was even remotely on my list of things to do today.

"I'm just going for a morning walk, officer," I mock him, using a sugary southern accent I picked up from some movie. I even throw in a curtsy, which looks lovely thanks to the A-line hem on my fabulous polka dot pinup dress. My red heels click on the pavement as I continue to walk away from him.

"Get in the car, Mischa!" *Oh! He's losing his patience.* "I'm not going to say it again." I look back at him to gauge his mood. He uses his index finger to push his reflective aviators up the bridge of his nose. He's a tall, slender man. Standing there with his hands on his hips, he looks like a straight line.

I sigh and roll my eyes behind my own Jackie Os. "Fine."

We take the long ride down the secluded road that leads back into town. I ride shotgun because I'm not under arrest. Plus, the cramped backseat would wrinkle my dress. I have to look my best for my grand resurgence in a school full of peers who hate me.

I stare out of the window of the patrol car at the town I call home. It's not very impressive. Just one main road that leads straight through town from a remote road off CA-120. It continues up into the wooded mountain overlooking the shops, diners, and three buildings that house the only elementary, middle, and high schools in town.

Grover, California. Current Population: 603.

Population in 181 days: 602.

Fergal laughs at my thought from the backseat, his yellowish teeth on full display through the metal grate dividing us. I don't tell him to shut up, because I know it'll upset Sheriff Freeman.

Freeman passes the police station and honks at the overweight officers loitering outside, doing absolutely nothing of the productive sort. We have to pass the elementary school and the middle school before we arrive at Grover High School, home of the Mighty Douchebags! I mean... Mountain Cats. The Mighty Mountain Cats...

I'm convinced that these people hate me more than I hate them, but I haven't really been taking tabs.

Sheriff Freeman insists on escorting me straight to class. I've already missed the first forty-five minutes of my first period. When Mr. Thomlin motions for us to come in, I let Freeman enter first before I saunter in with my chin held high. It's mid-October of my senior year of high school, and I'm just now starting my first day. I recognize every face in the room, but I pay them no regard. They aren't my friends.

I hear a few kids snickering and a couple of them whisper, *"What is she wearing?"* I dress the way I feel, and today I feel upbeat and beautiful. I feel like I'm riding on clouds. Tomorrow may be a different story.

Freeman clears his throat as I take the empty seat next to the window at the far end of the classroom. He winks at me and then turns to exit the classroom.

I notice he gives a quick nod to his son, Trey, who is sitting in the first column of desks with his fellow popular peers.

In Grover, you can count on one hand the number of Black families that live in the town. Sheriff Freeman, his wife, and their children are one of the few. Grandpa and I don't count since we're outnumbered in our house. Plus, no one in Grover even knows Grandpa exists. Mom always says Freeman is the most respected person in town because he's such a kind man, to which Joe always tosses in a joke about affirmative action. Joe is an asshole, but we'll get to that later.

"Ms. Lawrence, your surprising attendance has tipped the scales of equality," Mr. Thomlin quips with a weary smile. "We were just about to split into pairs for the midterm project. But since we now have one too many, one lucky group will have a third member."

"Trust me, I tried my damnedest not to come today." I deadpan.

Mr. Thomlin grunts. "Well, class, just give me a moment to reconfigure some things."

"Maybe it would be best to just let *Mee-sha* work in a group of her own," Alyssa Slade says, purposely mispronouncing my name.

My name is Mischa. Like Trisha with an *M*. And I know it's a stupid name, but it's my name. Alyssa Slade knows that. We've known each other since I moved to Grover. She's just being her usual bitchy self, so what's the point in blowing my high over her?

"While I'm sure everyone would agree, Miss Slade, I can't do that. So please, no more comments," Mr. Thomlin responds.

Gee, thanks a lot, Teach...

I'm not surprised by Mr. Thomlin's attitude toward me. Most of the adults in Grover despise me just as much as their children do. You'd think they'd be a little more discreet about it—being adults and whatnot—but everywhere I go in this town, I'm subject to snide remarks and disgusted glances from teenagers and grown-ups alike.

All because I'm *"strange."*

Oh, and that whole party situation freshman year...

I guess you could say that's when it all started.

The class breaks off into a quiet banter, no longer focusing on my presence, while Thomlin reconfigures his master plan of splitting twenty-one students into pairs. Because it's *that* hard to figure out. Maybe he's trying to figure out which two unlucky souls get to take me on as a third wheel.

Fergal is outside of the window. He's just standing there, grinning like the Cheshire Cat. As soon as that comparison leaves my mind, he gradually fades away, leaving behind only his elongated smile.

Thomlin stands up and hobbles back to the front of the class, clearing his throat to get our attention again. I don't bother giving him mine. Fergal is outside the window again. This time he's miming. Stuck in an invisible box. Thomlin reads off the pairs, and everyone either claps excitedly because they have been paired with their friend, or they groan in agony from being partnered with one of the lames.

"Jesse and Neil, congratulations. You'll have a third partner. You're with Lawrence," Thomlin announces last, and there is snickering amongst the peanut gallery. I'm still not paying attention. Fergal has escaped the invisible box and is now attempting to moonwalk outside the window.

He always stays outside of the school, never coming inside.

Chapter Two

"**W**here were you all day, bitch?"

My best friend Zoey calls me profanities as terms of endearment. She's technically my *only* friend, so by default, she's my best friend. Fergal doesn't count for obvious reasons.

"I didn't see you at school at all," she continues, hovering over me as I stock cans. "The only reason I knew you were back is because of Alyssa."

I roll my eyes and continue stocking. During the week, I spend four hours stocking cans and working the cash register at Brady's General Store after school. At six o'clock, Mr. Brady will come in, tell me that things are getting slow—it's always slow—and that I should head home. He'll give me twenty dollars' worth of groceries to take home for dinner tonight. We both know what he's really saying. *"Mischa, it's time for you to go home and cook dinner for your family because your mother is probably still lying in bed in her never-ending slump."* I won't complain, though. Mr. Brady is one of the few people who treats me like a human being.

"I didn't really feel like being seen," I tell Zoey without looking at her. "Still don't."

I'm positive she just rolled her eyes. "Whatever. You've been gone for like four months. I missed you." She's chewing bubblegum and making an occasional *'pop'* sound as she talks. She doesn't bother asking where I've been. She knows I won't tell her. I never do.

Zoey keeps holding a conversation with me, even though I'm not being very receptive. "How was your first day?" I shrug, standing up and smoothing the wrinkles on my dress. "Cute dress, by the way. Killer heels too!"

"Freeman forced me to come to school today, so I walked into first period just in time to be paired with Neil and Jesse for some traveling project." I ignore her compliment. I don't dress up for compliments. I got dressed up today because a voice in my brain told me I feel like a 1950s pinup.

That same voice in my head tells me that April 14th will be the perfect day to die.

"Jesse *Alford*?" Zoey's eyes pop out. I walk past her with the empty box that needs to be broken down and recycled and toss it toward the side door.

"The one and only," I shoot back dryly. Zoey follows me behind the cash register and sits on the bar stool that's normally reserved for the actual employee operating the register, AKA *me*, leaving me to lean against the counter.

"Hubba, Hubba!" She does this stupid shimmy dance and wiggles her eyebrows.

"Be my guest." I frown at her in disgust. "You guys *are* part of the elite crew, right?"

"Jesse isn't my type, and being popular doesn't make us elitists," she huffs. "You make it sound like we're better than other people."

"No, *they* make it seem like they're better than other people," I shoot back with a snort.

Even though Zoey is my closest friend—despite everyone telling her she's crazy for hanging out with me—she's still one of the popular kids. The Elites, I call them. Alyssa Slade, Chelsea Bright, Zoey Hall, Preston Wilcox, Trey Freeman, Nick Gillespie, and Jesse Alford are the poster children for Grover's elitism.

"Jesse's tolerable, though, right?" Zoey asks me as a customer walks in. It's Mrs. Gillespie, Nick Gillespie's mom. Zoey and Nick had a *thing* last year. "I mean, he's not an asshole like Preston or Nick." She's being loud on purpose, and Mrs. Gillespie shoots her a death glare.

"I guess he's never personally victimized me." I refrain from laughing at Mrs. Gillespie, and quote one of my favorite movies, *Mean Girls*.

"Alyssa's just jealous of you." Zoey pops her gum and inspects her nails. Before I can ask her how someone like Alyssa "Queen Bee" Slade would be jealous of me, she finishes her statement with, "Because you're cuter than her."

I snort. Like for real snort. Not with fake sarcasm. "Since when?"

"Since you moved here during middle school, and Jesse was the deciding vote in Alyssa's stupid poll of who was prettier, you or her." She winks at me. Zoey, with her glowing dark-brown skin and heart-shaped face, would put Alyssa and me both to shame.

"Oh, yeah, I almost forgot about that," I reply sarcastically. That was the day that Alyssa branded me with this big red target on my back. "Preston told me I was a lying repulsive piece of shit today. He's getting creative. Using bigger words."

"Well, you *did* almost send his older brother to jail with your lies," Mrs. Gillespie chimes in as she sets her items on the counter.

Zoey leans forward and grabs the box of tampons that are among her selections. "Aww, is Nicky having his first period?" she mocks in a baby voice.

Mrs. Gillespie glares at her, and I have to fight to contain my laughter. Mr. Brady has already warned me about poor customer service too many times. Mrs. Gillespie pays for her items and leaves the store in a rush. I'm sure she'll tell Mr. Brady how terrible I was to her. She'll leave out the part where she rape-shamed me.

"I can't believe I lost my virginity in the back of that woman's minivan," Zoey sneers.

"Doesn't Nick have a truck?" I ask her, scrunching my face. Like Preston Wilcox, Nick Gillespie is your typical asshole jock. Zoey was crazy about him for all of six months before meeting her current boyfriend, Anthony, who lives in Phoenix.

"Yeah, but he said his truck would be too cramped." She shrugs.

I shake my head and dismiss all thoughts of Zoey and Nick getting busy in the back of Mrs. Gillespie's minivan. I've got half an hour left of solace before

Mr. Brady comes in to dismiss me. Then, it's up the trail to the madhouse after I collect the Littles.

"So, you haven't been around to hear the news..." Zoey trails off, and I hear a hint of nervousness in her voice.

"What news?" I ask her curiously. She's finger-combing her neatly pressed hair, causing it to fuzz at the roots and stick out. She's hesitant about telling me whatever she's about to tell me.

"I'm doing this exchange program."

"Exchange program?" I furrow my brow.

"Yeah, I stay with this host family and attend a private school in their area," she explains. "I still get to transfer my grades here and come back for graduation. But it gets me a free ride to whatever college I want in SoCal."

"Where is the host family?" I ask her, feigning disinterest. On the inside, I'm feeling weird. I hear snickering and look down aisle three. Fergal is there, laughing at my plight.

"San Diego," she tells me sheepishly. My heart thumps hard, and now Fergal is rolling on the floor with laughter.

I swallow my emotions and try to ignore him. "You don't seem too excited."

"Oh, I am." She smiles genuinely. "I'll only be five hours away from Ant. He said he'll visit every other weekend from his college."

"But..." I already know what her hesitation is about. Me.

"I hate that I'm leaving you here. In this town, with these fucked up people," she tells me, looking out the window at Main Street. The venom in her voice tells me that she's seriously concerned about me. She's oblivious to everything about me, though. She has no idea how easy her departure will be for me. With my only real physical friend gone, there's one less thing keeping me from going through with my plan on April 14th. Zoey's absence will make things so much simpler. Fewer ties holding me here.

"I'll be fine. You just make sure you don't get pregnant out there," I half-joke. Zoey met Anthony at a party in San Francisco last Halloween. They've been in love with each other since. He's a freshman in college, and she thinks he's so mature. She rolls her eyes at me, just as Mr. Brady walks into the store.

"I heard you girls were very pleasant to Velma Gillespie," he greets us with playful sarcasm.

"She started it." I shrug at him.

"Welcome back," he tells me with a laugh. The brown skin around his eyes folds in as he smiles at me. He's an elderly Black man, with dark gray hair and a wrinkling face covered in moles and freckles.

I give Mr. Brady the rundown on all the stocking I did today, and he tells me to take the day-old pasta and tomato sauce and make spaghetti for the Littles. I grab a package of ground beef out of the freezer and a bottle of fruit punch to complete the necessities for dinner.

Once we're outside, Zoey hugs me. "You need help with the Littles?" she asks me, even though she knows I'll refuse.

"No, go home and call your boyfriend," I tell her with a smile.

She looks at me for a few seconds, pity in her eyes. "You should be going home and calling *your* boyfriend. Not taking care of your siblings and grandfather because your mom's a vampire and your stepdad's a deadbeat drunk piece of shit."

I want to tell her she's wrong. In order for my mom to be a vampire, she'd have to sleep during day and then actually wake up and move around at night. Not sleep the entire day or stay holed up in her room in a funk of depression, while her children run wild in this judgmental little town.

"Well, that's life," I tell her with another shoulder lift. "Besides. Boys are icky." We laugh together, and I promise her I'll find her at lunch tomorrow since we don't have any classes together. Then, I go on my usual routine of strutting through town, corralling the Littles so that we can head home.

The Littles are my younger half-siblings. The three children my mother had with Joe after she and my father split. I call them the Littles because *Little* is their last name, and they're significantly younger than me.

I can always find my sister Frankie outside of the arcade with the local middle school boys. She's twelve going on twenty-one and in this boy-crazy stage.

"Francesca, where is your brother?" I ask her in my sternest voice. She sucks her teeth and rolls her eyes, ignoring me in favor of giving her attention to one of her classmates. He'll be acne-ridden in a year, and she won't think he's so cool.

"Frankie, let's go!" I yell at her. "I've got to start dinner."

"Your sister is such a freak," Future Pimple-Face tells her with a laugh.

"Shut your mouth before I slit your throat, you little skid mark!" I scream at him. I'm not really mad, but if I embarrass Frankie enough, she'll follow me without a fight.

"Ugh!" She groans and bids her friends farewell. She's tall and skinny, like Joe, but pretty like our mother used to be. Because of our different fathers and ethnicities, we look nothing alike.

"Where's Teddy?" I ask her. She's walking behind me with her arms crossed and her lip poked out. It must suck having the town's aberration for an older sister. She doesn't respond, just points to Oldham's bookstore. Our little brother's favorite place to hide.

Theodore is eight years old, and the sweetest, most-timid kid you'll ever meet. That being said, he's an easy target for these quintessential small-town bullies. So, he spends his four hours of after-school time hiding in the old bookstore on Main Street. I finger-whistle once we're standing outside of the store. After thirty seconds, Teddy comes rushing out of the building, both of his skinny hands clutching the straps on his backpack.

"Hey Mischa, how was school?" Teddy greets me excitedly as he falls into place behind Frankie, who is standing behind me with her nonexistent hip jutted out and her arms folded across her chest.

"It sucked. How was your day?" Unlike Frankie, Teddy treats me like I'm a doting big sister. The apple of his eye, even when I'm short with him.

"It was okay. Tommy Brinkler pushed me on the playground," he tells me, and I note the hint of sadness.

"Did you punch him in his face?" I ask him. Tommy Brinkler and his crew of mouth breathers have been bullying my little brother since kindergarten. It's one thing for this town to persecute me. Teddy doesn't deserve it.

"You already know he didn't," Frankie replies with attitude.

"Fighting is prohibited in school. You know that," Teddy tells us, and I can picture him pushing his glasses up on his nose with his index finger. I'm sure his magnifying glass spectacles don't help his case.

"Well, until you fight back, Tommy Brinkler and his band of shit stains are going to keep kicking your ass." I shrug. I can't see his face, since he's behind me and Frankie, but I'm sure he looks pathetic right now.

Our last stop is to pick up the youngest of the bunch, Madeline, from the Bradys' house at the end of town. Mrs. Brady—who is obviously the wife of Mr. Brady—babysits five-year-old Maddie for me after kindergarten lets out. Maddie comes out of the old, wooden house and falls in line behind Teddy, and like the mother goose leading her goslings, I guide my siblings on the path to home.

Most of Grover's population lives in town, in the three neighborhoods surrounding Main Street. My family lives in a secluded house off of a winding path near the foot of the mountain that overlooks the east end of town.

The perfect location to hide a house full of secrets.

Chapter Three

It's easy to fall back into my nightly routine of cooking dinner and getting the Littles ready for bed. I've been doing it since I was eleven years old. It's basically second nature at this point.

I have already begged Frankie five times to get off the phone and help me. Maddie needs a bath, and I need to finish dinner and help Teddy with his math homework. Then, there's Grandpa.

"First day home and you're already back to raising these little hellions," my paternal grandfather, Henry Lawrence, comments gruffly from his usual spot, parked in the living room in front of the TV. Frankie sucks her teeth at him and rolls her eyes, still chatting away on the phone.

"Frankie, I need you to give Maddie a bath, *now!*" I remind her one last time. She huffs and tells whoever she's talking to that she'll see them tomorrow at school.

"Just because *you* don't have a social life doesn't mean you have to ruin everyone else's," she tells me, placing her hands on her waist.

"*I* don't have a social life because *I'm* always taking care of *you!*" I shoot back.

"Lies!" she sings as she makes her way toward the bathroom. "You don't have a social life because everyone thinks you're a *freak.*" Her words don't bother me. I'm just happy she's finally doing what I asked. Good help is impossible to find around here.

"I don't think you're a freak, Mischa," Teddy assures me from his place at the kitchen table.

"Thanks, Teddy. Now finish your homework." I give him a half-smile. My pot of water is finally boiling on the stove, so I pour the pasta in before dispensing the ground beef into the iron skillet to brown.

"Grandpa, have you taken your meds today?" I call to him over my shoulder as I attack the crumbling beef with my spatula.

He snorts. "Have you?"

"Yeah, I have actually." *No, I haven't.* "I take my meds every day, you know that."

What I actually mean is: *"I flush my pills down the toilet every morning when I wake up."*

"You know damn well that no-good mama of yours ain't woke up today," he tells me. That means he hasn't had his daily medications today.

Grandpa has to rely on his wheelchair to get around the house, which isn't very accessible. He takes seven pills a day, and with my mom constantly barricading herself in her bedroom, it's up to me to make sure he takes them.

"Be nice, Grandpa," I murmur. "It's not her fault. She's just sad."

"She wasn't too sad!" he huffs. "She laid around and had all these damn kids she can't take care of. I told Shannon about messin' with that white woman! I knew she wasn't worth a plug nickel!"

"Grandpa!" I snap through gritted teeth. "Not in front of Teddy!" I look back at my little brother to make sure he's more focused on his math sheet than my grandpa's insensitive words about our mother.

Grandpa completely ignores me. "I told him to marry a nice Black woman, but then he brings home Michelle. Your Grandma Sheryl was a real woman. Hardworking and knew how to rear children. She managed the hell out of our household whenever I was out on duty!" Everything this man says comes out mean, but I wouldn't change him for the world.

"Enough!" I cut him off, grabbing one of his nutrition shakes from the fridge and bringing it to him. "Drink this."

"Drinking a damn chocolate milk for dinner," he grumbles as I poke a straw through the lip of the can. "I want some red meat and potatoes."

"That's not good for your heart, Grandpa," I remind him and then go back to my spaghetti. I peek over Teddy's shoulder to make sure he's not making any mistakes. He's a smart kid, but sometimes he needs a little guidance. "Make sure you're writing those numbers neatly so your teacher can read them," I tell him before returning to the stove to make the sauce.

I'm putting my makeshift garlic bread in the oven when Maddie comes bolting through the living room completely naked. A nonchalant Frankie trailing behind her.

"Maddie, stop before you slip! What the hell, Frankie?" I yell at my sisters.

"She jumped out of the tub and started running around naked." Frankie shrugs and flops down on the couch again, this time grabbing the remote.

"Well, can you please get her dressed?" I'm fighting the urge to throw my spatula at her.

"No, I can't," she responds matter-of-factly, completely engulfed in the trashy reality show on the TV screen. I sigh and scoop up a slippery Maddie, carrying her into the bedroom she shares with Teddy.

"When you leave, I'm moving into your room with Frankie," my baby sister tells me as I slip her nightgown over her head. I'm sure she'll spill spaghetti sauce all over herself in a few minutes, but the four of us share a bathroom, so the earlier I can get bathtime started, the easier life is for me.

"What do you mean when I leave?" No one knows about April 14th, especially not my five-year-old sister.

"I saw your marbles in the fishbowl. You're counting down until you leave again, right?" My stomach lurches at her words.

"Why were you digging through my stuff?" I frown at her. I keep the fishbowl in the back of my dresser, in the room I share with Frankie. I keep it hidden so Mom doesn't grow suspicious during the rare moments she gets out of bed and roams the house.

"I was looking for my Lambie." She pouts, looking completely guilty.

"Why would your Lambie be in *my* drawer?" I ask her with a skeptical look. She shrugs and holds her hands out. She's so cute with her chubby cheeks and bright blue eyes.

"So, do I get to take your room with Frankie when you're gone?" she asks me again, and I can't help but laugh.

"Sure." I nod and run my fingers through her bangs.

The overwhelming smell of burning bread fills my nostrils, and I shoot up and bolt back into the kitchen. Black smoke is rising from the oven, and Frankie is still casually flipping through channels.

"Seriously Frankie?" I huff as I grab a baking mitt and pull the cookie sheet holding the burned sandwich bread out of the oven. "Would it kill you to help me out around here?"

She doesn't even bother looking my way. "I'm twelve. It's not my job to help you out."

I want to run over and smack her. I think about what my life was like at twelve. My mom was pregnant with Maddie, and my dad had just died. I was in charge of feeding and looking after Frankie, Teddy, and Grandpa.

"I guess we won't be having bread with dinner," I mumble to myself. "Teddy, go into the living room until this airs out. I don't want your asthma to act up." Teddy closes his math workbook and walks into the living room and sits opposite Frankie in Joe's cracked leather recliner.

"Are you okay, Grandpa?" I ask him as I walk over to the front door and open it. There's a screen door behind it, and I'm hoping the smoke will filter out while I set the table. I take notice that even with the smell of burning bread, my mom still hasn't bothered to wake up or leave her room. If a fire ever really broke out in the house, I'd be forced to leave her behind while I focus on saving the Littles and Grandpa.

"Fine, baby girl." He reaches out and squeezes my hands reassuringly. I'm not sure if he's trying to reassure me that he is okay, or that I am okay.

I was eleven when my dad died. I was living with him and Grandpa in Monterey. My parents weren't together. My mom was married to Joe and had already had Frankie and Teddy. I lived with my dad because Joe claimed he couldn't stand being around me with my *condition*. I would visit my mom whenever my dad was away on military duty. Even back then, I could tell my mom was different. She was always sad, and when she wasn't sad, she was in a haze. My stays with her were always spent babysitting Frankie and Teddy and staying out of Joe's way.

After my dad died, she got even worse. She was always crying, and Joe was always yelling at her. When I moved in with them, I was surprised to learn that Grandpa was coming too. Mom agreed to take over caring for him. She said she owed it to my father and Grandma Sheryl. Joe only agreed because it brought extra money into the house with Grandpa's social security checks.

At my father's funeral, a man, who I would later know to be Sheriff Freeman, approached my mother with a proposal. He said that he was my father's friend from the military, and that my father had given him special instructions in the event of his death. There was a home in Sheriff Freeman's town that my father purchased for me. It was completely paid for in the wooded area at the foot of the mountain. A few months later, shortly after Maddie was born, Joe lost his job, so my mom moved the family to Grover.

It's a small, three-bedroom manufactured home. The type that sits on a wooden foundation, so you can hear every step a person takes throughout the entire house. There's a deck attached to the exterior with a ramp. It was a beautiful house before we moved in and Mom gave up on the upkeep of things, and Joe started getting drunk and breaking shit, and the Littles started piling up their clutter.

I hear steel toes boots on the porch outside, just before hearing the screen door creak open and then slam shut as if someone just walked through it and let the door fly back. It pulls me from my thoughts, and I realize that I've been dispensing spaghetti on the plates I've set out.

"What in the fuck is that smell?"

Joe is home.

Fergal is sitting at the table now, where Frankie usually sits, and he's laughing at me.

Chapter Four

176

I wake up early Saturday morning to make breakfast for the Littles before I have to go into town to meet up with Jesse and Neil for this stupid history project. I perform my newest ritual of dropping a single marble into a fishbowl every morning since I've been back. The *clink* of the glass orb colliding with the glass bowl is like therapy for my inner thoughts. It's my countdown. One hundred eighty-one marbles for my last one hundred eighty-one days. There are now six marbles in the bowl.

I place the bowl back in my top dresser drawer where I moved it so that Maddie can't find it anymore. I go into the bathroom to shower and brush my teeth. It's seven-thirty in the morning, so the entire house is still sleeping, making it the perfect time to move about freely. After my shower, I go back into my bedroom, wrapped in one of our dingy white bath towels. The towels need to be replaced, but I have to be strategic about where I spend money and when. I stand in the mirror and examine myself, pulling the thick mass of curls that make up my hair into a messy bun on top of my head.

I look nothing like my siblings. They all have pale white skin with straight blonde hair and blue eyes. Blue eyes from our mother and blonde hair from Joe. My hair is an inky-black gathering of wild curls and waves that fall to the middle of my back. My eyes are the darkest shade of brown ever created, but I'm fine with that. They remind me of my father. I got my light-brown complexion from him too. Plus, the Littles look like the kids from that movie *Village of the Damned.*

Grandpa has never gone into town, so no one knows I am one of two Black faces in a house full of white ones. Not that they care. When the people of Grover see me walking down Main with my white siblings, our stark differences are the least of their concerns. They're too preoccupied with their glares and name-calling. Their focus is on me, not them.

I'm feeling pretty badass this morning. Fergal winks at me in the mirror's reflection. I do a little shimmy in my towel for him and turn to my dresser.

"You're so weird, Misch." Frankie's voice is groggy as she rolls out of bed. I ignore her and pull out a pair of cut-off shorts and a half shirt with a California flag logo I bought while hitchhiking in San Francisco last spring.

"What do you want for breakfast?" I ask her once she's back from her morning pee.

"Waffles," she responds as she flops down on her bed. "I can't believe you're hanging out with *Jesse Alford* today!" Her voice goes dreamy at the mention of the name.

I grunt as I slip on my shorts. "I'd hardly call it 'hanging out.' It's a school project."

"But you're going to be riding around in his awesome car!" she swoons, sitting up on her elbows. "Alyssa Slade's going to be so jealous!"

"How do you have so much insight into the happenings of my high school peers?" I roll my eyes at her and pull the crop top over my head.

"You're not wearing a bra?" She wrinkles her nose.

"Nope." I smirk at her as I slip on calf-high, faux leather cowboy boots. I walk out of the room and into the kitchen to start breakfast. Grandpa is up, sitting on the porch watching the world wake up. He has limited mobility outside of his wheelchair. He can handle his own bathroom activities, and get on and off the bed in the utility room, which was converted into a room for him, and into his wheelchair.

"Good morning, Grandpa," I call out to him through the screen. "I can make you eggs and toast. No bacon, though." I know he's going to protest, so we might as well establish it from the start. He's got heart disease and high blood pressure, and his eating limitations are hard on him.

"I'll be damned," I hear him grumble. He says nothing else, so I go into the kitchen and start breakfast.

The Littles all gather at the kitchen table just as I'm plating waffles, scrambled eggs, and bacon. I got the waffle maker for a dollar at a flea market in Stockton. The Littles love it so much, they request breakfast every Saturday morning.

"Frankie, I need you to keep an eye on Maddie for me while I'm gone." I put a small pile of eggs and two slices of toast on a saucer and take it outside to Grandpa.

I hear Frankie huff, and when I walk back into the kitchen, she's sitting with her arms folded. "I'm going to the football game this afternoon. Billy is playing. I *have* to be there."

"I need someone to watch Maddie," I repeat, not really caring about her social status or her need to impress her newest crush.

"We have a mother, you know?" she shoots back with wide eyes for emphasis.

"Yeah, well, you know she's not going to watch Maddie, so I need you to. I'll be back in a few hours. Then you can go to your stupid football game."

My sister huffs and starts eating. I hope she listens to me because we both know our mother isn't very observant in the comings and goings of her children. And Joe...

Joe's going to be gone all day, in the city somewhere, getting drunk.

"I want you two to stay inside," I instruct Teddy and Maddie as they eat their breakfast.

"Where are you going, Sissy?" Maddie asks me. She's only been at the table for two minutes, and her face is already sticky with syrup.

"I have to work on a school project." I tear off a paper towel and dampen it in the sink. I hand it to Maddie. "Use this when you're finished. Teddy, I want you to do the dishes. Frankie will make you PB&J for lunch if I'm not back in time."

Again, Frankie sucks her teeth. "What do you mean, *'if you're not back in time?'* I have to be at that game, Mischa! I can't miss it!"

"I'll be back Frankie, damn," I snap. I go to the fridge and pour Grandpa a glass of orange juice, setting the rest on the table for the Littles to help themselves.

I jog into the bathroom and open the medicine cabinet behind the mirror. I pick up each of Grandpa's bottles and dispense one pill from each in my palm. I look at the other two bottles left on the shelf. My clozapine and mood stabilizer. I take one of each out of their respective bottles and stare at them for a few moments before dropping them in the toilet and flushing.

I make it to the scheduled rendezvous spot ten minutes later than we'd agreed to. Neil and Jesse are standing there, not talking to each other and looking annoyed. We agreed to meet in front of Clement's garage since it's right at the entrance of Grover.

"You're late," Jesse tells me as he leans against his shiny black 1970 Pontiac GTO. He started restoring the old car when we were in the ninth grade, and it's his signature thing. Jesse Alford, the attractive jock with the panty-dropping classic muscle car.

Attractive is an understatement. Jesse is gorgeous. Tall and defined, but with soft facial features. Naturally neat eyebrows, deep-set brown eyes. Full lips and a nose sculpted perfectly for his face. We're about the same complexion. Freshly made caramel sauce as it cools in the jar. His hair is long and curly, usually styled in two-strand twists that stop at his jaw. He's the type of guy whose attractiveness comes from more places than just a perfect face and body. He's got that *"bad boy"* attitude without needing actions to back it up. Right now, his Hershey-colored eyes are fixed on me in disapproval. Even though he's got smooth features, his demeanor is demanding without trying. If I was a normal teenage girl, I'd be tempted to fall to my knees and apologize to him for keeping him waiting.

But I'm not normal.

I am a clinically insane, seventeen-year-old girl. And he's an Elite.

I don't owe him shit.

"Did I keep you boys waiting?" I turn on my sugary Southern belle accent and smile.

Jesse mumbles something under his breath, and Neil stares at me like I've got two heads. I fight the urge to look at my reflection in the car's tinted window because having a second head would be illogical, and I need to keep as clear of a head as possible right now.

"Can we just go, please? I want to end this day as quickly as possible." This isn't cool-guy Jesse talking, it's Neil. Neil, the super nerd who had to go dumpster diving for his retainer last year because Preston thought it would be funny to swipe it off of Neil's lunch tray and toss it in the trash. It was disgusting! The part about Preston touching Neil's slobbery retainer, not the dumpster diving part.

I switch my hips as I walk past Jesse and around to the passenger's seat. I'm not trying to be seductive; I'm just feeling amazing today. I doubt any other girl in town can rock cutoffs quite like me.

"Get in the back," I instruct Neil, who frowns at my harshness but still complies. I flop down on the cool, leather bucket seat, that I've seen Alyssa Slade sit in plenty of times.

Jesse enters his car with a groan. "Okay, so what's the plan?"

Thomlin's group project is to *"Appreciate Northern California."* This means he wants us to use our free time driving around looking for random things about our area that we should appreciate but really don't give a shit about. In three weeks, we're supposed to present our findings in a class presentation. Jesse is the only person in our group who owns a car, so he begrudgingly agreed to cart us around.

"I picked out a few places within a thirty-mile radius," Neil squeaks out from the back seat. He extends his hand out between Jesse and me to show us his list. "Mr. Thomlin said Yosemite National Park is off the table. It's too easy, and he thinks we're being lazy if we pick it."

"Considering Thomlin has never gotten up from his desk to actually walk around while he's teaching a class, I'm sure he knows all about being lazy," I reply sarcastically, and I'm surprised to hear Jesse chuckle.

I read over Neil's list. The first choice catches me off guard. "The Archerville Cultural Festival?"

"It's an arts festival where the entire town celebrates its diverse cultural background," Neil explains. "Archerville is about half an hour west of Grover."

"Archerville it is," Jesse says, expelling a breath and leaning in to turn the car key in the ignition. The car roars to life, and he pulls away from Clement's. Fergal is sitting next to Neil now, but I know better than to acknowledge him.

I'm feeling amazing.

Like I could fly!

I stretch my arms behind my head and prop my feet up on the dashboard as Jesse cruises down the two-lane road that leads to State Highway 120. The window is down, and the wind hitting my face feels incredible. I close my eyes and I'm transported to a place where everything is perfect. My mom is full of life. Joe is somewhere dead under a bridge. My dad is alive, and I don't see things that aren't there or think of things I shouldn't be thinking about.

"Seriously?" Jesse's annoyed tone brings me out of my daydreams. He's looking between me and the road like he's pissed off about something.

"What?" I frown. I note that this is the most amount of words we've spoken to each other in the six years we've been classmates.

He motions to my boot-clad feet, crossed at the ankle, and mounted on his dashboard. "Do you mind *not* putting your feet on the dash?"

I turn my frown into a smirk and giggle a little at him. "Oops, my bad." I slide my feet off of the dash, only to turn my body slightly and prop them on the seal of the window.

"How's that?" I ask, dropping my hands from behind my head to rest across my chest.

"You're determined to make these the longest three weeks possible, aren't you?" He shakes his head and looks back at the road. I only shrug and turn to look out the window. I've walked this stretch of road hundreds of times so that

I can hitchhike 120 into the bigger cities to shop for the Littles... or just to get away.

"I can't believe the fate of my history grade is in the hands of a football jock and the town runaway who's never in school!" Neil groans in the back seat, and I don't think he's talking directly to Jesse or me. Maybe he's talking to Fergal?

No. Only I talk to Fergal.

"Runaway?" I snap my head around and look at him incredulously. I'm leaning closer to Jesse so that I can see Neil from between the two front seats. My bun is almost touching the side of Jesse's face.

"Yes, *you*," Neil confirms, looking me square in my eyes through thick glasses that remind me of Teddy's.

"He's right," Jesse scoffs. "You are always out of school and disappearing for months at a time every year."

I give Jesse a fake smile. "I'm so glad you all noticed!" I say with faux excitement to match. So that's what everyone thinks? That I've run away whenever I'm gone?

"You literally got paired with us after walking into class forty-five minutes late a month and a half into the school year!" Neil is freaking out, and I think if I wasn't on such an emotional high, I'd be offended. "What? Are you doing stints in juvie or something?"

Nope. Beacon Pointe Mental Health Institution, actually.

My countdown was shorter this last time. Only thirty-three days. Fergal says in hindsight that probably wasn't enough time to prepare and get it right. I came home from work that hot June day, sealed up all the windows and doors in the house, and turned on the gas generators. Mom and the Littles were all in the city with Grandpa for one of his monthly appointments, and Joe was God-knows-where doing God-knows-what. So, I had the house to myself to lie in bed and suck in all the carbon monoxide I pleased. Or at least that's what I thought.

I'd been lying in bed for about five minutes when I heard coughing in the hallways. I dismissed it as just a hallucination until Teddy came bursting into my room, crying about not feeling well, and then threw up all over my wooden bedroom floor. I was able to snap out of it and call Sheriff Freeman to rush us to the hospital. I tried to play it off as an accident, but my mom and doctors read right through the lies.

I spent four months locked in a room with a blonde pyromaniac before being released on good behavior. Thinking about the Littles fending for themselves, and my grandpa not being cared for is enough to help me fake being well. Plus, I needed to be out in the world in order to complete my mission.

"Why are you sitting in the front seat if you're not going to navigate?" Neil snaps at me. Jesse is once again looking at me like he wishes I would fall out of the window and get run over by a semi. Maybe that's what I'll do. Go out via semi-truck like my dad.

I must have zoned out again because Jesse's expression tells me I missed the part where he asked me to give him directions. Not that I have a cell phone to navigate with anyway.

I ponder Neil's question and turn to him, producing that sugary smile again. "Because I didn't want to sit in Alyssa Slade's essence." I wink at him and turn to Jesse just in time to hear him make that *'tch'* sound and laugh heartily.

"Woooooow," he drawls in his husky voice. I fight the genuine smile that threatens my face at the triumphant thought that I made Jesse Alford laugh.

"You really are crazy," he finishes, and there's a hint of disgust in his voice, mixed with amusement at my expense. I frown and fold my arms across my chest again, dropping my feet from the window and resting them the proper way on the floorboard.

Yes Jesse, I really am crazy.

Chapter Five

JESSE

The last thing I want to do is spend my Saturday afternoon with Neil Gunderson and Mischa Lawrence. It's all any of my friends wanted to talk about last night after our game. Preston—who harbors a deep-rooted hatred for Mischa ever since she accused his older brother of trying to rape her three years ago—kept making sick comments about our town weirdo, while Alyssa and Chelsea laughed and threw in their hateful remarks. I just sat there and listened. It's bad enough I have to drive around with two of the lamest people in town. I don't need my friends making fun of me for it. I guess Neil isn't *that* bad. He's just your typical nerd. Comic books, science fiction, geometry club, and all that stuff.

But Mischa is a different story.

I haven't spoken many words to her since she first moved here, but she's public enemy number one to most of the town because she walks around like she's the only person who exists, and she dresses weirdly. My dad says it's probably got something to do with her family living in the woods under Mt. Grover.

I shoot her a dirty look when I see the heel of her small boots digging into the vinyl of my dashboard. It's October, and she's wearing these super short cutoffs and a shirt that stops at her rib cage. When I ask her for directions, she doesn't respond. It's like she's a shell of a person, and her mind is somewhere else.

This is why people think she's insane.

When she makes her snarky comment about me and Alyssa in my back seat, I'm almost amused. Annoyance wins the battle. This girl knows nothing about me, yet she's joking about what I do in *my* car. So, I tell her what I'm sure she's heard a million times from my friends, but never from me—*she's crazy.*

That shuts her up for the rest of the ride, and Neil stops complaining about his goddamn grade being in jeopardy. I may be going to college on an athletic scholarship, but I'm not stupid. That's what kids in Grover do. They excel in something, be it sports, academics, or trade. Then, we leave Grover and have bright futures, only returning to visit our families, and maybe to retire.

We arrive in Archerville just as the festival is starting. Without uttering a single word, Mischa walks off on her own. Her shorts stop just under the cuff of her ass, and every man, young and old, doubles back as she walks by and disappears into the crowd. I shake my head and follow Neil in the opposite direction.

There's a large stage in the center of the dying field of grass where the festival is being held. There's a folk band playing now, and tons of people ranging in age walking around with fair food and beer. I catch a few winks from a group of girls that appear to be my age. I smile back politely, even though they're not my type. I think about Alyssa and the other girls in Grover I've dated and wonder if I even *have* a type. If I did, it certainly wouldn't be these Archerville girls.

There are a lot of small towns in the Yosemite National Park area, and every town is different. I've never been to Archerville, but it's kind of like a poor man's Grover.

"For a cultural festival, there sure is a bunch of rednecks here," Neil announces, earning a few dirty looks from the locals. He's not lying, though. I'm not sure what culture they're trying to celebrate, but all I see are a bunch of drunken white guys in tank tops and camo pants. The ones that aren't chain-smoking cigarettes have tobacco tucked between their bottom lip and jaw, and everyone's spitting and looking at us sketchily.

"Let's try not to piss off the locals," I mumble to Neil. We haven't been here twenty minutes and I'm ready to leave already. We walk over to the stage and listen to a few acts, none of them ranging in anything different from the last. Neil's right, this whole *cultural* bit is a sham.

Next, we walk over to the art bazaar. There are only four booths, with about ten pieces of art between them.

"Archerville is kinda known for its abstract expressionalism," a toothless woman tells me as I stare at one of her paintings. She mispronounced *expressionism*, which this painting is *not*. It looks like a toddler's finger painting. I nod at the woman, giving her a weak smile and walking away.

Neil and I are standing near a building that has bathrooms in it when a group of guys approaches us. They're older than us, maybe nineteen or early twenties. They're all smoking cigarettes and holding half-empty beer cups.

"Hey man, you got a lighter?" one of them asks me after bumping into me from the side and hanging his arms around my shoulder.

I shrug him off and step aside a little to get some space. He's wearing a stained white tank top and khaki shorts and has a long reddish beard and a tattered hat with a folded bill.

"Nah, I don't smoke," I tell him. His buddies hover around us. They're dressed identically to him, except one, who is wearing a black tank top. Something is weird about them, considering the guy with the beard is asking for a lighter for a smoke that's already lit.

"That's cool. Straight-lace city boys, huh?" The guy with the beard, who I've dubbed Beardie, chuckles and puffs on the stick again. "What brings you all to the fine town of Archerville?"

"Just checking out the *culture*, man." I motion toward the stage, where a group of women wearing matching spandex dresses are getting ready to perform. I look over at Neil, who looks like he's about to piss his pants, as the other two guys lean against the wall beside him. His phone rings, and he pulls it out to answer it. Before he can put the phone to his ear, the flunky hits Neil's hand, knocking the phone up, and then grabbing it out of mid-air.

"Hey!" Neil protests in disbelief.

"That's a fancy phone you got there." Beardie steps forward. His friend tosses the phone to him, playing monkey-in-the-middle with Neil, who tries to grab the phone from them. Beardie tosses it between his palms and smirks.

"Where'd you say you were from again?" he asks, not really specifying which one of us he's talking to.

"We didn't." I sigh. "Now give him his phone back." I don't have time for this bullshit. I'm already sacrificing my Saturday morning to do schoolwork, which isn't fair at all. I'm using *my* gas and mileage to drive around with two of the least appealing people I can think of.

"What are you going to do if I don't, pretty boy?" Beardie isn't being aggressive, just putting on a show for his boys, who laugh harder than they need to.

"Look, man, we're not here for trouble." I put my hands up. Being the aggressive Black guy at the Archerville Cultural Festival is the last thing I need. "Just give Neil his phone back, and we can act like none of this happened." I've never been a pushover, by any means. I'm the cool, laid-back guy who doesn't like picking fights with hillbillies in an unknown town. But I really hate bullies, even if most of my friends are, in fact, bullies.

"I leave you boys alone for less than an hour, and you're already making friends?" It's Mischa, walking up from behind us using that oddly sweet accent. Beardie checks her out as she walks by and takes a drag from his cigarette, nodding in approval.

"Damn, Baby Girl. Where have you been all my life?" He licks his lips and approaches Mischa. She takes Neil's previous spot, leaning against the wall of the building and bending one leg at the knee to rest her foot on the wall.

"Wherever I was, it was nowhere near as interesting as this well-cultured little town." The sarcasm in her voice is painfully obvious. While I'm not here to pick a fight, Mischa arrives locked and loaded for a scene.

Beardie bites his bottom lip and nods again, apparently missing the sarcasm. He waves Neil's phone at Mischa and asks, "You got one of these fancy phones, baby? 'Cuz I'd love to get your number."

"Oh, really?" Mischa purrs seductively. I don't spend enough time with her to know if this is how she really flirts with guys, but it's kind of interesting. She's obviously being sarcastic but masking it with sex appeal.

"Okay, you guys can hook up or do whatever you want. Can I please have my phone back?" Neil stammers in a mixture of fear and annoyance. I've seen this side of him every time Preston torments him in the hallways at school.

"Nah, I think I'll hold on to this." Beardie grins and waves the phone tauntingly in front of Neil. I suck my teeth and groan. This is getting ridiculous! I'm just glad we haven't attracted a crowd.

Beardie motions toward me and asks Mischa, "Is this one your boyfriend, baby? Because I know a sexy chick like you wouldn't go for Four-Eyes."

Mischa chuckles lightly and I swear I hear her say, *"Four-Eyes, classic,"* under her breath. Funny, I was thinking the same thing. Her eyes meet mine and she smirks, twirling her finger around a loose strand of hair that has fallen from the messy bun. "Nah, he's not my type."

Beardie is eating her shit up with this big, toothy grin. His friends look like they wish they could get in on the action too, but I guess he's the leader, so he gets first dibs.

"Hey, Four-Eyes," he calls out to Neil, still staring at Mischa like she's a slab of meat and he's a ravenous carnivore. "Why don't you and the pretty boy get lost? We'll take care of Baby Girl."

"What's your problem?" Neil snaps. "We did nothing to you! Just came to your stupid hick town to write a report! You have no reason to steal from me!" I'm impressed by Neil standing up for himself. However, I think he's offended them this time. Beardie turns away from Mischa to lunge at Neil, grabbing his collar. His friends block Neil from behind. I'm about to interject when Mischa speaks up.

"Don't take it personally, Neil. They're probably just overcompensating for *something.*"

Beardie stops, loosens his grip on Neil's collar, and eyes Mischa suspiciously. He's finally learned how to read sarcasm. "What's that supposed to mean, Baby

Girl?" he asks her. He walks over to stand in front of her, blocking her in with his arms on either side of her head.

Mischa's smile never falters as she meets his gaze directly. "I'm just saying, usually guys act all big and tough, picking on the nerdy kid," she pauses and motions toward Neil, who glowers at her, "when they're... lacking..." She drags the last part out and then dragged her tongue across her full top lip. My eyes grow big. I can't believe she just said that to him!

"Lacking?" Beardie squints at her. "Lacking what?"

Now Mischa sucks her teeth and rolls her eyes. "Well, I was talking about your tiny penis, but I guess you're lacking a brain too."

"Tiny penis?" he croaks out in disbelief. He composes himself and laughs. "I can show you better than I can tell you, Baby Girl. I definitely ain't *lacking*," he tells her while tugging at his crotch.

"What's your name?" Mischa asks him. The smile has returned, and I'm having a hard time following whether she's joking with this loser or actually flirting. She's clearly insulting him, but she's also biting her bottom lip, and her thumbs are hooked through the belt loops on her rising shorts, making for a confident and kind of sexy pose. I've never seen her act like this before. Then again, I barely notice her most days.

"Jimmy," Beardie tells her in a tone that I'm assuming is meant to charm her.

"Well, *Jimmy*," Mischa mocks. She starts sensually running her hand down her thigh, continuing down the leg she has propped against the wall. Her other hand is sliding down Jimmy's chest before gripping his tank. "You know what you can do for me?"

"What's that, Baby Girl?" He leans in closer.

Within seconds, Mischa's entire demeanor goes from sugary sweet to spitfire as she tells him, "You can get the *fuck* out of my face!" As she speaks these words, she swiftly produces a switchblade from her boot and presses it against Jimmy's crotch.

"Woah, Baby Girl! What the hell?" Jimmy exclaims, and his friends make a move toward her, but she barks at them. I mean, literally *barks* at them. Like a dog.

"Tell them to back up or I'll cut your fucking dick off," she tells him calmly.

"Mischa, what the fuck!" I exclaim. There's a crowd forming now, curious to see what's happening with their local delinquents.

"Back up guys!" Jimmy squeals. "Baby Girl, calm down! We were just joking around!"

"Well, I'm not laughing," she says, pressing the blade deeper against his pants. She uses her grip on his tank top to maneuver them so that now Jimmy is pressed against the wall, and she's standing in front of him with the knife still pressed to his crotch. "So, here's the deal. Give me Neil's phone." She holds out her hand and Jimmy swiftly puts the iPhone in her palm. She tosses it to Neil, who fumbles to catch it without dropping it.

"Now apologize," she orders. When he tries to protest, she digs in deeper, and I'm convinced that she's one push away from tearing through his clothes and skin. "I said *apologize*," she repeats through gritted teeth.

Jimmy cries out in a panic. "Okay, okay. My bad, man!"

"*Neil*," Mischa presses. "His name is Neil."

"My bad, Neil," Jimmy corrects himself. "I was just dicking around."

Mischa giggles but doesn't remove the blade from Jimmy's lower region. "Funny analogy. Now give Jesse his wallet back."

"What?" Jimmy protests in confusion. "I don't—" He screams, and I hear a tearing sound that is his khakis shredding under the serrated blade.

"Give it to him now!" she growls. Within seconds, Jimmy's hand is shuffling into his pocket and pulling out the black leather wallet my grandpa gave me before he passed away. He pickpocketed me!

"Here man," Jimmy croaks out and tosses my wallet. Unlike Neil, I catch it perfectly. The small crowd opens up for an approaching police officer.

Mischa skillfully retracts the blade and tucks it back into her right boot. "Thanks, Jimmy, it's been fun!" Her head is tilted to the side and the sugary accent is back.

We walk back to my car with Mischa in the lead, bouncing as she steps. Neil must be in shock, just like I am. How did she do that?

"Well, I know what I'm writing about!" she tells us with a laugh. She's resting her forearms on the top of my car, waiting for me to unlock it. "Archerville is a hillbilly, piece of shit, white-trash town with about as much *multicultural appreciation* as a Mississippi race rally," she quotes herself.

I chuckle and nod as I turn my key in the lock. When I get in, I pop the lock on the passenger side, and Mischa lifts the seat for Neil to climb into the backseat before taking her seat. I stall for a moment, still envisioning Mischa pulling a knife out on that guy. She really is a psycho! But in the oddest sense, I'm saying that in a good way.

"Hey, Mischa?" Neil murmurs from the backseat. She turns her head to face him, and I look at his reflection in my rearview. "Thanks," he continues. "You're actually not that bad."

"Umm... I'll take that as a compliment." She smiles warily. "You're welcome, nerd. You really need to stand up for yourself. Assholes like that prey on the weak."

"I'm not weak!" he protests. "I just don't go around picking fights with random guys in random towns!"

I laugh, and Mischa looks at me curiously. "What's so funny?"

I start the car and shake my head. "I was thinking the same thing earlier," I say, throwing a motion toward Neil as I drive down the dirt road that will take us back to the state highway.

"Well, *excuse* me for standing up to injustices." She shrugs and sits back in the seat.

"Thanks though," I tell her, keeping my eyes on the road. "I didn't even notice that guy swiped my wallet. How did you know?" I take my eyes off the road briefly and look at her. She's looking out at the road, her fingers picking at the frayed edges of her shorts. She doesn't respond, just shrugs. She knows he did it because she's done it before.

As if reading my mind, she says, "I was also standing off to the side getting hit on by a toothless forty-year-old. I watched him do it. That's what made me walk over."

"Well, you handled it pretty badass." I give her a half-smile before returning my eyes to the road. I don't know much about Mischa Lawrence, besides seeing her switch her ass through the town as she corrals her little brother and sisters like a mother duck and her ducklings. I can count on one hand the number of times I've seen her mother since we were eleven, and her stepdad is always getting drunk and thrown out of Telly's Bar. That being said, it doesn't surprise me that a girl who dresses like a 50s pinup one day, wears a floor-length, long-sleeve Victorian-style dress the next day, and a pair of homemade cutoff shorts with a half top and cowboy boots in late October would have experience in pickpocketing.

Did I mention she isn't wearing a bra?

"I hate bullies. I hate guys who do fucked up shit for no reason." She punches her fist in her palm as she talks.

In the backseat, Neil snorts. "Careful, you're insulting all of *Pretty Boy's* friends."

Mischa laughs at his statement, and I glare at him in the rearview. We reach the on-ramp for the highway, and I gun it east, toward Grover.

"Aww, poor wittle Jesse can't help it that his friends are dicks," she baby talks, fake-pouting at me and tilting her head.

"Isn't Zoey, like, your best friend?" I shoot back, annoyed. I don't care if they make fun of my friends. I just hate being categorized with them and their antics.

"She is." Mischa nods. "But she's an exception. She'd never be mean to Neil, or anyone like that."

"What about Trey? He's never done anything to either of you," I point out. Trey's just as laid back as I am. Plus, his dad is weirdly obsessed with keeping Mischa out of trouble.

"Trey and Zoey are cool," Neil pipes up, "but Preston and Nick..." he trails off and I kind of feel bad. Neil has always been the brunt of all of Preston's pranks and mean jokes. Well, whenever Mischa isn't available.

"Preston can't help it either, Neil," Mischa surprises me by saying. For every Neil prank, Preston has got a thousand words of hatred for Mischa.

"Guys like Preston and our friend Jimmy of Archerville have a hard time coping with their baby dicks, so they take it out on those they see of lesser value than themselves." She smirks and looks at me. "Isn't that right, Jesse Alford?"

I can't help but laugh and return her smirk. "Wow…" is all I say.

"Nah, I'm just joking," she says with a smile and a wink. "I bet Jesse knows how to satisfy a woman. I mean, look at this badass car."

Her tone is so seductive I have to focus on the road so that I'm not tempted to look at her. It's creepy how she weaves in and out of conversation styles. One minute she's on a crusade to end bullying, the next she's talking about my sexual potential. I've never been the blushing type, but right now I feel my face warming up.

"Umm… am I missing something?" Neil speaks up from the back seat.

I'm still not looking at her, but I hear Mischa say, "I should probably stop. Wouldn't want to piss off Alyssa." I let out a chuckle and shake my head again. She's actually kind of funny. I see her smirking at me from my peripheral. She folds her arms across her chest and props her feet up on my dashboard. I don't protest.

Chapter Six

J esse drops Neil off at his house before dropping me off in front of mine. I thank him for the ride, and he thanks me again for saving his wallet. Inside, the house is silent, which means the Littles aren't here because they're *never* silent. I walk into the back room and see my mom is up and out of bed.

"Hey," I greet her, stepping partially into her bedroom. She's just finished slipping on her favorite floral print dress.

I have scattered memories of when my mom was lively and beautiful. She gave tight hugs, and her smile was warm. That was before Joe, and my diagnosis, and my dad's death. Now, her once bright blue eyes seem dull and sunken. What used to be wavy dark-brown tresses are now stringy dead strands that rarely get brushed. Her face is saggy and her collarbone protrudes. I bet she weighs about ninety pounds soaking wet, where she was once fuller and toned like I am.

"Hey, Misch." She smiles weakly at me. Her voice is deep and groggy with sleep. "How are you, baby?"

"I'm fine. Just got home from doing a school project," I tell her with a shrug. This is the first time we've spoken in about three days. She takes pills that help to sleep her depression away. Sometimes she'll be out for a week.

"That's good. I want to see you excelling, Mischa. Focus on school, not all of that other stuff." She yawns and bends down to pick up her ballet flats.

"Where are Teddy and the girls?" she asks me as if I've been here. Shouldn't she know where her own children are?

"I guess they're in town. I asked Frankie to watch the kids while I was gone, but she kept complaining about missing some football game. She must have taken Teddy and Maddie with her since I was running late."

Her room is atrocious, and it smells like cigarettes and beer cans, which are scattered all over the nightstand, alongside an ashtray filled with so many cigarette butts, it's overflowing. My mom doesn't smoke or drink.

"Well, I've got to take Grandpa to San Francisco tonight. He's got appointments on Monday." My mom and Grandpa stay one weekend a month four hours away in San Francisco so that my grandpa can spend the following Monday seeing his five different specialists. It's the one thing my mom has to do on her own since I can't drive while on the medications I'm supposed to be taking.

I give a sigh and sarcastically reply, "Well, I've got things handled here." God forbid their father watches them. "I'm going to go back into town to work for a few hours, then I'll bring the Littles home." I turn on my heels to walk out, but she calls out to me.

"Mischa." When I turn, she's giving the most pathetic smile ever. It's as big of a smile as she can muster, and no teeth are showing. "Thank you so much, Mischa."

I nod and leave the house, making my way toward town.

As I walk down the winding paved road leading into town, I add an extra switch to my step. A guy is whistling at me and telling me how sexy I am. He must be new to Grover, because I don't recognize him, and no one ever walks this road except me and Fergal. The cool teens drive up here to party at the shut-down lumber mill up the mountain.

The boy is gone now, but I can still hear him whistling.

Mr. Brady seems surprised to see me when I make it to the general store. He's standing at the register looking over inventory sheets. Busy work, since no one is shopping in the store today.

"I saw your sister dragging your brother and baby sister into town about an hour ago. I thought you and Jesse Alford were off doing some school project?"

I shrug and hop up on the counter. "We're finished for today. Ever been to Archerville?" Mr. Brady shakes his head. "Well, you're not missing much. That place is ass." I don't even bother reminding him that Neil Gunderson exists.

He chuckles. "Well, if you want to work, you can double-check this inventory for me. I'm doubling up on the Halloween candy this year." He sounds excited about that last part.

Mr. Brady lets me have control over the stereo, so I put it on the local hip-hop station, and go to work cleaning and doing inventory. I'm transported back to my father and I rapping Tupac lyrics in the kitchen together as we'd prepare dinner. Grandpa would complain and tell us to *"turn on some good music."* He preferred his Motown classics.

It's around 4:30 p.m. when the town starts buzzing again, and that's a sign that the football game is over. I'm sure Frankie is somewhere showing off for her new quarterback crush. That leaves Teddy to take Maddie with him to the bookstore. I'm bobbing my head to the beat of a song and dancing around in the freezer section when I hear Mr. Brady call out to me.

"It's good to see you back in high spirits."

'Is it?' I think to myself, grinning. If only he knew.

"Life's too short to be low," I call back. There's a double meaning, but he'll never know it. The cowbell over the door rattles, and I hear Mr. Brady greet someone, calling them *"Little lady."*

I crane my head to see down the aisle better. I see a little red ballet slipper that I recognize as Maddie's. Why is my baby sister walking into the general store alone?

"Maddie? Where are Frankie and Teddy?" I ask her once I've made it to the front of the small store.

"Frankie is talking to her boyfriend," she tells me softly. She has the cutest speech impediment that makes her *'Ls'* and *'Rs'* sound like *'Ws.'*

"And Teddy?" I press her after rolling my eyes at the thought of Frankie selling herself short for the sake of popularity. Maddie squirms.

"Maddie, where is Teddy?" I repeat, with a little more authority in my voice. I glance at Mr. Brady, who is frowning as well.

"Those boys keep pushing him. Frankie's boyfriend and his friend." She points a chubby finger toward the street that leads to the arcade and bookstore.

I'm out of the door without realizing it. My brain is firing off images, and I'm swearing under my breath. I hear cackling beside me.

Fergal.

I hear a commotion of laughter mixed with my little brother pleading with someone to stop. I hear Frankie too.

"Billy, cut it out. Leave him alone!" she's begging her little delinquent football friend to quit pushing her younger brother down in dirt and grass. Every time Teddy gets up, this punk pushes him back down.

What's even more infuriating? There are adults everywhere. Ignoring them. Boys will be boys, I guess.

Billy pushes my brother down again, and this time Teddy's inhaler flies out of his pocket onto the ground. Billy laughs and picks it up.

"Aww... wittle Teddy needs his ba-ba?" Billy taunts him. I'm jogging at this point. Fergal is having a field day beside me. He can feel it coming. All day I've been on high. My confidence was through the roof. I even pulled a knife on a guy today. And the sexual tension Jesse Alford was putting me through was insane.

This is mania.

My body is numb as I approach Billy Wessel, the pre-teen child of Satan. He drops the inhaler on the ground and stomps on it.

Fergal is screaming with laughter.

I grab Billy by the back of his smelly football jersey, catching him by surprise, and hip-toss him to the ground WWE-style. Then, I drop on top of him with my knee pressed hard into his chest and my hands pinning his arms above his head.

"Hey, you crazy bitch!" he screams out as he flails and kicks below me. I don't respond verbally, just smack him hard across the face to shut him up. Frankie screams at me from behind us, but I'll deal with her later. I keep my knee buried in his scrawny chest and look at the broken piece of my brother's newly purchased inhaler. It sends me further into a rage, if that's even possible.

I keep his arms pinned down with one hand and use my other to grab a handful of the plastic inhaler pieces. Clumps of dirt and grass come with it. I have my fistful, and while BillyBoy is in the middle of a vulgar scream, I shove it in his mouth, holding it there and shutting him up. Frankie is screaming hysterically now in defense of her stupid little boyfriend.

"Somebody stop her! She's hurting him!" I hear a woman scream from behind me. *Oh, **now** they're paying attention?*

"Touch my brother again, and I'll fucking kill you. Do you understand me?" I whisper harshly in Billy's ear. He gives a muffled yell and a nasty gagging noise under my palm.

"*Do. You. Fucking. Understand. Me?*" I press harder into his chest. He nods his head desperately and makes another gagging noise. I feel a pair of arms wrap around me and pull me upward.

"Dammit, Mischa, I'm too old for this!" Mr. Brady growls at me. "Get off that boy, now!"

Once I'm on my feet, I throw my leg back and kick Billy in the side.

"Mischa!" Mr. Brady barks. "Back to the store, now!"

I look around me with a cocky grin. The townspeople are staring at me and whispering amongst themselves like I'm a feral cat. I feel like a feral cat. *A mighty-fucking-mountain cat!*

When my eyes meet Frankie's, I snap again. "You're such a selfish piece of shit, Frankie!" I scream at her, causing her to jump slightly. "How could you stand there and let him beat up on your little brother?" Beside me, Mr. Brady and Mrs. Franklin are helping Billy up from the ground, patting his back roughly so that the bits of grass, dirt, and plastic come flying out of his mouth with a cough.

"Take Teddy and Maddie home!" I snarl at her. "Now!"

Tears are streaming down her face, but she does as she's told, grabbing Teddy by the arm and dragging him and Maddie toward the mountain trail.

I throw one last glance at Billy *Weasel*, and then casually turn on my heels and walk back to the general store. I'm sure it's only a matter of time before Freeman shows up. I should be worried about the kid's parents pressing charges against me, but I'm not. I'm feeling amazingly pissed off. Amazing, because I love taking retribution against bullies like Jimmy from Asherville and Billy Weasel. Pissed, because I shouldn't have to.

It sucks having to go through with my plan when I have the rational fear that my Littles will suffer without me. I can't have those distractions.

"Quite the show you put on there, girly," Fergal tells me with a laugh.

"Shut up," I mumble at him.

Chapter Seven

I make Teddy shower in Mom and Joe's bathroom, while I bathe Maddie in the hallway bathroom. I'm scrubbing cheap, apple-scented shampoo through her scalp when she lets out a soft sigh.

"What's wrong, Maddie?" I ask her flatly. I've got a pizza baking in the oven. It expires in two days, so Mr. Brady told me to take it home for dinner. That was after the sheriff came into the store accompanied by Billy's pissed-off parents, the Wessels.

They demanded I apologize, to which I told them both to shove it up their asses and teach their little hellspawn some decent human conduct. When they stormed out, Freeman frowned at me and shook his head.

"Are you kidding me, Mischa?" He scoffed at me, placing his hands above his gun halter. "Assaulting a twelve-year-old?"

"He assaulted my eight-year-old little brother! For fuck's sake, he destroyed Teddy's inhaler! I don't have the money to replace that shit! What is Teddy going to do for the next month?" I yelled back. Mr. Brady put his hand on my shoulder, attempting to calm me.

"I'll talk to Dr. Cosey on Monday. We'll get another one for him." Freeman sighed.

"But Billy Weasel doesn't have to apologize for beating up a kid four years younger than him? And Mr. Weasel doesn't have to pay for the replacement inhaler, right?" I shot back, leisurely leaning against the counter.

"The *Wessels* will refuse to pay for it, you know that," Sheriff Freeman told me with a mixture of exhaust and amusement. "I'll buy it. Just no more antics."

I snorted and shook my head. "*Antics,*" I mocked under my breath, though I'm sure he could hear me.

Mr. Brady sent me home early, with half a day's pay for the few hours I'd worked. He gave me the frozen pizza to feed the Littles along with some extra breakfast items for tomorrow.

Maddie shrugs her shoulders as I continue to massage her head. "You hurt Frankie's feelings when you beat up her friend. Fighting is bad, Mischa."

"Yeah? Well, Frankie's so-called friend was beating up Teddy, and Frankie did nothing to stop him," I retort, pouring water over her head with an old plastic drink pitcher.

"What's shellfish?" she asks me with her cute mispronunciation.

"Crabs and lobsters." I pour another pitcher of warm water over her.

She makes a scrunched face and looks up at me. "You called Frankie a lobster?" When she says Frankie's name, it always sounds like *Fwayne-kee.*

"No, I called Frankie *selfish,*" I correct her with a soft laugh. "That means she only thinks about herself. I told her to stay here with you guys today. She didn't listen because she wanted to be cool and show off for her friends, and see what happened?"

"But she was crying," she mumbles sadly. I don't respond, but my heart aches a little at the thought of hurting my little sister's feelings. We're all each other has.

I grab a towel from the rack behind me and dry Maddie's body. "Can you make the wrap-thingy on my head?" she asks. I grab a second towel, and gather all of her hair in it, twisting it and knotting it on top of her head.

"Let's get dressed and eat some pizza!" I tickle her towel-clad body, and she giggles hysterically.

Once I've got Maddie dressed and Teddy has finished his shower, I slice the thin-crust pizza and serve two slices a piece for each of the Littles.

"Aren't you going to eat the other two slices, Mischa?" Teddy asks me as I hoist my body up to sit on the counter.

I shake my head. "I'm not hungry. You and Frankie can have seconds."

Frankie hasn't spoken to me since I made it home. My mom was walking out with Grandpa, just as I was walking in. She didn't even notice that I was upset, or that Frankie had come home in tears with a dirty, disheveled Teddy.

I inwardly groan as rationality hits me. I'm such a hypocrite. Who am I to call anyone selfish? In less than six months, I'll be leaving them all in this hellhole world, with their crappy parents, in our crappy town. While I'm at peace.

But dying in 176 days is something I have to do. Don't ask me why. It just is.

After dinner, the Littles clear the table and go their separate ways. I stop Frankie just as she's walking out of the kitchen.

"Frankie."

She stops and turns her body toward me, but her face is focused on the kitchen window. There's a light pitter-patter of rain tapping the glass.

"I'm sorry I embarrass you." I don't use the past tense, because my very existence humiliates Frankie. "But we've got to stick together. What your little boyfriend was doing to Teddy wasn't cool. He's your baby brother. You've got to have his back!" I'm not yelling at her, just sternly pleading.

Frankie finally looks at me as she animatedly moves her arms to express herself. "I told Billy to stop. Just because I didn't power slam him and shove mud down his throat doesn't mean I didn't stick up for Teddy!"

"I'm not asking you to fight, Frankie. I'm asking you to look out for your little brother and sister. I'm not always here to do that." My voice softens.

Soon I won't be here at all.

I was eight when I was diagnosed with bipolar disorder. It started with me constantly sleeping throughout the day. Then I'd have episodes of unexplainable rage, which would lead to daily fights with the boys and girls at school and suspensions. Joe told my mom that he didn't want to deal with me anymore. My mom had just given birth to Teddy and couldn't handle me full-time. So, she got rid of me. I went to live with my dad permanently instead of on weekends and during breaks.

When I was ten, the hallucinations started, and I was given a dual diagnosis of mood disorder and schizophrenia symptoms. Schizoaffective disorder. Of course, back then I didn't know they were hallucinations. I would hear people say things that, apparently, they didn't say. I would see people and things that other people supposedly couldn't see. My dad was excellent at handling me because he didn't *handle* me. He just loved me.

Fergal showed up at his funeral. I thought he was a real person until he walked into school with me on the first day of sixth grade. I was the new girl at Grover Middle School, and the girls in my gym glass didn't take too well to seeing me talk to myself in the locker room. I was simply trying to tell Fergal that he wasn't supposed to come inside the girls' locker room. My mom immediately upped my dosage to a near-comatose-inducing level.

At the time of the carbon monoxide incident, it had been months since I'd taken my meds. I didn't explain to my mother or the doctors that taking the pills turns me into a zombie, and I can't be the sole provider for my siblings if I'm in a vegetative state.

I open all the windows in the house to let some kind of breeze in. It's raining, but there's a muggy heat in the air that's still lingering from the end of summer. I hate being hot. I rarely open the windows at night, since there are always mountain lions roaming around our property, and I'd hate for one to crawl through the windows and maul anyone besides Joe. I tried talking to Sheriff Freeman about it, but he refused to do anything. I guess that just comes with the territory of living in the woods.

There's an old Meg Ryan movie on TV that I remember watching with my mom when I was younger. She was always a sucker for these rom-com movies, and we always had to watch them with her. Dad was more into action movies and documentaries.

It's nearly midnight on a Saturday night, and I know most of my peers are up the trail at the abandoned lumber mill getting hammered. Zoey, who, while having a long-distance relationship with Anthony, still likes to party and make out with the local boys in town. She claims they have an *"understanding."* I say he's in college twelve hours away, so they're both sowing their wild oats until they're stuck with each other.

I've never been one for drinking. I don't need anything else altering my mental state. Though I have been known to dabble in the herbal goodness that is Purple Kush, which I purchase from this really cute Hispanic guy named Javi whenever I hitchhike to Stockton.

I've got my lips to the mouthpiece of my small water pipe, and my lighter to the bowl, when I hear the dreaded whistling sound.

It's not a hallucination, though. It's Teddy, stumbling down the hallway, wheezing in tears.

He's having an asthma attack.

The windows. They're all open, and the rain must have blown the dust and pollen from outside into his room. Or maybe it's mold. Either way, we're not well equipped for this. I drop the pipe on the table, scattering weed all over the surface, and scale the back of the couch in a one-arm vault.

"Teddy!" I scream. "Where is your... FUCK!" His inhaler is broken. Smashed by Billy Weasel. *How fucking convenient.*

Joe threw my cell phone against the wall last summer, shattering the screen. I was in a depressive episode, so I didn't stab him like manic-Mischa would have. I never replaced my broken cell phone because no one ever calls or texts me. Maybe Zoey, occasionally. I'm not even sure it still has service. I scream in frustration just as Teddy collapses.

"Teddy!" I run to him and check his head. He's not bleeding, but he's still wheezing terribly. This is a horrible situation for a seventeen-year-old to be in. Especially one with extreme psychological disorders. I'm not sure what I'm going to do, but I need to hurry. I bend down and scoop my lanky little brother into my arms. I'm wearing thin flannel pants and a spaghetti-strap tank top, and Teddy is wearing his favorite Batman sleep pants and T-shirt. Neither of us has on shoes, but I bolt outside with him bridal-style in my arms.

I may be planning my demise, and I haven't been inside a church in years, but all I keep repeating in my head is, *"Please God, don't let Teddy die."*

Chapter Eight

JESSE

I say a silent prayer that Alyssa is too preoccupied to notice as I slip away from the party and head to my car. It's raining, but the air is so stuffy that the inside of the factory we party in is nearly unbearable.

Everyone is drunk, dancing, and socializing under the music that's blaring from a rigged sound system that Lucas Hoffman set up when we were in the eighth grade. The liquor is always provided by Mason Telly, whose dad owns Telly's Bar, so Mason has easy access to swiping half-empty bottles of vodka and cases of beer.

I stop underneath the large, rusty awning outside of the building where Trey is talking to Nick and Preston.

"There goes the freak show chauffer now," Preston taunts as he sips from his plastic cup. At that moment, he reminds me of a cleaner version of that Archerville prick from earlier.

"Lay off man," I groan. I turn to Trey, who rode with me. "I'm heading out. Want a lift?"

"Nah." He downs the rest of his drink. "My folks are in Sacramento for the weekend for a wedding. I'm taking advantage of this free time."

"Alright, I'll—" I'm just about to bid them farewell when I hear someone slurring my name from behind me.

"Jesse, you're leaving already?" Alyssa purrs as she stumbles outside. She drapes her arms around my shoulders and leans her weight on me.

"Yeah, I've been up since eight this morning," I tell her, shifting out of her grasp and switching positions so that she's leaning against my side with my arm loosely draped around her.

"Spending the entire day with Liar Lawrence will do that to you," Preston seethes. "Stupid fucking bitch."

Alyssa sucks her teeth. "*Puh-leez,* Jesse wouldn't bother wasting a breath on that loser."

"You have to admit, Mischa is pretty fine," Trey chuckles lightly. I meant what I said to Mischa earlier. Trey never talks bad about her. Preston and the others know better than to give him shit about his dad and Mischa's weird relationship. Whenever anybody asks him about it, he always tells us he has no idea what their connection is.

"Yeah, she's *real fine.* Especially when she's beating up twelve-year-olds," Nick scoffs beside Trey.

"What are you talking about?" Alyssa laughs, just as Chelsea and Zoey come out of the factory.

"She, like, choke-slammed Billy Wessel after the game today." Nick shrugs before taking a gulp from his cup.

"Oh my gosh, it was so crazy!" Chelsea squeals, tapping Alyssa's shoulder. "She was shoving grass and dirt in his mouth, then screamed at her little sister and stormed off. I was having lunch with my parents and saw the whole thing!"

"Crazy bitch. They need to lock her ass in a cage somewhere." Preston tosses the red cup on the ground and crushes it under his shoe. I hear Zoey suck her teeth. She goes back inside the factory without a word to any of us. Mischa is her friend, so I doubt she appreciates Preston referring to her as a *crazy bitch.* No matter how accurate it may seem. I'm happy I didn't bother bringing up the fact that she pulled a knife on a guy in the name of justice for Neil and me today. That doesn't sit well after hearing she physically assaulted a seventh grader hours later.

"Hey." Alyssa nudges my side with her elbow. "I'll ride home with you." I know what that means, and I'm not in the mood.

Sex with Alyssa used to be a thrill. Now it just reminds me of that year I was addicted to mint chocolate chip ice cream and would buy a double scoop of it from Scoops Ice Cream Parlor every day. I got burned out and never wanted to eat it again.

"I'm just going to head home, Lys." My voice is low, trying to keep everyone out of what should be a private conversation.

"Hey, Lyssa. I'll take you home." Preston winks at her.

"I'd rather go home with Jesse." She rolls her eyes at him. She turns to me and gives me what's supposed to be a sultry smile, but ends up being a drunken clown face.

"I'll go grab my purse," she tells me, then skips off into the building.

When she's out of sight, I turn to Trey and give him a quick fist bump. "I'm out."

I'm down the walkway and in my car before Alyssa makes it out of the building.

My wipers are working hard to keep up with the rain as I cruise down the winding mountain road that leads into town. I'm happy I wasn't drinking much, or this would be an issue.

I drive past the secluded house that Mischa and her family call home. It sits about thirty yards off the main road, surrounded by woods. It's the only house out here. No one lived there before their family moved to Grover. Their home appeared out of nowhere one day, and Sheriff Freeman was maintaining the upkeep on it until they arrived six years ago.

Further down the pass, I see something staggering on the side of the road. In the dense rain, I can't make out what it is. A deer maybe?

It's not until I cruise past the figure that I see that it's Mischa.

I contemplate just driving on, not wanting anything to do with Mischa and her craziness. She's hobbling down the road in the middle of the night during a rainstorm. I shouldn't even care why. She's always doing weird shit during the day, so it doesn't surprise me she'd be a night stalker.

But then I hear her calling out. Not directly to me, but I swear I hear her screaming for help. I groan and pull off to the side of the road. When I look in my rearview, I see she has attempted to pick up the pace, but she's having a hard time because she's holding something in her arms. I open the door and the rain beats down on my head, instantly sticking my hair to my face and around my neck.

"Jesse!" Mischa screams out. "Please, help!" I can finally make out the form she's carrying in her arms. It's a little boy. Her kid brother.

"What happened?" I ask her frantically. I run around to my passenger side, opening the door without even thinking.

"He's having an asthma attack!" she cries out. When she makes it to the car, she flops down in the seat. I run back to the driver's side and put the car in drive, gassing it toward town. Mischa has her brother sitting parallel to her body on her lap. He's making this horrible wheezing noise, and his body is convulsing like he's trying to catch his breath.

"I need to get to Sheriff Freeman. Can you please take us to Sheriff Freeman?" Mischa asks me, now eerily monotone but still seemingly scared.

"The Freemans are out of town. We need to get to the hospital." I keep my voice as calm as I can. I glance at her and see her nod.

"Breathe with me, Teddy," she murmurs in his ear, placing her hand on his chest and taking long, deep breaths against his short, rapid ones. "Feel my breathing and breathe with me."

I'm seeing a different side of the town psycho, but now isn't the time to be fascinated by things like that. Both Mischa and her little brother are barefoot and wearing pajamas, and I'm not sure how long a person can have an asthma attack before...

"Doesn't he have an inhaler or something?" I ask her, trying to calm my nerves but failing miserably. We enter town and I stay on Main Street. It'll take us straight through Grover and to the interstate. The nearest hospital is the Mountain Region Healthplex, about half an hour's drive west of town.

"Shh..." Mischa shushes me and continues focusing on her mantra to her little brother. "Breathe with me, Teddy. Breathe with me." He's still gasping rapidly, but she doesn't give up on her slow breaths and tries to get him to follow her breathing patterns.

"Please, don't die Teddy," I hear her whisper. "I need you to live."

Chills run down my spine, and I swallow hard, slamming my foot on the gas and gunning it to the hospital.

Chapter Nine

The Mountain Region Healthplex is made up of several specialty health practices and a twenty-four-hour emergency care facility. It was built about ten years ago to serve as a closer medical center for all the small towns in the area. I guess they got tired of losing people on their way to the bigger cities' hospitals.

I slam on my breaks in front of the hospital twenty-one minutes after picking up Mischa and her little brother. I was punching well over ninety the entire way.

I jog around to the passenger's side of my car and hoist Teddy out of Mischa's arms as she tries to maneuver off of the low seat. We run through the sliding doors and practically slam against the counter. Mischa's little brother is still struggling to breathe in my arms as the uninterested receptionist looks at us over her reading glasses.

"He's having an asthma attack," I announce, even though it's painfully obvious.

She pops her gum and looks between me, Mischa, and the kid in my arms. "You'll need to fill these out. And I need an insurance card." She places a wooden clipboard on the counter with about five sheets of paper and a pen.

"I didn't grab his insurance card," Mischa mumbles, more to herself.

In my arms, Teddy takes a hard, labored breath, causing me to jump a little. "Can't you just take him back? He's been like this for like half an hour," I plead with her.

"I need these filled out, and if there's no insurance, then I need a guardian to sign right here." She points to a dotted line designated for the *responsible party*.

"I'll fill these out, but he needs a doctor now." I motion to the boy in my arms.

"I need you to fill out the paperwork, and then—" She doesn't get a chance to finish repeating her mundane statement, because Mischa completely flips out.

"We don't fucking have time to fill out paperwork, bitch!" she screams, sweeping her hand across the counter, sending pens and business cards flying in front of the middle-aged receptionist. "Get a doctor up here now and save my brother's life!" She's screaming at the top of her lungs and stomping around like a kid who was just told she couldn't have a new toy at the toy store.

"Young lady, you need to calm down this instant!" The receptionist backs up in her rolling chair, frightened. I don't blame her. Mischa's outburst startled me too.

"No!" Mischa shouts harshly. "*You* get someone out here NOW!" She points across the counter at the woman. Around us, a few patients and a couple of nurses are staring at Mischa like she's a rabid dog. Mischa reaches across the counter and swipes at the woman, but misses. She's just about to climb on the counter when, finally, an orderly comes out with a gurney and takes Teddy from me. Mischa tries to follow, but a nurse stops her at the double automatic doors, telling her she'll have to wait out here.

Mischa is pretty much in a trance at this point, so I walk over to her and place my hands on her shoulders to guide her to the seating area. I sit beside her with the paperwork in my hands, unsure of what I'm supposed to do with it. I know she calls her brother Teddy, but I don't know if it's short for something. Theodore, maybe? Mischa's last name is Lawrence, but I know that Joe-guy isn't her dad. But is he Teddy's? Do I put *Little* down as his last name? I can't even attempt to guess his birthday. And is there really an address for their house in the middle of the woods?

"His inhaler is broken," I hear Mischa whisper. It takes a moment for me to realize she's answering my question from earlier in the car. I sit the clipboard down on my lap and look at her.

"Billy Weasel stomped on it today," she continues. She's out of it, talking like a hoarse robot.

I can't help but snicker. "Is that why you beat him up?" Just asking the question out loud causes me to laugh harder.

Mischa looks at me and grimaces. "You saw that?" Her tone is almost accusatory, so I throw my hands up and shake my head.

"No, I just heard about it," I tell her, calming my laughter.

"Yeah. That's why I did it. He was beating up my little brother—four years younger than him, mind you—and everyone just stood there. He stomped on an asthmatic kid's *inhaler*, and none of those adults did anything. But when *I* stepped in, I was the *crazy girl*."

She's recounting the incident in a tone that tells me she wants me to understand her plight, and honestly, I'm pissed. The Wessels have always had a lot of pull around Grover because they donate a lot of money to the athletic programs, which is all Grover cares about. She turns away from me and looks toward the double doors that they wheeled Teddy through. With her profile to me, I can't help but give her a once-over.

She's soaking wet, causing her long, wavy black hair to stick to her shoulders and back, framing her round face. Her full lips are turned down as she pouts at the automatic doors. She's not even bothered by her hair dripping all over her. My eyes scan the length of her hair as it snakes around her arms and chest. That's when I see that her white tank top is clinging to her chest and her nipples are protruding against the fabric. I quickly avert my eyes back to the clipboard.

I clear my throat and hand her the clipboard. "You should fill this out."

She takes it from me and starts writing Teddy's information in her serial killer handwriting. Most girls our age have big, bubbly handwriting. Mischa's handwriting reminds me of a horror movie killer's ominous signature, written in blood on the walls of the victim's home.

We sit in silence for a few moments, and after Mischa is finished filling out the hospital paperwork, I take it up to the counter. I don't think it's safe for her and the rude receptionist to exchange any more words.

She's gone back to staring at the automatic doors as I make my way back toward her. She's leaned forward a little, so her hair is coving her breasts, which is a good thing because I've thrown the perverted old fart sitting across from us a few mean looks for licking his lips at her. I look down and see her wiggling her bare toes and turn back around and ask the receptionist to bring me a pair of socks and slippers they have for the patients. I know they have them. My grandfather died in this E.R.

"Here." I hand her the socks and the thin cotton slippers. She looks up at me in shock.

My cell rings just then, and I scramble to answer it before it irritates anyone in the waiting room. I swipe the answer bar before I even look at the screen, instantly regretting it once I realize who is calling.

"Where are you? You ditched me at the party in front of everyone!" Alyssa slurs angrily at me.

"I told you I was heading home alone," I reply, wondering why it took her almost an hour to call and chew me out. I sit down in my seat next to Mischa and watch her slip the thick socks over her painted toes.

I hear laughing in the background on Alyssa's end. "Sounds like you found a ride without me, though." I don't care what she does. I just like to throw her hypocrisy in her face sometimes.

"Yeah? Well, like I said, I would have rather left with you." She's with Preston, I assume. "Where are you, anyway? We rode past your house and your car isn't there." I don't answer her because I don't have to.

Just then, a doctor comes out and calls for Mischa to come back with Teddy. She doesn't acknowledge me at all as she jumps up and follows the doctor.

"I'll call you tomorrow, Lys," I lie. "I'm busy right now." I hang up before she has time to respond. Now, I'm just sitting here, not sure what to do. I've done my good Samaritan deed by bringing Mischa and Teddy here. Should I leave? What if the news she gets isn't good news? What if he...

I should stay and wait for her. Maybe they'll need a ride back home. I'm not sure where her mom or stepdad are. Maybe they'll be here soon.

Did Mischa even bother calling them?

I spend the next ten minutes internally battling over what I should do. The double doors open, and Mischa slowly walks out. Her arms are wrapped around her stomach and her head is down. The old pervert guy is grinning at her again, and my mind is made up. I'm not leaving her here alone.

I stand when she approaches me. "Is everything okay?" I ask her hesitantly, even though I'm trying to sound nonchalant for her sake.

She nods her head. "They're keeping him overnight. The doctor said we got him here just in time." She takes a long breath and looks up at me with big, sad eyes. "Thank you so much, Jesse. I don't know what I would have done if you hadn't shown up. Teddy would have..." She trails off and I feel like she's on the verge of tears again.

I shake my head and wave her off. "Don't mention it."

Her stomach growls, but I don't think she notices. She's looking around at all the people in the room with an uneasy look. These are the late-night interstate people who seem to always be questionable.

She sighs. "I guess I'll be spending the night out here so I can take Teddy home tomorrow."

"Well, I'm starving. There's a diner across the street," I say with a shrug. "Would you... maybe want to go grab a bite to eat?"

Her eyes widen, and she shakes her head vigorously, sending droplets of water everywhere. "Jesse, I can't hold you up like that."

I wave her off again. "I can't leave you here. Especially with that guy staring at you like a four-course meal." I point at the man, who tries to turn away from us and hide the fact that he's been staring at Mischa's ass.

She follows my finger and chuckles at the old man. "Eww, gross," she mumbles.

"C'mon." I motion for her to follow me. I leave my number with the receptionist, instructing her to call me if anything happens with Teddy.

The rain has slowed once we make it to the small diner that is directly across the highway from the emergency room. It's an old greasy establishment that's full of truckers and wanderers since it's right off the exit.

We sit down at a booth near the back of the diner, and both order sodas. Another awkward silence falls over us. Mischa is looking down at the smudgy tabletop and I can't help but watch her. She's so different from what I've always thought. I'm noticing that in the accumulative eight hours I've spent with her today, she's not insufferable at all. She looks so sad, and something in my chest is pulling for me to cheer her up. I've spent the past six years ignoring her entire existence, but right now, I want so badly to see her smile.

I rest my arms on the table and lean in closer to her. "My mom and I used to play this game whenever we got bored waiting around for my dad in the city." She lifts her eyes and looks at me. "Ever played that board game called *Clue*?" I ask with an encouraging smile. It's weird to see this firecracker of a girl look so defeated when less than twenty-four hours ago, she was holding a man at knifepoint.

She nods. "The Littles and I play sometimes, but they're not really good at understanding the rules, so we never get far." Her voice is raspier than usual. Probably from all the screaming she's done tonight.

"The Littles?" I ask her.

"That's what I call Teddy, Maddie, and Frankie," she explains, and I think I see a hint of a smile. "It's their last name, plus they're younger than me."

I nod and go back to my initial explanation. "So, yeah, we would play this game, where one of us would pick a random person around us, make up a life scenario, and then the other person had to guess which person it was.

She gives me a skeptical look, but at least she's not frowning anymore. "Sounds more like *Guess Who*."

I chuckle and nod. "Okay, I'll go first," I tell her, just as the waitress brings my cheeseburger and fries and Mischa's bagel. I want to tell her that the meal is on me and that she can order more food than just a plain bagel and cream cheese.

I look around the room and spot an old man with a long gray beard, eating a slice of pie and mumbling to himself.

"He's an undercover secret agent. He's in disguise, investigating a string of murders up and down Highway 120. He's stopped at the diner to take a break and gather his recent findings. Plus, he's got a sweet tooth."

Mischa gives a *'hmm'* sound and looks over my shoulder. Within seconds, her eyes land on the old man and his slice of pie, and she smiles brightly. Not that sly smirk she's been giving me all day, but a true, excited smile.

Trey was right. Mischa Lawrence is very pretty. Her smile is big and bright, and her eyes turn downward and crease as she does so.

"That old guy over there." She nods toward the man. "You made it too easy with that 'sweet tooth' part."

I nod in agreement. "Your turn."

She does that thinking sound again and looks around for her first pick. Her clothes are dry now, and her hair has morphed into a frizzy mass that suits her. Her slender shoulders are hunched as she surveys the diner.

"Okay." She clears her throat and looks at me with a challenge in her eyes. "She's a runaway bride. Everyone thinks she's just being difficult and ungrateful, but the truth is her soon-to-be husband is a total asshole who hits her. She's trying to live a quiet secret life in Archerville until she figures things out, but Archerville sucks, so she needs a new plan."

When she's finished, she rests her head on her palm and leans in to smirk at me. I look around the diner. There are only three women in the diner, not including Mischa. And one of them is the waitress.

"Sandra the waitress?" She seems like the obvious choice. Mischa nods her head slowly and I laugh softly. "That suits her, I guess. Those sweet, abused types."

We're exhausting our list of suspects by the time Sandra asks us if we're ready for the check. I tell her, yes, and not to split them. Mischa protests, but I tell her I have a twenty-dollar bill, and I'd like to spend the whole thing. It's bullshit and I can tell she knows it.

"It's my turn, right?" She smirks at me as Sandra walks away to print our check. I nod and give a curious look. I guess she likes this game more than I thought.

"He's not what he appears to be. From the outside, he seems like an asshole jock, just like his friends. But he's actually nice. Handsome too." She adds the last part with a wink, and my mouth goes dry. I regret denying Sandra's offer of a to-go drink. She seems to snap out of something. Shaking her head, she says, "Guess we'd better get back to the hospital."

We drive back to the hospital in silence, both lost in our thoughts, I'm sure. I'm caught up in her *Clue/Guess Who* description of me. Her mind is likely racing with concerns about her kid brother.

I pull into the drop-off area after Mischa insists I go home.

"I'm fine," she assures me. "Go home and rest. I appreciate everything you've done for us tonight."

She gets out of my car and walks through the emergency room doors without looking back.

Chapter Ten

174

I try to skip school on Monday, but Sheriff Freeman is at my house bright and early this morning to drive me and the Littles to school. He brought Teddy and me home from the hospital since Joe wasn't anywhere to be found, and I had sent Jesse away.

Images of Jesse laughing across the table flood my brain as I sit in the front seat of the patrol car. He does this thing where he runs his hands through his hair, pulling the twists back until they slowly fall back into place around his face. I'm not even sure he notices he's doing it, but five times that night in the diner, he ran his hands through his hair and smiled with teeth. Perfect teeth, wrapped in perfect lips. Perfect lips that he kept licking and biting as he waited for me to guess which patron he'd chosen for the game.

I shake the thoughts out of my head just as we pull in front of the high school. I turn around and bid the Littles farewell. Teddy's back to his normal self, and I'm thankful the hospital gave us a new inhaler to take home with us. That one, plus the one Sheriff Freeman promised to replace, will help tremendously.

The hallways are buzzing when I walk in, and I pray I make it through the day without incident. It's only been a week without the meds, and I can already tell that my mind is fighting to explode. Luckily, I'm used to it. Most people with my disorder don't start showing symptoms until they're my current age. My file at Beacon Pointe notes that I'm among 0.01% of the population who presented symptoms as early as I did. That just means I'm well-equipped with the ability to keep my mind stable until the very last snap.

Speaking of snapping...

"Hey Trey, you should be jealous." I hear Preston's obnoxious voice behind me as I spin the code on my locker. "You've got to bum a ride with Jesse, while your dad is chauffeuring this slut around." Trey doesn't respond, which doesn't surprise me. He's never been that type of guy. I don't know if he's naturally that cool, or if he knows better because of his dad.

"Back off, Preston," Zoey tells him. I slam my locker closed and turn to face Preston but pause when I notice his arm draped around Alyssa Slade, who is smirking at me.

"You are so weird." She's looking me up and down like I disgust her. My weekend wasn't ideal for a girl my age. Actually, that's my entire life. That being said, I'm in a bad mood today and my attire reflects that. Black leggings and an extremely oversized black sweater that might be my grandpa's. Black combat boots adorn my feet. I bought them from a second-hand store in Sacramento last year.

"I didn't know you two were sleeping together," I say inquisitively as I motion between Alyssa and Preston. Zoey and Trey snort to shield their laughter. Alyssa sucks her teeth and maneuvers her body from under Preston's embrace. I smirk before putting my final nail in the conversation. "I doubt Jesse would like that." I hear Alyssa and Preston call me a few choice words, and Nick shoulder-bumps me hard as I walk past him toward the class we all share. Zoey calls him an asshole as she follows me down the hall.

I take my seat near the window, opposite The Elites. When they file in, they throw me dirty looks, but I just wink at them. Zoey's not in this class, but I don't need her protection. I hear a familiar laugh and shift my eyes to the door just as Trey walks in with Jesse following behind him. I try to look away, but our eyes meet, and he walks toward me. My heart pounds a little harder, and I want to look away, but I'm interested in what he has to say, and he's got me captured with his demanding deep brown irises.

"Hey." He places his knuckles on my desk and leans in closer. He smells nice, like fresh soap mixed with some type of cologne.

"Hey," I croak warily.

"How's Teddy?" he asks me, and my heart melts without my permission. He's asking about my little brother? I glance over at The Elites and see that they're all staring at us curiously, so I don't think this is some weird prank. Jesse is really speaking to me in school.

"He's fine." I tear my eyes away from Alyssa's death glare, but I can't bring myself to look at Jesse again, so I stare down at the desk instead. Now Jesse's just talking to the side of my face, but that doesn't stop him.

"Did you stay at the hospital all day yesterday?" he asks. The bell rings and Mr. Thomlin hobbles in and clears his throat.

"Mr. Alford. Please have a seat so that I can start class."

Instead of returning to his side of the classroom next to Alyssa and Trey, Jesse glides past me and takes the seat behind me, forcing a late Lizzie Waiters to stop in her tracks and sit with The Elites. Preston looks like he wants to vomit at this point. If looks could kill, I'd be dead.

I'm on pins and needles in my seat during Mr. Thomlin's lecture on the American Revolution. Jesse's sitting behind me, and I can't help but feel like he's not paying much attention to Thomlin. I can feel him staring at me.

Then again, I sense a lot of stuff that isn't real, apparently.

I end up ditching Zoey at lunch again. This doesn't deter her, however, as she shows up at the general store after school. She's dying for information that is neither important nor juicy.

"It's nothing like that. Teddy had an asthma attack, and Jesse just so happened to be driving past while I was running into town with him." I shrug and press the label gun against the can of sliced carrots in my hand. "He only sat by me because he wanted to know how Teddy was doing." I label another can and then stack them both on the shelf. I often wonder if Mr. Brady gave me this job as a favor to Sheriff Freeman because a lot of this is just busy work that he could do himself.

Zoey sucks her teeth. "Alyssa and Chelsea made it seem like you two were stuck in some lovers' stare-down in the middle of class!" She's posted at the cash register, leaning against the counter, while I'm down the center aisle labeling prices on the new shipment.

"What does Alyssa care, anyway? Isn't she screwing Preston behind Jesse's back?" I snap.

Zoey laughs and shrugs her shoulders. "Who knows? She seems so stuck on Jesse. Maybe she's using Preston to make Jesse jealous?"

I don't mean to, but I give a sarcastic snort. "Jesse's too good for Alyssa, and there is no reason for him to *ever* be jealous of Preston."

My only friend gives me a skeptical look and poses with her hands on her hips. "Just last week, Jesse was an *Elite*. Now he's too good for something?"

"That was before he saved Teddy's life," I remind her.

"If you say so." She chuckles, grabbing a tabloid magazine from the rack and thumbing through it. I hear hissing, followed by a rattling sound. I walk away from the shelves and follow the sound. When I round the small corner that leads to the entrance behind the cash register counter, I see it sitting there on the floor next to Zoey's leg, preparing to strike.

A rattlesnake.

I gasp and immediately grab one of the inventory boxes, dropping it on top of the snake to block it from biting Zoey.

Zoey jumps in place, clearly startled by my sudden box-throwing. "What?"

I look at her as if *she's* the crazy one. I'm about to chastise her for not being very vigilant when a thought hits me.

"Hey, do you mind getting me a few paper towels from the restroom?" I ask her as casually as possible so that I can go through with my lie. "I killed a spider right here."

"Eww!" Zoey shimmies her shoulders in disgust and runs off to retrieve the napkins.

I lift the box, and the snake is gone.

Another hallucination. Some are harder than others to detect. Like the three months that my dad spent convincing me that the neighbors did not own a dog.

It would chase me to our door every time I walked home from school, and I was always too afraid to play in the driveway.

I refused to sit in the living room whenever Grandpa would watch CNN because I was convinced that the anchors were talking directly to me. There was a story about a hitman on the run for shooting at a politician during a rally in Washington, D.C. For a week, I tried to convince my dad that there was no way I could have flown to D.C. and committed the crime. I was only ten, and Anderson Cooper was telling the world that I was a murderer. They had even posted pictures of me, smiling in my fourth-grade school picture, wearing my polka dot jumper. My dad took everything in stride, never making me feel inadequate, or giving the impression that I was a burden on him. He never made me feel bad about being different.

"Here." Zoey hands me the napkin she found in the staff bathroom. I take it and pretend to wipe up spider guts as she returns to her place at the counter.

"I'm leaving Sunday morning," she tells me somberly. "So, if you want, we can meet up for some girl time on Saturday. There's a party at the mill on Friday night. It's my going away party." She shrugs.

"You don't seem too excited." I raise a brow at her. "Why leave if you're not excited about it?"

"I *am* excited," she groans, closing the magazine and facing me. "I can't wait to be closer to Ant. But at that same time, I'm going to miss hanging out with you."

I snort. "We barely hang out, Zoey. I'm always home with the Littles, and you're always with The Elites."

She frowns at me and shakes her head. "We're still friends, Misch. I'm allowed to miss you."

I toss the box over by the side door, refusing to make eye contact with my only friend. I don't want to be cold toward her, but relationships are tough when you're dealing with the mind I have. I take a deep breath and try to clear my mind before Fergal shows up. I haven't seen him since I almost physically assaulted that hospital receptionist, and I'm not looking forward to hearing him laugh at my friendship dilemma with Zoey.

I hear the rattling again and wait for Zoey to scream, but she doesn't. I've got to get this under control, or everything I have planned will fall apart.

Chapter Eleven

170

F riday night marks the end of another dull week, with plenty of attempted bullying at the hands of Preston, Nick, Chelsea, and Alyssa, but very few episodes of psychosis. I've been on such a high all week, wearing the brightest colors I can dig up and nearly skipping to school in the mornings. While all the girls in town are sauntering around in their fall burgundies, browns, and hunter-greens, I'm roaming the hallways in neon Lycra biker shorts and over-sized tunics. Frankie looked like she was going to die of embarrassment as we walked through town. I didn't care, because my fan club of new guys on the mountain trail kept telling me how sexy I looked.

I ask Teddy how he's feeling for the umpteenth time tonight before flopping down on the couch to watch TV. I'm on edge, but that's not rare for me, especially in mania. I can't shake the feeling that tonight's going to be another eventful night like last Saturday. I keep hearing Teddy gasping for air, so I run to his room seven times to shake him awake so that he can take his inhaler.

"Mischa, I'm breathing fine. Cut it out!" he groans and falls back asleep.

On my eighth attempt to save Teddy's life, I'm stopped by an angry, intoxicated Joe just outside the threshold of Maddie and Teddy's room, where their door meets Mom and Joe's bedroom door.

"Will you sit the fuck down somewhere, and stop running through my goddamn house!" he growls at me. "I'm trying to sleep, and your crazy ass keeps waking me up." He's standing halfway out of the door with no shirt on and his eyes are bloodshot.

His house? Last time I checked, this was *my* house he was living in.

"It's Teddy! He's—" I fall short and motion toward a gasping Teddy in bed.

"He's what?" Joe snaps, scratching his bony tattooed chest. "Asleep. He's asleep! Now, get the fuck out of here before you piss me off!"

I sigh and glance at Teddy again. His breathing is steady, so I turn and walk away from Joe. I make it back to the couch and stare at the television set, tuning out Fergal's laughter. He likes to give me the worst suggestions sometimes.

Like how I should end Joe's life before I end my own.

The excitement comes at two o'clock in the morning this time, and not as an asthma attack, but a phone call.

"Heeeeeeyyyyyy bitch, whatcha doin'?" Zoey slurs on the other end of my cell phone, which I replaced yesterday. After the horrors of Teddy's asthma attack last weekend, we can never be caught in an emergency without a working phone again.

"Are you sleeping?" she adds with a laugh. I can hear loud music in the background, accompanied by a bunch of voices and cheering. It would make sense for me to be asleep in the middle of the night, but who needs sleep when mania is causing adrenaline to pump through my body? I haven't slept longer than two hours at night since I've been home.

"If I was, I'm up now."

She laughs obnoxiously. "You are so funny, Mischa."

"And you are so drunk, Zoey. Did you drive?"

"Yep," she says proudly. "Nick keeps trying to get me to go upstairs with him. There's a mattress in one of the rooms. I told him to get over it." She gives another squealing laugh. "I want you here, Mischa! It's my last weekend in Grover. I want to spend it with my best friend."

My heart warms without my permission. We've established a friendship, sure. But she's never referred to me as her best friend. She's mine by default, but the emotional attachment is weak on my end, so I figured she'd given that title to Alyssa or Chelsea.

"I'm not welcome there. Not that I'd want to come anyway," I tell her indifferently. "And stay away from Nick. You're less than forty-eight hours away from being closer to Anthony. Don't screw it up over Nick the Dick."

"Nick the Dick!" she repeats in a loud fit of laughter, and I cringe, hoping no one can hear her.

"Please don't tell me you're driving back drunk," I groan. The road that leads up the mountain toward the mill is dark and winding, lined with enormous trees and rocks.

"How about this?" she halts her laughter. "You come up here for a little while, and then you can be my designated driver!"

I shake my head. "You want me to walk a mile up the dark mountain? What about the cougars?"

"Cougars?" Zoey repeats and laughs again. "Just c'mon, Misch. I want to party with you at least once in our life together!"

I snort. "We've been to a party together, remember?" This shuts her up, or maybe she slipped into a drunken sleep state or something.

"That's different and you know it, Mischa," she mumbles after a few seconds. "Look, I just wanted you to get out and have some fun with us. But I guess we're too *elite* for you. Enjoy the rest of your night." She doesn't wait for me to respond before she just hangs up. I toss the phone on the couch cushion and fold my arms across my chest. Is it too much to ask to just fall into a dull existence?

I go to my bedroom and slip on a black long-sleeve t-shirt and a pair of light gray oversized sweatpants, that I have to roll a few times to fit my small waist, and still, they fall to my hips. I slide on a pair of old sneakers and grab my phone on the way out, just in case I need to call 911 if I get attacked by one of the mountain lions. I keep telling Sheriff Freeman to get a ranger out here.

I make it to the lumber mill without incident, and I can already tell I'm not supposed to be here. I manage to slip inside undetected by the dozen or so teens outside, but the inside is packed. Every teenager in town is here, except me and Neil Gunderson's *Dungeons and Dragons* crew. I didn't see Jesse's GTO outside either. He must have skipped this one. Maybe he's somewhere on top of Alyssa.

I shake the mental image out of my head as I pass Whitney Kolger and Tyler Kendrick making out against the wall of the long hallway that leads to a room with old, broken conveyor belts and tables.

I shouldn't care what Jesse does with Alyssa or anybody else.

They say this lumber mill was one of the most successful commercial mills in the region, but then, a little over one hundred years ago, the town of Grover split up. Much of the population left with the town drunk to a new town. He was the brother of the founder of Grover, but he was a black sheep, so they exiled him from town. While stumbling around in the woods just opposite of Highway 120, he apparently decided to start his own township. He convinced most of the skilled residents in Grover to join him, mostly laborers. Thus, the lumber mill was closed. To this day, August Creek Township is a mysterious little village hidden in the forest that nobody really talks about. The lumber mill was gutted, so it resembles a large empty warehouse with a few rooms suspended upstairs.

Everyone's wasted, so they don't seem to notice me as I weave through the crowd of teenagers. I don't see Zoey anywhere, and I'm starting to worry. And then I hear an unpleasantly familiar voice over the blaring music.

"The fuck is *she* doing here?" Preston slurs, stopping in his tracks with Chelsea behind him. I'm standing at the threshold of a door that leads into a smaller room with a table scattered with red plastic cups and liquor bottles. I roll my eyes and prepare to walk away without responding, but he's garnered the attention of his buddies, and Nick is walking over with a wobbly Zoey.

Zoey sees me and starts screeching like Maddie whenever I bring home her favorite fruit chews from work. "You came!"

"Why are you here?" Preston approaches me. Before I can react, Zoey pushes him back.

"*I* invited her. It's *my* going-away party, and she's my best friend," she tells them confidently, and for a moment, I think her buzz has worn off. Chelsea sucks her teeth and rolls her eyes, while Preston looks at me like I'm covered in dog shit. I just stand there taking it all in, fighting the mania in my mind that tells me to grab the bottle out of Preston's hand, break it against the wall, and cut his fucking jugular open. Sheriff Freeman and the adults of Grover don't mind the high school kids coming up here to hang out, as long as they don't cause any trouble. If I start a fight up here and ruin that for them, I might as well kiss what little sanity I have left goodbye. They'd make my life a bigger hell than it already is.

"Yeah, well, just keep her away from the bedrooms," he shoots back sarcastically, taking a swig of his beer bottle. "Wouldn't want anyone getting accused of rape."

"That's not funny," Zoey whines and shoots me an apologetic look.

I just shrug and smirk, looking Preston square in the face. "What's wrong Preston? Mad that Blake got to it first?"

Zoey and Chelsea both gasp, and Preston advances toward me like he's about to grab me. I attempt to back up but slam hard into a taller body. An arm reaches out and pushes Preston back away from me. Not roughly, but enough to stop him.

"I didn't know you were into fighting girls, Preston." Jesse's voice is smooth above me. I'm pressed against his chest, and he hasn't attempted to push me away.

"You wish, you lying bitch," Preston spits out at me, completely ignoring Jesse's words. He walks away and Chelsea follows him. Nick is still standing there, holding Zoey around the waist and staring at me like he wants to finish what Preston started.

If Preston wasn't a complete dumbass, I'd use the analogy that Preston was the brains of The Elites and Nick was the muscle. But Preston's just their leader. He's the one who rallies them up to hate me, and he talks the biggest game. Nick is quiet, but there's intimidation there too. I don't know what Zoey sees in him. He's handsome, sure, in a meathead kind of way. He's massive in both stature and build, with short soft curls and ultra-light-bright skin because, like me, he's got a white mom and a deceased Black dad. Unlike me, Mrs. Gillespie's genes have a tighter hold on him.

Zoey shimmies from under Nick's grasp and takes my hand. "I can't believe you really showed up, Misch."

"I didn't want you drinking and driving," I tell her. I momentarily forget that I'm leaning against Jesse's inviting form until I'm harshly shoved against the wall.

"What are you doing pressing up on *my boyfriend?*" Alyssa yells at me.

"What the hell Lys!" Zoey gasps.

I push away from the wall calmly. It's the first time any of The Elites, besides Preston and his brother, have physically assaulted me. I'm going to chalk it up to Alyssa being drunk, and *not* beat her ass.

"I thought 'your boyfriend' just walked that way." I motion toward the room where Preston and Nick are still shooting daggers at me.

Alyssa rolls her hazel eyes. "You don't know what you're talking about. Everyone knows about me and Jesse." She motions between herself and Jesse, who is talking with Trey and completely ignoring her. I wonder if he even noticed me leaning against him. Hell, he doesn't even seem to notice I was just shoved into a wall. He must sense me staring at him because he turns and smirks at me.

"Yeah," I respond to Alyssa, but I keep my eyes on her supposed boyfriend. "Yeah, I guess they do."

She gives out a loud *'hmph'* and walks away. I break my staring contest with Jesse and call out to her.

"Oh, and Alyssa?"

She stops walking and whips her head around, causing her hair to swing dramatically. I motion for her to come back over, and she complies, curious about what I have to say. I lean in close to her, our chests almost bumping, only I'm a couple of inches taller than she is.

"If you *ever* put your hands on me again—me pressing against your *boyfriend* will be the least of your problems. I'll fucking gut you," I tell her through gritted teeth. I hear Trey Freeman choke back shock and laughter as Alyssa gasps and backs away from me.

I feel Jesse's strong arm wrap around my shoulder and pull me away from Alyssa. "I think you've threatened enough people lately." He's fighting a laugh, and I can smell the beer on his breath. He ushers me to the other side of the room where the old conveyors are, with Zoey following us.

"I'll be right back," he murmurs and then disappears into the crowd, toward the little kitchen area we were just standing near.

"I'm sorry they were being so horrible to you, but you handled it like a pro." Zoey adds the last part with a drunken giggle. Another girl from our high school comes over and grabs Zoey's attention, leaving me sitting on the conveyor belt alone to examine the room. No one seems to pay me any attention. I'm not sure if they're too drunk and it's too dark to notice, or if they just don't care.

I feel a presence behind me, and warm breath on my ear. I know it's Jesse before he even speaks.

"She's kind of strange, but she's really cute when she's mad," he whispers in my ear, and I feel the hairs all over my body rise. He offers me the plastic cup that he's holding.

I shake my head. "I don't drink." My mind is already screwed up. I don't need alcohol contributing to it.

"I'll take it!" Zoey happily snatches the cup from him and downs the mixed drink. She stumbles a little, and both Jesse and I reach out to stabilize her.

"We should probably get you home, Zo." I motion toward the front of the building.

She nods, agreeing with me, and then waves frantically at Jesse. "See you later, Jesse! It was nice knowing ya!"

"You're not dying, Zoey. Just moving away," Jesse says with a laugh. I wrap Zoey's arms around my shoulders, and she rests all of her weight on me as I grab her around the waist to help her walk toward the exit. Once we're outside, I pull her toward her car. It's a bright blue Ford Focus she got two summers ago.

"Hey!" Jesse calls out, and I pause and crane my neck back to see what he wants. "Can I catch a ride home with you guys?" I look at Zoey for an answer to his question. She nods sloppily and gives him a thumbs up.

He jogs over to us and scoops Zoey over his shoulder, causing her to laugh and scream. "I'll help you to the car." I smile and follow behind them. When we make it to the car, Jesse places Zoey in the back seat and takes the passenger's seat.

"I never thought I'd see you partying at the mill." Jesse is obliviously intoxicated. His words are slightly slurred, and his lids are low.

"You still haven't," I reply as we cruise down the road. "I wasn't there to party. I was there because Zoey asked me to help her."

"Yeah, it was *my* going away party!" Zoey sits up briefly and slurs before falling back across the seat.

Jesse laughs hard. "It's not her party! We won our game tonight!" They both laugh, and I wonder if it's some secret elite inside joke I'm missing, or if drunk seventeen-year-olds are always this weird.

"I'll side with Zoey since I like her," I mumble. When I look at my friend in the rearview mirror, she's snoring softly already.

"Oh? So, you don't like me, Mischa?" Jesse Alford has the sexiest voice I've ever heard. And he says my name correctly. When I look over at him, his head flops lazily toward me, and he's looking at me with those low eyes and he's biting his bottom lip.

"You're not a total asshole, I guess." I deadpan and then return my eyes to the road. The 3% of logic in me tells my brain not to feed into it. That he's been drinking all night, and he's just messing with me. The 97% of rising mania in my brain is screaming to pull over and mount him.

Logic wins.

"I ran the winning touchdown tonight," he tells me, and I can feel that he's still looking at the side of my face. "And you weren't even there to see it."

My breath hitches, and I swallow hard. He's flirting with me, and I don't know how much more I can take. "I never go to the football games."

"Well, you should," he replies in his stupid bedroom voice. "You should come see me play."

We pass my house, and I steal a glance past him to make sure there's no chaos. The mountain lions are gone, and I don't see any lights on in the distance.

Jesse is looking at the house as well, and when we pass it completely, he clears his throat. "How's Teddy?"

I nod, even though he's still looking outside. "He's fine. He was breathing funny before I left, but he should be fine." Jesse doesn't respond, just nods his head. Zoey pops up unexpectedly, scaring me nearly to death and causing me to swerve a little.

"Oh my gosh, guys!" she exclaims. "In two days, I'll be making out with Ant!"

I laugh after regaining control of the car. "Is he meeting you in San Diego?"

"Yep! That's the plan!" she sings out, swaying back and forth like she's trying to stay upright.

"Who the hell is Ant?" Jesse scrunches his face and turns to look at her and then at me.

"Her boyfriend in Arizona." I shrug. Jesse bursts out in laughter. "What's so funny?" Zoey and I ask at the same time.

"You have a boyfriend?" he asks between laughs. "You were just hooking up with Nick an hour ago!"

Zoey's eyes bulge, and she looks at me like a kid who got caught stealing candy at the store. "We kissed for like thirty seconds!"

"Zoey!" I scold her. We're entering town now. I know how to get to Zoey's house, but I'm not sure where I'm taking Jesse, who is still curled in the passenger seat, laughing hysterically at Zoey's plight.

"What?" Zoey whines. "We've got history. I don't love him, though."

"You don't just randomly make out with people you don't love, Zoey!" I tell her, even though I know it's bullshit. I've made out with Javi, my weed dealer, plenty of times. It gets me discounts.

Zoey flops back down in the backseat, leaving Jesse and me alone again. He's humming along and drumming his fingers to the melody of the song playing softly on the radio. His twisted strands are pulled back in a ponytail showing off the undercut. His fingers are copying the melody against the dark blue fabric of his jeans. He wears dark blue jeans and black shirts a lot. Oh, and can't forget his signature leather jacket.

"So, where am I taking you?" I ask him after finishing my personal assessment of him. We're reaching the part of Main Street where the road branches off to lead to the three different subdivisions.

"To my house, duh," he replies, folding his arms across his chest and shifting in his seat to get more comfortable in the compact car.

"No shit, Sherlock," I huff. "Where do you live?"

He smirks and raises a brow at me. "You really don't know where I live?"

"No, why would I?" I frown at him. Am *I* the crazy one, or is he?

"I know where everyone in town lives. Most people do," he retorts.

"Well, I never get the invites to visit, so I don't know where people live. Nor do I care."

He regards me for a moment. It's as if he's got something he wants to say. He shakes his head and points to the fork that goes left. "Middlebrook."

I snicker and accidentally speak my thoughts out loud. "Why do they call it Middlebrook when it's not even the neighborhood in the middle of town?" Springbrook is.

He laughs too. "I don't know, but that's random as hell."

"Random is what I'm all about," I reply, turning into his subdivision. His house is a two-story craftsman, nestled comfortably in the center of Middlebrook, way nicer than our double-wide in the woods. I see the GTO outside of the garage with a car cover over it.

"Thanks for the ride, Mischa." He groans and stretches. His head does that flop sideways thing again, and he flashes me a lopsided grin. "You suck at driving, by the way."

I suck my teeth and look away from him. Not because I'm angry, but because I can't keep eye contact with him anymore. He's sending my hormones into a frenzy, and all he's doing is *talking*.

"I'll see you in the morning," he calls back as he heads toward his house.

"So, you'll ditch me on my last day so you can hang out with Jesse Alford?" Zoey scoffs. She climbs over the center console and flops down in the passenger seat, just as I'm driving away from Jesse's house. I wonder how she keeps popping in and out of consciousness.

"I'm not hanging out with him. It's for that stupid school project." I wonder how Neil Gunderson would react if he knew people completely disregarded his existence.

"Whatever," Zoey murmurs and folds her arms like a pouting child. I know she's pissed, but this is for the best. If she moves away pissed off at me, it'll soften the blow for her when she finds out I'm gone forever.

I drop Zoey and her car off at her house in Springbrook. She offers to let me spend the night since it's so late, but I decline because I know her parents hate me, and I won't be sleeping tonight, anyway. Walking through our empty town back to the foothills is just what I need to clear my mind.

Chapter Twelve

The gravity hills of Northern California are next on Neil's list of places to explore. There's one about an hour away off of CA-108, so we gas up the GTO and hit the highway unpunctually at noon.

"How do you oversleep for three hours?" Neil whines from the backseat.

I laugh and prop my feet up on Jesse's dash, resting my hands behind my head. It's another mini-shorts day, only I swap my crop tops for a tank-top, and my boots for a pair of Converse sneakers.

"Because Jesse spent the entire night getting wasted and didn't make it home until three-thirty in the morning," I explain, throwing a smirk at the side of Jesse's face. I notice the corners of his mouth twitch as he tries to fight a smile. He hasn't mentioned last night or the way he was flirting with me at all, and now I wonder if I made it up. I once had a three-month relationship with our local news anchor, before Joe finally verbally bashed me enough to make me realize I'd never met the man before.

"It's not like you have anything better to do." His comment is directed at Neil.

"I'll have you know I have dinner plans with my girlfriend tonight," Neil shoots back defensively.

I twist my head back and give him a skeptical look. "*You* have a girlfriend?"

"Yes, I do." He frowns at me. "Why is that so hard to believe?"

Jesse laughs, and I continue to stare at Neil in disbelief. He's got these thick glasses and an acne-ridden face. His reddish hair is parted and styled to the side like an English schoolboy or something. He doesn't scream boyfriend material at all.

"Judgment from the most hated girl in town." Neil snorts and folds his arms across his chest. He's sitting in the middle of the backseat bench, and I briefly wonder why. Maybe he thinks we'll forget he's there if he doesn't make himself visible. "When's the last time you had a date?"

"Ha! Are you kidding me? Jesse here took me on a date last Saturday. Well, technically Sunday morning." I playfully smack Jesse's arm before nestling back into place. He doesn't respond, just shakes his head.

"Umm... did I miss something?" Neil asks, and I bet he's looking between the two of us, confused.

"It's too quiet!" I blurt out, reaching for the stereo knobs.

"You haven't stopped talking since we left town," Jesse reminds me with an incredulous tone.

"You know what I mean," I mumble, even though I don't even know what I mean. I turn the tuners on the radio until I land on a station that's not riddled with static. "Oh! I love this song!" I exclaimed just as "Mr. Blue Sky" plays from the speakers. I crank up the dial, but Jesse reaches over and turns it back down slightly.

"What the hell!" he huffs. "Are you trying to blow my speakers or something?" He seems a little annoyed, but I ignore him and start singing the lyrics to the song and bobbing my head around. Jesse tries to pretend like he's irritated with me, but I notice he's drumming his fingers to the melody of the song just like last night. When the chorus hits, I belt out the words, and I'm surprised to hear two other voices singing along with me. Granted, not as loud or animated as me, but still Neil and Jesse have joined in.

The rest of the ride goes on with my singing along to the radio, and the boys chiming in occasionally, but mostly, they're quiet. I steal an occasional glance at Jesse. I don't know why I'm so fascinated with him lately. It's like a weird aura that pulls my thoughts to him whenever we're around each other. I like the way he drives. Cool and confident, his elbow on the window, and his right arm stretched out as he grips the steering wheel and cruises down the empty highway.

He's wearing a long-sleeve black thermal, but I can still see the definition in his arms. The window is down, and the wind is blowing his hair back. I absently run my fingers through my unruly mane.

We follow the GPS until we start to see tourist signs pointing the way to the gravity hill roads and something called the Gravity House.

"It's a house that sits on a flat surface but gives you the feeling it's tilting when you're inside of it," Neil explains. A few cars are driving around slowly on the path to the gravity hill, but it's still pretty empty here. We stop at the information booth and ask for directions to the spot to get the best experience and then drive to a paved road surrounded by woods. Jesse drives to the bottom of the sloped road and parks the car.

"Okay, so you're supposed to put the car in neutral, and turn it off," I instruct Jesse, reading from the pamphlet I snagged at the info booth. He brings the gearshift down to neutral and then kills the engine. He relaxes in his seat, and I can already tell he's skeptical about the magic of the gravity hill.

"Now the car will roll up the hill, supposedly," I tell them. Resting the pamphlet on my lap.

"Do you actually believe in this stuff?" Jesse asks as we sit in silence, waiting for something to happen. My eyes are closed, and I nod my head. I see unbelievable things every moment of my life. Why should this be any different?

"The point is to have something to write about. I don't care if it's real or not," Neil chimes in, obviously a skeptic as well.

"Anything could happen." I wish they'd stop bitching. "Just shut up and concentrate." I hear Jesse grunt, but he says nothing else.

After another twenty seconds, it happens.

There is this feeling inside the car, like a force is pulling it backward up the hill. My eyes fly open and for a moment, I think I'm the only one feeling it. If I'm the only one feeling it, then it's the psychosis in me acting out. But then I hear Jesse murmur *oh shit,* and when I look over at him, he's leaning forward, looking at the speedometer.

"Okay, so you guys feel that too, right?" Neil stammers out. He is sitting stiff like a cat that just got thrown into a swimming pool.

I nod. "I told you!" I'm giddy and smiling brightly. These are things normal teenagers get to experience. Not forming a line to be force-fed their daily pills.

Neil scribbles down notes about what happened, and Jesse starts the car and drives down the road. The next set of signs points to the Gravity House, so we decide to check it out too.

"I'm going to pass," Neil groans as he gets out of the back seat from the passenger's side. "I'm getting motion sickness." Jesse and I give him matching disgusted looks and then laugh as we walk away.

The Gravity House is a log cabin that resembles something out of a slasher film. There's a dusty porch and boarded windows. I lead the way up the dirt path in front of the cabin, and Jesse trails behind me.

"Reminds me of home," I joke, and I hear him laugh behind me. The old, wooden steps creak as we take them onto the porch. The door is open already, so we're able to walk right in. Unlike the car, the force is ever-present as soon as we step into the house. My body is immediately pulled toward the back of the room, and I stumble to resist it.

"Woah!" I yell as I trip over my feet. Jesse grabs my arms to stabilize me as best as he can, but he's equally thrown off.

"I had way too much to drink last night." He chuckles. "I can't handle this again."

I laugh and steady myself, pulling away and attempting to walk straight. After a few minutes of walking like a newborn baby deer, I feel confident enough to walk around the small room.

"This is amazing," I murmur. There isn't much to look at in the dusty, single-room building, so I examine the short ceiling and the table and two chairs sitting in the center of the room. My eyes finally land on Jesse, whose tall form is taking baby steps across the room to keep from falling.

I try to stifle my laugh, but it blurts out anyway. He looks at me and grins sheepishly. "Shut up."

"It's not that hard once you get the hang of it." I gallop around him, only losing my footing once.

"You can walk in this freaky ass house, but you suck at driving," he mumbles, swatting me away.

I stop skipping and look at him with a smirk. "So, you *do* remember last night?" It's more of an accusation than a question.

"Of course I do." He shrugs. "What's not to remember?"

I'm not sure if he's really forgotten, and he's just playing cool, or if he's challenging my boldness. Either way, I've never been one to shy away from words.

"You were flirting with me." I shrug, standing in front of him, holding my hips. He smirks and chuckles a little, shaking his head, and looking everywhere but at me. "Don't worry, I didn't take it to heart." I laugh with him. "I know you were drunk."

We stand there for a few moments in awkward silence. He's still not looking at me, and I feel like this is the point where I'm supposed to be embarrassed by rejection. Good thing you can only feel rejected if it's something you wanted in the first place. None of this will matter in a few months, so knowing that Jesse Alford likes to flirt with me after a few beers, feels just as it did before we'd ever spoken words to each other. It doesn't matter.

I smile and get a surge of confidence out of nowhere, which wills me to reach out and grab his wrists. He looks at me oddly, but then I use all the weight I have to twirl us around.

"Mischa, hell no!" He's protesting, but he's also laughing, so I don't stop. Our feet stomp on the floor as I project us in circles, and Jesse tries to resist. We're both laughing so hard that we lose our footing, and I stumble backward.

"Oh, shit!" Jesse laughs and reaches for me. He falls short of grabbing me, so he has to resort to using his weight to press me against the wall before I fall to the floor. Now I'm pinned against the wooden wall by the force of the Gravity House and Jesse's body, laughing hysterically. I don't even notice that he's stopped laughing and is staring down at me, or that his left hand has slipped down my side and is resting on my hip. His other arm is bent at the elbow and resting against the wall.

When I finally realize what's happening, I calm my laughter and take a few slow breaths before looking up at him. Our chests and faces are inches apart, and I can smell the minty toothpaste on his breath.

"Jesse?" I breathe out.

He doesn't respond. He just closes the last few inches of space between us with his lips on mine. I moan and his tongue slips into my mouth, and it's all fireworks and sappy love music from there. His grip on my waist tightens, and he lifts me against the wall with one swift movement, never breaking our lip lock. I instinctively wrap my legs around his waist, and now we're in a full-on make-out session. This is more intense than anything I've experienced. I've never kissed a guy like this before. It's one of those kisses that could only lead to one thing. That is... if there was a bed in this dirty, little cabin. I squeeze his biceps harder at the thought.

Fuck it! We can do it right here against this wall.

I moan again at that thought.

I hear a disgusted *'ugh'* sound, and my eyes snap open. A middle-aged woman is standing at the threshold of the cabin door, shooting daggers at us.

"This is not some *hook-up spot* for horny teenagers!" she scolds us, placing her hands on her hips. "This is a place of history!"

Jesse puts me down and steps away a few inches. His head is hanging, and his twists cover his face, but I'm assuming his gaze is fixed on the floor.

I laugh at the woman's words. "Well, I think we just made it a little more interesting," I say with a shrug. Jesse lifts his head up slightly so that our eyes meet. He's got humor in his eyes, just like me.

As we make our exit, it feels like the Gravity House is trying to pull us back in.

Like it knows, we've reached a point of no return.

Chapter Thirteen

165

It's been four days since I've spoken to Jesse, and I'm not surprised. Guys like Jesse Alford don't kiss girls like me and then speak to them the next day.

I expected to see him in town Sunday when I met up with Zoey to say goodbye, but he wasn't there. Alyssa was there with Chelsea, giving me the evil eye. I wish I could have sent her my mental images of Jesse pinning me to the wall of the Gravity House, but what would it matter? It meant nothing to him.

The Littles are in a frenzy when I get home from work today. It's Halloween, my least favorite holiday because I'm forced to walk the Littles through town while they beg for candy from the very people who think our little family is scum. This year, Frankie is skipping trick-or-treating to go to the middle school's Halloween carnival.

"I'm so excited!" Maddie squeals while she jumps on the couch. I snap at her to get down, but she doesn't take it personally. She just jumps down onto the floor and starts running around the living room.

Frankie is walking through the house with her phone glued to her ear. I heard she dropped Billy Weasel for some basketball player at the middle school. She's apparently trying to date within the current sporting seasons.

"Where's Teddy?" I ask her, but she just walks past me without answering.

I walk down the hallway, stopping myself from checking Teddy's bedroom because I notice my mom's bedroom door is open. When I peek in, I find Teddy laying on his stomach watching TV while Mom snores softly.

"What are you doing?" I ask him, even though I already know the answer.

Every year there's a John Carpenter's *Halloween* marathon, where they play all the classic Michael Myers slasher films. I once told the Littles that those were our mom's favorite movies. Now, Teddy watches them with her unconscious body every Halloween. It's kind of morbid to me, but Teddy maintains that he's too afraid to watch them alone. When I'm in a bad mood, I like to spoil it for him and remind him that our mother is always sleeping during the marathon.

"She'll wake up during the good parts." He doesn't look at me as he speaks, just watches Michael stalk through the hospital.

"Well, go get ready for dinner, then we'll go trick-or-treating," I say. He rolls off of the queen-sized platform bed and dashes past me toward the kitchen. I'm just about to leave as well when I notice my mom stirring awake.

"Mischa?" she calls out in a groggy voice. "What time is it?" I roll my eyes and resist the urge to tell her she should be more concerned with what *month* it is. Time doesn't matter to the perpetually depressed.

She looks around for the alarm clock, but it's gone. Joe got drunk last weekend and threw it at the wall when it wouldn't stop beeping. It was another attempt by Teddy to get mom to wake up and spend time with us. Her eyes land on the gruesome scene of Michael Myers murdering a nurse in the hospital, and she gasps, probably realizing what day it is. Teddy was right. She always wakes up during the good parts.

"Oh my goodness, it's Halloween!" She shuffles to get out of bed but gets tangled in her sheets and ends up falling to the floor. I'm feeling disconnected today—a side effect of my condition, I guess—so I don't move to help her. I just stare down at her pathetic form. She starts frantically looking around, but for what, I'm not sure.

"Find my car keys. If we drive fast enough, we can make it to a Wal-Mart or something and get last-minute costumes." She's still sitting on her knees, hair messy, and wearing the same silk nightgown she's had on for the past week.

I roll my eyes and dryly inform her I've already taken care of that. "I bought their costumes two months ago." I had a free check back in August, so I ordered their costumes online and had them delivered to the general store so that Joe wouldn't ask questions. He doesn't like for money to be wasted on anything leisurely, except for beer and cigarettes. Frankie wanted to be a witch, so I bought her a discount witch's dress and hat that I found on the website and borrowed an old broom from the store. Teddy asked for a Darth Vader costume, and Maddie wanted to be a unicorn.

"Thanks, Sweetie. What would I do without you?" my mom says as she looks up at me pitifully, still kneeling on the floor. She stands and goes into the bathroom to shower, and I leave to feed the Littles.

After dinner, I send them to their rooms to get dressed so that we can get this stupid night over with. I immediately hear Frankie groan with frustration when she pulls her costume out of the cardboard box it came in.

"Mischa, what is this?" She sucks her teeth and throws her narrow hip out. She's standing at the entrance to the kitchen holding the black dress as if it were garbage.

"It's a witch's dress, Francesca." I sigh, trying not to lose my patience. My eyes catch the flickering of the light over the kitchen sink. I just replaced it yesterday, and it's already blowing out.

Frankie glares at me. "I thought you were buying me a cheerleading outfit? I wanted to be a zombie cheerleader."

"No, you specifically said a witch," I remind her, walking over and tapping the light bulb.

"That was *months* ago! I changed my mind a few weeks ago," she says, crossing her arms, still gripping the dress. "What are you doing?" she asks me in an annoyed tone.

"This bulb keeps going out. It's blinking," I explain as I attempt to tighten the bulb. It doesn't bulge.

"No, it's not." I turn to gauge her face, and she's serious. I look back at the bulb and it's still blinking.

Great.

"Frankie, just wear the damn costume or stay home!" I step away from the bulb just as Frankie huffs and stomps down the hallway. Fergal follows me down the hallway toward the room I share with my bratty little sister. I pull out the old trunk I keep in the back of my closet and fish through it. I find my old cheerleading uniform from the two weeks I spent going to practice at my school in Monterey. I told my dad I wanted to be a cheerleader, and he signed me up. After two weeks, I lost interest and told him I wasn't going back to practice. He didn't get upset, just asked me what I wanted to try next. He died before I made it to my first basketball practice.

"Here." I toss the uniform at Frankie, who is sitting on her bed, pouting.

"Where'd you get this?" she asks me as she examines the blue and white flyaway skirt and top.

"It's my old uniform," I tell her as I close the trunk and shove it back into the closet. "There's fake blood in the hallway closet from Teddy's vampire costume last year," I add, before going to help Maddie get dressed.

"I'm ready, I'm ready, I'm ready!" Maddie sings as she jumps on her bed. She's wearing a soft pink unitard and ballet flats. I couldn't find any cheap unicorn costumes, so I made hers. I can't help but smile as Maddie's eyes turn into saucers when she sees the multicolored tulle skirt I've pieced together.

"It's so pretty, Mischa!" She marvels at it and begins jumping again.

"There's a train on the back of the skirt. That's supposed to be the tail." She furrows her brows, confused. I gesture to the lengthy fabric, and she nods with appreciation. I bought the horn online for six dollars and then threw in a pair of butterfly wings to get free shipping.

Teddy comes out of the bathroom in full Sith lord regalia, just as Frankie appears in the hallway in my cheerleading outfit. She's older than I was when I wore it, but it fits her just fine. Frankie's tall for her age, long and willowy like a model.

"We'll need to come up with a code word, so that I'll know if you're making Darth Vader breathing sounds or having another asthma attack," I tell Teddy. I can't see his face, so I don't know if he liked my tasteless joke, but Frankie chuckles softly.

"Can you help me with the fake blood?" she asks me quietly, obviously humbled by my kind gesture earlier. I go into the hallway and take the tube from her, squeezing the fake blood all over the shoulders and chest of the uniform. I don't care if it messes up the fabric. In a few months, its sentimental value will mean nothing.

"What are you doing, Mischa?" Frankie screeches and backs away from me frantically.

I give her a curious look and motion toward the fake blood in my hand. "You asked me for help with the fake blood. I thought you wanted me to squirt some on you?"

"No, I didn't!" she huffs and holds her arms out. "I didn't even talk to you!"

I screw my face up and shake my head. "Stop messing around, Frankie. We're going to be late."

"You ruined my costume!" she yells at me, motioning to the red streaks of paint I've decorated on the top of the uniform.

"You wanted to be a zombie cheerleader. There you go!" I roll my eyes, growing more frustrated with Frankie and her dramatic antics. I screw the top on the tube and toss it in the bathroom trash can.

"*Zombie* cheerleader? What are you talking about?" she shoots back, frowning deeper. "I said a *sexy* cheerleader. How the hell did you get *zombie* out of that?"

"Frankie, you clearly said '*zombie*' in the kitchen about ten minutes ago." Now I'm yelling. Who in the hell does she think she's yelling at? "Besides, you're too young to be a *sexy* anything!"

"What's with all the screaming?" I hear my mother's voice from behind me and turn to see her standing at her bedroom door wearing a dingy bathrobe.

"Mischa's acting all crazy!" Frankie points at me and yells again.

"Don't call your sister crazy, Frankie," my mom snaps at her before yawning. "Mischa, what's going on?"

I hear another familiar voice, and when I turn to look inside the bathroom, Fergal's standing there laughing and mimicking Frankie's words in a sing-song way.

"Mischa's acting cray-zee, Mischa's acting cray-zee."

"She swears I said one thing when I said another!" Frankie explains with her voice still raised. "Then she squirted food coloring all over me!"

My mom gives me a funny look, but before she can react, I point out a valid fact. "Then why did you bring me the fake blood, Frankie? Huh?" I ask her triumphantly.

"*I* didn't bring it to you." Her jaw drops, and I can feel my mother staring at me intensely. "You were already holding it!"

As if on cue, my mom brushes past me, into the bathroom, and opens the medicine cabinet. She fishes through the bottles until she finds the clozapine. Fergal's beside her, telling her that her assumption is correct. That I haven't been taking my antipsychotics. She dumps the contents in her palm and stares at them, mentally calculating how many should be there if I'm taking them properly. My mother is a mathematic genius, but she's not coherent enough to think past the fact that just because the right number of pills are missing, doesn't mean they're inside my system. Maybe if she woke up every day before six o'clock in the evening, she could catch me flushing them.

"Mom, it was a mistake. I just misheard Frankie. That's it!" I plead with her after I've stepped into the bathroom. Teddy has left his discarded clothes and underwear on the floor in front of the toilet, but I'm sure she won't tell him to clean up after himself.

"Swear to me, Mischa!" She puts the pills back in the container and grabs me by the shoulders, shaking me a little.

"I swear, Mom," I reply softly. I'm struggling to meet her eyes because I'm literally lying straight in her face.

"Mischa, I'm ready!" Maddie sings out and hops inside the bathroom, showing off the butterfly wings on her back and the crooked horn on her forehead. "Look, Mommy! Mischa made me a unicorn!"

My mom stares at me for a few seconds longer before turning and bending down to examine Maddie's costume. While she's complimenting the colors and how beautiful Maddie looks, I squeeze past them and slam the door to Mom's bathroom so that I can shower. I don't really want to dress up for Halloween, but Maddie thinks it's more fun if I do, and I'd never want to ruin her fun.

I eye Joe's straight razor as I step out of the shower. I'm not sure how I'm going to do it in April. I guess it'll just happen.

When I step into our room, Frankie is sitting on the bed. She looks up at me and frowns. Not an angry frown, but an uncomfortable one.

"I'm sorry I got you in trouble," she murmurs.

"I'm sorry I dowsed you in red goo," I mumble with a deadpan face. I brush my wet hair into two slick ponytails before braiding them. My hair won't last in this style for long. Eventually, it'll crawl up toward my scalp and frizz into the mixture of waves and curls.

"What's going on? Why did Mom freak out back there?" she asks me.

The Littles don't know about my condition. Frankie just thinks I'm a freak like the rest of our peers in town, and Teddy and Maddie don't really notice. My stints in the psychiatric hospital usually take place after a huge fight with Joe, so they all assume I've been sent away by him every time I disappear. When I turned the gas on and almost killed Teddy, my mom told them I was just being irresponsible.

"Why does Mom do half the things she does?" I should feel bad for turning this on my mother when I'm the one who's supposedly hallucinating and causing all of this chaos. I have to keep my secrets safe, though. For my sake and the sake of the Littles. If I get hauled off to Beacon Pointe for good next time, the Littles and Grandpa won't have anyone.

"I guess being a sexy, zombie cheerleader isn't so bad." Frankie sighs and stands up. I put on the black dress and stockings that I already had in my closet. Yesterday, I sewed a white color onto the dress to complete the outfit.

I smile at her and nod toward the door. "Let's go before Maddie jumps off the roof."

We part ways with Frankie the Sexy Zombie Cheerleader in front of the gymnasium of Grover Middle School, then Vader, Rainbow Sparkles, and I head toward the neighborhoods.

"I want to go that way!" Maddie is still bouncing up and down, causing her fabric horn to flop around. There are miniature reflectors on the wings, causing them to glow in the night. We're standing at the fork that separates the three neighborhoods. Maddie's pointing left.

Middlebrook.

I try to protest, but Maddie is already taking off in that direction. Teddy follows close behind, and they both run up to the first house on the first street.

It's easy to find out where a person lives in Grover because they all have these obnoxious mailboxes with their family's name printed on them in fancy script and the unique insignia of each neighborhood. Middlebrook's insignia is a sparrow.

Luckily, Teddy's wearing a mask, and no one really recognizes little Maddie. Halfway down the street, we come across a mailbox that reads *'Wessel,'* and I inwardly cringe with rage at the thought of the Wessels being assholes to my trick-or-treating siblings all because I physically assaulted their son.

The Littles walk away from the Wessel house unscathed, though I swear I see Mrs. Weasel flip me the bird. They hit every house on the street before rounding the corner and blowing through the next one. After a while, they blend in with the other dozens of kids trekking the streets, and for a moment, I feel like they could be normal. They would be normal if it wasn't for me.

I'm shaken out of my thoughts by the sound of growling. When I look behind me, I see a black dog. Not just a normal dog, but a huge, snarling dog with its teeth bared like it's ready to attack. It lets out a sharp bark, causing me to jump and scamper backward, nearly tripping over the curb. It advances toward me, barking again, and I'm just about to scream when I feel someone tapping me on the shoulder.

"Hey." It's Jesse.

I turn to face him and then back to the dog. There are parents and children in costumes everywhere, and no one seems to pay Cujo any mind. He's not focusing on them either. Only me.

"You should warn your boyfriend about that dog, girly." I hear Fergal say. I look past the dog to find him leaning against a light pole across the street. He's laughing hysterically, and I frown at him.

"Hellooooo!" Jesse draws out, waving his hand in my face. I shake my head and turn my frown on him. He's giving me a smile that's both charming and amused as if he's been laughing at me.

When I turn back toward the street, the dog is gone. So is Fergal.

"Didn't you see that dog?" I ask him incredulously.

He looks around briefly, still wearing his amused look. "What dog?"

I give the street one more examination before deciding to drop the subject. That's when I remember I haven't seen my siblings in the past couple of minutes.

"Shit, where'd they go?" I mumble, walking past Jesse toward the last house I saw them walking up to. I read the name *'Alford'* on the mailbox and instantly want to die. Not my normal wanting to die. Of embarrassment this time.

"You looking for your little brother and sister?" Jesse calls out. I turn to him and nod. "What are they?" he asks next. I frown at him, confused by his question. He chuckles and adds, "Their costumes?"

"Oh, yeah, their costumes," I mumble. "Teddy is Darth Vader and Maddie is a unicorn."

Jesse points to a crowd of kids a few doors down. "I think they're at the Williamsons' door."

I nod and walk toward the crowd of kids. When they break off to head to the next house, I spot Maddie's wings reflecting in the streetlights. Teddy's holding her hand and dragging her to the next house with the other kids. It must be nice to feel like you belong. Even if you have to wear a costume so that no one knows it's you.

"Mind if I walk with you?" I hear Jesse call out to me. Before I know it, he's beside me, clad in his football uniform, minus that padding and helmet. I glance at him and then call out to Teddy and Maddie to wait up, but they ignore me and keep following the crowd of kids.

"Nice costume." I can hear the grin in Jesse's voice as he speaks, and it's hard to gauge whether he's making fun of me or really paying me a compliment.

"What costume?" I reply dryly. "This is how I always dress."

Jesse laughs and says, "Bullshit. You're clearly Wednesday Addams."

I peek at him curiously. He's the only person who recognized my costume. Even my mom and Frankie didn't notice I was dressed up. We walk in silence for a few seconds, following the kids to the next house. I speak up after the silence becomes deafening. If I'm quiet for too long, I hear the voices. When I hear the voices, it's hard to distinguish which ones are real, and which ones are supposedly only in my head.

"Pretty lazy, dressing up as a football player for Halloween," I comment, giving him a once-over.

"I'm not wearing a costume. I came straight home from practice and started passing out candy for my mom. I'd only been home about five minutes before you walked up," he explains with humor in his voice.

"How come you're never at the football games?" he asks me. A sense of curiosity fills me as we near the end of his street, wondering if he's going to follow us around the corner. Just two streets left in Middlebrook before we head home.

"Why do you think?" I snort. He asks a lot of dumb questions.

"Well, next week is Senior Night. You should come watch me play." His words catch me off guard, and I whip my head toward him with a curious stare. *What's his angle?*

"Why would I do that?" I ask him.

This time he snorts. "Why do you think?" he mimics. One corner of his mouth is lifted in a smirk, and I feel my insides warm. He's so damn fine. I can't handle it. Literal perfection. What the hell is he doing flirting with me?

I eye him suspiciously one more time. We're standing on the corner. Maddie and Teddy are at the last house on the street. When they see me standing with Jesse, they run over, leaving the other kids to continue around the corner.

"Sissy, we're tired," Maddie whines. "My legs hurt."

"Yeah, we're ready to go home now," Teddy confirms, nodding his head under the huge mask.

"Okay, let's head home then," I tell them with a smile.

"I can give you guys a ride," Jesse offers as we make our way back down his block.

"Yes, please Mischa, then we don't have to walk in the dark!" Maddie jumps again.

"No, we're fine." Jesse Alford has got some nerve. Making out with me and then ignoring me for almost an entire week, and now he's acting like nothing happened at all! I grab Maddie's hand and drag her along with me as I storm away from Jesse and his smug handsomeness.

"Are you mad at me or something?" I hear him call out as he jogs to catch up to us. Teddy's lagging, too preoccupied with his bag of candy.

I ignore Jesse and continue past his house, but he follows. He grabs my arm and pulls me back slightly. I whip around and snatch my arm away from him, glaring. He mumbles an apology and looks at me sheepishly. He's probably afraid I'll cry rape against him. I'm sure Preston has everyone convinced I'm a walking sexual assault case. I look down at Maddie and Teddy. They're both in their own world comparing candy sacks. I exhale and meet Jesse's eyes.

"Is this about Saturday?" he asks me with his own sigh.

I narrow my eyes at him and fold my arms across my chest. "What about Saturday?"

He chuckles slightly and looks back at his house. When his gaze meets mine again, he's biting his bottom lip—and damnit, he is so sexy!

"So, you *are* mad at me," he says with a nod. "That's why you've been ignoring me all week?"

I raise an eyebrow and scoff at him. "*I've* been ignoring *you*?" I give a short laugh and then turn on my heels to walk away with my siblings.

"I'll see you Saturday," he calls out, but I hear his voice further away, so I know he's not following me. Saturday is the last day we have to meet up to travel with Neil to God-Knows-Where, California. Then I'll never have to deal with either of them again.

I can go back to waiting out my demise.

Chapter Fourteen

162

One clink in the fishbowl, a flush of the toilet, and I'm out of the door just a little past noon.

Jesse's GTO is parked on the side of the road near the end of our gravel driveway. He's leaning against the driver's side door in dark jeans, a white shirt, and his dark-brown leather jacket. The crisp November wind flips his twisted hair around softly.

"Late again," he announces, not bothering to look up at me.

"Who told you to pick me up here?" I say with an attitude. I go to the passenger side and peek into the back seat. It's empty. "Where is Neil?" I ask him as he's opening his door to climb in.

"He's sick," Jesse replies with a shrug. I flop down into the passenger seat and prop my feet on the dash. Jesse speeds away from the curb and up the foothill road toward the mountain.

"Where are we headed? Thomlin said no Yosemite, remember?" I ask him curiously. He gives a smug look and continues to drive, the engine roaring as we cruise up the winding road.

"Oh yeah, I guess we forgot to tell you. Neil said the project was complete." He grins, and I furrow my brows and turn to him. "He said the gravity hill was perfect."

"So, Neil's sick, *and* the project is finished? What the hell is this, then?" I snap, motioning around the car.

"Relax, it's just a surprise." Jesse laughs at me. I stare at him, even though he's gone back to focusing on the road. I contemplate jumping out of the car. Tuck and roll. But then, I remember the mountain lions, and even though we're less than half a mile away from my house, I heard them roaring this morning, and I don't want to risk it. Plus, I'm curious to see where he is taking me. As we pass the mill, I briefly wonder if he's setting me up for some type of ambush. Maybe Preston and Alyssa are waiting for me somewhere, hoping to catch me off guard and jump on me.

I glance at the side of his face and dismiss those thoughts. I don't think Jesse is the type of guy who would do that. He's drumming his fingertips on the steering wheel and bobbing his head to the beat of a West Coast rap song thumping out of his speakers. His left arm is draped outside of the window, relaxed and cool, like he hasn't a care in the world. Like he's exactly where he wants to be right now.

In his car.

With me.

My heart races, and I pick at my thumbnail nervously. I'd much rather I was driving into a surprise attack by The Elites than to entertain the idea of Jesse actually *choosing* to spend his Saturday with me.

Just past the mill, we turn off the main road and down a thin dirt trail that most people probably would have driven straight past. I never venture this far into the woods because I'm afraid of things like snakes, and cougars, and cannibalistic mountain people out of a Wes Craven movie I watched once.

Jesse clears the small path, and we find ourselves in a dead-end flat patch of land that feeds into a cliff. He parks the GTO in the middle of the clearing and hops out of the car without saying a word. I watch him walk around and lean coolly against the hood.

"Let me guess, this is your special thinking place," I taunt as I get out of the car and walk past him toward the cliff.

"Yep!" he calls out from behind me. I keep walking until I'm able to see over the cliff. The view is stunning. Endless treetops and several mountain peaks for as far as the eye can see. A sharp wind blows, and the surrounding trees begin to howl and sway. The most peaceful place I've seen, just a few miles away from me this entire time.

After my dad died, and my mom moved us to this middle-of-nowhere mountain town, I thought I'd never stop missing the salty smell of the Pacific right in my backyard. I went from running a couple hundred feet to the beach in the backyard of our bungalow, to living in the middle of the woods surrounded by giant pine trees and mountain lions. I hated it here.

But this...

This place—*this*—makes me feel something I haven't felt in so long.

Alive.

Funny analogy from a girl who plans to end her life soon.

"You should jump," I hear Jesse's voice say from beside me. I didn't even notice him approaching. "Just end it all now, and jump. Why wait?"

His words shock me, and I consider them for a moment. I take another step toward the cliff, and the tip of my tennis shoes teeter on the edge, scrapping a few small pieces of gravel and knocking them over the drop. They disappear into the sea of dark green treetops and rocks hundreds of feet below us.

My father is dead, Joe is an asshole, and my mom is a no-show even though she lives in the same house as me. I have no friends. I live in a town that hates me as much as I hate them, and I'm forced to play caretaker to my siblings and sick grandfather, all while battling reality and severe mood swings.

That being said, I'm not suicidal. I'm not some angsty teenager who wants to die because her life sucks. I'm not sure that I even *want* to die. I just know that I *have* to. No reasoning behind it. I just know in my heart it's time. I've been instructed to end my life in five months, and I'm not even sure why.

"Hey," I hear Jesse call out. It's strange because he sounds further away than he did a few moments ago.

Maybe I'll do it here. On April 14th, I'll walk up here and jump off of this cliff. It's foolproof. There's no way I'd survive the fall. I'd be impaled by a branch or die from the blunt force of hitting the rocks below.

"Woah! Step back!" Jesse's voice sounds frantic, and I feel him pulling me away from the cliff. Only he's not pulling me to the left where he's been coercing me to jump off of the side of the mountain. He's pulling me backward now. When I look to my left, I see Fergal standing there grinning a yellow-toothed grin at me.

I shrug away from Jesse and walk back toward the car with my arms folded across my chest. I look around expectedly. *Where is the ambush already?*

"Are you okay?" Jesse asks me slowly, sounding rightfully confused.

"Why'd you bring me here?" I ask him instead, motioning around us. We're in the middle of a hidden paradise. A paradise that only we can appreciate.

"It's my favorite place." He shrugs. "I wanted to share it with you."

"But *why*?" I snap. Before he can speak, I keep digging in. "I get it. We made out. Cool. Add it to your list of conquests and move on." I huff and stomp away. I want to reach out and punch him in his stupid chest for bringing me here because now I love it here, and I don't want to love it here. I want to hate it here so that I don't go home and spend every waking moment wishing that I *was* here—peering over the edge of that cliff before plummeting off. Can't a girl plot her own death in peace, without some super handsome boy coming along and tempting her to speed up the process?

"Mischa, wait!" he calls out to me as I storm past his car.

"Move on, Jesse Alford. I'm warning you," I call back. Then a thought hits me, and it all makes sense now. I stop and turn around to face him with a suggestive smirk on my face. "Unless our little kissing session wasn't enough for you..." I bite my bottom lip a little and wink at him. "Is that it, Jesse? You brought me here to get a little action? Is this where you and Alyssa do it?"

He screws his face up in confusion and frowns at me. "What are you talking ab—"

"If that's what you wanted, you should have just asked, Jesse Alford," I cut him off, taking a few steps forward, biting my lip, and releasing it again. "I guarantee you I'm ten times better than Alyssa," I add in a sultry tone. His jaw drops, but he doesn't look excited or shocked. He looks pissed.

"I didn't bring you up here for that!" he scoffs at me. "I brought you here because I thought I liked you, and that I'd finally found someone to share this place with." And now it's out there. Officially in words. Jesse Alford likes me. Or at least he did.

For most girls in Grover, I'm sure that would be a blessing wrapped in a bow made of hundred-dollar bills and glitter. But for the girl planning to die in one hundred sixty-two days, it's a nuisance.

"Like I said…" I take a deep breath. "Move on, because we are *never* going to happen." I don't even bother giving him a chance to respond before storming off into the woods toward home.

I should have just hauled myself off the edge of the mountain to save myself from the inevitable invasion of Jesse Alford that is about to plague my mind for the rest of the night.

Chapter Fifteen

JESSE

There is zero correspondence between me and Mischa in the week after our fight on the cliff. If that's even what you want to call it. She went from being cute and curious to brash and accusatory, and then provocative and bragging about having sex with me better than Alyssa. It was a complete mind fuck! I didn't know whether to be pissed off or turned on!

That's what I get for convincing myself I had a thing for the town's pariah.

My mind kept reeling from our conversation in the diner after her brother's asthma attack and then the kiss we shared in the Gravity House. I thought there was chemistry there on my end, but I guess she didn't feel it. Maybe she's void of feeling like she is of friends and social interactions that don't involve people pointing and whispering at her. I don't even understand why we're expected to hate Mischa so much. She's strange and socially awkward, but is that really a reason to *hate* somebody?

I mean, Preston and his family have a pretty valid reason to not associate themselves with Mischa after the whole Blake thing. But what's everyone else's excuse? I think every school and town has to have an odd one out to function, and that person is Mischa for us. It's the balance of life, I guess.

Whatever, I'm over it.

I take Alyssa up on an offer to hook up at her house while her parents are sleeping, and by the middle of the school week, Mischa is a thing of the past.

Well... sort of.

There's an unspoken tension between us as Neil leads our gravity hill presentation on Wednesday. When he gets to the part about the mysterious Gravity House, I can't help but glance over at Mischa. Her head is dropped toward the floor, and her wild curly hair is hiding her face, but I can make out a smile between the strands. She's wearing a pair of oversized men's jeans with a black belt tied around the waist twice to make them stay on. We get an 'A' on the project, and then it's over. I never have to talk with Neil or Mischa again. My friends can get off of my back about hanging out with *"the geek and the freak"* as Preston has deemed them.

Senior Night in Grover is more important than homecoming, as it celebrates the senior players' last night playing football for the town. It's also the last home game of the season, and the last chance to get scouted by major colleges. Not that it matters to me. I've already got my future mapped out for me. I got my scholarship and acceptance letters in the mail last month. The University of Oklahoma, my father's alma mater. He was a walk-on for the Sooners before graduating from law school and moving to California. From the beginning, he'd drilled it in my head that I was supposed to follow in his footsteps. He'll be able to mount my law degree on the wall next to his, and I'll join him at the DA's office. How exciting...

I can hear the crowd cheering from outside the inflatable team tunnel, as we wait to make our grand entrance onto the field. Twenty high school football players hiding inside a giant replica of the helmets we're wearing. Black, blue, and silver, with a Mighty Mountain Cat pouncing on the side. Once the band plays our fight song, we'll rush the field like a bunch of warriors.

My parents are out there front and center, surrounded by the other football parents. Alyssa, Chelsea, and the other cheerleaders are outside the tunnel, chanting and jumping around. The girls who don't make the spirit squad pass out water bottles and do our laundry under the guise of football managers to maintain some type of social status. That's what life in a small town is all about, after all. Playing your part. Or at least *having* a part to play.

I know the entire town is out there in the stands or on the sidelines, ready to cheer us on to victory, but my mind wanders to one person in particular. Even she has a part.

The outcast.

I know she's not out there, but a part of me is holding on to the slight chance she shows up to watch me play. I don't know why it's so important to me. She made it clear that she wasn't interested in having any type of relationship with me. And I'd rather die than admit to my friends that I got dissed by her of all people.

Still, I can't get her out of my head.

The band plays our fight song, and the managers turn on the fog machine just before we all run out onto the field. Thoughts of Mischa Lawrence are pushed out of my brain. God forbid I have to hear my father's mouth at the dinner table tonight because I didn't have my head in the game and played like shit.

During half-time, the senior players and cheerleaders parade around the field with our parents, while the student council snaps pictures. The MC reads off our accolades and plans for college.

"Jesse is the son of Michael and Kelisa Alford. In the fall, Jesse will attend The University of Oklahoma with a scholarship to play football. He also plans to pursue a degree in law."

That's actually my father's dream. I'm not sure what I want to do with my life, but I know I don't want to be a lawyer. My dad spends most of his time at his office two hours away in Sacramento. That leaves my mom alone to do mindless things around the house until he comes home, and me to fulfill his strict plan for my future.

By the fourth quarter, the score is in favor of our rival team by four points, and during our last timeout, Coach tells the line to get the ball to me for a touchdown. It's a risky play, but I'm not too concerned. I catch the ball just before the fifty-yard line and gun it toward the end zone. The defensive players try to stop me on more than one occasion, but Trey is there to get them off of me. In a momentary lapse of time, I lose myself in my thoughts as I run. I think about Mischa with her feet propped on my dashboard with her cocky smile and wild hair blowing in her face.

The winter formal is in a few weeks. I wonder what she'd look like in one of those fancy dresses the girls always wear to the dance. I wonder what it would be like to go to the dance with her, holding hands and dancing close. I'm sure it would drive Preston insane to see me arrive at one of the biggest events in town with his self-proclaimed archenemy on my arm. But who cares?

I like Mischa Lawrence. There's no denying it. To hell with what Preston and my other friends think. The only thing stopping me from pursuing Mischa is Mischa.

The sound of the crowd going wild and my teammates rushing me brings me back into the now. I've just run the ball fifty yards and scored a game-winning touchdown.

Trey is bear-hugging me. Alyssa has her arms wrapped around my neck, screaming in my ear, and trying to kiss me. I'm too excited to push her away, but I turn my head to avoid contact with her lips on mine. While Nick is tousling my hair around, and Alyssa is still trying to kiss me, I look toward the end zone and see Mischa standing against the fence. Her chin is resting on her folded arms across the top of the fence, giving me her signature smirk. I want to run over to her, but my coaches and teammates have a death grip on me. She actually came to see me play, despite our weird exchange on the cliff.

When I finally break free from everyone's embraces, Mischa's already gone. I'm pretty sure I know where to find her, though. And I intend to find her.

After posing for a few pictures for the yearbook and school paper, I'm able to sneak away from everyone and head to the mountain. I find her walking on the side of the road not too far from her house. Upon first glance, I swear she's talking to someone, but there's no one around. They're all still at the field. Her mouth is moving quickly like she's arguing with someone, and occasionally she looks to the left as if she's waiting for a reply. I pull up beside her, and she doesn't look my way. She's got a look on her face like she's listening intently to something. We move forward another ten feet before I decide to honk the horn and break her trance. When I do, she looks over at me with wide brown eyes.

"What the hell?" she breathes out, but she doesn't stop walking.

"You came to the game," I state, chuckling lightly. She's wearing a pair of women's jeans today, but they're still slightly oversized, and her white long-sleeved shirt is fitted and tucked in. She looks like she jumped out of one of those '90s fashion magazines in my mom's collection.

"So what?" she responds, turning away from me and focusing her eyes on the road ahead. She's walking against the traffic, forcing me to talk to her from across the oncoming lane.

"You came to see me play." I'm using her signature smile against her. She shrugs and continues to walk. We don't speak for a while as I slowly coast up the hill to match her walking speed.

"Are you just going to stalk me the entire way home?" she asks in an annoyed tone. "It's kind of creepy."

"Be my date to the winter formal," I call out to her instead of answering. This finally stops her in her tracks.

"Wh—what did you just say?" She looks at me like a deer caught in head-lights, standing stiffly with her arms weighted to her sides. I put my car in park and hang my arms out of the window to face her better.

"Come to the formal with me. I need a date," I repeat, giving her my most charming smile, hoping to win her over.

She shakes her head fiercely, and I wonder if she's saying no to me or herself. "Take your girlfriend."

I laugh. "I don't have a girlfriend."

"Yeah, she's probably going to the dance with Preston, anyway," she mumbles, more to herself, but I hear her. I wonder what kind of dirt she has on Preston and Alyssa since she brings up their supposed relationship behind my back a lot. I don't ask her though, because I don't care about that. Right now, I just need her to agree to be my date.

"Look, I'm not going to the dance with you, Jesse. I shouldn't have shown up to the game today, but I was looking for my little sister, and..." She trails off, unable to finish her lie.

I'm about to call her out on it when I hear music blaring from behind me. I look in my rearview and see Preston's Jeep cruising up the road behind me. Behind him are Nick's pickup and a whole caravan of other kids heading up the mountain to the mill.

Mischa sees them as well and sucks her teeth. She starts walking up the road again, so I put my car in drive and continue to cruise beside her. I wonder what it must be like to not be able to walk home in peace.

"You left us hanging, man," Trey calls out from the passenger seat of Preston's Wrangler after Preston has driven around me to coast between me and Mischa in the oncoming lane.

"Trying to start the party without us?" Alyssa jokes from the cramped backseat. There are two other cheerleaders squished in beside her, so I assume Chelsea is in the pickup behind them with Nick.

"Nah, I think he's trying to get a piece of Skanky Lawrence over here," Preston chimes in, nodding toward Mischa, who is still trying to advance up the road as quickly as possible. Alyssa frowns and looks between Mischa and me, confused.

"What's up, Lawrence? You enjoy the game today?" Preston asks her coolly, hanging one arm out of the driver's side window and coasting beside her. Mischa doesn't respond, she just keeps power walking up the road.

"What are you talking about, Preston? She doesn't go to the games." One cheerleader in the back seat tries to correct Preston.

He shakes his head and laughs. "Nah, Bitcha was there today." He purposely mispronounces Mischa's name to insult her. I feel myself growing angry. "She was all giddy, jumping up and down behind the fence cheering for Jesse when he was running the ball."

His words surprise me. I didn't even notice she was there until the very end. I bite my lip to fight the smile that wants to spread across my face at the thought of her cheering for me. Alyssa looks like she's about to lose it at any moment. She's looking at me like I've betrayed her in some kind of way. Maybe I have? I'm not sure.

"I'd watch my back around this one though, Jesse. Can't have you getting locked up for rape before you go off for that fancy scholarship," Preston presses. Mischa shakes her head and picks up her speed a little. At this point, she's one more advancement away from sprinting up the mountain.

"Why don't you just leave her alone, Preston?" I finally come to her defense as I continue to coast beside them. Nick and the rest of the teens from town finally catch up, and now it's all eyes on Preston and his usual tormenting of Mischa Lawrence. "She's not even doing anything to you." Mischa doesn't look at me when I speak up for her. Instead, she looks past me, like something beyond my car has piqued her interest. I glance over and there's nothing there.

"I guess you're right, Jesse." Preston shrugs, but he never takes his eyes off Mischa. "She nearly ruins my family name. I make her life a living hell. Two wrongs don't make a right. Isn't that what they say, Lawrence?"

"Yeah, take your parents for example," she responds, turning to walk backward as she winks at him before flipping him off.

"What did you just say, you stupid bitch?" Preston growls, and I feel the situation escalating. I think Mischa's about to repeat herself, but Preston doesn't give her a chance. He revs his engine and jerks his jeep sideways over the side of the road where Mischa is walking. There isn't a curb to separate the main road from the dead grass that serves as the *side of the road*, so he easily almost hits her.

"Are you insane, man?" Trey bellows and hops out of the Jeep. The girls in the backseat screech and then giggle as he tries again to ram her. Mischa lets out a yelp as she nearly dodges the bull bars in front of his Jeep.

I throw my car in park and jump out. I jog over to Preston's Jeep, reach through the open window, and turn the key off. This causes the car to jump forward one last time before Preston scrambles to put it in park.

"What the hell, man! You're going to ruin my engine!" he cries out. I want to tell him that his power steering is actually in jeopardy, but that's not important.

"You're joking, right?" I yell at him as I back away from the Jeep. "You're just going to run her over out here?" I motion toward Mischa, but she's already running up the mountain and nearly out of sight. I intentionally left the stadium early to get her alone and ask her out; but as usual, my friends had to mess everything up.

Preston laughs. "Calm down, man. I was just fucking with her." Nick and the others take the newly opened space between our cars and continue up the road while Preston and I continue our stare-down. Well, more so that I'm staring him down, and he's still laughing as if almost committing vehicular manslaughter is funny. I briefly wonder if Nick will finish what Preston started with Mischa up the road out of my sight.

"C'mon Jesse." Trey pulls me back toward the GTO. "Too far this time, Preston," he calls out as he rounds the front of my car to get in the passenger seat. I launch Preston's keys in the tall grass before getting back inside of mine.

"It was just a joke, man!" Preston calls out, as I'm snapping my seatbelt. "Who gives a shit about Skanky Lawrence, anyway?" That's the last thing I hear before I roll up my window and peel off up the road.

At the mill, I keep my distance from Preston and the others, hanging out with Trey and a few girls from our senior class instead.

"So, what's the deal with Mischa?" Trey asks, tossing me a beer and taking a swig from his own.

I pop the top open on the side of the old conveyer belt where Mischa, Zoey, and I sat a few weeks ago. I shrug. "Nothing, I just—" I attempt to lie, but Trey is my best friend. He knows me better than anyone.

"Bullshit, man. You like her, don't you?" He laughs.

"So, what if I do?" I shoot back defensively. I don't see the big deal with me liking Mischa. She's cute. Actually, cute is an understatement. She's gorgeous! Always has been since she first moved here in junior high. I remember Alyssa had this childish survey, where she wanted all the boys in school to vote on whether she was prettier than Mischa. I didn't know that I was the tiebreaker in the vote at the time, but I was like twelve, and Mischa was the first girl I'd ever seen in school with that thick curly hair and actual boobs. She had big, almond-shaped brown eyes and looked like she was pouting all the time. So, I shrugged and said, *"Mischa."* Ever since that day, Alyssa has hated Mischa, and things didn't get any better after the incident with Blake. Now that we're older, she's even prettier, with a nice body to match. Aside from her good looks, there's something about her personality that's refreshing once you get to know her. She doesn't give a fuck, and in a town like Grover, where status is essential, it's nice to meet a girl who doesn't care about the usual shit.

Trey throws his hands up and shakes his head, laughing softly. "No judgment here, man. If you like her then you like her. What's the big deal?"

I sigh and down half my beer. I sit the glass bottle on the belt table and cross my arms. "I asked her to the winter formal."

"Wow." Trey raises his brow, finishing his beer. He'll only drink the one, for the sake of not being the odd one out. He never gets too drunk because his dad is the sheriff, and he'd probably kill him if he came home wasted. "So, you're taking Mischa to the dance? Alyssa is going to flip. And you know Preston will never let you hear the end of it."

I frown and shrug. I don't give a shit what Preston thinks. To be completely honest, I don't care how Alyssa feels, either. We're over for good this time. "She said no, anyway," I mumble, picking up my bottle and gulping down the brown liquid.

Trey cracks up laughing. *"Jesse Alford* got turned down by *Mischa Lawrence?"*

I shush him and look around to make sure nobody is listening. "I'd like to keep that to myself, thank you!"

"My bad, man." He chuckles and smirks at me. "So, what now?"

I shrug again and finish the beer off. "I asked her to come to the game today. She said she wasn't coming, but she showed up anyway." I shrug.

Trey considers this for a moment but holds up a finger to contest. "Yeah, but it's going to be hard for her to just show up to the formal without a definite answer."

He's right, she'd have to get a dress, which I doubt she has because she's never attended any of the formals or parties thrown in town.

A thought hits me, but before I can express it, I hear a commotion outside. It's after midnight, and the party should be winding down soon. Plus, everyone knows not to cause a scene out here if we want Sheriff Freeman to keep letting us use the place.

We follow the crowd outside and find Preston standing next to his jeep with his hands weaved tightly in his dirty blonde hair, gripping the roots in frustration.

"Stupid bitch slashed my fucking tires! I know it was her! Somebody *had* to see her do it!"

He's screaming and pacing back and forth in front of the driver's side tires that are sitting flush with the ground with a deep gash in the rubber. I imagine the serrated blade that Mischa pulled on Jimmy in Archerville and chuckle silently to myself.

Payback's a bitch, Preston.

Chapter Sixteen

JESSE

Trey insisted on tagging along to Mischa's house so I could make one last attempt to ask her to the winter formal. I figured my best bet would be to catch her off guard. So, I'm coming to her house—her comfort zone—instead of the school where she's tormented by my friends. This will show her my intentions are genuine.

We drive up the gravel path that leads to her house. It's one of those double-wide manufactured homes that sits on a foundation with a large deck. Completely different from the craftsmen-style houses in town.

Her younger sister, Frankie, is walking around outside the front of the house talking on her phone. In the distance are the two youngest siblings. When Frankie sees us approaching, her jaw drops. She tells whoever she's talking to, "Oh my gosh, I need to call you back. Jesse Alford is walking up my driveway!" She pulls the phone away from her ear and hangs up.

"Is Mischa home?" I ask her, and she nods slowly, mesmerized.

"Mischa!" she calls out, but she's still looking at us. Teddy and their youngest sister stop chasing each other and stare.

"Oh, look Teddy! It's Mischa's friend with the cool car!" The baby sister, I think her name is Maddie, points at me.

"You're a celebrity around here, man." Trey nudges me, and we both laugh.

Maddie takes off running and calls Mischa's name. That's when I see her, dancing to the beat of the music that must be blaring in her headphones. She's walking up the stairs of the deck and into the house, and I swear I see her look me dead in the eyes before disappearing inside the house. Maddie follows her, calling her name over and over. A second later, Mischa reappears outside, hands on her hips, narrowing her eyes at us. "What are you doing here?"

I'm eying her body, so it takes a moment for me to answer. It's like fifty-nine degrees outside, but she's wearing tiny cotton shorts and a sports bra. Not that I'm complaining. Mischa's maybe about five-foot-five, and she's curvy like an hourglass. I don't let my gaze linger too long on the way she's filling out the shorts and sports bra, for fear of making things even more awkward.

"I wanted to see you," I tell her with a shrug.

"Well, you see me." She makes a shooing motion with her hand. "Now leave."

Trey laughs, and I can't help but laugh with him. "Are you always this mean?"

"Only to guys who nearly get me run over," she shoots back. She starts frantically swatting away at something. I assume it's a gnat because I don't see anything there.

"Preston's an asshole. I'm sorry he did that to you," I tell her genuinely. The memory pisses me off, but I don't focus on it. "You've been avoiding me for weeks. The dance is in two weeks. I need an answer."

"I gave you an answer, Jesse Alford," she groans. "The answer was 'no.' Several times. Now, I'd like to stay and chat, but I've got an entire house to clean." With that, she turns on her heels and walks into her house, giving me the briefest image of her ass hanging out the bottom of the shorts.

Trey and I stand there awkwardly, wondering what to do next. This didn't go as smoothly as I imagined. Mischa has turned down my advances about five times in the past few weeks.

I feel someone tugging at my shirt sleeve, and when I look down, Maddie is standing at my feet. "Wanna meet Sissy's grandpa? He's funny." She's inviting us inside the house, so I follow because it gives me a chance to get through to Mischa again.

"You sure about this man?" Trey asks, and I nod beckoning him to follow me up the ramp and inside the house.

It's cramped inside the house and full of dingy, outdated furniture. When Mischa sees us walking in, she glares at Maddie. Frankie slips in behind us and watches us in awe like we're celebrities or something.

"Grandpa Lawrence, wanna meet Mischa's boyfriend?" The chubby-faced little girl walks over to an old Black man in a wheelchair in front of the TV. He's watching one of those daytime courtroom shows and not facing us.

"Boyfriend?" he replies gruffly and turns the chair around to face us. His eyes meet mine, and he grins a toothy smile and claps his large hands once. "My baby girl is bringing the bloodline back!" Trey laughs hysterically, and I take a moment to register what he's saying. "I knew you'd make me proud, baby girl! I can die happily knowing that there will be another round of Black babies with the Lawrence blood," he adds, and he's dead serious. He's proudly shifting his eyes between Mischa and me.

Mischa is laughing now too. She's standing on the other side of the living area, giving me an amused look. "Jesse's just a classmate, Grandpa." She grabs a zip-up hoodie from the coat rack next to her and slips it on. Her attempt at making herself decent, I guess, even though we showed up announced.

"Grandpa, this is Jesse Alford, and that's Trey Freeman. Guys, this is my grandfather, Henry Lawrence."

"Freeman? You, the sheriff's son?" Mischa's grandpa asks Trey with a scowl.

"Yes, sir. Maurice Freeman the Third. Everyone calls me Trey, though." Trey nods, reaching out to shake the older man's hand after me.

Mischa's grandpa snorts. "*Free-man*, my ass. Black sheriff in a white town? He's somebody's *boy*, I tell ya that."

My eyes nearly bulge out of my skull and beside me, I hear Trey choke back a shocked laugh. I can't believe he just said that!

"Grandpa! You're being rude! I'm warning you!" Mischa snaps. She throws an apologetic look at Trey, who waves her off, and then motions for us all to go back outside.

"It was nice meeting you, Mr. Lawrence," Trey and I say in unison, before following Mischa outside. Mr. Lawrence just grunts. His back is already facing us again, and his attention has returned to CourtTV.

"You'll have to excuse my grandpa. He can be pretty militant," Mischa tells us once we're outside on the deck. "He gets ruder as the years go by."

"Nah, he's funny." I smile at her. She raises a brow, silently telling me once again to leave. "All you have to do is say you'll be my date to the formal, and we'll leave." I shrug, giving her my most charming smile.

"Why?" She sucks her teeth and juts her hip out slightly. "So Preston and Alyssa can douse me in pig's blood, and everyone can laugh at me?"

Again, we laugh at her sarcasm. "I'm not trying to set you up, Mischa. I'm being serious."

"But why, Jesse?" she snaps, cutting me off. I'm just about to respond when she cuts me off again. "You know what? I don't care why. The answer is still no! So, leave!" She turns and storms back inside of her house, slamming the screen door behind her. I can hear Frankie screaming at Mischa.

"Are you crazy? That was Jesse Alford!"

"Well, that was a bust." I bite my lip and shrug my shoulders, still staring at the door.

"I need more time with that old man. He's hilarious," Trey cracks, turning to walk down the ramp and back to the car. I'm just about to follow him when I feel a presence walk over and stand beside me. I look down, and Teddy is standing there, staring at the door as well. He's small but lanky, and his glasses are too big for his face. He reminds me of Neil Gunderson in elementary school.

"You really like Mischa, don't you?" he asks me and glances up to meet my eyes.

"Yeah, I do," I tell him with a smile because it's true. I don't know why I like her. She's the strangest person I've ever met. She dresses weird, albeit very sexy sometimes. Like last Monday, she wore oversized, dingy, men's overalls and a long-sleeved plaid shirt that swallowed her arms and hands. She looked like a scarecrow. Then on Tuesday, she was dressed in sheer black stockings under an extra-large sweater and beat-up Doc Martens. Chelsea said Mischa looked like a wannabe high fashion bum, but she looked good as hell to me, and I noticed Preston couldn't stop staring at her either.

I sigh and shake my head at Mischa's little brother. "But I don't think she likes me back."

"She does," he tells me simply, and I raise a brow in question. "She talks about you all the time."

"She does? To who?" I ask him curiously, growing excited. Inside the house, Mischa is screaming for Teddy to come inside and wash up for dinner.

Teddy shrugs and replies, "To herself." Then, he walks up to the door. "See you later, Jesse Alford."

The Freemans insist I stay for dinner, and since my parents are having dinner in the city, and Mrs. Freeman is the best cook in Grover, I take my usual seat next to Trey at the dinner table.

The Freemans are like a second family to me. The Black population in Grover is scarce. The Freemans, Alfords, Halls, and Bradys are the only fully Black families in town. Nick, like Mischa, has a white mother and a deceased father who was Black. We all naturally gravitated to each other, under a silent understanding that we are the minority in our small town. Somehow, that grace has never been extended to Mischa.

"So, what did you boys get into today?" Sheriff Freeman asks us after Trey's little sister, Trinity, finishes praying over the food. "Dale Redding said he saw you guys heading up the mountain."

"Oh, nothing. Jesse wanted to go visit Mischa Lawrence," Trey tells his dad nonchalantly, causing me to elbow him.

Sheriff Freeman finishes the mouthful of steak and potatoes and eyes us both suspiciously. "What for?"

I don't respond right away, so Trey answers for me. "He's trying to get her to go to the winter formal with him, but she keeps turning him down. It's actually quite funny." He laughs and looks at me, ignoring my glare.

"Why would you want to go to the winter formal with Mischa Lawrence?" Sheriff Freeman asks. His narrowed gaze remains solely on me, and I can read the distrust in his expression.

"Why wouldn't I?" I shoot back defensively, pushing my steak and potatoes around my plate. My tone is probably disrespectful, and my mom would have a fit if she heard me respond to an adult that way. But I'm already confused enough about my feelings for Mischa. I don't need anyone judging me for it.

Sheriff Freeman only laughs and puts his hands up in his defense. "I don't mean it like that, son. I just don't understand why the *'most popular guy in school'* would want to take the least popular girl in town to the winter formal." He puts air quotes around his description of me. In a more serious and authoritative tone, he adds, "You guys aren't trying to pull some type of prank or anything, are you?"

"Maybe Jesse actually *likes* Mischa?" Trey's mom chimes in, giving me a knowing look.

"It's not a prank. I'm being serious." I neither confirm nor deny Mrs. Freeman's allegation.

"So, you went to her house. What did she say?" Sheriff Freeman nods and takes another bite of his food. I do the same, so Trey answers.

"She was pissed, I think. Then, her little sister invited us in to meet Mischa's grandpa," he tells them with a mouth full.

"You met Henry?" Sheriff Freeman looks shocked.

"You know him, Dad?" Trey asks before spearing a piece of broccoli with his fork.

Sheriff Freeman nods and finishes chewing before wiping his mouth with his napkin and elaborating. "Mischa's father, Shannon, was one of my closest friends back in the day. We were in the same platoon in Kuwait before we had families. He saved my life once. Shortly after his passing, Mischa and her family moved here. Henry is Shannon's father. Great man, if not a little rough around the edges sometimes," he adds the last part with a chuckle. Trey tells them about his excitement over Mischa possibly having a Black boyfriend, and we all share a laugh.

"Mischa's such a sweet girl. She just gets a bad rap around here." His mom sighs. "But I'm glad you boys are being nice to her." She winks at me, and I'm sure I blush a little.

"Just make sure you're not up to no good with that girl," Sheriff Freeman tells us seriously. "If I hear about either of you causing any trouble for Mischa, it's going to be serious trouble, you understand?" He looks at us, and we nod in unison.

After dinner, we meet our friends at the mill for a random get-together. However, after an hour of listening to Preston being a belligerent asshole, I decide that I really want to be alone. So, I head to my secret spot. To my surprise, it's occupied.

She doesn't even move when I pull up. She's just standing on the edge of the cliff staring down, and for a moment I wonder if she's going to jump.

Chapter Seventeen

fter a mental battle with myself, and encouragement from Fergal and the voices in my head, I ended up going to that stupid football game. Against my better judgment, I started cheering like a silly little schoolgirl with a crush when Jesse started running in my direction with the football and scored the winning touchdown.

Then mania took over and provoked me to slash two of Preston's tires while he was inside the mill, bragging about trying to run me over. That was almost a month ago, and now I'm constantly watching my back. I'm not afraid of Preston. If push comes to shove, I'll just stab him in his liver if he comes near me with physical harm. It's those thoughts that scare me, however. I can't afford to get sent upstate because I had a rightfully deserved psychotic moment with Preston, Satan's lovechild.

When I'm not tuning out Preston's hateful words, I'm fighting the butterflies I get every time Jesse Alford comes around. And it seems like he's always around me. He has now permanently taken Lizzie Waiters' seat in Mr. Thomlin's class. In fact, he switches seats in all of our shared classes, sitting behind or beside me every chance he gets. We rarely speak, and when we do, he's asking me about the stupid winter formal that I will not attend with him. Sure, he saved Teddy's life and defended me when Preston tried to mow me down on the mountain pass. But I don't owe him a date. Jesse Alford's liking me doesn't fit into my life plan—which is to end my life. He'll end up being an attachment to this physical world, and I need to rid myself of those. Zoey's gone, and even though I have the Littles and my grandpa, I'm still on a good track to go through with it in a few months.

Nope, can't let Jesse Alford ruin that for me.

And then he shows up at my house today and throws me completely off-kilter. I thought they were hallucinations when I first saw him walking toward me with Trey as I walked from the shed to the house. I should have known something was up when Fergal kept appearing and laughing at me. At one point he even told me, *"You've got company, love,"* and I still didn't believe it was true. I've got to get control of this without the medicine before I lose it completely before April.

It's the last weekend of decent temperature, so I kept the Littles away from town today and focused on thoroughly cleaning the house before we're all locked inside for the winter. Plus, I didn't feel like dealing with the townsfolk and my classmates. I'm having manic episodes, and I haven't taken my pills in two months. There's no telling what might happen.

After dinner, I put the Littles to bed early, just as Joe comes stumbling through the house drunk. His hand is bandaged and bloody, but he's still whistling and singing to a tune that only he can hear. My mom's been on another week-long sleeping binge, so it's the Littles I'm worried about him waking.

"What happened to your hand?" I ask him in an unconcerned voice.

"None of your fucking business," he mumbles and keeps on stumbling back to the bedroom. He smells like sweat and booze, and I'm hoping he plans on showering.

I don't have time to ponder that for long, as the ground starts to shake violently. An earthquake? I stumble to the back and try to keep my balance as the ground beneath me continues to rock side to side. I've never felt an earthquake this strong, and I wonder why the hell no one in the house is waking up and freaking out! This magnitude of shaking should even wake up my near-comatose mother!

When I finally make it to the room I share with Frankie, I find her sleeping soundly in bed, despite the bed bucking around and jerking her body back and forth.

"Frankie!" I call out, and she groans and rolls over, muttering for me to shut up and leave her alone.

Maddie and Teddy are next door, still fast asleep as well. Maddie is terrified of even the smallest earthquakes, yet she's able to sleep through this! I'm walking gap-legged around the threshold into Teddy and Maddie's room, using the walls to stable myself. Fergal is laughing hysterically at me when suddenly the turbulence stops, and everything goes silent. I take a moment to catch my breath and regain my equilibrium.

As I'm making my way back into the living room to see if the news has a report on the Richter reading, I hear a muffled voice calling my name. I follow the sound until I'm standing in the space that separates the kitchen and dining area from the living room.

"Mischa, help me!" A small voice cries, and I recognize it as Maddie's. But that's ridiculous because Maddie is in her bedroom room sleeping. I turn on my heels and walk back down the hallway to Teddy and Maddie's room. Teddy is snoring softly, but Maddie's bedspread is disheveled and she's nowhere to be found. The voice in the living room screams louder and my heart drops painfully. *"Mischa! Help Me! I'm scared!"*

"I'm coming, Maddie!" I call out as I run down the hallway and out the front door. Once I'm on the deck, the voice sounds distant. It's coming from behind me, inside the house. I follow the screaming voice inside until I'm standing in the same spot as before, just outside the kitchen. The screaming is frantic, and I drop to my knees and scratch away at the wood flooring. Maddie is hysterical, somewhere under the house screaming about how afraid she is and begging for me to help her.

"Mischa! Please!"

"Maddie, where are you? Try to crawl away, Maddie!" I scream.

"Sissy, what are you doing?" Maddie asks me in a calmer voice now, but I can somehow still hear her screaming. I stand and run outside to the storage shed where Joe stores his tools. I grab the axe that he usually uses to chop firewood. He hasn't done it this year.

I make it back inside, and Maddie is still screaming for me. I swing the axe down, splitting the wooden boards with a loud '*CRACK.*' I bring the axe down again and a section of the floor caves in a little. I drop the axe, wanting to avoid accidentally striking Maddie with it. I drop to my knees and yank at the floorboards, trying to free my little sister.

All at once, the screaming stops, and a strange gurgling sound resonates through the room, like the sound of oil boiling. I've got my fingers wrapped around a plank of wood, and I'm just about to pull it up when I see the blood. The entire space under the house is a pool of dark, thick blood, and it's rising and bubbling through the seams of the surrounding floorboards. My hands are covered in the sticky red liquid, and the metallic smell suddenly hits my nostrils hard. It sways back and forth in waves until finally it sloshes up and covers my chest. I scream and scurry backward until my back hits the back of the couch, and I curl into a ball of tears.

Maddie screams again, and I slowly crawl back to the hole I've created in the floor, looking down at it.

"Maddie?" I whisper, and then I scream at the top of my lungs. "Maddie!" I yank at the board again, trying to create a hole large enough for me to fit through. I'm screaming and crying, and I've almost got it broken up enough for me to slip down into the bloody pool when I'm roughly shoved aside.

"What in the hell are you doing to the floor, you psycho bitch?" It's Joe.

I look up at him in horror and then down at my blood-soaked hands and chest. "The—floor, and Ma-aaa-Maddie, and the b-b-blood!"

"Look at the fucking floor! Are you in-fucking-sane!" Joe screams. This time when I look at the floor, there is no blood. Just an ugly display of broken polished wood and a hole where chunks of the flooring have caved through.

"I told your fucking mom those pills don't work!" He grabs me roughly by my hair and yanks me to my feet, dragging me to the door. "Get the hell out of here!"

He throws my body out on the deck and stands at the threshold, scowling at me. "Sleep outside since you wanna act like a fucking animal." He spits at me, but it doesn't make contact. As he's closing the door, I see a wide-eyed Maddie standing outside the hallway bathroom.

"Why are you barefoot and not wearing a coat? It's freezing out here." I don't know what possessed me to come here, but after Joe kicked me out of the house, I went straight to the secret spot Jesse showed me over a month ago. I'm standing on the edge of the cliff, mesmerized by the beauty of the trees, the layer of fog, and the potential for death below.

I should do it here next. I should come to this place and jump off this cliff in 134 (well, it's after midnight, so 133) days. Back of the napkin, I calculated about eleven seconds of falling and reflecting on this wonderful life I've had. I hope only the best memories will replay as I descend. Living in Monterey with my dad and Grandpa. The time they took me to San Diego, and we swam out as far as we could, only to get pushed back onto the shore by a giant wave. That was the last summer Grandpa spent walking before he was bound to his wheelchair. Or the day Frankie was born, which I remember through scarce memory and home videos. I remember the day Teddy was born, however.

He was blue. Mom said his lungs weren't working properly, so he couldn't breathe. She was so calm about it. When I asked her why she wasn't crying, she told me that God would take care of Teddy. She was right because, for most of his life, only fate and I have cared for Teddy, while my mom checked out and took a backseat.

I want to remember last week's Thanksgiving dinner because, for the first time in years, my mother woke up and spent an entire hour of dinnertime with us before she popped her pills and passed out. I cooked Cornish hens, mashed potatoes, green beans, and macaroni and cheese. Joe wasn't around, and she showed up at the table, having not showered and still wearing her nightgown, but it still felt like a family meal. Mrs. Freeman sent over a sweet potato pie for Grandpa since I'd declined to have dinner with the Freemans for the fourth year in a row. It was the last Thanksgiving I'll share with my little siblings, so I wanted to make it count. I tried to show Frankie a few cooking tips so that she'd be able to care for the others once I'm gone, but she was being a brat, so I dropped it.

The last vision I want to see before I hit the ground is me kissing Jesse Alford in that wacky Gravity House.

I feel a heavy weight on my shoulder, and the memory of putrid blood from an hour ago is replaced by the familiar smell of Jesse's car. He's placed his thick leather jacket on my shoulders. It smells earthy, like the wind blowing through the open windows of his car when he's cruising, mixed with the musky scent of his cologne. It's comforting and sexy.

"Thanks, but I'm not cold," I tell him, pulling the jacket tighter around me.

"Then why are you still wearing my jacket?" he retorts smugly.

"Because it smells like you." He wasn't expecting that answer.

"What are you doing out here?" he asks. "This is supposed to be *my* secret place."

"I guess you'll have to share." I shrug, finally turning to regard him. He's wearing the same black joggers, gray thermal, and expensive-looking Nikes that he wore earlier when he visited. He must have run out of dark-wash jeans.

"I don't mind sharing it with you," he tells me. "It's freezing out here though, so maybe we can talk in the car."

He's standing next to me, about seven inches taller with such an alluring presence, that I have to turn back toward the cliff, so I don't get trapped. "Who said I wanted to talk to you, Jesse Alford?"

"Why do you call me by my full name, Mischa Lawrence?" He chuckles, and out of my peripheral, I see the puff of cold breath coming from his mouth. It's weird because to me it feels like it's about seventy-five degrees, too warm to freeze your breath.

I shrug in his heavy jacket. "It's a small town. That's what we're supposed to do."

"Well, *I* want to talk to *you*, but it's freezing, and I don't have my jacket on, so will you please get in the car?" He's waiting for an answer, so I shrug the jacket off and hold it out to him. He scoffs. "Are you kidding me? You're in pajamas and barefoot! You have to be just as cold as I am."

"You're not used to rejection, are you, Jesse?" I laugh while simultaneously swatting away a bat.

"No, I'm not actually. And why do you keep doing that?" He takes the jacket and shrugs it back on.

"Doing what?" I ask, eying the large tree to the right of us suspiciously.

"You keep fanning your hand at something," he tells me. I look at the dozens of red glowing eyes in the tree. A horde of bats wrapped up in themselves. All at once they take flight and I squeeze my eyes shut, turning to Jesse and absently burying my face in his chest, gripping his thermal.

"I'm not used to rejection, you're right" His chest vibrates when he speaks. "But you also keep sending me mixed signals, Mischa." He's not even flinching. Because he can't see the bats. But I can. I can see them, hear them squealing, and even feel the rush of air as they flap around us.

"I'm sorry," I muffle in his shirt. "I just don't understand *why*. Why do you like me all of a sudden?"

"Do I have to answer that while you're hiding your face?" he asks me with humor in his voice.

I tell myself that the bats aren't real. That Jesse is real. And then, mid-flap, they all disappear.

I loosen my grip, but still hold my hands to his chest, and look him in his eyes. He smirks and tells me he's not sure.

"After that night at the diner, I saw a different side of you," he tells me, and I can hear his sincerity.

I let him guide me to the car, and we sit together, listening to the engine purr and the cicadas buzzing. I'm pretty sure he can hear them too this time.

"Aren't you worried about what the other Elites would say if they saw us together?" I ask him, propping my bare legs up on the dashboard and crossing them at the ankle. I feel my little cotton shorts rising up my hips, leaving my thighs exposed.

"Elites?" He scrunches his face and stares at me, waiting for me to elaborate.

"You, Preston, Trey, Alyssa, Chelsea, Nick, and Zoey." I shrug. "You're The Elites."

"How so? Because we're popular?" he sounds offended.

"That and because you carry yourselves like you're above the rest of us," I add matter-of-factly.

"I don't! Neither do Trey and Zoey!" he shoots back frantically. "We're just a group of friends. I don't see how we act like we're better than people."

"Well, try looking at it from the bottom of the social chain," I say with a snort, and fold my arms across my chest.

He ponders my words, and I can feel he's got a rebuttal. Instead, he says, "Well, to answer your question, no, I don't care what my friends think about me hanging out with you. This has nothing to do with them."

There's a long silence, but for me, it isn't uncomfortable. When you're constantly hearing voices, silence is always welcome.

Jesse is the first to break the silence. I hear a hint of reluctance in his voice when he asks, "So, do you need to get home to your siblings? I can give you a ride."

I shake my head. "Nope, they're tucked away in bed counting sheep as we speak."

"So, what's your story?" he asks me next. He's texting on his cell phone. If I really cared, I'd have to assume it was Alyssa, probably prowling for a late-night snack. I'm suddenly more compelled to stay here with him, just to keep him away from her.

"I don't have a story."

He chuckles. "Everyone has a story, Mischa."

I suck my teeth and press the back of my head harder into his leather headrest. "It's the weekend. Shouldn't you be sucking face with your girlfriend? I'm sure she's wondering where you are?"

"I already told you I don't have a girlfriend, and are you reading my texts?" he asks me in an accusatory tone, pulling his cell phone further away from my view.

"It was actually just an assumption. But thanks for the confirmation." I snicker at him.

"What do you care, anyway? You won't even talk to me most of the time," he huffs at me and returns his attention to texting Alyssa back. This time I *do* read the text.

> **Jesse:** Can't. In for the night.

"My dad died when I was a kid, so I got sent to live with my mom. She was already married to Joe and had the Littles, but my dad dying really messed her up." I can tell him pieces of my story, but never all of it.

"Is that why you're always taking care of your little brother and sisters?" he asks me. He's genuinely interested, giving me his full attention now instead of his phone, which keeps vibrating in the cup holder.

I nod. "Yeah, my mom spends most days doped up on antidepressants and sleeping pills. So, it's up to me to take care of the Littles and Grandpa."

"That sucks," he mumbles. He's right. It does.

"Be thankful you're an only child," I tell him blandly. I reach out and try to warm my hands with the warm air flowing from the vents. This is strange. I'm actually... cold.

Jesse reaches into the backseat and pulls a blanket up to the front for me. "Being an only child is *okay*, I guess. My parents put a lot of pressure on me for the future." I eye the blanket suspiciously, and he laughs. "My mom always insists I keep a blanket in my car, just in case I get stranded somewhere."

"I'll take the jacket, instead," I tell him, and he shrugs the coat off again and hands it to me. He cranks up the heater, but I tell him to cut the engine. No use wasting gas.

"Can I ask you a personal question?" Jesse asks me as he wraps the fleece blanket around his shoulders.

"I probably won't answer, but shoot."

He takes a moment to laugh at my words—even though I meant them truthfully—and then he rolls his head in my direction. "The whole Blake thing..."

"Yeah, what about it?" I reply indifferently. He's referring to the night a party at the mill was broken up by the sheriff after a call came into the station that I was being assaulted in one of the closed-off rooms.

"What really happened?" he asks nervously. I'm not sure if he's just concerned that his best friend's brother is a rapist, or if he is worried that I'm a serial rape accuser.

"You've heard the stories? What do you think?" I retort smugly, smirking at him.

"I *heard* that you had a lot to drink that night and persuaded him to go upstairs with you, and then when you guys were having sex, you called Sheriff Freeman and cried rape," Jesse tells me, but I can tell he wants to call bullshit on the story. Everyone knew Blake Wilcox was a menace, no matter how much of a façade he put on for the adults. He was eighteen, and I was fourteen when we were in school together, and he always had a thing for me. Not a genuine *thing*, a sexual one. He'd smack my ass when we crossed paths, and he'd make lewd comments about me whenever I walked through town or at school.

"Well, I guess that's the story." I shrug, turning toward the window.

"Yeah, well. I believe your side," he tells me softly. "Blake was a dick."

"I've never told my side." I remind him because I haven't. I've never once told people Blake tried to rape me, but I've never denied it either.

"Yeah, well, I always knew you hated Blake, so there wouldn't have been a reason for you to have sex with him willingly," he tells me.

I'm caught between the swell in my chest at the thought of Jesse believing in my character as something other than a weirdo, and the need to change the subject from that fateful night, so I blurt out the first thing that comes to mind.

"I don't want to go home tonight."

Jesse gives me a lazy smile, and I feel the mania and psychosis creeping back in. No hallucinations. Well, at least I don't think so. No, this is something else. I squirm in my seat a little to fight it.

"Me neither." He licks his lips, and even though I know it's an unconscious gesture, my insides start to do flips. "I say we stay right here all night and get to know each other."

"Or we can sit here quietly and listen to the music," I say softly, facing him the same way he's facing me. Slightly turned in the bucket seats, heads hanging to the side with smiles on our faces.

"You want me to turn on some music?" He moves to turn the key backward. I reach my hand out to stop him, placing my palm on the back of his hand.

"Not that kind of music," I whisper. He furrows his brows, and I giggle. "Just listen."

He sits back in his seat again, but instead of moving my hand, he grasps it and relaxes. The cicadas and mountain wind sing a song outside. Maybe they're singing about us?

Two social opposites, sitting together in silence, falling asleep together in a secret place where no one can find us.

A place where one of us plans to die soon.

Chapter Eighteen

JESSE

Mischa is gone when I wake up the next morning, and she's taken my vintage leather jacket with her. I'm about to freak out, but then I notice the scrap of paper with a message written on it lying in the passenger's seat. I didn't even hear her leave this morning, but when I look at my cell phone, I see it is almost eight o'clock in the morning. I'm definitely missing church today because while staying up and listening to the sounds of nature around us was refreshing, I didn't sleep comfortably in the GTO's bucket seat. I still have a few more hours of snoozing to complete.

I'll bring your precious jacket to school on Monday. But after that, you're not allowed to talk to me until you've picked me up for the formal. And you can't tell ANYONE!

I can't fight the smile and short fist pump I do at the realization that she's agreeing to go to the formal with me. Maybe she's coming around to feeling the same way I feel about her. Trey thinks it's just a phase.

"She's something different from the girls that are always hanging around, but do you really like her, like that?" he asked me last night at the party. I just shrugged because, even if this is just a phase, I like Mischa. Last night was a strong test of that. We sat in silence for hours until we fell asleep, and I thought nothing of it.

When I pull into my driveway, I jog around the side of my house and lift my unlocked window, slipping through and collapsing on my bed. I've barely dozed off when my mom pounds on the door, demanding I wake up and get dressed for church.

"You don't get to stumble in the house after dawn and sleep through church. Get up now, Jesse!" she yells, and I groan and do as I'm told.

I have to keep from dozing off as Reverend Daniel drones on in his sermon. I recall a service when I was in sixth grade when he called Mischa to the front of the congregation and announced that she was possessed by a demon because a few girls caught her talking to someone in the locker room that nobody else could see. The boys all assumed the girls' locker room was haunted, and maybe Mischa was talking to a ghost. At the time it was fun, but now that we're almost adults, we know it's not true. We still tell the middle schoolers that the gym is haunted, just for kicks.

Sheriff Freeman was livid that Sunday morning. He walked up, grabbed Mischa by the arm, and told Reverend Daniel, in front of everybody, that he should be ashamed of himself. Mischa never comes to service anymore.

After church, my group of friends, or *"The Elites"* as Mischa likes to call us, meet up for lunch at The Strip, a local restaurant that's 50s diner-inspired and known for the best chicken strips in the Yosemite area. It's our usual hangout spot, in the largest booth by the picture window looking out at Main Street.

"I bought a black dress," Alyssa tells me sweetly, leaning on her bent elbow, and chewing a French fry. She's sitting across me, both of us in seats closest to the window. Preston is beside her, in between her and Chelsea. On my side of the booth is Trey, and Nick has pulled up a chair to occupy the end of the table. Nick is tall and stocky, more muscular than the other teenagers in this town. He almost looks like a pissed-off, grown man, hanging out with a bunch of teenagers.

"For what?" I ask her, cocking a brow.

"The formal, duh." She giggles, and I feel my stomach knot up. "I heard you were wearing a black tux. So, I figured we'd match."

I look around the table to make sure our friends are preoccupied. I'm over Alyssa, but I still care about her feelings. I don't want to embarrass her.

"Uhh, Lys. We're not going to the formal together," I tell her as quietly as possible. I'm trying to keep our conversation between the two of us, but she's got other plans, I guess.

"What do you mean, *'we're not going to the formal together?'*" she asks me loud enough to pull the others into our conversation.

I shrug. "I mean, I didn't ask you for a reason."

She huffs and then flinches when Preston wraps an arm around her shoulder. "Don't worry, Lyssa, I'll take you to the formal."

She makes a disgusting face, and I can tell that whatever happened between those two, Alyssa's not feeling it. Preston gives me a smug look. He doesn't really like Alyssa. He's just trying to get under my skin. That's not going to work, though.

"I'll pass, Preston." She rolls her eyes and looks out the window. When she stares through the glass, her face screws up with even more irritation, and she sucks her teeth. I follow her line of vision and my eyes land on a familiar form prancing down Main Street in a pair of red straight-legged jeans and a silky, button-down black top with little yellow pineapples printed all over it. Her hair is pulled back in a wild ponytail, and she's marching forward with her shoulders slightly hunched and her eyes focused straight ahead like she's on a mission to get somewhere.

It's Mischa. Behind her, Teddy and Maddie are struggling to keep up.

"She's so fucking weird, I swear," Alyssa mumbles, and I figure now wouldn't be a good time to mention that I'm not taking Alyssa to the formal because I'm taking Mischa.

Preston sings, "One of these things is not like the other," causing Chelsea to laugh.

"I wonder if she's mixed with Black?" Chelsea says, still laughing at Preston's offensive joke. A dumb question because Mischa is clearly Black. Her skin is even darker than Nick's. Almost the same shade as mine.

Alyssa does a snort-laugh, like she's just thought of something funny, and then says, "That would explain her gross, nappy hair."

Preston laughs obnoxiously at the comment, and Chelsea stifles her laugh. Nick—who I'll remind you is *half Black*—doesn't react at all. He just stares intensely at Mischa as she walks out of the frame. Maybe his hatred for Mischa outweighs his contempt for racist comments.

Trey and I? Oh yeah, we're pissed!

"What the hell is that supposed to mean?" Trey asks Alyssa, slamming his palm on the table.

"I—I didn't mean to—it was just a joke, Trey. Calm down," she stutters before regaining her composure and smiling at Trey. "I mean, c'mon, it's *Mischa Lawrence*. She's a freak!"

"Yeah, whatever," Trey mumbles, scooting out of the booth. He exchanges dap with Nick and then storms out of the diner.

Preston has taken digs at Mischa plenty of times, and aside from the jokes he's made about her not fitting in with her white family, no one has ever made an outwardly racist comment about her. At least, not around me. I doubt they do it around Trey and Zoey, either. I wonder if Alyssa has said those things about Trinity, Trey's younger sister, who wears her hair in tight natural curls. What does she say about my mom, or Zoey, or Mrs. Freeman? Because if she could say something like that about Mischa's hair, there's no telling what she's thinking of theirs.

I stare at Alyssa in disgust and shake my head. "*That* is why you're going to the formal alone." I'm not sure if by *"that"* I'm referring to Mischa or

Alyssa's attitude, but I guess they both work in this case. I follow Trey's example and scoot out of the booth. Just like in Archerville, we can't afford to be the aggressive Black boys in a Grover diner.

I catch up to Trey, and we decide to go to the arcade and take out our frustrations on the old Street Fighter machine they have in the back. On the way, I fill Trey in on my encounter with Mischa last night and that she agreed to be my date to the formal.

"She probably swore you to silence so that Preston and the others won't torture her for the next two weeks." Trey rolls his eyes, but then I see the smirk on his face. He's happy for me. "Besides, it's none of their business."

He's right. It's not their business. In a few months, we'll all go our separate ways and high school will be a blur. Their opinions on who I took as a date to the winter formal will be null and void.

Chapter Nineteen

132

onday morning, I saunter down the hallway clad in Jesse's leather jacket. It swallows me, but I think it looks kind of cool over my plaid pleated miniskirt and sheer stockings. I even threw on a pair of Mary Janes with a three-inch heel for a little extra flair. My hair is slicked up in a wavy bun on top of my head, and I even put on makeup. I look as good as I feel, and even though I've forbidden Jesse from talking to me for the next two weeks, I'm looking forward to seeing him, and him seeing me when I give the jacket back.

It would be nice of fate to allow me to share that moment with Jesse in peace and solitude, with no one watching, but as I walk through the crowded hallways with my head held high and my hips switching, I find that I don't care who sees me talking to Jesse and wearing his coat.

Alyssa's eyes look like they're about to pop out of their sockets when I wink at her as I pass. I walk over to Jesse, who is across the hall at his locker, talking with Trey and Nick. Luckily, Preston is nowhere in sight.

I walk right over to him and tap his shoulder. He stops talking and turns around to look down at me. When he sees that it's me, he smiles brightly, and I ignore the punch in the gut that is my hormones flopping around at the sight of such a handsome smile.

"This..." I draw out with a sigh as I shrug the jacket off of my shoulders, "belongs to you." I hand it to him with slight reluctance. Last night, Frankie nearly lost her mind when she caught me snuggled in bed wearing what she had recognized as Jesse Alford's vintage leather jacket. She pressed me for half an hour about why I had it, and I finally spilled the beans. That he'd asked me to the dance. I swore her to secrecy, with the promise that I'd stand outside her school yodeling, something I'm not skilled in.

Jesse eyes me up and down and smirks. He likes what he sees. I don't blame him. I told you I look good! He bites his bottom lip as he examines me. Not sensually, the way it's playing in my head, but another Jesse quirk I've studied during our brief... *whatever-ship.*

"Why are you dressed like a preppy schoolgirl?" He chuckles.

I narrow my eyes. "I'm sorry. Are you *talking* to *me?*"

Jesse laughs again and does a zipper motion with his lips. I walk away without another word, but I hear him dismissing himself from his friends and following me. I can't see Alyssa anymore, but I'm sure she's blowing steam out of her nose. No, seriously. I bet if I looked at her, there would be literal steam shooting out her nostrils like a cartoon bull.

"Spill, bitch!"

I'm standing behind the counter of the general store, lazily flipping through a catalog with tons of prom and formal dresses. The dance is in a week. I know I don't have the time or the money to order anything from this high-end magazine, but I can at least get a few ideas. Zoey's phone call is a needed distraction from all the daydreaming I'm doing as I visualize myself in one of these dresses. My body comes equipped with a nice pair of boobs and cleavage, and I'm not as thin as the teeny models in the catalog with their narrow hips and flat chests.

"Spill what?" I ask her, sliding the magazine aside and giving her my full attention.

"You, strutting through school wearing Jesse's jacket!" Her tone is a mixture of excitement and accusation.

"I borrowed it Saturday night. I walked home, and it was cold," I half-lie. "And how did you even hear about that?"

"Nick told me," she states matter-of-factly.

"Why were you talking to Nick?" Now it's my turn to accuse her.

She sucks her teeth and tells me that information isn't important. "Rumor has it Jesse isn't taking Alyssa to the winter formal this year."

"You're five hundred miles away and still keeping up with Grover's gossip?" I laugh. The town is dead because it's so cold outside. It's nice of Mr. Brady to still let me watch over the store and earn my pay. I've already got my eye on the frozen chicken breasts that need to be thrown out in place of the newest shipment. They're not expired, just in the way.

"But you're right. Jesse's *not* taking Alyssa to the winter formal," I tell her with a smile. My mood is high, and I feel like bragging. "Because he's taking me."

I have to pull the phone away from my ear as Zoey screams hysterically on her end.

"You're kidding me! You're going to the winter formal with *Jesse Alford*?" she yells, and I wonder what her host family thinks about her screaming. "He asked you to the fucking formal? What have I been missing?"

"Not much, trust me," I reply nonchalantly, staring out the window at the empty Main Street.

"Bullshit! I leave for less than two months, and you're dating Jesse Alford!" she exclaims.

"I'm not *dating* Jesse Alford. We kissed once and spent one night together talking in his car. Calm down." She's more excited than I am.

"YOU WHAT!?" she screams in my ear, and I once again pull the phone away and stare at the receiver. She's always so over-the-top about everything. "You're telling me that you *kissed* Jesse!"

"Technically, he kissed me. But I've kissed plenty of guys." I shrug to myself. Of course, my drug dealer and random motorists as I hitchhike the interstates aren't nearly as thrilling as kissing Jesse.

"I can't believe this!" she screams. Alyssa and Zoey have been friends way longer than either of them even knew I existed. I'm not sure why she is excited about me making out with Alyssa's ex-boyfriend. Friendships are weird like that, I guess.

We spend the rest of the afternoon chatting about the winter formal, well actually Zoey does all the talking, and I half listen to her dress ideas and how I should style my hair. The other half of my brain is fixed on the large tawny creature prowling down Main Street. A mountain lion on a mission.

It's stalking through the town, looking from left to right like it's reading the signs and looking for something. The way its muscles flex under the tan fur is almost mesmerizing, and I'm entranced, completely ignoring my friend's yapping on the phone. Mrs. Hatcher at the sewing and alteration shop across the street comes outside and is locking up the shop, completely oblivious to the predator behind her. I'm just about to drop the phone and run to the window to scream a warning to her when the beast stops and locks its eyes on me through the large window.

We're caught in an intense stare-down, and behind the animal, Mrs. Hatcher walks away down Main. The cougar holds its stance, trapping me in its pale eyes.

"He's going to ruin everything we've planned," I hear a disembodied voice say. A normal instinct should probably be to assume it was coming from the girl on the phone against my ear. But I know that voice so very well, and it's not Zoey. It's *that* voice.

The voice that tells me it's time for me to end my life soon.

"Seafoam green." Zoey's voice breaks through all the other distractions. The mountain lion releases me from its gaze and continues down the street and out of sight. Oddly, it's not walking in the direction of the mountain pass. It's heading out of town.

"What are you talking about?" I ask Zoey with an exhausted sigh. I walk over to the window and draw the shutters closed. I take my seat behind the counter again, trying to push the mountain lion's words out of my mind. I know what it was saying. That Jesse is going to impede on my goal to die in four months.

"Your dress, duh!" Zoey scoffs. "Are you even listening to me?"

No, I'm talking to mountain lions about all the reasons I *shouldn't* go out with Jesse Alford.

"Of course, but what the hell is seafoam green?" I chuckle instead of saying what I really want to say.

"Google it, bitch." Zoey laughs. "It'll look great with your complexion. Oh, that reminds me! Apparently, Chelsea asked the table what they thought you were mixed with during lunch on Sunday, and Alyssa and Preston made some remarks that pissed off Trey and Jesse."

"What kind of remarks?" I feel my blood boiling at the thought of Alyssa and Chelsea making racist jokes at my expense.

"Nick didn't really say." Zoey's lying, but I don't call her out on it. The door chimes, and Mr. Brady walks in and goes to the back freezer. He returns with a bag of frozen chicken breast and a few cans of peas and carrots. "But it all makes sense now, why Jesse walked out on her like that. He's clearly into you!"

Or maybe he realized his girlfriend is bitch.

"I've got to go, Zo. A customer just walked in." I give her a chance to say goodbye before hanging up.

I thank Mr. Brady and ask him if it would be alright for me to take next Saturday off. "I need to go into the city for a couple of hours."

"I'm sure I can handle things without you." He smiles. "How are you getting there?"

"The usual." I shrug, grabbing the bag of chicken and heading out the door. "See you tomorrow."

Chapter Twenty

I relish the sound of the marble falling onto the stack of fellow glass spheres in the fishbowl. That, mixed with the sound of my clozapine and lithium plunking into the toilet water, is music for a good day.

The Littles are having waffles again for breakfast, partly because it's their favorite, and because it's quick and easy. The earlier I start down the highway, the faster I can get picked up, and the quicker I get to San Francisco. Once everyone is settled, I'm out the door. I zip through town without a single run-in with the rogue mountain lion from earlier in the week.

It doesn't take long for me to get picked up. It's early December, but I'm wearing my shorts and a low-cut top, so someone is bound to stop for me. He's a decent-looking guy in a Ford pickup, maybe early thirties, blaring overwhelming volumes of heavy metal music at 9 a.m.

Mr. Brady and Sheriff Freeman hate it when I hitchhike, but I don't have many other options. I can't just take the van and drive into the city without a license. So, whenever I need to re-up on weed and essentials for the house that I can't get in Grover, I take to the highway in my shortest shorts and a thumb out.

"Where are you headed?" the blonde driver asks with his cigarette hanging out of his mouth.

"As far west on 120 as you're going. I need to get to San Francisco," I tell him, leaning toward the window to put some space in between us.

"I'll take you as far as Oakland. That's where I'm going." He grins at me. I give him a fake smile and thank him. I should be grateful to have lucked up on a ride that's headed basically the entire way, but riding with the same driver can be exhausting. I like the switch up of personalities during the longer commutes like San Francisco.

I understand the sheriff's and Brady's apprehensions. That's almost three hours on the road with a stranger who could be a serial rapist or something. That's why I keep my switchblade tucked neatly against my hip.

"So, what's your name?" he asks me. He's inhaling and exhaling smoke from his cigarette, which smells disgusting.

"Alyssa," I tell him confidently.

"That's a pretty name. I'm Barry. Are you from the Bay Area, Alyssa? Or around here?" He motions to the mountains. He's going well over the speed limit, which means we may have a chance of making it to our destination earlier than expected.

"I'm from the South, actually." I put on a fake southern accent, "Alabama, honey."

"Long way from home, aren't you?" He grins.

"Wanderlust." I shrug, looking out the window. The trees and hills zoom by in a blur as we cruise down the highway. I'm not in the mood to chitchat with this guy. I'm tempted to tell him to stop in Stockton to shorten the ride, but I know I won't find what I'm looking for there.

Jesse may act like he's one hundred percent into me the way I am, but I know appearances must mean *something* to him. He's popular, and popular people care about appearances, especially at school dances. That being said, if I'm going to do him any type of justice, I need to find a decent-looking dress. So, San Francisco it is.

"Don't tell me you're on some epic journey to complete your bucket list?" he says with a laugh, but I notice that he's continuously dragging his eyes across my body at every chance.

"Yeah, I am." I smirk, hoisting my legs up on his dusty dashboard like I do in the GTO. "I want to scope out all the best suicide spots in the world. Today's target is the GGB."

He frowns at my nonchalant attitude. "That's morbid."

"I'll be dead by April." I shrug.

"Huh?" He twists his head and looks at me, but this time he's not staring at my tits.

"Yep." I nod, smiling proudly. I cross my hands around my chest.

"Are you, like, sick or something? Like, cancer?" he asks in a nervous tone.

"I am definitely sick." I nod. "But aren't we all?"

"I'm not sure what that means, but I'm sorry to hear that," he tells me somberly. I've successfully killed the mood, so maybe he'll shut up and just drive. If he thinks I'm crazy, maybe he won't try to pressure me into exchanging any *favors* for the ride. Those rides usually end up with me giving them the Jimmy from Archerville special. "Life is so beautiful. Everyone should be allowed to live it to the fullest, you know? To experience all the beautiful things life has to offer." Instead of going into an uncomfortable silence, I seem to have unleashed the philosopher in this guy.

"Life is pretty dull." I shrug again, looking at the side of his face. "We're kind of all just waiting around to die. At least I know how long I have to wait."

Barry shakes his head and laughs. "You don't *have to* wait around to die. You have the choice to live any life you want before that happens. You can travel, you can meet all kinds of cool people, and do all the things you enjoy. You can even fall in love and wait out that inevitable death with your soulmate."

That last part makes me think of Jesse, and I want to kick myself. I don't want to fall in love with Jesse, no matter how incredibly attractive he is, or how my hormones start begging for him whenever I'm in a manic state. I don't care if he treats me like a normal human being and sticks up for me against his friends. I don't want him to like me. No, I want him as far away from me as possible. That mountain lion was right. Jesse will ruin everything if I fall for him. He'll be something physical that exists to keep me grounded in this life. I can't die in peace if I'm in love with him.

I combat Barry's nonstop conversations with a series of grunts and hums. If I were a sane person, I might be concerned enough to jump out of the car. He's giving me life advice while simultaneously ogling my body. Yeah, I don't care about this... *thing* with Jesse. I'm just going through all of this trouble for... what, exactly?

Barry was kind enough to drop me off at the BART station in Oakland, so I put an extra switch in my ass to give him something to dream about as payment. I catch the BART to San Francisco, and an hour later, I'm standing outside of a small formal boutique with sparkly dresses on sassy-posing mannequins.

Glitter and sparkles are a definite no.

The bell chimes as I walk in. I'm expecting an overly made-up, fake-smiling, forty-year-old woman to greet me. Instead, I get a bored, distant grunt from a college-aged, brown-skinned girl flipping through a magazine. She reminds me of myself at the general store, and I feel myself relax a little. I can browse in peace, without the discomfort of having someone realize I have no sense of style.

I find a rack of dresses and shuffle through the assortment of random styles lazily. I'm not big on shopping or fashion, but I want to put in some effort for Jesse's sake. I pick up a black strapless dress and examine it, deciding to try *something* on.

"Oh, no. Your tatas are way too nice for a strapless dress," the sales associate speaks up suddenly. I look over to find her smirking at me. I glance down at my newly coined *"tatas."*

I place the black dress back and then pull out a poofy, purple dress that has thin straps on both shoulders. It's hideous, but I don't care at this point. Ten minutes into dress shopping and I already want to call it quits and tell Jesse Alford to shove it because going to the dance with him is bullshit, just like kissing him is bullshit, and falling asleep in his GTO with him is bullshit.

The cashier gives me an exaggerated sigh and closes her magazine, pushing it aside as she stands to round the counter she's sitting behind.

"You need something with a halter top. It'll make your boobs look amazing!" She pops her gum and shuffles through the rack in front of me. Her name tag says Meka, and she's pulling dresses from the rack and draping them across her arm without even blinking.

"Follow me," she demands in a short tone. I do as told, following her across the store to a stall with a flimsy curtain that serves as a dressing room. She shoves six dresses inside with me and draws the curtain.

"So, what's the occasion? Early prom shopping?" she calls out from outside the dressing room.

"My school is having a winter formal next Saturday," I reply, undressing and pulling on the first dress, a form-fitting, stretchy red dress with one shoulder strap.

"Come out so I can see you," she orders. I oblige. She scrunches her face when she sees it. "Eh, I don't know about that one. It doesn't scream *school dance*. And you need to show off those tatas, girl!"

I retreat into the dressing room and the next time I emerge, I'm donning a royal blue ball gown that halters around the neck and pushes my *"tatas"* up to my chin. Again, Meka frowns and shakes her head.

"Too much cleavage, plus it hides that cute body of yours."

I shuffle back into the dressing room and strip off the giant gown. I have to admit, this is kind of fun. It's what I'd imagine I'd be doing with my girlfriends if I had any. It feels… normal.

"Oooh, girl! That is the one! That's the perfect dress for you!" Meka grins and simultaneously chews her gum when I resurface in the third dress.

It's a pale blue. So light, it almost looks silver. The column-style dress has a deep neckline, accented by little rhinestone chains that connect both sides, allowing my *"tatas"* to sit naturally. It's haltered and the thin material clings to my body before pooling on the floor.

"There are still three more dresses in there." I throw my thumb back toward the curtain.

"That's the dress girl." Meka beams. "Trust me. Your man is going to love you in that dress!"

I turn on my heels and pull the curtains back to hide me again. "I don't have a man!" I yell out to her as I undress. I toss the light blue dress over the door, and she catches it and takes it to the register.

"So, you're going to the dance alone?" she quips. When I walk out of the dressing room, she's smirking again.

"No, I'm actually going to the dance with the most popular guy in school. But *I'm* not popular at all. Therefore, we are not a couple. He is not my man."

"Oh? So, like one of those movies where the hot, popular guy makes a bet that he can turn the geeky girl into a cool girl?" She could be on to something. Except I'm not a geek like Neil Gunderson, and I really hope Jesse's asking me out isn't part of some giant scheme between him and The Elites.

"I need shoes," I tell her to change the subject. There's a small selection of shoes near the back of the small boutique, so I walk over and pick up a pair of strappy silver sandals with rhinestones all over the straps and stiletto heels. I toss them on the counter alongside the dress and wait impatiently for Meka to ring me up. My mood is in a frenzy and the fun of dress shopping is lost suddenly. I'm ready to get home to the Littles. I'm ready for this stupid dance to be over with. I'm ready to end my life.

"What's your name?" Meka asks me as she scans the price tags that I didn't bother to look at. Impulse shopping.

I feel compelled to be honest with her. Maybe it's because she helped me out today without judgment. It felt good to be treated nicely for once. In Grover, I can't walk into any of the shops and stores without being ridiculed.

Or maybe I'm just crazy and like to give certain people the name of my sworn enemy and others my real name. Who knows?

"Mischa."

"Well, Mischa. I like you, so I'm going to give you a discount and throw in some costume jewelry for free." She grabs a pretty crystal earring, necklace, and bracelet set from the jewelry rack next to her.

"Thank you for everything today," I say as she puts the dress in a black garment bag. I tell her to just throw the shoes in the bottom of the bag and thank her again.

"Don't mention it. I hope you have fun at your formal. Hope your man shows you a good time." She winks and hands me the garment bag over the counter. I want to remind her that Jesse isn't *my man*, but it's not important to her. I'll never see her again after this.

"See you around, Mischa," she calls out as I open the door and sound the chime again. I pause and wave back at her shortly.

"Goodbye, Meka."

Chapter Twenty-One

Main Street is bustling when I make it home later in the afternoon. I hurry through the town with the garment bag draped across my arm, focusing straight ahead, hoping to attract as little attention as possible. When I finally make it home, I'm not given a moment's rest before Maddie and Teddy come barging in with their requests.

"Sissy, we want ice cream!" Maddie sings in her high-pitched voice just as I'm plopping down on my bed.

"You haven't even had dinner yet," I murmur, covering my face with my pillow. It's only late afternoon, but I'm exhausted from the day's events.

"But Teddy and I want ice cream now! Can we go to Scoops?" she whines, pulling the pillow away from my face. Her inability to pronounce her 'Rs' distorts the word *cream*. It's almost cute, but I'm irritated and tired.

"No!" I growl and snatch the pillow from her. I place it over my face again and shoo them away. I hear Maddie huff and stomp her feet as she makes her way out of the room.

"C'mon Teddy, let's go play. We never get to do things like the other kids do."

Her words sting me right in the chest. All they want is to do normal things like normal kids. Normal kids eat ice cream on Saturdays and play hide and seek around town with the other kids. Just because I hate Grover with a passion, and would rather not spend more time there than necessary, doesn't mean they have to suffer.

I pull the pillow away from my face and groan. "Put your shoes on. I'll take you to get your stupid ice cream."

Teddy's still standing at my bedside, staring at me, but a smile creeps across his face when I concede. From the hallway, Maddie squeals with delight, and I hear her feet padding down the hallway into their bedroom. Frankie walks in and goes straight to the garment bag in our closet. She immediately unzips it and examines the blue dress.

"This is cute."

I toss the pillow, and it hits the back of her head. "Get out of there!"

"Ow!" she yells and turns to pick up the pillow and throw it back. I roll to the side, and it misses me, bouncing off the bed and falling onto the floor.

"We're going to Scoops for ice cream," I tell her, standing to slip on my tennis shoes. "You're more than welcome to join us."

Frankie shrugs, but she follows Teddy, Maddie, and me out of the house.

Scoops Ice Cream Parlor is one of the many family-owned businesses in Grover. Like the other stores in Grover, it's named after the man who owns it, Mr. Scoops. I guess you don't really have any other choice but to sell ice cream for a living with a name like that.

There's an old 1950s tune playing, and the lobby of the small parlor is cold and outdated. The teenagers of Grover typically hang out across the street at The Strip—named after the chicken strips instead of the Fredrick family who owns it—so Scoops is usually empty or busy with come-and-go traffic.

Today, the Littles and I will be dining in, however.

Maddie has her nose pressed against the glass of the ice cream display, standing on her tiptoes to get a better view of the barrels hosting the fourteen different flavors, mesmerized.

"Can I get two flavors, Sissy?" she asks.

"Me too!" Teddy chimes in. "I want cookies and cream and raspberry!"

"Gross." I scrunch my face. Mr. Scoops is standing behind the glass, staring at us like we're stray animals with rabies. I ignore him and start to order. Behind me, the door chimes, so I don't want to hold up the line with all of my siblings' complicated orders.

"We'll take four double scoops. Chocolate and vanilla in a cup for the little one. Cookies 'n cream and raspberry in a waffle cone for Teddy. I'll take caramel and chocolate on a waffle cone, and Frankie, what do you want?" I pause and turn to Frankie for her order, but she seems to notice, like I have, that Mr. Scoops hasn't moved to start our orders.

"I'm not serving you," he tells me simply. He's standing straight up with his arms crossed, staring at me.

My mental thread begins to tighten. "Excuse me?"

"You heard me."

"Look Scoops, I've got money to pay for it, so just give my kids their ice cream before I—"

"I'm not serving them because they're with you, plain and simple." He shrugs again. I feel my heart beat faster, and I know I'm about to jump over the counter when he says, "Your money's no good here, Lawrence. Now leave."

"Listen, you stupid fuc—" I'm just starting my verbal assault when the person in line behind us steps in.

"Well, surely my money's good here, Scoops." It's Jesse, and he's standing right over my shoulder. He extends his hand out with cash in it. "So go ahead and give them what they're asking for, on me."

Scoops frowns at Jesse but does as he's told. This town is built on football, and Jesse Alford *is* Grover football at the moment. He scoops Maddie and Teddy's flavors and asks Frankie what she wants. Jesse orders cookie dough ice cream in a cup, and hands Mr. Scoops a twenty-dollar bill and a few ones.

He follows us to the round table near the window and sits across from me, with Maddie and Frankie on either side of him. Frankie's staring at him like he's some type of deity, not even paying attention to her ice cream cone.

"Thanks for buying us ice cream, Jesse," Maddie tells him cheerfully, smearing chocolate ice cream across her face.

Instead of being disgusted, Jesse smiles at her and nods. "You're welcome, Maddie."

I take a napkin from the dispenser in the center of the table and reach across Teddy to wipe Maddie's mouth. "Maddie, you're making a mess." I sigh, cleaning the smudged chocolate away. "And Frankie, stop staring at him like that!" I snap. Jesse laughs.

"So, I saw you walking down Main with a garment bag." Jesse smirks at me. I watch as his plastic spoon disappears between his gorgeous lips. I squirm a little in my seat as my hormones fire off. "Did you find a dress?"

"You're not supposed to be talking to me, Jesse Alford," I remind him flatly.

He scoffs and shakes his head, turning his gaze to Teddy instead. "Teddy, can you ask your sister if she found a dress for the winter formal?" Teddy frowns briefly but relays the message to me.

"Yes, I did," I answer shortly. I run my tongue around the mound of caramel ice cream suggestively, and I notice Jesse stifling a smile.

Maddie starts wiggling in her chair and waving her tiny hand around. "Me next, I wanna talk for Jesse next!"

Jesse releases his chuckle, but he is still watching me lick my ice cream. "Okay, Maddie. Tell your sister that I'll be picking her up Saturday night at seven. Sheriff Freeman is renting a limo for Trey and me."

I stop licking the ice cream and eye him seriously while Maddie translates his message to the best of her abilities with her speech impediment. *So much for low-key.*

"Won't your friends be a little perturbed to see you arriving at the dance with *me* in a *limo*?" I watch him skeptically to gauge his response. He says he doesn't care about what everyone thinks about his sudden interest in me, but he has to know he'll be committing social suicide next weekend when he arrives at the dance with me on his arm. Whatever plan he and The Elites have up their sleeves must be pretty spectacular. Worth twenty-three dollars in ice cream for my Littles and me.

"Teddy, tell her I don't really give a damn what my friends think about it," he instructs my little brother, still looking me in the eye.

Teddy gasps and looks between us frantically. "I—I can't say that word, Jesse," he stutters softly, seemingly ashamed to be letting Jesse down with his inability to relay the naughty message.

"Oops, my bad, man." Jesse laughs again. His white teeth are on full display and his twisted hair swings casually, and that stupid swirling in my lower gut returns at the sight of his gorgeous smile. I've been dealt some pretty shitty cards, and I rarely complain. That being said, it's still hard to believe that this gorgeous creature would *actually* be interested in me.

I resume my sensual assault on my dessert, shaking my head at Jesse. What do I care if his friends all desert him for *"liking"* me? I won't be around long for the aftermath.

Chapter Twenty-Two

I examine my dress again for the thousandth time this week. The formal is tonight. In about nine hours, Jesse Alford will be here to pick me up. I hate to admit it, but I'm actually nervous. Maybe even excited.

Wednesday, I nearly set the kitchen on fire trying to cook a pack of ramen noodles with no water in the pot. My brain immediately went down the list of things to save—number one being the Littles, and then Grandpa, and finally, I thought about my dress being all charred and mangled, ruining Jesse's winter formal plans.

My mom didn't even make the cut over the stupid dress.

Of course, Joe threw a fit when I doused the entire kitchen in water from the faucet sprayer. He claimed there wasn't a fire and threatened to call *"the folks up at the loony bin"* to come and get me.

Since I won't be home tonight, I make extra sandwiches for Teddy and Maddy, one for lunch and another for dinner.

"Frankie will make you a bowl of cereal if you're still hungry later but try not to drink all the milk. I won't be able to buy anymore until next week," I warn them as I sit their sandwiches in front of them. They're sitting in front of the TV watching some colorful cartoon.

I've been doing my best to kill time and stay busy until it's time for me to get ready for tonight, and even after serving a late lunch at two o'clock in the afternoon, I've still got about five hours.

"Umm, shouldn't you be getting ready for your date tonight?" Frankie asks me as she shovels a corner of her ham sandwich in her mouth.

"I don't need five hours to put on a dress, Frank." I scrunch my face at her.

She returns the gesture and drags her thin body off the recliner. "You're hopeless," she huffs.

I follow her and her sandwich down the hallway to our bedroom. She places the sandwich on the corner of her dresser and tells me to sit on her bed.

"For what?" I fold my arms across my chest defiantly. She's pulling out her ceramic flat iron and unraveling the cord.

"We need to do something with that." She points at my mass of frizzy tangles before turning to plug in the iron. "Now go shower and wash your hair, and then I'll straighten it for you. I think it'll look really pretty if we just leave it straight with a part on the side." She seems excited about this. Strange, considering my sister acts like she hates me every chance she gets. I eye her suspiciously, but eventually, I give in and gather my things for my shower.

I may not need five hours to put on a dress, but it takes me nearly an hour to blow dry and detangle my mane. I finally finish and come back into the bedroom, walking over to the bed and flopping down in a kitchen chair Frankie has brought in.

Frankie sits on her knees behind me on the bed and takes out some of her grooming supplies.

She parts sections of my thick hair into smaller portions, and then clamping it in between the hot panels of the flat iron. The hair magically goes from frizzy and curly to straight as she drags the iron downward and puffs of smoke fly upward. An hour in, she's halfway through my hair and has had to stop several times because of her hand cramping.

"You have way too much hair, Mischa!" she groans while flexing her sore carpal tunnel.

"Sorry, we weren't all born with naturally silky straight hair like yours, *Frankie*," I snap back sarcastically, wincing when she touches my scalp with the hot ceramic plate. I'm not so sure it was an accident either.

Frankie snorts and pulls the flat iron down the next slice of hair. "I wish I could get my hair to curl like yours."

I furrow my brows because that's almost a compliment from her, making two almost-compliments from Frankie in one day.

What is happening here?

I'm just about to respond when I hear the screen door screeching open and slamming. I hear heavy boots stomping through the living room toward the hallway, and then Maddie greeting her father.

"What the hell is that smell?" he bellows out instead of returning Maddie's greeting.

Joe's standing in our doorway before either of us has a chance to answer. Not that I was planning on responding to him, anyway.

"What are you doing to her hair?" he asks Frankie, who is now working on the last quarter section of my hair.

"I'm straightening it." Frankie shrugs. She doesn't even bother to look up at him.

"What for?" he presses. He's got a tall can of beer in his hand and brings it to his lips. He's looking at me with hate in his eyes, and suddenly Fergal's behind him making knife-to-throat motions. I shake my head, willing Fergal to leave, but Frankie just ends up scolding me.

"You're going to make me burn you," she warns, even though she's already nicked me with the flat iron several times today. "She's going to the formal tonight," she finally answers Joe's question, "with Jesse Alford!"

"What kind of dumbass would take *her* to a school dance?" Joe laughs and sloshes beer across the floor of our bedroom when he points the can toward me.

"Jesse is like the most popular guy in school." Frankie sucks her teeth. Joe snorts again and walks down the hallway into his bedroom. "He's right though. It's weird that *Jesse Alford* wants to take you to the formal. You sure it's not some kind of prank?" she continues talking and straightening my hair in Joe's absence. "One time we watched this old movie with Mom, and the popular guy took the weird psychic girl to prom, and the bullies poured pig's blood all over her." She's speaking matter-of-factly, tossing a section of newly flattened hair over my shoulder. The heat stings my skin a little.

"The movie is called *Carrie*, and I already made Jesse promise not to set me up with the old *"blood in a bucket"* trick," I respond dryly.

"So, I guess you won't go on a psychic rampage, either?" she jokes as she drags the iron down the length of my hair.

"Nah." I chuckle more to myself. "I don't have telekinesis."

Just a lethal concoction of schizophrenic symptoms and manic/depressant mood disorder.

Once my hair is completely straightened, Frankie busts out her giant makeup collection and starts painting my face. She uses my foundation since she doesn't have my shade in her collection, but everything else is from the stash of beauty products that I've gifted her over the years. Makeup and beauty products are all she's ever requested for her birthday and Christmas since she was ten. She's not even a teenager yet, and she wears better makeup than Alyssa or Chelsea ever dared to.

"You're really good at this," I comment, wincing as she plucks at my disorderly eyebrows. Her own perfectly sculpted brows are furrowed in concentration. She plucks a few more hairs and then steps back to examine them. A part of my brain wonders if she may have purposely shaved off one of my brows with her arching blade.

A smile peaks through her serious face, which means she is proud of her work.

"One day I'm going to move to L.A. and work with celebrities," she reveals confidently. It's the first time I've ever heard her talk about what she wants to do in the future. Lately, I haven't cared much about the Littles' future, because I won't be there to see it for myself.

"Francesca Townes: *makeup artist and stylist to the stars,*" she recites, dramatically creating stars in the sky with her outstretched arms.

"Townes?" I chuckle at the mention of her using our mother's maiden name.

"Yeah, Frankie Little sounds like some hick, not a celebrity stylist." She shrugs, pulling the plug on the flat irons and wrapping the cord around them. I watch her with an admiration that I've never displayed for my little sister. Not because I dislike her, it's just not the relationship we've ever had.

"Aren't you going to look at the finished product?" She sucks her teeth, bringing me back to reality. *I think.*

I get up and make my way to the mirror on the other side of the room. I almost don't recognize the figure staring back at me. She's stunning!

Frankie has parted my hair on the left side, and my hair, which usually falls to the middle of my back in its normal curly state, is now hanging down to my waist in uneven straight points. My face looks neat with light blue and silver eye shadow and dark liner making my dull eyes appear bright brown. I'll occasionally wear makeup during my highs, but I've never looked this good.

"Wow," I breathe out, running my hands through my hair. It feels light and silky. "Thank you so much, Frankie." I turn to her, wrapping her in a tight hug.

She stiffens in my embrace but eventually pats me on the back. "Don't mention it. You're my sister, which means you're a reflection on me, so I can't have you ruining my high school reputation before I even get there. After tonight, I'll be known as the girl who beautified *Jesse Alford's* date to the winter formal."

I want to tell her that no one will remember Jesse Alford's date to the winter formal because high school isn't that big of a deal, but why rain on her parade?

"Shit, Mischa! Jesse will be here in half an hour! You need to get dressed!" Frankie squeals, wiggling out of my embrace and running over to the closet.

She forces me to paint my toes in the matching sparkly silver polish that she has, and then she helps me into my dress and heels.

"Mischa, you look like a princess!" Maddie gasps when she sees me all dressed up. Frankie is behind me, dousing me in hair spray to stop my hair from clinging with static. I'm not sure how long this straightening will last, but I pray it gets me through the night.

"He's here!" Teddy screams from outside on the porch, and I feel my stomach drop with nerves. I'm not supposed to be nervous about tonight because I'm not supposed to care about tonight.

"Well, here goes nothing!" Frankie announces with a dramatic exhale. "Do us proud, Mischa!" She pushes me toward the door and then runs around me to grab her phone.

Grandpa is stationed in front of the TV watching his usual court shows, but he spins the chair around when he hears my heels clicking against the wood floor. He wolf-whistles and flashes me that rare toothy grin.

"My beautiful grandbaby." He nods, and I feel my nerves falter. "I sure do wish your daddy was here to see you right now. He'd be so proud of you."

With a weak smile, I walk over to him. "Thanks, Grandpa." I lean down and place a soft kiss on his cheek.

Frankie bolts out the front door mumbling something about a red-carpet photo shoot, and I take one more deep breath, smooth the invisible wrinkles on my dress, and follow her.

Chapter Twenty-Three

The limo arrives at Mischa's house promptly at seven, but the driver claims the car won't make it up the gravel path, so he parks against the curb where I have in the past and honks the horn.

"I'll be right back." I sigh at the man's rudeness and crawl past Trey and his date, Briana. She lives two hours away in Sacramento, but the two have managed to keep a steady long-distance relationship.

I'm making my way up the path when I hear Teddy calling into the house that I've arrived. A few seconds later, Frankie dashes out the front door with her phone in her hand.

"Just in time for the red carpet, Jesse!" she calls out before snapping a quick picture of me. "Looking good," she adds with a nod of approval, giving me a once-over.

I stop walking and stand a few feet away from the porch with my hands in my pockets. "Thanks, Frankie." I smile. "Is she almost ready?"

"Yep." Frankie smirks. "She's been prepping all day," she adds, dragging out the word *all*. I chuckle, and she screams for Mischa to *"Hurry the hell up!"*

Thoughts of Mischa, with her dry humor and nonchalant attitude, spending the entire day preparing for a date with me is doing wonders for my ego. I spent weeks trying to get her to agree to be my date to the formal, and she's actually excited!

I just pray that Preston and the others don't ruin this night for her. For us.

My date to the winter formal has been a mystery that has been driving my group of friends crazy ever since I told Alyssa we weren't going together. Preston made a joke about me taking Mischa after word got out that I'd bought ice cream for her and her siblings after Scoops tried to deny Mischa service.

I've never felt hatred for Grover the way I felt while watching Mr. Scoops refuse to serve Mischa and the Littles. Sure, I'd watched my peers torment Mischa for years, but we were all kids. To see an adult doing it was disgusting.

I lied to my parents and told them that Alyssa was my date for tonight because I could only imagine the shitstorm that would have hit dinner that night if I'd told them I was taking the most hated girl in town. My dad is all about order and image. Everything has to be perfect, and Mischa is everything disorderly and imperfect.

At least that's what I thought before she walked out of her house.

The first thing I notice is her hair. The normal curly mane is now flat and smoothly cascaded down her body, stopping around her midsection, just above where her dress hugs her waist and hips.

And her dress...

It's simple, but it looks incredible on her. It's a pale, silvery-blue color, and it somehow flows loosely as she walks down the stairs but is clinging to her body at the same time, accenting the roundness of her hips and butt well.

Her heels click against the old wooden stairs as she descends them instead of taking the ramp. She keeps fidgeting with her hands, clasping them and pulling on her fingers, and I'm amused at the thought of her being nervous. She hasn't even looked up at me.

Frankie is snapping pictures like the paparazzi, even though Mischa's not looking up from the ground. She swats at Maddie, who is mimicking an airplane, running in circles around her oldest sister with her arms stretched out. The youngest Little spots me and grins, and I see that she's recently lost a lower front tooth, making her even more adorable than usual.

"Oh, Jesse! You look really handsome!" Only her *"really"* sounds more like *"wheelie."*

"Thanks, Maddie." I smile at her and return the hug that she gives my leg.

"Doesn't Sissy look pretty?" she asks me, and I fix my eyes on her sister again. She's standing before me, still pulling at her fingers anxiously.

"Yeah, she does," I answer Maddie's question. Mischa finally raises her head to meet my eyes, and I notice that her eye makeup matches her silver shoes and makes her eyes sparkle brighter. She looks almost angelic, save for the tease of open fabric that displays the valley of her breasts.

"You clean up nice, Mischa Lawrence." I smirk at her, bouncing on the balls of my feet and trying to contain my goofy smile. I really like this girl. I don't think I've ever been this giddy over a date.

She chews on her glossy lower lip and looks down at her feet again. "You don't look too shabby yourself, Jesse Alford."

"Okay, you two, picture time," Frankie instructs, motioning for us to stand near each other. I snake my arm around her waist and pull her closer, smiling for Frankie's picture.

She snaps one photo and then looks down at the digital display and frowns. She looks between the phone screen and us and then huffs in frustration. "Mischa, can you please pose a little? You're going to the winter formal with the hottest guy in Grover. Act like it!"

I stifle a laugh as Mischa mumbles, "Shut up, Frankie."

Frankie walks over and pushes Mischa's body closer to mine and plants her left hand on my chest, making for a much more realistic couple's pose.

"Perfect!" she squeals after stepping back and snapping another picture.

Mischa sucks her teeth but doesn't move away from me. "We need to go."

We bid the Littles goodnight and make the trek down the makeshift driveway toward the waiting limo. We're about halfway down the path when we hear a woman calling Mischa's name, and Mischa turns around in shock.

A woman with stringy, unkempt brown hair and giant bags under her eyes is frantically running down the ramp and toward us, gripping the folds of her flimsy robe together.

"Mom?" Mischa questions, knitting her brows together.

The woman stops short of us and bends over to catch her breath. When she stands up straight again, she smiles weakly and exhales.

"You look so beautiful, Mischa. Both of you look great." She stops and nods toward me, and I return her smile with a little more pep. "Have fun tonight."

Mischa seems lost for words, and I can see the emotions etched across her face. She'd mention that her mother wasn't around much, and I imagine that put a strain on their relationship. But right now, Mischa looks like she's about to cry. She smiles, matching her mother's somber expression, and leans in to embrace the older woman, breaking away from my hold. They hug and Mischa murmurs a *"thank you,"* before backing away and continuing to walk with me.

The driver gets out of the car and opens the door for us, and I allow Mischa to climb in first.

Getting to the dance was the easy part. Surviving the night Preston and Alyssa-free will be the real challenge.

Chapter Twenty-Four

I f you had asked me a couple months ago what I'd be doing the night of Grover High School's precious winter formal, my answer would definitely not have involved Jesse Alford and some fancy limo ride into town.

I'm fidgeting with my hands because I'm not sure what to do after crawling past Trey and his date and taking a seat on the long bench seat perpendicular to them.

"Lookin' good, Lawrence," Trey compliments me after Jesse gets in the limo, and we take off toward town. There's humor in his voice, but I don't think he's mocking me. The pretty, dark-skinned girl next to him smiles at me and nods in agreement. I've never seen her before, so she must be from out of town.

Or maybe she's a hallucination?

She's wearing a shimmery gold dress, matching tall heels, and glittery gold eye makeup. She looks too perfect to be attending a high school social event in a town with only twenty Black people and one stoplight. When she extends her hand out to mine, I notice Trey is looking at her as well, a sign that she's not a figment of my overactive imagination.

"I'm Briana." She smiles at me, shaking my hand. "Meesha, right?"

"Mischa," I correct her softly. "And it's nice to meet you, Briana."

"Oops! Sorry. Trey told me that a million times, and I still messed it up." She lets out a cute laugh, and I feel myself relax a little. This girl seems friendly enough.

I want to ask her if she's Trey's girlfriend, but she starts firing off questions and compliments about my hair and makeup that seem pretty genuine.

"Wow, you drove all the way to San Francisco to find a dress and shoes?" Briana gushes.

"Drive is a bit of an overstatement," I mumble and turn my head toward the tinted window behind me. We've made it out of the foothills and onto Main Street. We pass by Brady's, where I notice Fergal standing outside smoking a cigarette. His eyes meet mine, despite the dark tint, and his jaw drops. He seems angry and starts running alongside the limousine, shouting profanities and telling me that I'm ruining everything.

"How did you get to San Francisco if you didn't drive there?" Like a snap, Jesse's words cause Fergal to disappear.

I turn to him, and he's giving me a skeptical look. I shrug. "I caught a ride."

"As in hitchhiked." Trey's words are more of a statement than a question. I'm sure he's heard his father complaining about me risking my life catching rides with highway motorists. I don't confirm his accusation with words. Instead, I just smirk at him.

"You *hitchhiked* three hours to San Francisco?" Jesse chokes out in disbelief. I simply shrug and he continues. "You really are crazy, Mischa."

I don't like being called crazy, but I give Jesse a pass for some reason. Maybe because he looks so damn good in his black-on-black tuxedo. Clean edge-up and his twists are shiny and pulled back in a ponytail, showing off a freshly tapered undercut. And oh my God, he smells like heaven. Like some kind of expensive cologne. I squirm in my seat as I feel the warm, tingling feeling in my lower belly.

"You should consider yourself lucky, Jesse." Briana chuckles. "She must really like you if she's willing to go through all of that to find a dress for this date."

I feel Jesse's arms come around my shoulder, and the mere brush of his skin against mine sends my hormones into a frenzy. I absently squeeze my thighs together and cross my legs at the ankle.

We arrive at the school's gymnasium, and the dance is already in full effect. There's music blaring from inside the building and teenagers filing inside in all types of formal attire. The limo stops in front of the walkway, and now my stomach is flip-flopping for a different reason.

Trey and Briana exit the limo first, then Jesse. He waits patiently outside the door, holding out his hand for me while I sit in my seat, trying to wring the nerves out through my hands.

"I won't let anyone mess with you, Mischa. I swear."

He's standing outside of the limo, slightly bent, holding one hand out to me. It reminds me of the scene from Disney's *Aladdin* when Aladdin holds his hand out to Princess Jasmine and asks, *"Do you trust me?"* Only the look on Jesse's face is serious. He's no Disney prince, but in this moment, he feels like one to me. And I want so badly to trust him.

I scoot over to the door and place my hand in Jesse's, and just like Aladdin and Jasmine, we take off on the carpet. We thank the driver before he gets back in the black stretch town car and drives away. I'm not even sure if he's coming back after the dance is over. It's fine. I'll need to walk off this sexual frustration, anyway.

We follow a few couples into the small corridor that leads into the gymnasium. There's a line to sign in, and for the first time since Jesse started harassing me about this stupid dance, I remember that I never purchased a ticket.

"You paid for my ticket?" I ask him absently.

"Of course." He laughs. "Haven't you ever been on a date?"

"What do you think?" I frown, though I'm not looking at him. I'm scanning the room for signs of sabotage. We've come this far, but that doesn't mean I'm not on my toes when it comes to Jesse's involvement with The Elites. I think back to Frankie's *Carrie* reference, and the words of Meka, the boutique clerk in San Francisco. It's possible this is all a prank.

"Don't worry, I'll let you pay for our prom tickets," he says with another chuckle. In front of us, I notice Trey laughing too, but I don't know if it's because Jesse's being sarcastic about making me pay for prom or because he actually plans to go to prom with *me*.

When we get to the decorated cafeteria table, that serves as the check-in table, Sheriff Freeman is standing there while his wife and Billy Wessel's mom take charge of the sign-in sheet and wristbands.

They briefly acknowledge their son and his date, before turning their attention toward me. Mrs. Wessel looks like she's seen a ghost. Her eyes bulge in disbelief.

"Well, look at you!" The sheriff beams at me proudly, and I'm reminded of my father for a split second. "You look beautiful, Mischa!"

"That dress is gorgeous, Mischa." Mrs. Freeman's sing-song voice compliments. "You two so look cute together!" She points at Jesse and me, and I realize that he's wrapped his arm around my waist. "I want a copy of your picture together, so make sure you go to the photo booth." She turns to Trey and Briana and relays the same instructions.

"You kids get in there and have fun." Sheriff Freeman nods his head toward the entrance to the gym. The way he looks at Jesse reminds me of how a father would look at his daughter's first date. A silent warning that tells me he's not very trusting of Jesse's intentions either.

We walk through the long, shimmery, metallic fringe curtain to enter the dimly lit gym. The student council committee has transformed it into an icy winter wonderland. There is blue and silver tinsel cascading from the ceiling, and decorations hanging on the walls. Two large ice sculptures sit in the center of the room. One in the shape of the letters *GHS*, and the other in the shape of a cougar, or *mountain cat*, I guess. The DJ is playing a song that I vaguely recognize from the nights that I allow Frankie to blare her music in the bathroom while she showers whenever Joe's not home. He hates loud noises that aren't his own. My peers are doing dances I don't know how to do, and have never seen before, and while I'm wearing a plain formal gown, some girls are clad in elaborate, multicolor dresses that you see at galas.

Everything about this event is perfect. Though, I don't understand the need for all the secret service style security. About a dozen men are standing around the room in black suits, black shades, and earpieces. They're standing with their feet firmly planted, and their arms crossed behind their backs as they survey the room. Is it really *that serious*? You'd think Sheriff Freeman and his chubby deputy could handle a little school dance.

"All eyes on you two," Trey announces and winks at me, before disappearing into the crowd of people with Briana.

It's weird that I hadn't noticed everyone watching us, considering I always feel like people are watching me. They're all whispering to each other and pointing at us. Or maybe just at me.

"Is that Mischa Lawrence?"

"Yeah! And she's here with Jesse!"

"Is this some type of joke?"

"Why would he take her?"

"That is a pretty dress she's wearing."

"Look at her hair!"

"That can't be Mischa."

"She looks ridiculous!"

"Jesse must have lost a bet."

"I thought he was going to the dance with Alyssa?"

I blow out a deep breath as Jesse guides us toward the refreshments table.

"Don't worry about them." He nudges me softly and smiles down at me. "Thirsty?"

I shake my head. I'm already over this night. I want to be home with my Littles, mentally plotting my death. I don't want to be a spectacle to a room full of people who despise me.

"Do you want to dance?" he asks me next, and again I shake my head. It's not that I don't *want* to dance with Jesse. I just don't want to dance with him in front of these people. We can dance somewhere more private, preferably naked.

"Well, then..." He chuckles lightly. "What do you want to do?"

I shake the naughty images from my head, even though those are the things I want to do. Instead of telling him that, I shrug. I look up at the rafters in the ceiling, hoping to find Alyssa and Chelsea up there with their bucket of pig innards to drop on top of me in front of everyone.

"What are you looking at?" Jesse asks, scrunching up his face and following my line of vision.

"Oh, nothing," I drag out and cut my eyes to him with a hint of a smile. It's strange how I go from fantasizing about having sex with him, to not trusting him in a matter of seconds. I guess it's not the strangest thing my brain has done, but it's still amusing.

"Maybe we should go check out the ballots," he suggests.

"The ballots for what?" I ask him.

He tilts his head like the answer should be obvious. "For the winter formal king and queen."

Now it's my turn to laugh at him. I let out a hearty laugh that causes me to double over slightly, and I think a couple of people stop and stare at us.

"What's so funny?" he asks me, looking around at the attention I've drawn.

"What's the point of a winter formal king and queen?" I ask him through giggles. I stand up straight and try to suppress my laughter by chewing on my lip while I wait for him to respond.

He shrugs, but I think he shares my humor. "It's just something to brag about for the next week, I guess."

I nod, still biting my lip to stifle my laughter. "Let's go see these ballots."

He takes my hand and leads me to the voting table, which is being run by Lauren Daniel, the daughter of Reverend Daniel. Lauren likes to pretend that she's holier-than-thou, but she is your stereotypical preacher's kid. When she spots Jesse approaching, she cheeses from ear to ear and perks her boobs out, which are larger than I'm certain her daddy was hoping for.

"Hey Jesse, you look nice," she squeaks out. If I were the possessive type, I would jump over the table and claw her eyes out because she's practically eye-fucking my date in front of me. But I'm not possessive of Jesse. I'm not even sure I have genuine feelings for Jesse. He's a fun way to pass the time until I expire.

"Thanks, Lauren. You look pretty too." Jesse doesn't even spare her a glance, so I'm not sure how he's able to compliment her.

Lauren hasn't bothered looking at me for longer than a second, so I'm confused when she asks, "Who's your date? Someone from out of town, like Trey's?"

Jesse frowns just as I scoff at her. He looks at me and then back at her. "You mean, Mischa?"

Lauren's eyes go wide behind her glasses, and I see the recognition register in them as she stares me up and down.

"Oh, my God!" she spits out harshly, but it's not in shock or surprise, but more like disgust.

I make a *'tsk, tsk, tsk'* sound with my tongue and wag a finger at her. "Shouldn't be using the Lord's name in vain like that, Lauren. You know better."

Beside me, Jesse lets out a snort-laugh and passes me a ballot. He seriously thinks I'm going to involve myself in stupid shit like voting for high school royalty. I glance down at the rectangular card to see whose names are printed on there. My eyes zero in on Jesse's first, and then I notice Preston's and off-handedly scribble a checkmark next to Jesse's name. Anything to spite Preston. Jesse lets out a *'hmph.'*

"I thought you said it was all pointless?"

"It is." I shrug, placing the ink pen back on the table. "I mean, what great attributes must one possess to be nominated for such a prestigious title?"

He can tell that I'm making a playful stab at him, and he takes it in stride. "You're right, it's a popularity contest. But it's nice to know you want to see me win." He winks and motions toward my ballot.

"Don't flatter yourself."

He slides his own paper back to Lauren, who is still gawking at us like an idiot. I notice he has voted for Trey and Zoey. I didn't even bother to look at the girls' side of the ballot, because I already knew the names that would be there. Alyssa, Chelsea, and a bunch of other bitchy, mean girls from Grover. I didn't expect to see Zoey, because Zoey is supposed to be in San Diego.

"You have to vote for a queen too," Lauren huffs and pushes my ballot back to me.

"I don't *have* to do shit," I snap back at her. She gasps and turns to my date with giant puppy dog eyes. He just shrugs at her, as if to say, *"What do you expect me to do about it?"*

I get an idea and snatch the ballot back, grabbing the ink pen off the table again. "So, whoever wins the queen gets to stand up on that stage and pose with the king, right?" I ask her, pointing at the structure erected for a coronation. Two thrones on a red carpet-covered stage.

Lauren nods proudly. "Yep."

I look down and find Lauren's name at the top of the list of queen candidates. Of course, she'd put herself at the top of the ballot above the Queen Bee herself, Alyssa Slade.

"So, if you win, you get to stand up there and snuggle up next to Jesse Alford, right?" I press with a mischievous smile. Under the icy blue strobe lights, I can see Lauren blush and glance at Jesse briefly. She's got a crush on him, and that's adorable, I guess. Too bad she's a bitch, just like all the other girls around here. She doesn't deserve Jesse.

Lauren nods, and I bend down to check off her name on the paper. "In that case, I'll vote for you!" I say in an overly chipper voice. I pass the ballot back for good and hook my arm with Jesse, dragging him away from Lauren and her prying eyes.

We find Neil Gunderson by the refreshment table with a Vietnamese girl in a green satin halter dress. She's actually really pretty, nothing like what I'd imagine Neil's girlfriend to look like.

"What's up, Neil?" Jesse nods at our former project partner as he grabs a plastic tumbler of punch and hands it to me.

Neil seems shocked that Jesse is speaking to him, despite our adventure this fall. He returns the head nod to Jesse and introduces his girlfriend, who smiles politely.

"So, this is the mysterious girlfriend we've heard so much about," I say, taking a sip of the punch I didn't ask for, but that Jesse handed me. Neil squints at me before realization sets in, and he gives me the same look Lauren did.

"Mischa?"

"The one and only." I raise my newly sculpted brows and outstretched arms.

"You look... different..." He looks me up and down. He does that dorky thing where he pushes his glasses up the bridge of his nose with his index finger. His girlfriend clears her throat, and he snaps out of his examination. "Mischa, this is Thùy. Thùy, this is Mischa." Thùy gives me a small wave, which I return.

"I knew something was going on between you two!" Neil accuses while pushing his glasses up his nose again.

I narrow my eyes at him. "There's nothing going on between us."

"There isn't?" Jesse chuckles, wrapping his arm around my waist again, and I punch his arm.

"No, there isn't. It's just a stupid dance." I turn to Thùy and smile cynically. "Jesse's the super popular football star, and I'm the outcast. There's nothing going on between us!"

Thùy scrunches her face at me and nods slowly. "Umm... okay."

Trey and Briana walk up, and Trey has an oddly amused expression on his face when he leans into Jesse and whispers something. Good thing I'm excellently skilled in reading lips. He says, *"Heads up,"* and nods behind us.

No need to squint and try to figure out my identity. These people have spent the past six years tormenting me. They could point me out in a crowd at the Super Bowl. I feel my stomach churn when Jesse turns us both around to face them. Nerves prickle my skin, and I feel bile rising in my throat. This is it. The moment that the pig's blood drenches me. I hold my breath, anticipating the onslaught.

And then I see Alyssa's face.

Chapter Twenty-Five

I'll start by saying she looks absolutely stunning in her sleeveless black cocktail dress, which sports a black beaded bustier top and poofy tulle material at the bottom. Her face is made up to perfection, but it's the mixture of shock and disgust on her face that makes me grin and lean into Jesse harder.

She's surprised to see me here. They all are. Which means this isn't a setup. Jesse was sincere when he told me he wanted to take me to this stupid dance.

"What in the *fuck*, Jesse?" Preston groans, running his hands down his face. I'm assuming he's not here with Alyssa since his tacky red tuxedo matches Meagan Burns' red mini-dress.

"You ditched *me* to go to the dance with *that*?" Alyssa points at me and stomps her stiletto-clad foot once. "Is this some kind of joke, Jesse?"

I wink at Alyssa again, and her nostrils flare as she huffs in response. Here she is, the prettiest, most popular girl in Grover, and she's here at her precious winter formal alone, while I'm wrapped in Jesse Alford's arms. Oh, how the mighty have fallen!

Preston is opening his mouth to insult me, I'm sure, but he's interrupted by a squeal of excitement.

"Holy shit, Misch!" Zoey runs up and wraps her arms around me tightly. "You look good, girl!"

"Hey, Zoey," I mumble into our embrace, which completely severed my connection with Jesse. It feels strange, but I'm already itching to get back into his arms.

"I thought you were joking when you told me you were coming here with Jesse." She pulls back and glances at Jesse, who has yet to speak to his group of friends.

"Why would I lie about something like that?" I shrug and step back toward Jesse. She keeps on alternating her look of suspicion between Jesse and me and then looks back at the pack of predators that are waiting to jump me. It's a good thing those Secret Service guys are here because I don't think I can handle all of them without my blade.

"I'm borrowing her," she tells Jesse and pulls me away from everyone. "I'll be right back," she mumbles to Nick, patting him on his chest. She pulls me through the crowd and into the restroom. A few girls are congregating at the sinks, drinking out of a shared flask. They smile at Zoey, but when they see me, their eyes pop out of their heads.

"Are you here with Nick?" I accuse my only friend.

She bites her lip and rolls her big, round eyes. She's wearing a purple dress similar to Alyssa's, only it halters into a choker around the neck and is backless. Her hair is pinned up in a neat updo, and her pretty face is made up naturally.

"Anthony and I broke up." She shrugs. "When you told me about Jesse asking you to the dance, I decided to come so we could party together." She smiles brightly, and I feel my heart soften a bit. "I had to be there for your first school dance!" she jokes, and we laugh together.

"Yeah, well, I'm probably the worst date ever. I spent the entire night thinking Jesse was trying to set me up."

"Set you up for what?" She frowns, cocking her hip to the side.

"So, what happened to Anthony?" I ask, ignoring her question and my previous statement. She sucks her teeth and tells me about the many times he canceled on coming to San Diego to visit her before she found out he had a college-age girlfriend in Arizona.

"So, you're back with Nick? I'm sure Mrs. Gillespie was ecstatic." We share a laugh, and I have to admit that it feels good to see my only friend again. I should dread seeing her again. Her absence in my life helped ease the fact that I'm about to end it. But being here in the girls' bathroom laughing at Velma Gillespie like old times feels comforting.

Zoey suggests we return to the dance and find our dates before some other girls steal them from us. She says it playfully, but suddenly thoughts of Jesse slow dancing with Alyssa invade my thoughts, and I'm out the door before Zoey can finish suggesting we snap an obligatory selfie.

I shove my way through the throngs of my dancing peers until I spot Alyssa and Jesse talking near the ice sculptures. She's pouting and rolling her eyes, and he's lovingly stroking her arm.

Okay, so maybe The Elites weren't in on a plan to embarrass me at this dance, but Jesse and Alyssa obviously still have a *thing* going on. Why else would he be standing there, trying to cheer her up no sooner than I step away?

Alyssa must feel me staring at her because she turns toward me and cuts her eyes my way. The hatred is evident and very mutual. Jesse keeps talking to her, completely oblivious to my presence only a few feet away. I decide to storm over and give them both a piece of my mind. To hell with Jesse Alford and this entire town! He's just another small-town asshole like the rest of them. I'm only able to take one step before I feel someone gripping my arm and pulling me softly toward them. I assume it's Zoey catching up to me—until I hear his voice.

"There you are."

I turn around, and now Jesse is standing behind me with a lopsided grin. I turn back to Alyssa, who looks like she's about to cry. The other Jesse is now Dillon Scoops. I whip my head back to the new Jesse, and his smile warps into one of confusion.

"You look like you've seen a ghost or something. What's wrong?" He looks up at Alyssa and frowns at her. "Did she say something to you?"

I look back at Alyssa, who is completely ignoring Dillon's advances in favor of staring at Jesse. "No, it's nothing."

"You sure?" He's still watching Alyssa cautiously, and when I turn back again, Preston is standing in place of Dillon, but I'm not sure if it's a hallucination or if Dillon finally gave up and walked away. Chelsea is with them now, clad in a bright pink illusion dress. My brain is going haywire, and I want nothing more than to be away from all of them.

"I want to dance now," I tell him, pulling him into the crowd just as the song selection slows down. Talk about good timing. I turn around and wrap my arms around his neck like I've seen in movies. When I was a kid, my father and I used to slow dance in the living room whenever I was having an episode. He'd pick me up and sway around the room with my legs dangling to the melody of 90s R&B.

Dancing with Jesse is nothing like dancing with my father. When he snakes his arms around my waist and pulls me flush with him, I feel the warmth return inside of me and fight the urge to squirm. Instead, I bury my face in his chest and allow him to lead us in the slow dance.

"You don't seem to be having much fun tonight." His chest rumbles as he speaks, breaking me out of my thoughts. His warmth envelops me like a comfy blanket, and his cologne is a heavenly scent.

"I am now," I whisper, and I wonder if he can even hear me over the noise of the music and the talking around us.

"What changed your mind?"

I bring my face up to rest in the crook of his neck now, to ensure he can hear me. "Seeing The Elites surprised to see me here."

"What's that supposed to mean?" he asks me. My eyes are closed, but I can almost imagine his look of confusion.

"It means this wasn't some elaborate scheme to trick me."

His shoulders drop a little and he sighs, taking his arms away from me and planting his hands on both of my hips. He pushes me back a little, trying to get me to look at his face. I drop my head instead.

"Why is it so hard for you to believe that I simply wanted to take you to the dance? No tricks," he asks, exasperated.

I shrug but keep my face turned down at our shoes. We're still swaying side to side as the slow song croons on. "Because you've spent the last six years tormenting me with your friends."

"I've *never* tormented you," he cuts me off, and his voice sounds slightly offended. He's right, I guess. He's done nothing malicious to me in all the years we've lived in the same town.

I roll my eyes. "Okay, you've spent the last six years ignoring my very existence while your friends tormented me," I correct myself sarcastically. "And now, suddenly, I'm supposed to just be fine with the fact that you've kissed me and want to take me to the biggest social event of the year. Of course, I'm going to think you're trying to set me up!"

"Or it could mean that I like you, Mischa." He sounds so frustrated in his response that I know he's being sincere.

I told myself several times I believed in the authenticity of Jesse's feelings for me, but I always held onto the possibility that he was trying to pull something over on me with his friends. So, I kept a wall up. That wall comes crashing down when I look up and my eyes meet Jesse's. His gaze is so intense, and while I love that look in his eyes, the disappointed frown is something I never want to see again.

So, I crane my neck upward and close the gap between us with a soft kiss. It catches him off guard, and I pull back before he can respond.

"We should head over to the photo booth. We promised Mrs. Freeman we'd take a picture together." I pull his arm and drag him toward the booth. It's one of those rented photo booths you see in the malls. I guess they're saving the photographer for prom.

We slip inside the booth after Trey and Briana come out in their matching gold ensembles, and Jesse pulls the privacy curtain closed.

It reminds me of a bright padded room at Beacon Pointe. There are Xs made of tape on the floor in front of a white shimmery wall across from the automatic camera. There are props hanging near the camera, but we don't give them a thought.

Jesse hits the timer button on the camera and then steps back to pose with me. I wrap my arms around his neck, and he rests his hands on my hips, mirroring our slow-dancing position.

"Traditional is boring," I murmur after the flash pops and the camera snaps the picture. The camera counts down for the next picture, and before he questions it, I tighten my grip on his neck and jump up in his arms, forcing him to catch me bridal style. We both laugh, but just before the camera snaps the picture, I press my mouth against his.

He tries to deepen the kiss, but I pull away again, bringing my feet back to the ground and stepping away from him. We stand there awkwardly for a moment. The camera flashes again, capturing our graceless moment, and Jesse's the first one to break our gaze. The little machine beneath the camera sputters, and Jesse walks over as it dispenses the pictures.

He shuffles through the stack of 5x7 photos with a smile on his face and then turns to me and hands them over.

The first one is that perfect, cheesy high school dance picture. Fake smiles and all. Mrs. Freeman can definitely keep it.

The second one is more genuine. Our lips are pressed together in our third kiss since this crazy courtship started, but we're both still smiling from the laughter. We look like a happy, carefree couple, and I like the thought of that.

But the third photo is my favorite. I'm staring up at Jesse with an impish smirk, and he's staring down at me longingly, obviously disappointed that he couldn't kiss me more. The candid moment isn't awkward at all. It's pure.

It tells a story about us. One that's about to unveil tonight.

We just need to get the hell out of this dance.

Chapter Twenty-Six

JESSE

After local events like the winter formal, most of us go hang out at The Strip, and then there's usually an afterparty at the mill. I know Mischa's not going to agree to either of those options, but I'm hoping she isn't ready to end the night either.

"I grabbed double the amount of liquor I usually get, man," Ethan Telly brags to me after Mischa and I exit the photo booth with our pictures.

I was surprised when she jumped in my arms and kissed me, and disappointed when she pulled away before I could really kiss her back. She seemed to like the accidental third picture, where we're staring at each other. After I handed them to her, she plucked that one out of the stack and said, "This one's mine."

"We'll probably skip the afterparty," I tell Ethan with a shrug. He frowns and gives me and Mischa a weird look. Well, I guess it's not too weird. It's how everyone's always looked at *her*.

Just before ten o'clock, we decide to split. We've endured all the dirty looks required to get the hint. No one approves of seeing Mischa and me together. Even our teachers are giving us shitty looks. I swear I heard Mrs. Franklin tell Mrs. Crabtree that I was *"making a huge mistake showing up with that girl."*

It's unnerving knowing that Mischa has been dealing with this type of treatment her entire life in Grover.

We find Trey and his date near the refreshment table talking to Nick and Zoey.

"See you at the mill?" Zoey asks Mischa, who seems to have checked out completely.

I answer for her when Mischa fails to speak up. "Nah, we're not going up there."

Zoey pouts and grabs Mischa by her shoulders. "Aww man, I wanted us to party together a little more."

Mischa gives her a weak smile and shrugs her shoulders.

"C'mon guys, come party with us," Zoey presses. "Is it Preston and the others? Don't worry about them, Misch. Nick won't let them pick on you."

Mischa raises an eyebrow and shoots a highly skeptical look at Nick. I'm sure my expression matches hers, and Trey is looking at Zoey the same way.

Why would Nick protect Mischa from Preston?

Nick just snorts and looks on into the crowd like Zoey's words have no effect on him.

"*I* wouldn't let them mess with her," I tell her confidently. "But I'm sure she doesn't want to go up there."

Zoey turns her frown on me briefly before turning back to Mischa. "Well, have fun, whatever you decide to do. I'm leaving in the morning, so I probably won't see you."

Mischa gives another weak smile, and this time pulls Zoey in for a hug. She whispers something in Zoey's ear, and Zoey smiles and tightens the hug. They pose together for a selfie that Zoey insists on taking, and then we walk away.

When we leave the gym, Mischa stops at the registration table and hands the photo from the photo booth to Trey's mom. Her eyes widen and she smiles at us.

"You two are the cutest couple ever!" she gushes. "Look at this picture, Moe!" She shoves the photo in her husband's face, and he, too, gives it a genuine smile. When he looks at Mischa, he beams at her like a proud father.

"You two be careful up there at that mill," Sheriff Freeman warns us. There's an underlying message in the look he gives me that says: *Don't let Preston and the others mess with her.*

"We're not going to the mill," I assure him. "Just going to grab a bite and then take Mischa home." I partially lie. Everything in me is hoping that Mischa isn't ready for this night to end, either. I'll even settle for another night of staying up late, silently listening to nature. Anything to squeeze in a little more alone time with her.

We bid the Freemans farewell and head out into the parking lot where I'd parked my car earlier, so we'd have a ride home after the dance. We don't even bother to stick around for the king and queen announcements. The last thing I'd need is to possibly win and have to stand beside Alyssa. We don't speak as we cross the parking lot. Just the click of her heels on the pavement and music seeping out of the gym in the distance. I open the door for her and then round the front of the car once she's settled. Starting the engine, I leave the car in park and turn to Mischa.

"Do you want me to drop you off at home now?" I ask her. *Please say no. Please say no.*

She bites her lips and shakes her head. "No, but I understand if you want to go party with your friends."

"I'd rather spend the rest of the night with you," I tell her. "I didn't even get a chance to really kiss you," I add, and she laughs. "Are you hungry?"

She shakes her head no.

"Well, where to?" I ask her, pulling my seat belt across my chest.

"You know where." She folds her arms across her chest and kicks her bare feet up on the dash. I nod and switch my gearshift to drive, pulling out of the parking lot and onto the road that leads to Main Street.

We end up at my secret spot, which is quickly morphing into our shared secret spot with each passing rendezvous we have there. I kill the engine, and we both get out of the car. I grab a blanket from the trunk and spread it out across the damp grass. I don't know what my mom's deal is with keeping blankets in my car, but at the moment I'm thankful for her overabundance of old comforters in my trunk and backseat.

I sit on the ground and reach out for Mischa's hand to help her sit with me. She molds herself between my legs with her back against my chest. Something about being this close to her seems natural. I bring my arms around her middle and pull her closer.

"What's your middle name?" she asks, nestling into my embrace. Her demeanor has changed now. She's more relaxed than she was at the dance. I take that as a sign that she's comfortable with me, even though she spent the entire night expecting an ambush from my friends that I may have orchestrated.

"Mikel. Michael and Kelisa combined." I think about the full story and laugh. "It was a compromise."

"How so?" She tilts her head back and regards me curiously. I'm tempted to kiss the corner of her mouth, but I don't want to make the moment awkward if she's not ready for me to kiss her again.

"My dad wanted me to be Michael James Alford the Third, but my mom wanted to name me Jesse—her maiden name. She said the world would be full of Michaels. It needed more Jesses. My dad conceded but wanted some part of his name included, so he suggested James as my middle name."

Mischa cracks up laughing. "Your dad was going to name you—a Black kid in Northern California—*Jesse James*?" she mocks in between laughs.

I laugh with her, shaking my head because this story will forever be cringe. "Yeah, on some seriously corny, country, Oklahoma shit. My mom quickly shot that down. My Gramps—her dad—suggested Mikel."

"So, the college you're going to, is that in Oklahoma?" she asks me next. There's a slight chill in the air as the wind picks up. I try to wrap her in my tux jacket tighter, but she doesn't seem to mind the cold.

"Yeah, OU," I tell her blandly. "The plan is to play football for four years, and then get into law school there, and then come back here to work with my dad."

"You don't seem too excited about that." I can hear the sarcasm in her voice.

I shrug. "It all sounds nice. But I'm not sure it's what I want to do, or if it's just what my dad wants me to do."

"The best part about living is that we all have options. We have the ultimate say-so in how our life goes."

"So, what's your grand plan in life?" I ask her.

She chuckles softly, as if I've asked her something funny before answering. "To live out a mundane life in my stupid double-wide, raising my mom's kids."

I frown and look down at the side of her face. She's staring out at the view of the treetops and mountains just off the cliff. The sunrise here will be amazing, and I hope we're around to see it in a couple of hours.

"So, you're not going to college?"

"Nope," she replies nonchalantly.

"That doesn't bother you?"

She shakes her head. "It is what it is. So, what's your favorite color?"

She's changing the subject. "Black."

"This is fun. Getting to know each other, I mean."

We continue to trade mindless information about each other. Stuff that I never knew about Alyssa or any of the other girls I've dated in Grover. She's afraid of mountain lions, which isn't completely irrational, but is random since we rarely ever see mountain lions in Grover. Her favorite food is pizza, her birthday is July 7th, so I'm older than her by almost five months since my birthday is February 27th.

I'm just about to ask her more about her interests when she suddenly stands up. It's like someone has called her name, or a magnet is pulling her toward the edge of the cliff. She slowly walks over to the edge and stands there for a moment.

And then she starts taking off her dress.

Chapter Twenty-Seven

My condition has given me an abundance of different emotions and sensations over the years, and since my mother has taken out a patent on depression, I'm typically left living with mania. It's convenient since I'm able to function pretty well when it comes to caring for my siblings. There are the obvious symptoms like mood swings. Bursts of anger, like slashing Preston's tires—which I still consider a normal reaction to nearly being run over by him. Then there are the "positive" symptoms. The hallucinations and the delusional thoughts, like the life I'd planned with Dennis Randall on Channel 12, or thinking Jesse was out to get me tonight. There are the "negative" symptoms, such as my constant lack of appetite. I'm a walking PowerPoint of psychiatric symptoms.

Lately, a new one has emerged, and Jesse Alford is solely to blame.

"So, what's your grand plan in life?"

"To die before my eighteenth birthday," I want to tell him. Instead, I tell a vague truth, because if I didn't already plan on dying in a few months, that's what I'd be doing. Parenting the Littles until my mom got her shit together. Which will never happen.

I try to follow along with his game of questions, but he's touching me. Innocently drumming his finger against my stomach like I'm his steering wheel. Then, he'll occasionally splay his palm flat against my stomach or tighten his embrace. All innocently over my dress. Still, mania takes over, and before I know it, I'm standing on the edge of the cliff in the place I'm pretty sure I'll take my last breath soon.

Completely naked.

"Mi—Mischa?" I hear him stammer, but I keep looking straight ahead.

My hair is blowing around my body, but I can't seem to feel the wind. There are giant bats in that tree again, but they're not moving. Their red eyes are watching us. Waiting to see what happens next.

When I turn around to face Jesse, he's still sitting frozen on the pallet he made on the ground. My hair is long enough to cover my breasts, but I'm completely exposed everywhere else. Still, Jesse's looking at my face. He seems nervous. I wonder if he's always this nervous, or if he fears the local rape accuser. To be fair, I'm sure Alyssa gave him some sort of sign before she took her clothes off for him. Maybe he's just stunned.

I take a few steps toward him, and he scrambles to his feet.

"He seems excited." Fergal laughs, and I cut my eyes at him. He's standing a few feet away from Jesse, pointing at the tent forming in his pants.

I stop walking when I feel Jesse's hands on my bare shoulders. I look away from Fergal and find that I'm standing right in front of Jesse. He's looking me in the eye still, but now his gaze occasionally drops to my chest, which is inches away from being pressed against his suit jacket.

"What are you doing, Mischa?" he asks me in a shaky voice, and I swear I can hear his heart beating, whereas mine feels like it's not pumping at all. I feel hollow, like a shell of myself. The only thing I can feel is his hands on my shoulders and the pressure in my lower body telling me I want Jesse.

"What do you think, Jesse Alford?" I whisper, and then I wrap my arms around his neck and crash our lips together.

He's got his hands on my sides, and he's kissing me back, but I feel numb. It's pissing me off because I want to *feel* him.

I run my fingertips up his shoulder blades, to his chest, and under the open blazer, pushing it back and off his shoulders. It falls behind him on top of the hood of his car. I go to loosen his buttons, but he grabs my hands and stops me.

"Mischa, are you sure about this? I mean—"

I huff, cutting him off and grabbing at his shirt again. "Positive."

There's a white tank top underneath the black dress shirt, so I go to work on the clasp and zipper on his pants. Again, Jesse stops me.

He chuckles a little like he's in disbelief about what's happening. I'm sure Jesse's had sex dozens of times, so I'm not sure why he's overreacting so much with me. He motions around us. "Out here?"

I look back at the bat-infested tree and consider his apprehension. He's probably right. I'd hate to get attacked by those Peeping Tom rats with wings, or a rattlesnake, or worse.

A mountain lion.

I bite my cheek and look at Jesse briefly before shifting my gaze behind him. He follows my line of sight and chuckles again.

His car.

"You're not one for romance, are you?" he asks, running his fingers over his hair. He's standing there in a white muscle shirt, and his slacks hanging loosely on his hips, contemplating doing something that he *so obviously* wants to do.

I shrug. "Not at the moment."

I walk around him and open the car door, snaking my body behind the driver's seat and onto the back bench seat. Outside, Jesse hesitates, looking around and mumbling to himself. I know that he's nervous about my sketchy past with guys. More specifically, my past with Blake Wilcox. Eventually, he follows suit, though. Picking up the blanket from the ground and dusting it off, Jesse walks around to the driver's side of his car, pulls his bucket seat forward, and climbs in to join me in the back.

My mind swirls when he kisses me, and I don't even notice that he's undressing, until he's pushing my body backward so that I'm lying on my back with him hovering over me, his eyes searching my own for a sign of hesitation. He won't find it. I want this. I want *him.*

My arms have been glued to my sides during our stare-down, but I bring them up and run my fingers through his twists, releasing the band that's holding them back so that they fall naturally around his face. I smile at him, and his eyes seem to light up as well. He brings his lip down to mine and kisses me passionately. He pauses and reaches across the front seat, into his glove compartment. I hear him fumbling with a foil packet, and I'm pretty sure my heart is pounding. I still can't feel it.

All the numbness goes away when Jesse pushes against me and our bodies connect. I clench my teeth because he definitely didn't hold back. I don't blame him, though. He's going into this with a completely different understanding of me, and it isn't his fault. I feel him freeze briefly, and I know that he's just realized it. I'm relieved when he moves again. I hold back the tears and relish in the bliss of finally feeling something, *anything*. Even if it is pain. He's kissing my neck, and his hands are roaming across my body, and I can feel every movement. Even Fergal—who was just beating on the windows and wolf-whistling as Jesse kissed me—has disappeared.

I arch my neck and look out the window at the bat tree. No more glowing red eyes are watching us.

And I know this moment. Right here. Right now, with Jesse.

Is real.

Chapter Twenty-Eight

The small sliver of sunrise stirs me awake. Jesse and I didn't speak after we were finished with our backseat extra-curricular. Instead, we laid in silence under the blanket, my head resting on his chest, listening to him drift off to sleep until finally, I followed. I didn't sleep long, maybe five hours, but it's more than I normally sleep. Sleeping on Jesse's chest, cramped in the backseat of his car, was refreshing.

He's not in the car when I wake up, but he's not far away. He's redressed in his slacks and tank top, sitting on the hood of the car wrapped in a blanket. He's left his black dress shirt hanging on the back of the driver's seat. I assume it's for me to wear. I stretch and then slip the shirt on before getting out of the car.

My once silky, straight hair is now frizzing at the roots, probably from the body heat of being in the backseat, and it's tossed across my head chaotically. My dress, which I'd left in a pool at the edge of the cliff, is now draped across the front seats neatly.

He doesn't look my way, so I lean against the hood beside him. My mind is whirling with what I'm supposed to say in this situation, and his ignoring me isn't helping.

"You always such an early riser?" I ask him with a stupid giggle. He doesn't respond, and when I read his features, I can tell he's upset. Not necessarily angry, but something is bothering him.

"Did you sleep well?" I try, growing somewhat irritated. I'm standing beside him wearing his oversized shirt and nothing else, yet he's still managing to ignore me.

I suck my teeth. "What's wrong with you, Jesse? Did I do something wrong?" Panic sets in and I start to imagine that he's just a hallucination. Maybe I had sex with a complete stranger last night? I'm a *20/20* special in the making.

But then he finally speaks.

"You're a virgin," he tells me, still staring out at the first light of the soon-to-be rising sun.

I laugh and fold my arms across my chest. "Well, I *was*."

Jesse doesn't share in my humor. "You know what I mean."

"Okay, so I was a virgin." I toss my arms out, part in frustration and partly to get him to look at me. "What's the big deal?"

"You didn't tell me. That's the big deal," he snaps back without raising his voice at all.

"Well, I'm sorry I'm not the slut your buddy Preston made me out to be. I thought guys were into virgins, anyway. What's your problem?" I huff. He's being ridiculous!

"You lied about Blake," he says in almost a whisper, causing me to stop my inward ranting and stare at him. He finally turns to me, and I can read the confusion in his eyes so well now.

So that's what's bothering him.

Now it's my turn to ignore his stare and gaze at the approaching sunrise. This isn't a conversation I want to have *at all*, let alone after such an amazing night like last night. I can feel Jesse's eyes on me. It's making my skin crawl because I know he's not looking at me the way he did last night. He's looking at me with a painful look that I'm sure few people have seen before.

I blow out a hard breath and groan. "Honestly, Jesse. I don't even remember that night."

He grunts, and I can tell he doesn't believe me. It is a pretty cliché thing to say. But it's the truth.

"The only visuals I have of that party—*of that night*—are because of the stories everyone tells. I don't even remember *talking* to Blake, let alone having sex or being raped by him." I face him now, hoping he'll take it for what it is and drop the subject.

"Then why lie and tell the sheriff that he did?" Jesse snaps, but he's not angry. It's more of a plea for understanding.

"I don't remember any of it, Jesse. Not even the conversations with the police."

"How is that possible, Mischa?" He rolls his eyes and sucks his teeth. "You couldn't have been *that* drunk."

I want to explain it to him. I want to tell him the truth about me. That I drank for the first time that night. That I'd just taken my pills, and they don't mix well with alcohol. But I doubt he'd take well to me being a manic-depressant with a touch of psychosis, and I can't risk him telling our peers about it.

I'll be dead soon, so telling him is pointless, anyway.

"I'm not going to run to the station and tell Sheriff Freeman that you raped me if that's what you're worried about." I shrug and turn my gaze back to the view of the trees, where the sunrise is about to start. Jesse Alford is a distraction, so maybe it's a good thing that things between us are about to go sour. I don't need him fogging up my mind while I try to focus on the plans in my head.

I hear grunting and see a pair of arms planting themselves on the edge of the cliff. Fergal pulls his body up and over. He stands and dusts off his tattered pants, before looking up at me and grinning. He gives me a thumbs up.

"Told you," he taunts me.

"Yeah, you're right. This whole thing was bullshit anyway," I tell him with a sigh.

"I never said it was bullshit," Jesse groans because he thinks I was talking to him. "And I don't think you're going to accuse me of... *that*."

"I'm just confused by all of it," he continues. "But I think I know you well enough that I trust you. I know you wouldn't falsely accuse someone of something they didn't do."

I shake my head and laugh. He thinks he knows me, but he has no idea. He reaches out and tugs gently on my upper arm, willing me to slide up the hood of his car with him. He wraps me inside the thick comforter, and I instinctively snuggle against him. Is this how normal teenage relationships go? Arguing about your first time together one minute, and then snuggling and preparing to watch the sunrise together the next? Is that even what I should call this... *thing* that Jesse and I have going on? A relationship?

The sun peeks up over the horizon just as Jesse nuzzles his chin in the crook of my neck, and Fergal dramatically teeters over the edge of the cliff before plummeting to his death.

I briefly envision my own body standing at the edge of the cliff, the wind whipping through my hair as I hold my arms out and fall forward gracefully down the mountainside.

But then Jesse Alford kisses my neck, and I'm brought back to a place I rarely visit.

Reality.

Chapter Twenty-Nine

JESSE

My dad has always been a no-nonsense, straight-to-the-point kind of guy. He's a lawyer, though, so I guess that's expected.

Gramps used to say, *"You don't become a reputable district attorney by being the nice guy."*

Of course, he was being sarcastic. My maternal grandfather and father were complete opposites. My mom and her father were always fun-loving and cheerful. While my dad was commuting to the city for work, Gramps and I were outside building the GTO, until he died two years ago.

Where my mom and Gramps were always encouraging me to be myself and excel in whatever made me happy, my father had a vision. He saw me—*and our family*—as someone above everyone else. An *elitist* is what Mischa would call him. Who needs to spend time getting dirty building cars, when you could simply make six figures and buy a brand-new car?

He decided that I'd be a lawyer, just like him. I'd graduate from his alma mater and work for the state, following in his footsteps in every way. He's overbearing like that, and there's usually no going against his expectations. He expects everything we do to be practical and perfect.

So, when I walk into the house in the late afternoon on Sunday after dropping Mischa off at her house, I know he's not turning his nose up at me because I missed church. I'm not ready to argue just yet, so I nod at him and go straight to my bedroom, where I pass out until dinner.

At the table, my father is still shooting daggers of disapproval at me, and I try my hardest to dodge them. My mom's nervous fidgeting isn't helping at all. She keeps looking between us, and I know she's silently praying that we keep the peace.

Her prayers go unanswered.

"So how was the dance, Jesse?" My dad asks sardonically.

Here we go...

I groan and roll my eyes, pushing my food around the plate, suddenly no longer hungry even though I haven't eaten since before the dance yesterday. I tried to get Mischa to go to breakfast with me. Most of the town would be in church, and we could have snuck over to one of the restaurants to eat in peace. She declined, though, stating that she needed to get home to the Littles and feed them.

"It was cool, Dad. Just the usual Grover antics," I reply.

My mom chuckles and tries to steer the conversation in the most positive route possible, and I feel sorry for her because I know it's all in vain when dealing with Dad.

"One year, they'll realize that it's okay to do things a little differently around here. Maybe gymnasium school dances are getting a little outdated," she jokes, and I give her a weary smile.

"Speaking of *'doing things a little different,'* Jesse, you were the talk of the town this morning." My dad snorts and then takes a big gulp of his red wine. "You and your choice of date."

I suck my teeth and drop my fork on the ceramic plate with a loud *clank.* It's hard enough having to stick up for Mischa against idiots like Fred Scoops. I don't want to listen to my father berate a harmless teenage girl, especially one that I'm falling for.

"Don't be upset with me, Jesse. You're the one that thought it would make sense to lie to us about going to the formal with Alyssa when you were really taking the local crackpot," he says the last part with a sarcastic laugh.

I slam my fists on the wooden dining table out of reflex.

"Jesse!" Mom pleads with me to calm down. She turns to my father with the same pleading eyes and asks, "Can we *not* talk about this at the dinner table? Jesse missed today's sermon. Maybe we can talk about that."

But my dad doesn't miss a beat. "Jesse also missed the part where his friends informed us he left the dance with that girl, and they didn't see him for the rest of the night. Which leaves me to believe that you were out racking up a new rape case for me?"

All the air in the room seems to dissipate when he says those words. I hear my mother gasp, and her chair screeches against the wood floors as she stands up abruptly. This time it's her flat palms that smack against the table. This poor table is suffering so much unnecessary abuse tonight.

Kind of reminds me of a certain firecracker outcast.

"Michael James Alford, have you lost your mind?" she scolds my father through gritted teeth.

"Our son is out gallivanting with the Lawrence girl, and you're asking *me* if *I've* lost *my* mind?" My father scowls at her.

"And you think rape shaming is healthy teaching for our son?" she retaliates. The anger is clear in her tone, but I can tell that my dad doesn't plan on backing down.

"It didn't mean anything, Dad," I tell him before the war starts between my parents. My mom has never expressed a liking or disliking for Mischa. She's never really mentioned her at all. But she seems really pissed off right now, and I'm not so sure she appreciates my dad's harshness toward Mischa's sexual assault.

My dad eyes me suspiciously, and I can tell from the look on my mom's face that she doesn't believe me either, but she also seems relieved by my words. I wonder if she's thankful that I'm lying for the sake of defending the relationship, or if she hopes that I'll snap out of my infatuation with the most hated girl in town.

"I just wanted to break things off with Alyssa, and she wasn't taking the hint, so I took Mischa to the dance to piss her off," I lie effortlessly.

"Stay away from that girl, Jesse. I mean it," my dad warns me in a demanding tone. "You're a few months shy of getting out of here, and you've got a full-ride scholarship. Don't mess it up for some crazy girl with no future."

His words upset me, but I hold my tongue for the sake of Mom's hard work on dinner tonight. I'm not sure what pisses me off more, his comments about Mischa or the way he thinks he can just run my life.

It's the last week of school before Christmas break, and I'm excited to have three weeks to spend with Mischa, away from my friends. I didn't hear from her again after I dropped her off at home yesterday. This morning, she walked into class and sat in front of me without so much as a glance.

Of course, Preston couldn't wait to confront me with an onslaught of questions and *"What the hell, Jesse? You hooking up with Hoe-Bag Lawrence now?"*

"Do me a favor, Preston." I stop him short of more insults in front of my locker after first period. "Try to refrain from calling Mischa out of her name whenever I'm around."

My words stop him in his tracks, and when I turn away from my locker, I see Chelsea and Preston staring at me in wide-eyed disbelief. I smirk at them and walk past with a wink.

Alyssa stops me outside of our third period, and I can't fight the annoyed look on my face.

"Jesse, I think we need to talk," she tells me dramatically, and I groan and throw my head back. I'm not even halfway through Monday, and I'm already over all the looks and whispering gossip about my date on Saturday. I can't believe Mischa deals with this on a daily.

"There's nothing to talk about Alyssa, we're—"

"I talked to your dad this morning," she cuts me off, and I scrunch up my face and stare at her oddly.

"You what?" I ask her. The late bell is about to ring, but I need to know where this is going.

She shrugs and says, "He came into the coffee shop this morning."

Of course he did. My dad has a daily routine of grabbing a black coffee at the Slade family's coffee shop before heading to the city for work. But what could he have possibly had to say to Alyssa?

"He told me you explained the situation with... Mischa." She has to pause and almost force herself to say Mischa's name, as if it physically pains her to say it.

"What situation?" I can feel myself growing angry. I can already tell my dad has crossed another line.

"The winter formal. You took *her* just to make me mad." She's smiling when she tells me this, like she finds it amusing or something. Obviously, my dad didn't believe my little declaration at dinner last night. He's trying to use Alyssa to get me away from Mischa, but I'm not falling for his tricks. He may have a chokehold on my future, but he can't control my love life.

"Alyssa, I like Mischa." I sigh and look her square in the eyes. "I asked her to the formal because I really do like her. That's not my dad's business, and it's not yours." I tell her this firmly so that there is no confusion, and I notice the falter in her confident smile. It's as if she was really buying my father's words. Hearing them repeated to me, I'm not surprised that my dad didn't believe the words when I said them to him.

The late bell rings, and I turn and slip into third period before Mrs. Slattery notices me. I can't focus on the English lesson today because my mind keeps drifting to the girl sitting across the room from me.

She's wearing a green plaid, long-sleeved flannel shirt, open over a black tank top, and her fishnet stockings under a pair of black cut-off shorts. Her hair is no longer straight, it's curly again and swept up in a massive ball on top of her head.

She's staring out the window, and every now and then she smiles and laughs silently. I wonder if she's thinking about me.

Chapter Thirty

I manage to stay under The Elites' radar for the first three class periods. After third period, I guess they've had their fill of letting me go about my day peacefully.

I'm heading down the hallway in the opposite direction of the cafeteria because I *never* eat lunch in the cafeteria. Why would I? Even the nerds and the goths don't like me.

Fun fact, before she made out with Nick Gillespie freshman year and became part of The Elites, Zoey Hall was an emo-goth chick. The night of the party, she had just made the transition from Black alternative chic to preppy popular girl—her own worst nightmare.

She's not the only member of The Elites who wasn't always so high and mighty. Preston's only living in his brother's shadow. He only got popular after he started tormenting me. Before my supposed rape accusation, I'm pretty sure Preston had a thing for me too. He would do those annoying little things that boys do when they like a girl. Pull my hair and bump into me on purpose, but never anything harmful. Nowadays, he's a tad bit more hostile with his bullying. And Alyssa, while always having her incredibly bitchy attitude, couldn't live down the fact that she had a boy's chest until tenth grade. She called me a cow in the eighth grade after Preston pointed out that I had boobs, and she didn't.

Anyway, I'm heading toward the girls' bathroom upstairs, where I spend every lunch period because I don't eat during lunch because I'm rarely hungry, and I get to hide out and hear the latest gossip. I've got tunnel vision, not really paying attention to my surroundings when suddenly I'm face-planting into the linoleum.

Someone tripped me.

Everyone's laughing hysterically, everyone except Alyssa, who is leaning against a locker with her arms crossed and a condescending smirk on her face.

I'm attempting to sit up on my knees when I feel a foot on my back and my body being forced back down by a stomping motion. This time it's Preston.

"Stay down, bitch!" he snickers. He is literally physically assaulting me, and people are *laughing*. I'm glad I'll be stone-cold when this generation meets its fate. We're a doomed society. I try to sit up, but he's got his foot firmly on my back. It doesn't hurt, but it's enough to make me struggle a little.

"Preston, if you don't get your foot off of me, slashing your tires will look like a favor," I growl. There are no metal detectors in the school. I have my blade in my boot.

"Shut up and stay down, you stupid—" The last part of his insult turns into a *"woah!"* before he collides into the lockers. I'm kind of bummed because I was interested in hearing what he could come up with next, but I'm also relieved to have the pressure of his sneaker off my spine.

Once again, it's Jesse to the rescue as he bends down to help me stand. He's giving his friend the biggest *"go-to-hell"* look, and Preston has the nerve to have this look of shock on his face. Like he doesn't understand why Jesse would push him into a locker. For a moment, I don't understand it. Then I remember our night together in the back of the GTO, and it hits me again that Jesse Alford *likes me*.

Everyone has stopped laughing, and now they are whispering. They're talking about Jesse now, and how they can't believe he just did that to his *best friend*. I don't even bother dusting off the dirt on my shirt. I just take off down the hall as if there was no interruption at all. I do glance at Alyssa, who is now staring somberly at Jesse.

I'll have to cook up something extra spicy for my revenge against her.

Jesse catches up to me just before I make it into the girls' bathroom. He grabs my arm and spins me around to face him. His eyebrows are knitted together, and he's wearing a deep frown on his face.

"You've been ignoring me all day."

"Yes, I have." I shrug, folding my arms across my chest and meeting his gaze challengingly. I hate upsetting Jesse, but I will not fall victim to his domineering aura.

"You're really sending me mixed signals here, Mischa," he groans, and I inwardly celebrate breaking his bad-boy façade.

"Jesse, you got what you wanted. What's the big deal?" I briefly extend my arms out in mock exasperation before dropping them to my sides.

"That's bullshit, and you know it, Mischa. I like you, and you know that so, what's *your* deal?" he shoots back, and I can tell he's getting frustrated with my runaround.

I roll my eyes and point down to the floor. "*That* is my *deal*, Jesse." He looks down at the floor, confused, and not comprehending that I'm referring to the situation downstairs with Preston just three minutes ago. "Those are your friends, and they hate me. If you keep trying to make this happen," I pause and motion between us, "then they're going to hate you too."

He smirks and gives a snort-laugh. "I don't care about that. Preston's a dick. He always has been. My friends that matter won't judge me for who I choose to date."

I smirk at him. "Prove it."

"Prove it?"

I nod. "If you really like me, then prove it." And with that, I turn around and march into the restroom.

To my surprise, Jesse actually follows.

Chapter Thirty-One

Jesse

I think I've done more than my fair share of things to prove to Mischa that I really do have feelings for her. I guess taking her to the biggest school event in town, making love to her in my favorite hideout, and nearly kicking Preston's ass for assaulting her isn't proof enough.

Nope, she needs me to hang out in the girls' restroom with her during lunch, cramped up in a stall with only a lidless toilet between us.

"I'm going to be expelled and on the front page of the Grover Gazette," I huff, folding my arms across my chest and ducking down awkwardly because if I stand up straight, I'm taller than the walls of the stall. "I can read the headline now, ***Local football star Jesse Alford found making out in the girls' bathroom at Grover High School.*** My dad would have a field day with that one."

Mischa laughs, and my heart skips because lately, it's the single most beautiful sound in the world to me. They should record it and play it on one of those relaxing sound apps. The ones that play white noise and thunderstorm recordings to help people sleep at night. I think about Mischa a lot when I can't sleep at night. Last night it wasn't her laughter I was thinking about, but another sound from my memories of Saturday night after the formal.

"You need to learn to live a little, Jesse Alford. Besides, I'm definitely not making out with you in a high school bathroom. I may live in the woods, but I've got way higher standards than that."

Now it's my turn to laugh. I relax a little, standing up straighter and resting against the wall. Everyone's downstairs in the lunchroom, anyway.

"Then what do I stand to gain from all of this?" I ask her with a smirk.

She shrugs and leans against her side of the stall. "Who says you have to gain something from everything? Sometimes it's just nice to *happen*."

"Is that what you do? You just *happen*?"

"Basically."

"So then, why can't *we* just happen?" I ask her motioning between the two of us.

It doesn't seem like she's going to answer, but it doesn't matter because the sound of the bathroom door opening and two girls giggling catches us off guard. I immediately duck down, but it's probably in vain because if these girls bother to check under the stalls, they'll see my feet. I look up at Mischa frantically, but she's just leaning nonchalantly against the wall, smirking at me.

I step up on the toilet and crouch down, causing Mischa to laugh silently. She takes her feet and extends one leg out and presses against the opposite wall and the other foot she plants next to mine on the toilet seat. Now she's awkwardly suspended in the air, still wearing a calm smirk.

"Oh my gosh, I can't believe that happened! Do you really think Jesse Alford is dating that freak?" I recognize that voice as Amber Pemberg, a fellow senior who lives down the street from me in Middlebrook.

"I can't imagine. It has to be a freaking joke or something. He can't seriously be dating her!" The other voice belongs to Claire Parker, Amber's best friend. They do everything together, so I'm not surprised that gossiping in the bathroom is on their list of bestie activities.

"But he took her to the winter formal. The *winter formal*, Claire! That's like social suicide. You think they hooked up afterward?"

My eyes snap up to Mischa's, and she's grinning at me. Is this an everyday occurrence for her? Hiding in the girls' restroom listening to all the latest gossip?

"He wasn't at the mill that night, and then today he nearly beats up his best friend for her. Of course they did! We all know she gives it up so easy."

Amber makes a sound of disgust and stomps her foot. "How could someone like *Meesha* Lawrence get lucky enough to hook up with Jesse *freaking* Alford? It doesn't make sense!"

"I'm sure he's just using her for sex."

Amber chuckles this time. "Yeah, guess he got bored with Alyssa."

"She totally cheated on him anyway," Claire snorts.

"Maybe that's the real reason Jesse wanted to kick Preston's ass. Nothing to do with Lawrence." They giggle hysterically, and then their voices fade as they exit the bathroom. Mischa drops her legs to the ground as the door swings closed, and I step off the toilet and stretch my cramped limbs.

"*That*—" She points in the general direction that Amber and Claire were just standing. "—is why '*we can't just happen,*' *Jesse freaking Alford.*"

I can't help but laugh at her mocking tone. "Okay, so people talk about us. So what?"

"Trust me Jesse, you don't want the problems that come with associating yourself with me." She shakes her head. There's dust smeared across her black tank top where her cleavage is displayed perfectly, and the flannel she's wearing is way too big. It stops at her knees, and she's wearing shorts and fishnet stockings again, so it almost looks like she's not wearing any pants from the back. I wonder why she's never cold in the winter. She almost always dresses the opposite of the season. Her hair is curly again, and she has it slicked up in a messy bun, which I'm surprised Amber and Claire hadn't spotted during their play-by-play analysis of our love life.

She's beautiful, though. No matter how weird she dresses or acts sometimes. And she's playing hard to get, which makes me want her more.

I reach out and wrap my fingers around one of her wrists, pulling her to me. She stands in front of me, not in the least bit shy about meeting my gaze. It's like we're in a constant battle for dominance. I thought I was winning on Saturday because she was out of her element, and she was being so timid and nothing like her usual self. But now she's back to normal, and she's not giving in. That's fine because I don't plan on backing down either.

"You've got about two minutes to get out of here before the hallways fill up," she warns me with another smirk. "So, what's it going to be, Jesse?"

"I like you, Mischa," I tell her, returning the simper and still gripping her wrist. "I really like you a lot. And you like me too."

Her smug expression doesn't falter. If anything, it grows even more mischievous. "Yeah, I do. So what?"

I don't respond with words. I just dip my head down and press my lips against hers. She wiggles out of my grasp on her wrist and fists my T-shirt, kissing me back.

With my hands now free, I place them firmly on her small waist. A small, hormonal part of me wants to lift her up and press her against the wall, like our first kiss in the Gravity House, but the rational part of my brain remembers that we're in school, in the girls' bathroom, minutes before the bell for fourth period rings.

Mischa breaks the kiss first. She lets go of my shirt and places her palms flat on my chest, but my hands remain on her waist.

"There go my standards." She shrugs, feigning disappointment. I lick my lips because I want to kiss her again. She waves a finger at me and shakes her head. "No more kissing. We've got to get you out of here."

I want to protest, but I know she's right. I release my hold on her, and she turns around and leads me out of the stall. She walks out first and makes sure the hallway is clear before beckoning me out.

"That was really exciting or whatever, but next time, can we do something different?" I ask her as we walk side by side toward our next class.

"Next time?"

"Yeah, next time. Tomorrow maybe?" I shrug just as the bell rings, signaling that lunch is over. "I want to spend lunch with you, but not in the bathroom."

She side-eyes me and then nods. "Okay, how about the roof?"

"How about the cafeteria? It's the middle of December." I laugh at her. When I look over at her, she's frowning.

She stops walking and folds her arms across her chest. "I'm not eating in there. Not with those people." The way she says it lets me know it's final.

I put my hands up in defeat. "Okay fine, but maybe we can find a place in the courtyard or somewhere it's not against the policy. I kind of hate getting in trouble. My dad can be a real dick sometimes."

"Fine, but somewhere private." She's not showing any signs of moving until I agree to all the terms of our new lunch dates. Students climb the stairs on their way to their classes, so I nod eagerly, trying to get her to walk with me. She smirks again and starts walking with her arms still folded like a child who just successfully threw a tantrum and got her way. I just shake my head and laugh.

Chapter Thirty-Two

According to Northern California standards, it's freezing outside, even though it's only fifty degrees. That being said, nobody eats outside in the courtyard during the colder months, so Jesse and I have had total privacy during lunch for the rest of the week.

It's the last day of school before we're out for three weeks of winter break, but I'm not as excited as the rest of my peers for the break. There's no winter break for the seventeen-year-old girl who has to raise her three younger siblings. That's just more hours in the day that I'm responsible for feeding and entertaining the Littles.

"So, I'll take that as a *no*." Jesse's words snap me out of my stupor, and I look at him with a confused scowl.

"What?"

He chuckles and bumps my shoulder with his. "I asked you if you had any plans for the break."

I roll my eyes and turn away from him. "Oh yeah, so many wonderful plans. All of which include playing mommy to my siblings."

"Well, hopefully, you'll have some time to spend with me," he states in a sultry tone. He's so damn gorgeous that it's hard to resist that charm he's seemed to master. Of course, there is a part of me that wants to spend the entire break wrapped up in the back seat of the GTO, but other parts of me know it's not a good idea. He's a distraction from so many more important things I've got going on already.

"What are you thinking about?" I hear the amusement in his voice. "You just smiled and frowned at the same time."

"I have a ton of wood to chop." I shrug. I'm starting to really love this spot in the courtyard. Every time we're out here, my head feels clear. It's quiet. There aren't the dozens of voices of my classmates in the hallways or the whispers that supposedly aren't real, according to Dr. Zakarian. I haven't seen Fergal all week either.

"Need some help with that?" he asks me next.

I shoot him a skeptical look and shake my head. "I can manage."

"Is that your way of telling me you *don't* want to hang out with me over the break?" He's laughing, but I can't tell if he's amused or if he's nervous about my answer.

I sigh. "You should spend the break with your friends, Jesse." I focus my gaze down on our feet. My dingy, white Converse swing back and forth above the ground next to his planted Nikes. "Not tagging along while I babysit the Littles or waiting until I have free time away from them, which I rarely have before midnight."

"Well, I'd rather spend it with you." He shrugs, staring at the side of my face. He wants me to look at him.

"Your loss," I mumble. I hop down from the stone ledge that we're sitting on and stretch my arms up in the air. When my shirt rises to expose a section of skin above my waist, Jesse reaches out and pokes me in the rib, causing me to buckle a little and giggle.

"So, you're ticklish." He laughs mischievously. I stand up straight and give him a look that says, *"Don't even try it."* Of course, he ignores my threatening glare and reaches out for me. He's got me wrapped in his arms before I can get away, and he's drumming his fingertips on my sides and stomach, causing me to screech with laughter.

"Jesse, stop!" I beg him, still giggling hysterically and struggling in his embrace.

I remember Teddy tried to tickle me once, and I couldn't even remotely feel his fingers on me. I yelled at Teddy to stop being annoying, and he ran into his room, crying. Sometimes I feel nothing at all. Most of the time, my skin feels so numb that a simple touch is transparent. When Jesse touches me, I feel it.

The bell rings and Jesse finally stops his assault on my sides, but he continues to hold me in his lap while his palms are planted on my waist. Once I've calmed my laughter, I attempt to stand, but Jesse holds me steady on his lap.

"I mean it, Mischa. I'd much rather spend the break with you," he tells me softly. I can feel his breath against the skin of my neck, and I bite my bottom lip to contain my smile. He lets me go, and I follow him through the courtyard and back inside the school.

It's not that I don't *want* to hang out with Jesse for the next three weeks. It's just that I have so many things that I need to get done before the spring, and I'm running out of time. I know my mom will never change, so I have no choice but to find a substitute caregiver who will ensure that the Littles are taken care of and stay together once I'm gone.

My mother has a sister. Her name is Cassandra, and the last time my mother heard from her, she lived *somewhere* in California. My Aunt Cassandra ran away from home when she and my mom were still teenagers, and the sisters haven't kept steady contact since.

Last summer, I snuck inside Dr. Zakarian's office and read my files, which had been transferred from my doctor in Monterey. On my medical history sheet, my father had marked that mental illness runs on my mother's side of the family. There was a letter in which my father explained that my mother's sister, Cassandra Townes, suffered from bipolar disorder, and has been missing for most of her adult life. Not much was known about her, and we've never heard from her.

One day, the house phone rang, and there was a man named Kevin on the other line asking for my mom by name. After I told him my mother was unavailable, he briefly explained that he was an acquaintance of my Aunt Cassandra and that he needed to speak with my mother about getting Cassandra and her daughter help, before *"things got worse."* I never told my mother about the phone call. She's never been able to take care of her own kids, so I wasn't going to give her the chance to be further distracted by someone else's.

Aunt Cassandra taking the Littles after I'm gone is out of the question. I'm crazy enough, I can't send them to a crazier stranger.

Next on my list of potential foster parents for my siblings is Mason, Joe's son from a previous marriage, and the Littles' oldest brother.

Mason is two years older than I am, but he's been alone his entire life. After his mother died, he lived with Joe and my mom briefly. But just before Frankie was born, Mason went to live with his aunt in Vacaville. He hates Joe, and I don't blame him, but I've never known why. He only comes to visit the Littles once a year, and he refuses to stay long if he knows his father is around. He and I have never been close. I was forced to take over caring for the Littles after Joe and my mother tapped out. I resented Mason because he should be here helping me.

After April 14th, he'll have no choice.

Chapter Thirty-Three

Jesse

The weather forecast is calling for snow tomorrow, but today I have something special planned for Mischa.

My parents wanted to get away for the snowy weekend, so they've planned a two-day trip to San Francisco for the three of us like we used to do when Gramps was alive. I decline, however, because I've got something much more interesting laid out for this chilly Saturday.

I see my parents off with an excuse that I want to hang out with my friends at Winterval, a Christmas carnival held a few miles outside of town in the heart of Tuolumne County that brings the few surrounding towns together to celebrate the holidays. The plan is to attend Winterval, and I'm sure my friends will be there, but I won't be arriving with them.

Mischa's so focused on her task that she doesn't even notice me when as I make my way up the trail. Once again, I'm bundled up in my leather jacket, thermal, jeans, and boots trying to combat the whipping icy wind, while Mischa stands before me, chopping wood in tiny shorts and a tank top.

She's small, but she's able to bring the old, faded wooden-handled axe over her head and into the cylindrical pieces of wood with skill. At least she's wearing eye protection.

The wood goes flying to the sides after being sliced in half, and then Maddie appears from behind her sister to gather the wood and carry it to a small pile a few feet away. She's wearing oversized gloves that are supposed to be preventing splinters.

I stand there and watch Mischa chop a few more pieces of wood before Maddie finally spots me. She inhales sharply and squeals with excitement.

"Hi, Jesse!"

She runs over to me with her arms spread out for a hug that I accept. I don't have any siblings, and I have no experience with little kids, but there's something about the Littles that draws me in and makes it easy to show affection toward them. I've even gotten used to speaking to Frankie when I see her in town, hanging out with her latest boyfriend and the other kids her age. She used to blush and shy away from me, but now she coolly greets me like I'm her brother or some part of her family.

Mischa startles when she realizes I'm there. She looks like a deer in headlights as she holds the axe in mid-swing and stares at me.

"What are you doing here?"

"I came to help you with the firewood." I point toward the pile of chopped wood with an impish grin.

Mischa returns the gesture and lowers the axe down into the chopping block. "Well, too bad. I just finished up."

"Good, because I was just heading to the Christmas carnival, and I was hoping you'd join me," I tell her, keeping my smirk aimed at her.

Instead of the excited grin I'm expecting from her, Mischa frowns at my proposition. She releases the axe handle completely and plants her hands on her hips.

"I can't," she states simply, lifting her chin proudly.

"Why not?"

Mischa motions to Maddie, and then toward the house, as if the reason should be clear as day. I shrug and shake my head, not understanding her apprehension.

Mischa rolls her eyes. "The Littles, Jesse. I can't just go to some fair with you and leave them here alone."

I laugh and look down at Maddie, who I can tell is excitedly fidgeting at the thought of going to the carnival.

"They don't like carnivals?" I reach down and lift Maddie into my arms. "Don't you like carnivals, Maddie?"

"Yeah!" Maddie squeals and hugs me tight around my neck. "I love cawni-fulls!"

"You've never even *been* to a carnival," I hear Mischa mumble as she glares at her little sister.

"Well then, I think it's time for you to go to a carnival, Maddie." I bounce the small girl in my arms, and she giggles excitedly. She wiggles down and out of my embrace and runs toward the house.

"I'm going to tell Teddy and Frankie that we're going to the cawnifull!" she yells back at us as she dashes across the yard. I smile proudly as I watch her scale the ramp and call out to the other two siblings in the house, *Jesse is taking us to a cawnifull!*"

The sound of Mischa clearing her throat brings my attention back to her, and she looks annoyed.

"What the hell, Jesse?" she shouts at me in an accusatory tone. Her arms are outstretched, and even though she's obviously pissed and yelling at me, I want to kiss her. "You can't just make decisions like that for *my* little sisters and brother!" she continues. "Why get their hopes up like that?"

"Get their hopes up?" It's just a local Christmas festival. Why is she making such a big deal out of it?

"Yes. I can't afford to take them to that stupid carnival. Plus, you know the whole town will be there. I'm not in the mood for people's shit today."

"Look, the carnival is free. I'll pay for anything else they want to do." I offer with a shrug. She doesn't move, just stares at me coldly.

I know girls can be moody, but Mischa's mood swings are intense. She's always annoyed or irritated, but when she's relaxed, she's the coolest person I know. That's why I need her to go to Winterval with me today. I need to experience fun-loving Mischa again. I'm craving it.

"Are you wearing that to the carnival?" I point at her shorts and tank top, which are covered in debris from the wood chopping. She deepens her glare but shifts it behind me to the beat-up truck that's bouncing across the gravelly road. I'm pretty sure the shocks are busted.

The brakes screech as the rusty red pickup truck comes to a halt, and the driver hops out. His boots crunch on top of the gravel, and he stops and stares Mischa up and down like she's old garbage.

Mischa returns his look of disgust and then turns to me and mumbles, "I'll be right back." She sprints inside the house, leaving me outside with her obviously drunk stepfather.

Joe Little sizes me up while taking a hard swig from the liquor bottle in his hand.

"You the boyfriend?" he asks me in a condescending tone.

"Yeah," I respond, and I can feel my voice deepening. Not because I'm trying to sound tough, but because I don't like this guy, even though I've just met him for the first time, and I'm trying to control my growing anger toward him. I don't know why, but he's giving me a bad feeling. I don't like the fact that Mischa and her family have to be alone with him.

He snorts and then snickers at my response. While he's sizing me up, I'm making my own assessment of him. He's about my same height, but he's thinner than me. There's a display of yellow teeth, and he looks like he hasn't shaved in weeks. All in all, if I wanted to, I could take him.

But why would I even *want* to fight this man? I don't know him.

He finally breaks eye contact with me to spit a wad of saliva on the gravel and then ventures off to the house. As soon as he enters the house, the door swings open again, and Mischa's grandpa comes rolling outside.

"Well, if it isn't the local celebrity," he calls out. I laugh and approach the ramp.

"Good afternoon, Mr. Lawrence." I nod to him. He returns the gesture and grunts. He wheels down the ramp. An eerie thought hits me, and I briefly wonder why Mischa's grandfather came outside no sooner than her stepdad came home.

"You know why I stay up here cooped up in this raggedy ass house?" Mr. Lawrence asks me as he comes to a halt at the bottom of the ramp. There's only gravel and dirt from this point, so I'm not sure what he's hoping to accomplish.

"It's got nothing to do with this damn chair, either. I was always moving around in this thing before that dumbass ex-daughter-in-law of mine moved us out here with her good-for-nothing husband and lazy kids."

I laugh at his words but listen intently. I'm interested in what he has to say and relieved that he's actually giving me the time of day. Mischa loves the Littles, but her grandfather seems to hold a special place in her heart. Maybe it's because of his relation to her father. Either way, I can relate. Gramps was my best friend. Closer than my father and I ever dared to be.

"I'd rather rot away in this shitty little house than watch those bastards treat my grandbaby like garbage, all because she's not some blonde-haired, blue-eyed kid." He shakes his head.

I grimace at his words. Everyone in town treats Mischa like crap. Not just the white residents. And most of that is because of the Blake situation. "I don't think Grover is *racist*," I tell him, but then my mind wanders to Alyssa's comment about Mischa's "*gross nappy hair.*"

Mr. Lawrence scoffs. "What makes you think that? Because they love you so much? They always have loved a nigga who could throw a ball."

"Grandpa!" Mischa's voice bellows from the porch. I'm about to explain to her I'm not offended, that I enjoy talking to her grandfather, but when I look at her, I'm temporarily stunned.

She's standing with her hand on her hips, glaring at her grandfather disapprovingly. Her light blue skinny jeans are tightly fitted, accenting her curves and stopping high on her waist, where a sliver of skin separates the top of the jeans and the frayed bottom of her tan cropped sweater. Her curly ringlets are pinned up neatly, and her eyes have dark makeup around them.

Teddy runs past his older sister and down the ramp. Gripping the handles of the wheelchair, he tries his hardest to pull Mr. Lawrence back up the ramp.

"Grandpa Lawrence, we have to leave now. You have to go back inside." The small boy grunts as he attempts in vain to move the chair containing a man who is more than three times his size. Mr. Lawrence is hunched over in the chair, but I can tell he was once a tall, strong man.

"I don't want to be in that house with that drunk redneck," Grandpa Lawrence fusses back. "Just leave me out in the shed." He points to the small structure about twenty yards across the land.

"No, Grandpa. You'll get attacked by mountain lions," Mischa tells him in an irritated tone. Her full, painted lips turn down, and I want to kiss the frown away from her face, despite the risk of smearing the burgundy lipstick.

"Girl, if you don't shut the hell up about those damn mountain lions!" Her grandfather waves her off. He shrugs his shoulder backward, a gesture meant to signal that he wants Teddy to stop pulling on his chair. I walk over and move Teddy aside, effortlessly pulling the wheelchair backward, up the ramp.

"It's too cold to leave you out here, Mr. Lawrence," I tell him as we travel backward up the ramp and back onto the porch.

Mischa holds the door open, and I take the old man back inside the house. He shrugs me off like he did Teddy, so I let him go, and he wheels away from me to his normal spot in front of the TV.

Mischa walks over and kneels in front of him. "We'll be back in a few hours, Grandpa," she tells him, gripping his hands and willing him to make eye contact. "Joe's probably going to head out to the bar soon, anyway."

I watch the heartfelt exchange with a mixture of emotions. While it's sweet watching Mischa care for her siblings and her grandfather, it's also kind of sad. We're kids, we're supposed to be having fun and doing things that teenagers do all the time. But Mischa's stuck living like an adult, and not a glamorous adult life, either. She should be running out the door to attend the carnival and have some fun. Instead, she has to get all of her little siblings dressed and talk her near-senile grandfather off the ledge in order to leave the house. All while her mother sleeps, and her stepfather prepares for a night of getting hammered.

I wonder if Alyssa and Preston would treat her better if they could see this side of Mischa. If they knew what she deals with at home.

In the car, Mischa's feet are propped up on the dashboard again, and her little brother and sisters are huddled in the backseat excited about their first time going to the Winterval.

"You know you don't have to do stuff like this just to get me to sleep with you again," Mischa blurts out, motioning toward the backseat.

I nearly choke on my breath at her declaration. "Excuse me?"

"Mischa!" Frankie screeches, and I see from the rearview that she's covering Maddie's ears with her hands. Teddy's eyes are glued to the window, watching the trees whirl by on the mountain pass.

"It's true." Mischa shrugs. "You don't have to pretend to want to spend time with me and the Littles, just to get me in bed. Or the backseat, or whatever?"

"Backseat?" Frankie spits out in disgust. She starts shifting in her seat in an attempt to not sit in the spot where Mischa and I shared our intimate moment last weekend.

I reach over and turn up the music. "Don't you think that's a little inappropriate?" I ask her as I shuffle through songs on my phone.

"Teddy and Maddie have no clue what I'm talking about, and Frankie's not stupid." She shrugs nonchalantly.

"You have definitely lost your marbles," I reply with a laugh.

"What did you say?" she asks me, furrowing her eyebrows and frowning.

"You've lost your marbles," I repeat. "My grandpa used to say it all the ti—"

"Turn the car around!" she yells at me suddenly, and I swerve a little from the shock.

"What?" Now it's my turn to knit my brows together. "Mischa, I didn't mean anything by it, I swear. It was just a joke, I—"

"Jesse, turn the car around. I need to go back to my house," she presses, frantically looking around for God-knows-what.

"Mischa, I'm sorry. I—" But again she cuts me off.

"Jesse!" She pauses and then looks at me with pleading eyes. I slow the car down, and her demeanor changes. "I forgot my phone. I need to go back and get my phone, Jesse."

I eye her suspiciously, but I do as she asks, hitting a U-turn and driving back up the mountain to retrieve her phone.

When I pull up against the curb in front of her house, I fight the urge to watch as the tight material of her jeans forms snuggly against her ass as she runs up the gravel path.

When I give in, and chance a glance, I notice the imprint of her cell phone in her back pocket.

Chapter Thirty-Four

*H*ow *long has it been?*

That's the thought that keeps racing through my mind as I sprint across my yard and into the house.

Grandpa is already fast asleep, slumped over in his chair in front of Judge Judy, as she screams at two ex-roommates. I slam the bedroom door behind me and rush over to my dresser, pulling out the fishbowl and bag of marbles.

How long has it been since I've heard the clink of the stained-glass orbs falling into the bowl? I haven't even bothered to flush my meds. I'm still not *taking* them, but it's unfathomable that I'd forget to perform these sacred rituals. I quickly count the marbles in the bowl and use the calendar on my phone to count the number of days left until April 14th.

How many days has it been?

Fourteen days. That's two Saturdays. The day I went to San Francisco to find a dress for the formal.

I count out fourteen marbles in my palm and fist them tightly, silently apologizing to them for my neglect before sprinkling them into the fishbowl. I go to the bathroom and flush the pills next.

We're down to 113 days.

I'm wrapping a blanket around Grandpa's shoulders when I hear Joe's boots coming down the hallway. I dart out the door. I've got enough going on right now. I don't need his shit today.

Jesse is sitting patiently in the car with the Littles as I approach them, but it's obvious he's in deep thought. I know he's trying to figure out what just happened.

Fergal was right. Jesse *is* a distraction. He's managed to run Fergal away, and I haven't seen any mountain lions ever since our ice cream date two weeks ago. Add that to the fact that I haven't been counting down my days and flushing my pills, and that spells trouble for my plan.

"Ready now?" Jesse asks me, throwing a wary smile my way. I return the gesture and nod my head. He puts the car in drive and takes off down the road.

Teddy and Maddie make a beeline for the row of bouncy houses, and I slide Frankie a twenty-dollar bill I swiped from Joe's wallet while he was in the shower last night. Now Jesse and I are alone, slowly making our way to the giant inflatable dragon where Teddy and Maddie are now jumping inside of his stomach. I'm just about to make a comment about the morbid concept when I feel his arm around my waist, pulling me against him. His warmth and scent are so inviting that I can't help but relax in his embrace.

"Are you ever going to drop this whole *Jesse is just trying to use me* thing? I know you don't really believe that."

A smirk plays on my lips, and I shrug a little. "It's more fun making you chase me."

"Yeah, but it's exhausting for me." There's humor in his voice, but I'm sure he's being serious.

We stop in front of the disemboweled dragon, but Maddie and Teddy slide out, and sprint past us to the inflated castles next to it. I step out of Jesse's embrace and walk over to the mesh netting on the side of the castle. Maddie is screaming excitedly as Teddy bounces next to her, making her fly higher in the air.

I need to end this with Jesse before things get out of control and he ruins everything. But for some reason, I can't. It's like deep down I don't want to, so every time I push, and he pushes back, I give in. It's curiosity. Only this time, it won't kill anyone, and that's the problem.

"Watch this, Jesse!" Maddie calls out as Jesse approaches and stands beside me. She does nothing at all. She just jumps up and falls on her back, giggling wildly.

"That's so cool, Maddie!" Jesse tells her excitedly. Maddie gets up and grins her toothless smile at him, obviously proud of herself for impressing him. The two smaller Littles take turns trying to impress Jesse, and I have to admit it makes my heart melt. They like him.

I like him.

After two more turns in the bounce houses, Jesse convinces the Littles to go to the midway so that we can play games. He pays for them to play round after round of ring toss and whack-a-mole. It takes him four tries to knock over three milk bottles—which I'm positive are glued down to the wooden shelf—and wins me a stuffed monkey.

"Sissy, play this one with us!" Maddie demands, stopping at the next game. It's the water gun game, where you aim the sprayer at the red dot, and the marker goes racing to the top as the tube fills with water.

I take a seat on the stool next to Jesse and grip the handles. Jesse hands the worker a few dollars, then turns to Teddy and Maddie and explains how the game is played.

We all take aim at our red dots and within seconds, the bell rings and the pressured water comes spraying from the guns. I purposely sway my stream away from the red dot so that my tube doesn't fill up as fast as Maddie's and Teddy's. Jesse's doing the same, and again I feel those butterflies people talk about. He really is something special. The alarm goes berserk, signaling the end of the game, and Teddy jumps up and waves his hands excitedly.

"What do you want, kid?" the worker asks him, lazily chewing dip.

"You pick one, Maddie," Teddy tells our baby sister. She points to the row of stuffed pigs, and the guy pulls one down and tosses it to Teddy.

We find Frankie on the row of food stalls with a group of her friends from school. To my surprise, she excuses herself from the giggling girls and joins us at a picnic table where we all share funnel cakes and popcorn.

"This is the best day ever!" Maddie gushes with her mouth full of fried dough. There's powdered sugar smeared around her face. "Thanks for bringing us here, Jesse!"

"Thank you for coming here with me. It would have sucked having to play midway games all by myself." Jesse winks at her. He leans against me and bumps my shoulder. "Are you having fun yet?"

"Yes, I've been having fun the whole time," I tell him matter-of-factly. I reach across the table and wipe Maddie's messy face with a napkin.

"You came in last place in the water game, and you didn't even cry, Sissy," Maddie informs me, and I think it's her way of complimenting me.

"See, I told you so," I tease Jesse, shaking my head in his face. He only returns my smirk. His eyes shift down to my mouth, and I know he's thinking about kissing me, but he's too much of a gentleman to be *"inappropriate"* in front of the Littles. I lick my lips to tease him, and he bites his to keep it in check.

"I'm going to take the kids on the Ferris wheel," Frankie announces, causing our sensual stare-down to end.

"We'll go too," Jesse suggests, and we all stand up and toss our trash in the rusty garbage can. We walk over and stand in the short line for the ride.

"Maddie, are you going to be afraid?" I kneel in front of my baby sister and pull her collar tighter around her neck. It's late afternoon, and the wind is picking up with a chill.

She shakes her head, and her pigtails swing. "Nope. I won't be scared, I promise."

"Stay right here after the ride is over," I tell them. They nod and sprint up the ramp where a teenager helps load them into the red gondola-style car. Maddie and Teddy wave excitedly as the car rises away from the platform, and Frankie leans back and calls out to us.

"You're supposed to make out at the very top!" She points at the top and sticks her tongue out at us. Jesse laughs while waving back at Teddy and Maddie, and I flip Frankie the bird.

"I hate her so much."

"C'mon." He places his palm on my lower back and pushes me softly up the platform where a blue gondola is waiting. Jesse helps me into the rocking car before getting in and sitting beside me. The gondola is round and has room on the opposite bench for the Littles, but it's just me and Jesse under the umbrella as the car rises behind the Littles.

"Looks like you've finally got me alone, Jesse Alford."

He laughs and brings his arm around my shoulder. "That was the plan, right? Get rid of the Littles, and then get you all alone on the Ferris wheel."

"Was it?" I side-eye him with a smirk. I know he's joking, but it's fun to play along.

"Actually, I was hoping to kiss you on the Scrambler, but I was afraid you'd hurl funnel cake all over me."

I punch his arm playfully and we laugh together. "Gross."

"Your Littles are cool. I mean it, Mischa. I don't mind having them around, as long as I get some alone time every now and then."

"They like you," I tell him absently, watching as his smile grows bigger. "Teddy thinks you're some kind of superhero."

"He's so quiet, but Maddie sure can hold a conversation."

"He's got a wall built up. I don't blame him. Kids are assholes, especially in Grover. He spends most of his time hiding in that bookstore. As for Maddie, she spends her days with Mrs. Brady, who is senile and thinks Maddie's one of her girlfriends from the sixties. They sit on the porch all day drinking lemonade and gossiping about people and things that Maddie doesn't even know about."

"Well, then I guess it's a good thing they tagged along today."

The wind picks up the higher we climb in the air, so I snuggle closer to him, and he holds me tighter. I lay my head against his chest and listen to the thumping of his heart as his fingers dance against the skin of my side.

Below us, there's a chorus of laughter, screaming, and music from the midway. There's a band playing, but I don't recognize the song. Probably some local band from one of the surrounding towns. I tune all of it out in favor of listening to my new favorite sound.

Jesse's heartbeat.

If I'm being honest with myself, I enjoy it more than the sound of those marbles dropping into the glass bowl, or the *'plunk'* of the pills falling into the toilet water.

It's the sound of normalcy. It makes me wish I was normal.

It's a sound that I'll miss when I'm gone.

When we're close to the top, Jesse finally speaks, and his voice rumbles against my ear on his chest.

"So, if I kiss you, will I have red lipstick all over my lips?"

I shake my head, but now my own heart is beating rapidly. "It's a matte. Less transfer."

"Whatever that means," he murmurs and tucks his index under my chin to lift my head up.

The car comes to a stop at the top of the wheel, and Jesse leans in and captures my lips with his own. His hands drop to my waist, and I bring mine up to grab onto his shoulders. He's trying to be romantic, but I want more. I deepen the kiss with my tongue, and he happily complies.

It's like my whole body is alive again. Something only Jesse can do. Just a touch or a kiss from this boy and I'm on fire. A girl who walks around feeling numb from the head down—I feel all tingly and warm whenever Jesse is around.

His thumbs run circles on my stomach, and I moan in his mouth. I'm suddenly burning up in this sweater, and it's not psychosis. I consider pulling my shirt off, but maybe *that* is the psychosis.

No. This is real.

These feelings he gives me. They are real.

"I hope you two are keeping the tradition up there," Frankie calls out from below us. Jesse laughs into the kiss, ultimately ending our little session.

"I really, *really* hate her," I mumble against his lips, giving him one last peck.

"Mischa look! It's Santa!" Maddie is going bananas as Jesse and I walk off the platform of the Ferris wheel.

Maddie and Teddy still believe that a jolly, old, fat guy breaks into our house every year at Christmas and leaves them presents. Frankie fell prey to the little assholes at her school, so she's been my accomplice in keeping the magic alive for the other two for years.

There's a winter wonderland just opposite the area designated for the carnival rides. There's a man dressed up as Santa Claus with a couple of disgruntled-looking elves walking around him.

"Mischa, can we go see Santa? Please!" Maddie jumps up and down. Teddy nods in agreement with his magnified eyes glued to me.

"Frankie?" I look to my little sister for help, but she just shrugs and backs away.

"I've got to go find my friends again." And with that, she's gone, sprinting across the dead grass onto the midway.

I don't feel like faking it for Santa right now. The kiss with Jesse and the elevation of the Ferris wheel has my already jumbled head spinning.

"I'll take them," Jesse offers nonchalantly.

"Jesse," I trail off with a weak smile. "You don't have to..."

He waves me off. He bends down to pick Maddie up and sits her on his shoulders. She giggles and squeals and wraps her arms around his forehead.

"C'mon Teddy, let's go see Santa." He takes off toward the wonderland with my Littles, leaving me to watch alone on a bench across the way.

I laugh to myself as I watch Jesse try to corral Maddie in place in the line after taking her off his shoulders. She's so excited, and I can tell Teddy is trying to help Jesse explain that she has to wait her turn. It's like birdwatching, only the subject is a sexy, six-foot, caramel-brown cutie instead of a woodpecker.

"He's not serious about you. You know that, right?"

I'd recognize that voice anywhere. Usually, I'm in a constant state of paranoia, and she would have never been able to sneak up on me like this. But I was Jesse-watching and got distracted. *Typical.*

"What do you want, Alyssa?"

"You're temporary, *Meesha,*" she spit out in a condescending tone. "He may pretend to like you, and play house with your weird little family, but it's all a ploy to make me jealous."

"Well, looks like it's working." I don't even bother to face her. I don't want to see the pathetic, smug look on her face. She's desperate. It's painfully obvious.

She makes a *'pssht'* sound. "Yeah, right. Like I'd ever be jealous of you."

"Whatever you say, Alyssa." I roll my eyes. It's Maddie's turn to talk to Santa, and I wish I was up there now so that I could hear her wish. That'll help me with my last-minute shopping.

"Like I said, you're temporary," my arch-nemesis presses.

I decide to give her what she wants. I turn to face her and shoot her the smuggest grin I can muster. "Good thing *he's* only temporary as well," I tell her confidently because I mean it.

The look she gives me lets me know I've satisfied her. Her smile is as sweet as a lemon, and she stands and leaves with her newfound information that I'm sure she'll relay to Jesse later.

"Bye," I call after her, waving and smiling as fake as possible.

I turn back just as Teddy is climbing down from Santa's lap, and the three of them make their way toward me. Unlike the smile I was giving Alyssa that caused my cheekbones to grow sore, Jesse's smiling face is genuine as he listens to Maddie and Teddy gush about meeting Santa.

He's an amazing guy.

A girl like Alyssa doesn't deserve him. None of these girls in this piece of shit town deserve him. Not even me.

I decided then and there that, while Jesse may be a dangerous distraction to my plan, I'll gladly occupy his time if it means keeping him away from Alyssa Slade.

Chapter Thirty-Five

113

My condition never really bothered me before.

I mean, of course, it has affected my life, and I certainly don't enjoy seeing snakes in my bed sheets and mud spluttering out of the showerhead, only to scream and then be told that everything is fine. That no one else can see these things.

But I've never wondered, *"Why me?"*

Or asked God, or whoever, *"Can't you just make me normal?"*

I've always just rolled with the punches because I never really knew what *normal* was.

When I'm off my meds long-term, I'm supposedly out of control. My hallucinations and delusions become harder to identify, and the voices become so loud I can't hear myself think. Or maybe I am just thinking? Maybe when I'm thinking, it's really the voices. Without my medication, I increasingly start to feel as if I'm being watched. I once scoured the entire exterior and interior of the house in search of cameras that I'm positive federal agents had placed around the house, because once again Anderson Cooper was on the TV screen, warning me of a government conspiracy. There were no cameras, but I'm sure that's because the government had them removed once they realized I was on to them.

When I'm on my meds, I'm a zombie. Locked away in my white room at Beacon Pointe Mental Health Facility with Leala, my roommate who set her family home on fire with a butane torch and gasoline-soaked tennis shoes because she didn't want to move into a new house two blocks away.

After sixty-eight days without my meds, I am now in a space I like to call the *between*. It's a state where I'm able to pinpoint most of my hallucinations as being false, but they still occur regularly.

So when I'm cooking dinner for the Littles after Jesse drops us off, and Teddy walks over asking for help to fix his action figure's broken arm, I'm temporarily stunned by the deep, warped voice that's coming out of his small mouth. He sounds like a distorted recording on a tape. Almost demonic.

I take the action figure from Teddy and examine the damage while trying to convince myself that this is just another hallucination. Auditory hallucinations are my most frequent with this disorder, falling second only to mood shifts.

Teddy's hazy new voice is firing off in a frantic, yet slow, tone as he tries to explain that this is his favorite wrestling figure, and that Maddie broke his arm off. I'm fighting desperately to ignore his voice, but he won't stop talking and it's becoming too much. What little rationality I have isn't enough to combat the delusion and I snap.

"The joint is broken, Teddy. I can't fix it." I shove the plastic man and his amputated limb back to a tearful Teddy.

"But Mischa, he's my fav—"

"I don't care, Teddy. Shut up!" I scream at him. My head is spinning now, and the ground beef and pasta meal I'm attempting to make, with only half of the amount of ingredients I need, is sticking to the bottom of the skillet. I only had one can of pasta sauce, and I'm using sliced sandwich cheese instead of shredded. I went to that stupid carnival today instead of going to the store and stocking up on groceries.

Teddy stops talking, only to start crying instead. Now the distorted talking is distorted wailing, as he holds the little man's body in one hand and his arm in the other, both at his sides. His mouth is wide open, and he's crying like a cartoon baby.

"Seriously, Teddy?" I yell at him while simultaneously scraping the pasta from the bottom of the skillet.

I move around him and start piling the pasta on plates for each of the Littles and Grandpa, just as Frankie comes in and shouts at Teddy to be quiet.

"What's wrong with him?" she calls out to me over the sounds of Teddy's sobs.

"Maddie broke his stupid toy," I tell her as I grab the bread from the oven and spread butter over them with a butter knife.

"It's not stupid! It's my favorite!" he whines, and his voice still hasn't changed.

"I did not break it! It was already broken!" Maddie's squeaky voice calls out as she stomps into the kitchen with her hands on her hips and her new stuffed pig under her arm. "It was already broken!" Her rolled speech is almost as irritating as Teddy's wailing.

"Was not!" Teddy growls deeply and lunges for the piggy, ripping it from Maddie's arms and holding it over her head.

"Give it back, Teddy!" Maddie screams. Now they're all screaming! Maddie's screaming at Teddy, Teddy's screaming at Maddie, and Frankie's screaming at both of them.

And then Joe walks in.

"What in the fuck is all of this goddamn noise?" he bellows, and they all instantly stop bickering and stare at him with wide eyes.

"Maddie broke my wrestler and—" Teddy begins, but then Maddie jumps in defensively.

"Nuh uh, Daddy. I didn't!" she squeals, pleading with her father to believe her.

This time, Joe cuts her off. "I don't give a fuck! All of you shut the hell up before I—"

"Don't talk to them like that!" It's my turn to scream at him. He's crossing the kitchen floor in a flash, pushing Teddy aside roughly to get in my face.

"Don't push him either! You fucking drunk—"

"What the fuck are you going to do about it?" His spit barely misses me as he harshly growls in my face. He's inches away from me, but he's not so big that he's intimidating. Just a scrawny, hillbilly alcoholic.

"Kill him."

He doesn't scare me, not in the sense that he'll hurt me.

"Kill him."

It's what I could do to him that frightens me.

"Kill."

Teddy's warped voice was annoying, but I don't hate it as much as I hate Joe Little, and I'll be damned if I let him threaten the children that he refuses to raise, despite being their biological father and living in the same house as them.

"KILL HIM!"

I look down at the knife in my hand as the voice grows more demanding. It's not a blunted butter knife anymore. It's a sharp, serrated cutting knife, and it feels light. Easy to bury in Joe's bony chest.

"KILL HIM!"

The voice is deeper now. Much deeper than the one permeating out of Teddy a few seconds ago. It's not Fergal, but I know this voice well enough to know when it's losing its patience with me.

I stare at Joe, and he's still yelling at me, but I can't hear him. All I hear are the two words repeating over and over, and I can almost imagine the exact spot I'd have to stab him to ensure that he bleeds out for good. I could hit him in his aorta, or even his jugular for more fanfare.

He'd be gone forever. Just like me.

"Mischa!"

That's Grandpa, fighting against the murderous voice in my head, trying to bring me into the present. I toss the butter-smeared knife into the sink. Joe calls me more names, and then he walks away just as I'm coming down from visions of killing him.

I slam the plates onto the table and tell Frankie to pour everyone something to drink after they're finished eating. I serve Grandpa his dinner on his tray in front of the TV, before storming out of the house in socks and the same clothes from the carnival earlier.

It's not until my feet hit the hard frosted grass that I realize that the snowfall the weather anchor predicted has come early. That doesn't deter me, though. I just stomp across the frozen yard until I reach the road.

I'm almost to Main Street when Joe's raggedy-ass pickup goes barreling past me. I flip him the bird and continue down the road to Brady's General Store.

I stop behind the store and fish out the joint I left wrapped up inside the recycled boxes. I pray that the snow hasn't dampened it because I really need to get high.

And that's not all I need.

I grab a lighter that I keep on the windowsill, place the white rolled paper between my lips, and light it. I inhale deep until my lungs burn, and then I swallow and exhale, instantly feeling the euphoria that the weed brings me.

I need to control myself, or everything is going to fall apart. If I lose it on Joe, they're going to haul me off to Beacon Pointe again, and that's not good for my plan or my Littles.

Neither is leaving them alone with Joe, but I can't think like that either.

I pull out my cell phone and send a quick text message to Mason.

> **Mischa**: We need your help. Come to Grover ASAP.

He can't ignore me forever. He'll have to come back, eventually. He may be a flighty douchebag, but he loves our little siblings.

A thought hits me as I stare at my phone screen, waiting for a reply. I know I won't get one for a few days, if at all. I'm sending out another text now, this time, to Jesse. I take off toward Middlebrook in wet socks. I'm numb, and in desperate need to feel.

> **Mischa**: I can't sleep.

He responds almost immediately.

> **Jesse**: Me neither.

I don't respond again until about ten minutes later when I'm standing on the side of his house, looking at what I'm hoping is his bedroom window.

> **Mischa**: Open your bedroom window.

> **Jesse**: Okay. It's open now… Why?

Shit! Wrong window, I guess. I trudge through the now thick snowy ground around to the other side of the house. When I reach the other side, Jesse and his twists are hanging out the window looking around. There's snow falling on his nose and long eyelashes, and he looks so young and innocent. I can't help but giggle, catching his attention.

"What are you doing out here?" he asks me in a shocked, accusatory tone.

"Why else would I want you to open your window? I went to the wrong window, though." I shrug sheepishly. Just seeing him brings my nerve endings alive, and I'm now feeling the cold under my feet.

"That was probably my parents' bedroom. Good thing they're out of town." He chuckles as I approach the window. *That's not the only good thing about them being gone.* As I get closer, I notice his smile fade, and now he's frowning at me.

"Why the hell aren't you wearing shoes? It's like thirty degrees outside!" He scrunches his face and switches between staring at my face and my feet.

I'm standing directly in front of him now, outside of his window, inches away from his face. I can't tell him about the argument with Joe and the knife incident. I can't tell him about how stressful it is making dinner for the Littles and listening to them bicker back and forth in distorted voices, and that I'm freaking out over trying to find someone to take care of them after I'm dead. No, I can't tell him any of that.

So instead, I shrug and say, "I couldn't sleep, and I wanted to see you."

I watch the smile break through his confused scowl, and then he extends his arms out to grab me and pull me up and through the window.

His bed is positioned against the wall under the window, so when he falls back, I land on top of him on his queen-sized bed. Much fancier than the twins that Frankie and I sleep on inside our cramped little room. I give him a quick Eskimo kiss before rolling off him and looking around the room.

His room is way bigger than the room I share with Frankie, and it smells like him. It has all the decor one would expect from Jesse Alford. Posters are scattered across the wall, mostly cars and overly sexy celebrities. There's a nice metal desk at the foot of the bed, with an expensive-looking laptop on it and a few picture frames. I pick up a black-framed picture of an old man posing in front of a beat-up muscle car next to a younger Jesse.

"Me and Gramps the day we bought the GTO," he tells me at the same time I hear the window sliding shut and the cold air disappears from the room.

"That's your car?" I tap the glass frame in disbelief.

"Yeah, we bought it and then gutted it and rebuilt it from the inside out." He relaxes against his pillows.

"You two were close?" I ask him absently, peering at the picture one more time before sitting the frame down exactly where I found it.

"Yeah, he was my best friend," Jesse tells me quietly. I'm sure he doesn't want to talk about his grandfather, but making people comfortable has never been my style. Plus, I want to know more about him.

"I remember seeing you guys around town together," I tell him as I finger the model cars and statues on his bookshelf.

I'm surprised to hear him laugh. "He was a fan of your rain boots. He'd say, *'There goes the Lawrence girl in those rain boots.'* whenever we'd see you around town."

I laugh because I remember my rain boot phase. They were bright yellow, and I wore them with every outfit for an entire year when I was thirteen.

"You're lucky to still have your grandpa around. Even if he's a little mean." Jesse chuckles again, and I shake my head. There's a picture of him standing with his parents on Senior Night this past football season, and I trace the frame with my fingers lightly.

"You're lucky to have a living father and a coherent mother," I tell him dryly.

He snorts in response. "My dad can be a dick."

"At least he's alive."

"Come here." I turn and see him relaxing on his bed, beckoning for me.

I kick off my damp socks and crawl onto the bed. We lay side by side, staring at the ceiling. There's a ceiling fan rotating on low, almost putting me in a trance until I feel Jesse drop his arm down next to where mine is resting at my side and intertwining our fingers.

"Tell me about your dad," he says, and I feel my heartbeat skip. I'll never get used to this feeling Jesse gives me. The actual ability to *feel* is abnormal as it is, but the way I lose my breath and my heart drums against my chest for even the briefest of moments confuses, scares, and excites me all at once.

"Tell me about your Gramps," I challenge.

Jesse sighs, but to my surprise, he starts talking. "He was one of those people that saw the good in everything. He was always smiling and cracking jokes. I never heard him raise his voice, and I never saw him worried or stressed. Not even angry. He would always let me be me. My dad's always going on about my future and how cars aren't going to get me far in life. But Grandpa always supported me. He loved cars too. I guess that's where I got it from."

"My dad was like that too," I mumble after he falls silent.

"Did you live with him before he died?" he asks me, and I'm sure he's done the math on Frankie's age and the small gap in time that allowed us to have different fathers in such a short period.

"I lived with him and Grandpa in Monterey until he died."

"How old were you when he died?"

"Eleven. A truck driver fell asleep behind the wheel and hit him head-on while he was driving home from work."

"Damn," he murmurs, and I feel his thumb rub circles on my knuckles. He doesn't have to go into detail about his grandfather's death. Grover is a tiny town. Everyone knows everyone's business. Jesse's Gramps died from cancer. Like me, he was fortunate to know that he was going to die, even if he didn't know the exact date. At least he got to prepare for it.

"I take it you and the Littles' dad aren't close." His tone is nonchalant, but I can almost hear the wheels spinning in his head.

"Where are your parents?" I ask him instead, twisting my body so that I'm hoisted on my elbow on my side.

He furrows his brow. "San Francisco until tomorrow."

I nod my head in approval and sit upright completely. I swiftly pull the sweater over my head and roll over to straddle him.

"No more talking, Jesse Alford," I breathe out before pressing my lips against his. I move my hands under his T-shirt, and he plants his palms on my hips. And we once again fall into our newfound rhythm.

And it feels so good to feel.

Chapter Thirty-Six

He's waiting for me at the end of the gravel path, like usual. The evening snow is falling, but my body is on fire as I approach the car and see Jesse coolly nodding his head to the music inside.

Today was Christmas, and unlike most Christmases in the past, it was the best day of the year for the Littles and me. Joe was gone. Somewhere getting hammered in the city, I'm sure. Grandpa was in a good mood and ate his dinner without complaint. He even smiled at Maddie as she handed him the wrapped present the Littles had picked out for him. A new, thick quilt for him to drape across his lap.

Teddy got most of the action figures he'd requested from Santa, and Maddie spent the entire day gushing over her stuffed pet dog. It's a knockoff of a popular overpriced toy that she was obsessing over every time the commercial would come on while she was watching court shows with Grandpa. It's thirty dollars cheaper than the fifty-dollar name-brand puppy and carrier set, but Maddie doesn't seem to notice the difference.

I didn't even bother looking at the price tags as I strategically shoplifted tubes of liquid lipstick, foundation, an eye shadow palette, and a couple of other random cosmetic items from the MAC counter at Macy's. Shoplifting is second nature to me, but it's still risky this time of year, so I was relieved when Frankie squealed as she opened her present from me.

My mom stayed in bed all day, but she was awake long enough to watch a couple of Christmas specials with us before taking her pills and crashing again.

We drive up the mountain road to our secret spot, and he parks the car in the same spot he did after the formal.

"Did the Littles have a nice Christmas?" he asks me, cranking the heat higher and then relaxing in his seat.

I nod and prop my feet up on the dash. The warm air travels up my exposed thigh and under my dress.

He shuffles around in his jacket, causing me to side-eye him as he produces a flat rectangular box from an interior pocket.

"For you." He grins and holds it out for me. "Merry Christmas."

"Jesse..." I glare at the box in his hand.

"Just take it." He sucks his teeth and laughs.

I take the box from him warily and slowly tear away the shimmery wrapping paper to reveal a black velvet box. Inside is a necklace. A thin silver chain with a silver arrow pendant attached.

"The lady at the jewelry store said that the arrow represents *'courage when moving forward.'* Seems pretty symbolic for you. For us." His smile is shy. Unusual for Jesse Alford.

I take the necklace out of the box and secure it around my neck. "Us?"

"Yeah, us."

"There is no *us*," I tell him with a snort. I give him a sly smile and bring my fingers against the arrow on my chest. "But I appreciate the necklace."

Jesse just shakes his head. We eventually crawl into the backseat, and after, lie wrapped in each other's arms. Jesse tells me all the things he's got planned for us for the next week and a half. He seems enthusiastic about it, and I find it absolutely adorable.

This thing with Jesse may be temporary, but I'm sure there are worse ways to pass the time until you die.

Chapter Thirty-Seven

53

By late February, my involvement with Jesse Alford is a known fact around Grover, but it seems to come with some reprieve. It's like Jesse is the president, and I'm the Thanksgiving turkey that he has pardoned. People still stare at me and roll their eyes when I walk by, but for the most part, they're quiet about it. I still prefer to keep the interactions I have with Jesse as private as possible. We don't speak in the hallways or during class, and we only eat lunch together in the courtyard. Most of our time on the weekend is spent up the mountain trail in Jesse's secret spot.

"Our secret spot," he likes to correct me.

"Today Lynsie Slade shoulder-bumped me in the cafeteria. She totally hates me now!" Frankie is oddly excited as she brags about being assaulted by Alyssa's little sister during lunch. We're all seated at the dinner table, and Frankie has volunteered to tell us about her day.

"You're happy she hates you?" Teddy narrows his magnified eyes at her as he chews his meatloaf.

"Duh! She's totally jealous of me since *my* sister stole *her* sister's boyfriend." It's one of the few times I've heard Frankie refer to me as her sister.

I shake my head at her, but I can't fight the smile that threatens my face at the thought of the Slade family being in shambles now that their princess has lost her promising meal ticket.

That's what those types of people do. They pawn their daughters off on boys they deem worthy of taking care of them. Jesse comes from a wealthy family, and he's a football prodigy. It's obvious he's going places, and now, thanks to me, Alyssa will not be along for the ride.

Not that I'm too interested in anything other than a physical way to pass the next few weeks. Still, I have to admit that I do *sometimes* think about Jesse whenever he's not around, and the other countdown in my life is waiting for our moments spent together.

After dinner, I put the Littles to bed and nestle into the tree behind the house. From my vantage point, Grover looks like a field of fireflies glowing in the night. The businesses and neighborhoods are still bustling since it's just before 9 p.m. on a Wednesday night.

I stare out in the general direction of Middlebrook, wondering which firefly is Jesse's and what he's doing right now.

I'm in the general store, flipping through magazines and waiting for Mr. Brady to come in and relieve me. I've been taking over the morning duties on Saturdays, so that he can have some time to sleep in. He's been mumbling about selling the store, but we all know that's going to be impossible. Grover is so small that anyone without a business already isn't going to buy an old general store. Not when everyone is fine with driving to the Walmart Supercenter forty-five minutes away in Tuolumne.

It's sad, though. This general store is Mr. Brady's life. He spends every day here, even after Mrs. Brady retired from teaching at the high school.

"We've got to take breaks from each other," Mr. Brady told me one day while I was stocking cans, and he was counting the till. *"That's how you keep your marriage healthy."* It was weird advice, but I was so focused on the halo of moths surrounding his head that I didn't even ask him about it.

The phone rings and I pick up. "General store." But there's no response, just heavy breathing. It's been like this all morning. Stupid prank callers, or nearly senile Mrs. Brady.

"Why do you keep playing with the phone, Sissy?" Maddie asks me, stopping in front of the counter to stare between the old landline phone and me.

"Because someone keeps calling and not saying anything," I respond dryly. Maddie frowns like she wants to say something in response, but then shrugs and gallops down the aisle.

It's cold outside again, but people are buzzing about on the streets doing their usual Saturday afternoon routine. Frankie is probably somewhere reveling in her newfound popularity as a result of being what she calls *"Jesse Alford's girlfriend's sister."* Teddy is at Oldman's reading comic books, even though he's probably safe to walk the streets again after Jesse gave him a high five when he saw us walking on Main Street, effectively warding off most potential bullies. Even when I'm ignoring him around town, he always stops the Littles and talks to them.

Everyone's got a routine in Grover, but it seems like Jesse and I have caused a rift in the normality of this piece of shit town.

The door chime sounds, and I don't even bother looking up. I hear Maddie greeting someone, with a badly pronounced, "Welcome to the general store!" and a woman chuckles lightly and says, "Hi."

When the woman approaches the counter and places the loaf of bread on the counter, I finally look up at her and meet familiar brown eyes.

Kelisa Alford.

"Hi. Mischa, right?" Her smile is uneasy. Something that doesn't match her beautiful face. She's got the same deep brown eyes as her son, but her skin is a darker brown, like Zoey's. Her hair is cut in an immaculate bob that stops at her neck in sweeps and waves. She looks youthful, though I'm sure she's in her forties, like my mom. The result of good genes and the drive to get out of bed more than twice a month.

I don't respond. I just stare at her, dumbfounded for a minute.

"I've heard a lot about you," she speaks again, offering a brighter smile.

"I'm sure you have." I don't mean to be rude, but the Alfords *never* shop in the general store, except for Jesse when he's trying to woo me. Why is she in here buying bread instead of getting it from the big Walmart?

"From my son, I mean," she clarifies.

"Are you Jesse's mommy?" Maddie asks her, excitedly jumping up and down in place next to Mrs. Alford.

Jesse's mom looks down at my baby sister and nods. This time her smile reveals teeth. Her teeth are perfect, and her smile reminds me of Jesse's. Big and heartfelt. "I am."

"I'm Maddie! Does he talk about me too?"

I try to shoot mental messages to Mrs. Alford, willing her to say yes, even if it's a lie, just to preserve Maddie's feelings. My Littles are obsessed with Jesse, Maddie being the most enamored.

But to my surprise, Mrs. Alford nods her head immediately. "Yep, you too Madeline."

She looks at me again. We're caught in another awkward stare before she finally clears her throat and speaks again. "I guess you and Jesse have been spending a lot of time together." Her smile and words are meant to be encouraging, I think, but she still seems uncomfortable.

"Frankie says that Jesse is Mischa's boyfriend!" Maddie tells her excitedly. I throw her a look that screams, *"Shut the hell up!"*

Mrs. Alford smiles at her, another unsure smile, and I can tell that my friendship with Jesse isn't very welcomed in the Alford home.

The door chimes, and when I glance at the door, Mason Little is standing there brooding. My heart drops, and I stare at him while Maddie continues to talk Mrs. Alford's ear off, not even noticing her big brother standing there.

"I'd like to have you over for dinner, maybe tonight?" When I face Mrs. Alford again, I can see that she's seriously asking me to dinner. The look on her face is still very nervous, something I wouldn't expect of Jesse's mother.

I shake my head. "I can't." I grab the loaf of wheat bread and type in the barcode numbers. She seems taken aback by my answer, and when her eyes shift over to the stranger staring at me like he's annoyed, I think she gets the wrong impression.

"Jesse seems to think you're really special, Mischa. I just wanted to..." She stops short and looks at me sadly before pulling out her wallet and handing me three one-dollar bills. "Just think about it."

I have zero intentions of ever stepping foot in the Alford house while the parents are present. Jesse says his dad is an asshole, and I believe it. And while Kelisa Alford seems like a wonderful, shy person, I can't chance it.

I'm not even going to be here in fifty days. She'd be better off waiting until he brings home some hick from Oklahoma next Christmas.

She gives me one last hopeful, sad glance before smiling at Maddie and leaving. When she walks past Mason, I can tell she wants to look at him. He's wearing a long-sleeved shirt, but you can see the dark greens, blues, and reds from his full sleeves of tattoos extending onto the back of his hands. Mason resembles his father, only a sober, less gross younger version. Green eyes, dusty hair, thin build.

"You've been blowing up my damn phone for months. Don't just stand there looking stupid!" he huffs. I notice his demeanor soften when he spots Maddie over the counter.

"Hi, Mason!" Maddie waves and runs up to him. He immediately scoops her up in his arms and hugs her tight.

"Hey Maddie, long time no see." They exchange back-and-forth banter, and Mr. Brady comes in and stares at Mason like he's got ten heads.

"I need to leave, Mr. Brady," I tell him as I round the register and storm past Mason and Maddie out of the store.

"What's your deal, Mischa? Why do you keep asking me to come here?" Mason calls out, following me toward the bookstore. Mr. Oldman tells me that Frankie came by and picked up Teddy about an hour ago, so I continue up the road to the foothills. I ignored Mason all the way up the mountain road. I can sense his frustration as he follows me, even though Maddie is talking his head off about nonsense.

"He's in jail," I announce as we come into view of the driveway. Mason never comes around when Joe is home. He hates his father just as much as I do.

"I know. I checked before coming." When I look back, he's still scowling, and his hands are shoved in the pockets of his jeans.

The screen door swings open, and Teddy comes bolting out, with an equally excited Frankie behind him, with her phone attached to her ear.

"Are you staying for dinner?" I ask Mason as he mushes Teddy's unkempt hair and side-hugs Frankie. "We're having lasagna," I add with fake enthusiasm.

"I'm not here for fun, Mischa. What did you want from me?"

"We'll talk later." I nonchalantly wave off his obvious irritation. "Enjoy your siblings."

At dinner, Mason eyes the oven-ready lasagna as if it's beneath him to dine on anything but the finest of Italian cuisine. I know he's just trying to get under my skin, though. Last I heard, he was bumming it on the coastline with a group of stoners in a pedo-van.

"Sissy has a boyfriend!" Maddie announces proudly. She's got marinara sauce smeared around her cheeks, and she's talking with her mouth full.

"Maddie, shut up!" I frown at her. I'm sitting at the table, but I'm not eating. I don't trust the weird color the sauce turned after I took the lasagna out of the oven. The Littles don't seem to notice the greenish-brown color, and I have nothing else to feed them, so I don't mention it.

"Boyfriend? Who the hell would date you?" Mason teases. Mania is begging me to tell him he sounds just like his father when he says that. I don't, because that will piss him off, and he might leave before I get a chance to talk to him.

"Jesse Alford," Teddy chimes in this time.

"Okay, who the hell is that?"

Frankie sucks her teeth, annoyed as if it were a crime to not know who *Jesse Alford* is. "Only the hottest, most popular guy in the world!" She rolls her eyes.

"I mean, he's no Michael B. Jordan." I shrug.

"Mischa stole Jesse from Alyssa, who is also super pretty and popular. Her little sister hates me now," Frankie brags.

"Is that what this is about?" Mason accuses me, pointing his fork at me and flinging brown tomato sauce on the floor. I'm briefly reminded of the blood-soaked floorboards from a few months ago and shake my head violently. Mason thinks I'm shaking my head in response to his question and sucks his teeth.

He tells the Littles about the waves he caught last fall and other stupid vagabond adventures, and they tell him about going to the carnival and other mini adventures they've tagged along on with Jesse and me. After dinner, I put the Littles and Grandpa to bed, and I meet Mason outside on the deck.

He sparks up a joint and inhales deeply. "What's going on? Why'd you call me here so frantically? Ya missed me?"

I snort and pluck the joint from his fingers, taking a drag. "I need you to take over for me," I tell him after exhaling. I take another drag and repeat the process before passing it back. "I won't be able to take care of them much longer."

"Why? Seems like they did alright the last time you were gone."

"No, they didn't. Teddy started randomly wetting the bed again out of nowhere, and they lived off junk food and microwave pizza."

He hits the joint again and passes it back. "You think they're going to ship you off again? Why aren't you taking the meds?"

I shake my head as I inhale. "I'm skipping doses. I can't be doped up and take care of the kids. That's why I need your help."

Mason gives me a skeptical look. "Does this have something to do with your boyfriend? That Jesse dude?"

At this point, I'll say anything to get him to help me, and I've never been one to hesitate on a lie.

"He wants me to go to college with him."

"You want to go to college?" he scoffs, and I can tell he's still suspicious.

"I want to be with him," I reply, and it sounds so convincing that, for a moment, I think even I believe it. I'd be a complete liar if I said Jesse doesn't make me feel good. The fact that he makes me *feel* speaks volumes. When we're together, I'm at peace. Almost as peaceful as I imagine dying will bring me. And I must admit that it feels good to feel wanted for once in my life.

Yeah, Jesse is fun, but Jesse is an interruption, so I can't think too deeply about this... *thing* between us. I can, however, protect him from the evils of being Alyssa Slade's meal ticket. Jesse's going to be an amazing man in the future. He's different from the boys Grover breeds.

Too bad I won't be around to see it.

"Look, I hate to be an ass, but I can't be here with him." Mason sighs. I find the first part of that statement unbelievable. Being an ass is second nature for Mason. "Besides, I'm not their dad. Hell, you're not their mom. We don't have to raise them."

"Then who will? Maddie's five, Mason, she—"

"Exactly!" he cuts me off. "I'm barely an adult myself. I can't raise a five-year-old, an eight-year-old, and a twelve-year-old!"

"Teddy's nine now. His birthday was last week. You missed it. There was cake," I respond dryly, partly because I'm pissed and partly because that's just me.

Mason is nineteen. He's right, he can't raise the Littles. He can barely take care of himself. But in fifty days, I'll be dead, so they've got a better chance with him than with me.

"I can't do it, Mischa. Michelle and Joe aren't going to just give them to me, anyway. Sorry, but you'll just have to figure something else out."

He gets up and goes inside the house, letting the screen door crash behind him.

So much for that plan.

Chapter Thirty-Eight

JESSE

Before I started spending all my free time with Mischa, my Sunday routine revolved around tinkering with the GTO at Clement's garage. Gramps and I would order parts to be delivered to the garage, and then use Clement's tools to upgrade and fix up my car. It was my way of keeping a piece of Gramps with me after he died. Since Mischa's been a little preoccupied this weekend, I revisited the old tradition.

That's what I'm doing now. Under my car finishing up an oil change, when I hear gravel crunching. I look over and spot a pair of worn-out Chuck Taylors, the right one impatiently tapping.

I roll out from under the car on one of Clement's creepers and there's Mischa, clad in her favorite shorts and a tank top like it's not fifty-two degrees outside. It's cloudy, and she's wearing sunglasses. The arrow necklace I gave her for Christmas is resting against her chest. She hasn't taken it off since I gave it to her.

"Well, aren't you going to stand up and greet me?" I give a little snort, but oddly enough, I do as I'm told. I stand in front of her with my arms folded, smirking at her.

"You didn't call." The way she says it doesn't make me feel like she actually cares. Something catches my eyes just past her head. Teddy and Maddie are walking out of the bookstore with the same guy I saw Mischa walking through town with yesterday. I've never seen him before, so I doubt he's from Grover. I fix my gaze back on Mischa. I'm jealous, but I'm trying not to show it.

"What's your problem?" She frowns, but almost like she's confused. I don't respond, but my damn jealousy forces my eyes to cut back to the grungy-looking guy walking into The Strip with Mischa's little brother and sister. I recall a conversation with Alyssa a couple of months ago. *"She said you were temporary, Jesse!"* I wrote it off as Alyssa's manipulative ways. Now I wonder if she was on to something.

Mischa follows my gaze. "What? Mason?" To my surprise, she turns back around to face me and she's grinning. "Gross! You think I'm fucking Mason?"

My eyes bulge. "What? No. I—"

"I would never fuck Mason! He probably got a tiny—" I clamp my hands over her mouth and drag her away from the garage. The other guys working at Clement's are trying to stifle their laughter. I doubt anyone actually gets shocked by anything Mischa does anymore.

She squirms out of my hold and stands in front of me with her hands on her hips. There's oil smeared across her cheek where I covered her mouth, but she doesn't seem to notice or mind.

"You seemed preoccupied yesterday," I tell her with a shrug. She puts her hand up and grimaces as if to say, *"No more."*

"Mason Little is Joe's oldest son. The Littles' big brother. My stepbrother. I don't know what kind of porn you're into, Jesse Alford, but I would never!"

"Can you chill with all the vulgarities? People are staring at us," I tell her with a nervous laugh.

"So now you care what people think again?" she asks me, feigning hurt. At least I think she's faking. Her eyes are hidden behind her sunglasses, but her moods seem to jump around like that with ease.

"No, I just think it's a little inappropriate to talk like that on a Sunday afternoon."

She starts playing with the fringe in her cut-off shorts and digging her foot in the gravel. "Well, if you don't want people to see us, we can always go up the mountain."

I look down at my oily coveralls. "I need to change first."

Mischa reaches up and strokes her thumb across my cheek, wiping away some oil on my face. "I think it's kind of sexy."

I can't help but laugh at her words. I reach out and do the same to her cheek, only I make it worse. It causes her to smile even more, though. "I'll go home and shower, then meet you up there later."

"Don't keep me waiting. It's cold up there." She winks and then turns on her heels and heads down Main.

This thing with Mischa, it's fun. It's exciting and I'm a teenager with hormones and whatnot, so her frisky attitude is definitely a turn-on.

But sometimes I feel like I'm in over my head with Mischa. Like I'm on some kind of ride, and she's the one in control of the brakes. Not that I want things to stop. I just want to know what these feelings mean.

I wake up at 6:15 on the morning of my eighteenth birthday. It's a weekday, so the biggest plan I have is going to school and sitting through seven lectures while girls pass me *'Happy Birthday'* notes, and I anticipate my friends' birthday punches.

My phone pings, signaling that I've received a text message. I grab it off my nightstand and read the message.

Mischa: We're not going to school today. Make a left on Main and pick me up.

I chuckle and roll onto my back with the phone above my face.

Jesse: I've got a calc quiz today.

Mischa: You've already been accepted into college. Who cares? Stop being a wimp. You're a MAN now Jesse Alford.

Jesse: What are we going to do instead?

Mischa: Just pick me up outside of the middle school at 7:38.

Jesse: Why 7:38?

Mischa: Dammit Jesse! Just meet me there!

I sigh and roll out of bed. I take a shower before meeting my mom and dad downstairs for breakfast. My mom always cooks a huge breakfast on birthdays. Pancakes and waffles, eggs, bacon, sausage, toast, and potatoes. She calls it *Jesse's Choice'* because when I was a kid, I changed my favorite breakfast food every week. Some weeks I wanted pancakes, other weeks, I wanted waffles and toast. I guess she got tired of guessing. Mom is creative like that.

"My birthday boy is a man now." She smiles as she kisses my cheek and sets the table.

"Thanks, Mom."

"This is just the beginning! I want you to text me what you want for dinner. Whatever you want, I'll go pick it up and have it ready for dinner."

My dad is reading emails on his phone, but he puts it down and winks at me as I take a seat at the table. "Happy birthday, son."

"Thanks, Dad." I nod back. I feel guilty, sitting at the table with them, knowing that I'm about to ditch school to spend my birthday with my girlfriend, whom they aren't very fond of.

"Honestly, Mom, whatever you make for dinner will be fine."

"But it's your last birthday at home. It has to be special," she protests.

I give her an appreciative smile. When I leave in a few months, she'll be alone. My dad is always in Sacramento working, and even though I'm usually out with my friends, I'm still *here.* After I move away, I wonder what she'll do to fill the void. That thought immediately makes me think of Mischa, and the void that separating will cause in both of our lives. She acts nonchalant, but I know the time she spends being a normal teenager with me has to mean something. Is she really just going to sit around and raise her siblings after the summer ends?

She's got to have more of a plan than that.

I make it to the middle school at 7:37 a.m., and Mischa stands outside the car in the cold until the minute changes.

"Early or late, I can't win," I comment as she flops down into the passenger seat. She doesn't respond, just points to Main Street in the direction that takes us out of Grover. Once we're outside of town, I decide to ask her where we're going, even though I know she's not going to respond with a simple answer. I'm learning that Mischa is all about the mystery of life.

To my surprise, she proves me wrong.

"Sonora. Snow tubing."

"Snow tubing?" I furrow my brow in amusement.

She looks at me with a sly smile. "You got something else in mind?" She shimmies in her seat, and I laugh.

"No, I just didn't expect you to answer, and I didn't expect that answer."

"Just don't tell the Littles. They'll be jealous," she tells me before leaning across the console and kissing my cheek. A warmth grows in my chest, and I don't try to fight the smile that spreads across my face.

"Just one more time!" Mischa pleads. I've just checked my rental tube back in, and she's stubbornly holding on to hers.

"We've been out here for almost three hours, Misch. We've got to get back."

She pouts and I'm a sucker for her pouty face, but I have to show some restraint. "Just one last round?"

"I already checked my tube in." I point to the shack where the white-haired woman is watching our exchange with humor in her smile.

"We can both go on mine. We've been racing all day. Let's just do one together. Then we'll leave. I promise!"

I sigh and fold my arms across my chest. Mischa's begging me. Mischa never begs. Usually, it's hard to tell if she even actually likes me. How can I honestly say no to her like this?

"*One*," I hold up my index finger, "and then we're going home."

She claps and jumps twice before grabbing my hand and dragging me away from the rental booth and back to the snowy hills. She chooses the highest one, and we wait in the short line. When it's our turn, I sit in the tube first and then Mischa flops down on my lap.

"You should hold the handles." The attendant tells Mischa, motioning to the plastic handles on either side of the giant round tube. He motions to me. "And you can hold on to her and stabilize you both."

I wrap my arms around her slender torso and pull her against me so that her back is flush against my chest. She tilts her head up and smiles at me. It's a smile I rarely see from her, but one that I'm sure she doesn't give to anyone else.

"Hold me tight." Her instructions are almost a whisper. I tighten my hold on her. The feeling of her relaxing in my arms makes my heartbeat quicken before our descent downhill even begins. I nuzzle my face into the crook of her neck. This moment with Mischa feels like forever. Like we're on the same page and we could actually work out. No hateful classmates, no overbearing parents, no Littles to look after. Just two teenagers in love.

In love...

The attendant braces his foot on the back of the snow tube and pushes us down the hill. The cold wind whips around us, and Mischa's relaxed body tenses again, but I'm still stuck on my self-declaration. I love this girl. For the first time, I realize that what I'm feeling is *love*. For all of her mood swings and strange behavior, Mischa is the only person I've ever felt comfortable around. She expects nothing from me. She just lets me be me. Teenage hormones aside, something has to be said about how we're only truly comfortable when we're alone together.

We've spent months navigating this weird relationship we have. She won't kiss me, or even talk to me sometimes, in public. Sometimes she'll randomly crawl through my bedroom window, not caring if my parents are home. I got into the habit of locking my bedroom door after my mom came home while Mischa was lying in my bed. She skillfully tumbled through the window, and in a rush of risky judgment, turned around and hoisted herself back through it, refusing to leave unless I gave her a kiss goodbye. She was out the window again milliseconds before my mom opened the door.

And then there are the nights at our secret spot.

Those are the nights we spend wrapped up in a blanket in the backseat of the GTO, talking about anything. I do most of the talking, I guess, but Mischa soaks it all in and it's great to have someone that I can be vulnerable with. When she does feel like opening up to me, she tells me stories about her dad and their life together before he died.

Throughout it all, Mischa's behavior hasn't gotten any less strange. If anything, she's gotten stranger. Her mood swings are sudden, and she still talks to herself like she's done since we were kids. But even that is something I love about her. She's *her*. Her entire life, everyone has told her how she should act, and Mischa doesn't care. She continues to be Mischa.

And that's what I love. I love Mischa.

The descent down the hill is only about thirty seconds long, and as we slide across the base of the hill, my lips find the corner of Mischa's mouth and I kiss her softly. She turns her head and molds her full lips with mine. Even after the tube bumps against a tree and completely stops, the kiss isn't broken. Our tongues wrestle with each other, and when she releases a brief moan, I want to tell her how I feel.

It's not until we hear the screams of the next couple sharing a tube behind us that we stand and move out of the way. I press another chaste kiss to her lips.

"This has been the best birthday ever," I breathe against her mouth.

"Yeah." Her breaths come out in white puffs. "Well, this was only part one."

I drop Mischa off at the elementary school since she declines my offer to drive her and the Littles home. My mom texted me asking me to pick up my birthday cake from the bakery on my way home from school. I'm walking to the door of the bakery when I hear my full name being called out.

"Hey! Jesse Alford." It's the guy I saw walking with the Littles on Sunday. Their oldest brother, Mason. He's walking toward me with a swagger that suggests he's angry, but I think he just has an aggressive exterior. Maybe the effects of having the town drunk as a biological parent?

"Is it true?" he asks me.

I frown, turning to face him. "Is what true?"

"Mischa says you're going off to some fancy college, and you're taking her with you," he huffs. His hands are shoved into the pockets of his hoodie and he stands before me, tapping his foot impatiently. *What is he talking about?* I'm not going to a fancy college, but those are definitely the words Mischa uses to tease me about moving to Oklahoma. Why would she tell him she was going to college with me? Is that what she wants?

A few townsfolk call out to me with birthday wishes, and I smile politely at them, but I'm still pondering Mason's question which is laced with new information about my relationship with Mischa. She wants to be with me after high school? She's making plans to move with me? I'm excited, concerned, and confused all at once. What about the Littles? Why hasn't she talked to me about this? My thoughts are interrupted by Mason's impatient grunt.

"Look, man, I don't know what you see in her. And I don't really care, but I'm not taking over for her."

I scrunch my nose in annoyance at his insult of Mischa, and confusion because I still don't know what the hell he's talking about.

"She wants me to come here and take over caring for Frankie, Teddy, and Maddie. I ain't doing that," he clarifies with another huff. "I keep telling her to let the state take them. But I'm not coming anywhere close to this town as long as Joe's around."

He's throwing more information at me than I can process because I don't think I fully understand the dynamic of the Little-Lawrence residence.

"Whatever man," Mason shrugs, "I'm out. Sorry to bust up your plans with the nutcase."

The nutcase?

I'm finished showering and redressing by the time my dad is home and dinner is ready. We sit around the table and my dad takes over the conversation as usual. This is *Jesse's Birthday Edition* though, so the topic is all about how I'll be moving away in four months, and how he's already purchased season tickets to see the Sooners play next year. To watch me play next year.

I've already made up my mind, though. I'm not leaving. It hit me on the snowy hills this morning, and again after my run-in with Mason. I don't want to leave Mischa, and Mischa can't leave her siblings. Maybe if I stay in California, we can make it work. I've got several other colleges in Northern California I could consider before I officially commit to OU. I'd be close enough to Grover to visit still and vice versa.

"Maybe we can look into UC Davis?" I croak out before I have a chance to stop myself.

My mom freezes with her fork halfway to her mouth. Her eyes are wide with concern and she looks between me and my father. Dad is calm. He takes the time to chew his steak and even sip his wine before he responds.

"Look into UC Davis for what?" he asks nonchalantly, but I know he knows what I'm talking about.

"College." I shrug. "So I can be closer to home," I add.

Now Mom sits her fork down completely, and the concern in her eyes intensifies. "Are you nervous about being away from home?"

I don't even get a chance to answer, because my dad starts laughing almost maniacally. "It's that girl."

A chill runs up my body, and I can feel my heart rate speed up like it did as I held Mischa at the top of the snowy hill. But unlike that time, it's beating in anticipation of anger. I know where this is going.

"Michael..." Mom's voice is both a warning and a plea. "Not today. Of all days, not—"

"It's a man thing," Dad cuts her off. "You see, Kels, there's something about crazy women that cause men to do crazy things. Risk their freedom and give up their future to fuck the local lunatic."

My mom gasps. I briefly see red, and I stand up from the table. My dad follows suit and now we're two titans, about to wage war at the dinner table again. Only this time, I have no more restraint left.

"If you think I'm going to let you throw your life away after everything we've worked for, you're as crazy as that little whore you're chasi—"

My fist meets his teeth, and I feel the skin split before he even finishes the statement.

"JESSE!" my mom screams, but I keep advancing on my father, who is now lying on the floor holding his busted lip. I grab him by the collar of his shirt, preparing to hit him again, but my mother grabs me from behind. This leaves my father the perfect opening to backhand me so hard across the face that I know it's going to bruise. The slap stuns me, causing me to fall backward against my mom on the floor.

"Stop it! Both of you!" My mom cradles me in her arms to console me after the blow of my father's slap, but also to hold me back from retaliating. "Michael, if you hit my son one more time, I swear!"

My dad stands and wipes the blood from his mouth. For a moment I think he's going to hit me again, anyway, but he reaches past me and pulls my mother to her feet, forcing her to leave me sitting on the floor.

"Jesse just... wait there." Mom holds her hands up, motioning for me to stay seated on the kitchen floor as she follows my father out of the dining room. As soon as she leaves, I'm off the floor and pushing out the side door, heading to my car.

Mischa is already at our spot when I arrive. She told me to meet her here later for what she calls "part two" of my birthday surprise. I wasn't supposed to be here for another hour. She's wearing a thin white sleeveless dress. She looks angelic, but it's below freezing. I'm reminded of all the times she's dressed opposite of the weather this past winter. She's no stranger to being barefoot in the snow or wearing shorts and tank tops when it's thirty or below.

The roaring of the GTO's engine should announce my arrival, but she doesn't turn around. She just sits on the edge of the cliff and stares out at the endless tree line below. I'm also reminded of the feeling I get every time she sits like that.

Like she's thinking about jumping.

Chapter Thirty-Nine

46

I 'm staring out at the dense tree lines below the cliff I love so much when I hear Jesse's GTO come through the clearing. This place—*this view*—is so peaceful. Something beautiful will happen here, but my brain is fuzzy on the details because Jesse's here and my body is buzzing with the need to feel him. The need to feel has always been a yearning for me all my life. Jesse fulfills that need. When he kissed me today, my body caught fire. Not even the chills that covered my body could combat it. I was fire and ice. My body was calm and electric all in one. So many feelings at once. It's overwhelming since I'm not used to feeling anything. Nevertheless, it's so blissful.

I stand when he cuts the engine, and I hear his boots crunching against the frozen leaves as he approaches me. I can feel his aura warming my skin as he gets closer. I smile and bite my lip before speaking.

"My Juliet."

"Juliet?" There's amusement in his voice, and I know he's smiling without looking at him.

"Yep. I'm Romeo in this affair." I grin, still looking out at the setting sun over the cliff.

"Care to elaborate? I don't really see how I'm the thirteen-year-old girl in this scenario."

No, Jesse is definitely all man, and we're about to climb into that backseat as a reminder. I shake my head and quote, "Sin from thy lips? O trespass sweetly urged! Give me my sin again."

Jesse is standing right behind me as I say this, so I spin around and reach for his face to draw him into a kiss. When I turn to him, my eyes land on the bruise forming next to his left eye.

"Jesse, what the fuck happened to your eye?" I lightly run my finger over the welting skin, and he winces slightly. He grasps my hand with his, and I see his knuckles are busted up and bleeding on the right hand. "Did you get into a fight?"

He bites his lip and stares at me, but I can't read past the intensity in his eyes. Something is wrong.

"What are your plans for us after graduation?" he asks me.

"What?" I scrunch my face and crane my head back to look at him. Even with his brooding expression and bruised eyes, he's so handsome it's almost unreal.

"I need to hear something good because this went from the best birthday in my life to the worst in a matter of seconds." His voice is breathy, and I can't tell if he's about to cry or if he's about to laugh.

"Jesse, you're bleeding, and your eye is swelling. What happened?" I tear the bottom of the white summer dress I'm wearing into a long strip of fabric and then wrap it around his knuckle.

"I punched my dad in the mouth for calling you a whore." I pause my wrapping and look up at him to gauge how truthful that statement is. He's staring at me with a blank expression. "He hit me back, and then my mom broke it up."

I shake my head and go back to tying the fabric around his hand. "Why would you do that? Why would you even talk about me to your parents?"

"Because I love you, and I want to be with you."

I feel like someone has punched me hard in the chest, knocking my soul from my stupid, weak body. My head spins, and I absently take a step back from him. This isn't happening.

This isn't happening.

"You want to come with me when I leave, but you can't, because of the Littles," he continues. He inspects the makeshift medical wrap I've performed, and I see that it's already staining with his blood.

"Who—who told you that?" I frown. I suddenly don't want to feel anymore because my heartbeat hurts. It's beating too fast, too hard.

"Mason. He said you want to go with me, but he's not going to take over caring for the Littles."

"Jesse..." I can barely hear him over my heart pounding in my eardrums. I do hear something else. Something I haven't heard in months.

Laughing. Dry, hysterical laughing.

"I told my dad I wanted to stay in California. Maybe go to UC Davis. It's only a few hours away and—"

Fergal's climbing over the cliff now. The last time I saw him, he'd fallen over it. He'd... fallen over...

The cliff...

"Oi, you forgot about our plan, girl?" Fergal's laughing at me. *"I think he's got other plans. Big plans, girly."*

"Shut up." My words are directed at Fergal, but Jesse can't see Fergal, so he stops talking and looks at me with confusion and pain written all over his bruised, handsome face.

I read a quote once on the cover of a TIME magazine in the general store. *"We're not frayed at the edges—we're ripped at the damn seams!"* The article was about U.S. war tactics in Central Africa, but right now I relate that quote to me and Jesse. Our relationship isn't some small, teenage puppy love gone wrong. It was a huge building mess of a mistake that has led us to this very moment. I recite another appropriate quote as I stare at Jesse's desperate brown eyes.

" *'Go confidently in the direction of your dreams. Live the life you have always imagined,'* Henry David Thoreau."

"Dreams change. And now mine is to be here with you." His rebuttal comes with no hesitation. No second thought.

"Jesse, go to college. You can't stay here for me because I—" *I'm not going to be here.*

"Tell him, girly. They'll have you up at the looney bin in no time."

"Shut... up!" I snap at Fergal.

"I didn't even say anything." Jesse's frown deepens, and he holds out his arms in frustration. I eye the bloody bandage made of my dress. He's hurt, and he's fighting with his parents because of me. All I wanted was to keep him away from Alyssa. I just wanted to pass the time until I left here. And now...

Now, he thinks he's in love with me.

"I thought you felt something too, Misch."

"You don't feel. You can't feel. Stupid boy thinks you feel."

"Fergal, shut the hell up!" I scream at the top of my lungs, and Jesse startles and backs away from me. There's more distance between us now than there's been in the past four months.

"Fergal?" he questions. He's staring at me and running his uninjured hand through his twists. "Mischa, what's going on?"

My breathing turns shallow, and I struggle against my labored breaths as Fergal skips circles around us.

"Tell him what's happening! Tell him! Tell him! Tellhimtellhimtellhim!" he sings obnoxiously.

Tears spring in my eyes, and I continue to gasp for breaths. "Fergal, please shut up. Stop it!" I swat at him as he passes me.

"Mischa, are you okay?" Jesse's voice pulls my attention to him. He's stopped backing away from me, and now he's approaching slowly. Like I'm a wild animal. A mountain lion.

"Jesse. Just go." I don't know if I mean for him to leave the cliff, or if I'm still talking about his decision to stay in California after graduation.

"Mischa, I—"

"Just leave! Jesse. You need to leave!"

"I'm sorry, Mischa. I—I didn't know—I didn't mean to upset you." He doesn't even know why he's apologizing. He did nothing wrong.

Fergal walks over and stands in Jesse's face, mocking his words and blowing raspberries. I attempt to push him away, but I only end up awkwardly pushing Jesse instead.

"What is going on, Mischa?" He grabs my waist in an attempt to stop me from fighting off what he sees as thin air, and I see as Fergal.

Fergal sidesteps me and runs around to the edge of the cliff again. I turn out Jesse's grasp to follow, but Jesse grabs my hand.

"*Remember this?*" Fergal says before diving off the side of the cliff like an Olympic gold medalist. "See you in forty-six days."

Forty-six days.

I pull away from Jesse and drop to my knees. There's too much stimulation. I'm not used to seeing Fergal and feeling the fire and ice that Jesse brings. It's too much. I don't notice I'm screaming until Jesse backs away.

"Just go..." I beg him, and he runs away from me.

Chapter Forty

JESSE

When I make it home, the house is silent. My mom is curled up on the couch, and the chocolate cake she had me pick up earlier is sitting on the coffee table untouched. There are eighteen unlit candles perfectly lining it. My father is nowhere to be found.

"I'm sorry," I tell her hoarsely.

She looks at my bruised face and then looks away quickly, shaking her head and biting back tears.

"Where were you?" she asks me calmly. "I told you to stay put."

"I was up on the mountain... with Mischa." Just saying her name causes a shiver to run down my spine. I don't know what that was up there. She completely lost her mind. That was a part of Mischa I've never seen. Even when she does weird stuff like talk to herself and laugh at nothing, she's never that intense. It was... scary. And who the hell is Fergal?

Maybe Mason was lying to me? Maybe Mischa never wanted to go away with me. Maybe everything in the past four months meant nothing to her.

My mom sighs. "Let's just light the candles and try to salvage what's left of your birthday." She picks up the lighter next to the cake on the table, and I sit on the floor across from her. The light from the candle flickers in the dim room. Mom stares at my eye before reaching out and stroking the bruised skin the same way Mischa did before things went to shit.

"I don't have any voice left, so no song this year. Just make a wish."

I want to call Mischa. Maybe I should go back to the mountain and check on her. What if she was having some type of panic attack? That's it. A panic attack. She was having a panic attack. My declaration of love was probably just too much. I'll tell her it was the truth, but that we can take it slow if that's too much for her.

I'm inhaling a big breath to blow the candle out when a knock sounds on the front door. I make a quick wish for clarity on this situation with Mischa, then blow out all the candles before standing to answer the door.

It's Sheriff Freeman.

"Jesse, happy birthday, son." He's regarding me with caution, so I know he didn't come all the way over here to wish me a happy birthday.

"Thanks," I eye him suspiciously. "What's going on?"

"What happened to your eye, Jesse?" Sheriff Freeman surveys my face, and then his eyes roll down my body until they fall on my hand and the dried blood staining the fabric wrapped around it. "And your hand."

I whip around to my mom and frown at her in disbelief. "You called the sheriff on me?"

Mom stands and comes to my side. "I didn't call him. What's going on, Moe?" She directs the last part to the sheriff.

"Jesse, Deputy Rodgers said he heard a disturbance up the mountain. Then, he saw Mischa Lawrence running down the trail, crying. Said her dress was all ripped up and bloody."

My mom takes in a sharp breath and shakes her head. "Nope. You aren't doing this without a lawyer present. How could you—"

Sheriff Freeman puts his hand up and interrupts my mom politely. "Kels, you know I'd never do anything to hurt Jesse. This isn't *that*." He pauses and looks past us with a knowing expression. "Plus, it looks like we've got a lawyer present." We both turn and find my father leaning on the threshold of the entrance to our living room. Even with his busted lip, he's still smirking.

"Anyone want to tell me about the busted lips and bruised eyes?" Sheriff Freeman's eyes land on mine again, but my father speaks up, and he immediately diverts his eyes back to him.

"You aren't here to investigate a family dispute between me and *my son*, Moe Freeman. You're here about the Lawrence girl. Let's stick to that." Dad scoffs, and he shakes his head. "I knew this was going to happen."

"Like I said, it's not that type of visit. I just need Jesse to tell me what happened up there," Sheriff Freeman tries to reason, but my dad keeps talking.

"That girl's bloody dress. Is it white?" He's asking Sheriff Freeman, but I'm the one who really knows. I nod at the same time the sheriff does.

"Jesse left out of here after our fight with a bloody hand. He came back with it wrapped in white fabric. Do your job, Freeman," my father arrogantly spits.

"Jesse, you're eighteen now. I don't need your parents' permission to question you. Can you step out and talk to me, son?"

"I don't like this, Michael." Mom looks back at Dad, who advances toward us.

"Jesse..." There's a warning in his voice. Not a threat, but a lawyer's warning. "*Don't say anything incriminating.*"

"Mischa's not hurt. I haven't even spoken to her. This isn't an accusation of anything." There is sincerity in Sheriff Freeman's eyes. I've always been able to trust Trey's dad. More than I've trusted my own. I nod and follow Sheriff Freeman outside and down our driveway. My parents stand at the door, so we walk to the back of the GTO for more privacy.

"Jesse, how was Mischa when you saw her tonight?"

"She was fine." I shrug.

"Jesse..."

"She was," I press him to believe me. "Earlier at least. We ditched school and went snow tubing. It—she was fine. Better than fine. She was laughing and kissing me and smiling. We were good."

"And then what?" Sheriff Freeman doesn't seem phased by my admission of ditching.

"I got into a fight with my dad. I told him I didn't want to leave California. He insulted Mischa and I—"

"Are you okay? Did he hurt you?" His words are weighted with more sincerity. He's here on behalf of Mischa, but he cares enough about me to make sure I'm alright after my dad blacked my eye.

I nod. "I went to the clearing up the mountain where we always hang, and Mischa was there waiting. I told her my plans to stay here to be with her and she..." I stop because I don't even know how to put it into words. I don't even know what Mischa was doing.

"She what?" Sheriff Freeman urges me.

"She just started screaming *'shut up.'* I thought she was talking to me, but then she started getting hysterical and calling me Fergal, and she was fighting the air. She just went..."

Crazy.

"Jesse, are you sure you're okay here tonight?" Sheriff Freeman looks toward my house and glares at my father.

"Yeah, I'll be fine." I nod. "What about Mischa? Is she—"

"I'll handle Mischa. In the meantime, you should probably keep your distance from her. Just until things... cool off." There's a lie somewhere hidden in his words, but I don't challenge him. He leaves in his truck, and I go back into my house.

"If I hear about you going anywhere near that girl again, there will be consequences." My father's threat lands on deaf ears as I pass them both and head straight into my room.

Chapter Forty-One

45

Fergal's voice is still echoing in my ears as I sneak into the school today. I wanted to stay home to avoid Jesse, but I couldn't risk the sheriff showing up and experiencing mania during a truancy check. I can't tell if Fergal's voice is a memory or if he's somewhere in the empty hallway. After performing a twisting dive off the side of the cliff, Fergal followed me home, taunting me. I spent the entire night lying in bed with a pillow clamped over my head to drown him out. I didn't even feed the Littles breakfast. When I finally pulled the pillow away from my head this morning, they had already dressed themselves and walked to school.

A poster on the wall catches my eye as I make my way to class. It's a prom poster. I'm transported back to the night of the winter formal when Jesse joked about taking me to prom. The theme is *Enchanted Forest*.

The date is April 13th.

It would have been a nice last hurrah for Jesse and me before I died. Too bad he'll probably never talk to me again. I could tell by the way he peeled out of the clearing last night that he was terrified. I don't even know what to say to him when I see him today. I've never endured a breakup before. Is this even a breakup? Was Jesse Alford ever really my boyfriend?

"You won't be stepping foot into prom, so stop gawking at that fucking poster."

The voices in my head are right. I need to spend that last night tying up any loose ends before I die. Hell, maybe breaking up with Jesse will finally allow me some time to get the Littles ready for my absence. Frankie will need to step up since Mason is a deadbeat, just like his father. Teddy's wetting the bed again, so I need to get that figured out because Frankie won't be as nice as I am. Someone needs to show Maddie how to tie her shoes and wash her own hair. I'm sure Frankie can handle that. But then there's Frankie, herself. I can't teach her how to handle her first real heartbreak because maybe I did love Jesse Alford, and I'm numb to the realization that he's not my boyfriend anymore.

"You think Jesse really cares about you? You're just an easy fuck."

Mom can't teach Frankie about love. She left the only good man who ever cared about her and married Joe Little, a drunk who hates her child and neglects his children. Hell, *she* neglects her children. Frankie will have to find her own way. The same way I did after I lost my dad. She'll have to choose Frankie in a way that I wasn't allowed to choose Mischa. In forty-five days, Mischa will choose Mischa.

"Bitch, are you ignoring me?" I'd thought that the voice I was hearing was a newbie in my head who'd manifested in all the chaos. But there's actually a person standing behind me as I stare at the prom poster with the knockoff Sleeping Beauty silhouette. It's mimicking Aurora and Prince Phillip dancing in the woods. Frankie used to love that scene when we would watch the old DVDs I'd brought with me from Monterey.

A hand grips my arm so tightly that I should be yelping, but ever since Jesse told me he loved me, I've started losing the sensation of touch again. The hand pulls me and turns me around before slamming me against the poster-covered wall hard. I don't feel the pain, but I do lose my breath before I can register that it's Preston Wilcox assaulting me.

"First my brother, and now Jesse. You're a real fucking piece of work, Lawrence." Spit flies from his mouth as he grunts the words out in my face.

My chest rises and falls as I try to catch my breath. "What—what are you talking about?"

He doesn't answer me, he just keeps on his tangent as if I'm following along. "But you know, that's what Jesse gets for ditching his friends to fuck with you."

Once I've recovered from the blow against the wall, I attempt to sidestep him, but he just blocks me in with his arm. He leans in millimeters from my face, and I'm surprised to find that he actually brushes his teeth in the morning. He presses his index into the bridge of my nose and through gritted teeth tells me, "But I guess that's what it all comes down to. A dirty, nappy-haired slut like you is exactly what he wanted. There's no way Blake would have touched *you*. But Jesse? Gotta go back to his *roots*, huh?"

Preston has verbally and physically assaulted me so many times in my life I've lost count. He's called me whore, slut, bitch, and did a terrible job of mixing those insults with my name. This is the first time he's ever gotten blatantly racist—at least, to my face.

I'm so stunned by his words, and he's still staring at me menacingly, that neither of us notices we aren't alone until Preston is stumbling sideways from a blow to the side of his face. He holds his cheek as he tries to regain his composure, but before he can recover, Jesse grabs him by his neck and slams him against a row of lockers. He slams him so hard that the locker dents in behind Preston's head, but Jesse doesn't let up. He throws another punch that hits Preston square in the nose with a crunching sound. He's not saying words, he's just brutalizing Preston's face. He's about to throw a fourth blow when I wedge myself between the two of them, wrap my arms around Jesse's torso, and use all of my strength to push him back.

"Jesse, stop!" I scream at him as he presses against me to get to Preston again. My scream must have alerted the teachers in the nearby classrooms, because one of them roughly pulls Jesse out of my grasp and another helps Preston, who is slumped on the floor, get to the nurse.

I sit outside of the front office for half an hour waiting for Jesse to come out. The hallways fill and then empty, and I guess the gossip of Jesse breaking Preston's nose has already made its rounds. When Jesse storms out of the office, he walks past me without even a glance my way. I reach out for him, but he snatches away from me and continues to storm down the hallways.

"Jesse, wait. What's happening? Did you... did you get in trouble?" I'm chasing him down the hallway. He doesn't respond, and he doesn't stop walking. And then Sheriff Freeman rounds the corner ahead of us. Jesse stops walking and frowns.

"You're going to arrest me?" he scoffs, and my heart drops.

Words fall from my mouth because I'm so afraid of Jesse being arrested over me. "Sheriff Freeman, Preston was—he was attacking me. Jesse was just protecting—"

"I'm not here for Jesse," the sheriff cuts me off. He's looking directly past Jesse, at me. I recoil.

"C'mon, Mischa." Sheriff Freeman stops just past Jesse and stands in front of me. Behind him, Jesse's frown deepens into one of confusion as he looks at us.

"Come where? What is this?" I ask him. He reaches a hand out to me, but again I back away.

"C'mon, Mischa. This isn't the place for this conversation. Come with me." Sheriff Freeman looks exasperated, and I don't understand what is going on.

"You're arresting Mischa? For what?" Jesse asks, but Sheriff Freeman ignores him and continues to stare at me as if I've betrayed him in some way.

"Mischa, you don't want to do this here. Not in front of Jesse. Come with me and we'll talk about everything." I recognize the tone he's using. He's trying to compose himself.

"Mischa?" Jesse's voice draws my attention to him, leaving me open for Sheriff Freeman to grab my arm and pull me down the hall.

"What the hell? Let me go!" I try to use my free hand to pry his hand off my arm, but he doesn't release his grip. I buck wildly, trying to get loose from his grasp. "What the fuck are you doing? Let me go!"

"Sheriff Freeman, where are you—" Jesse doesn't get to finish his sentence because the sheriff turns around and glares at me.

"You lied to me, Mischa!" I stop fighting him and furrow my brow. Before I can ask him what the hell he's talking about, he continues to drill into me. "You're up there on that cliff yelling at things that aren't there? I went to the house. Pills missing from the bottle, but I know you're not taking them. You flushing them, huh? Oh, and the marbles? Another countdown?"

His voice becomes warped as I try to figure out a way to talk myself out of this. I'm so close to the date, I can't afford to be caught. I look back at Jesse, who looks even more confused. Sheriff Freeman's words don't make sense to Jesse because for the past few months, I've been really good at hiding the fact that I haven't been taking my meds.

"No—I've been taking them. Yesterday, we just had an argument. The marbles... they..."

Sheriff Freeman sighs and looks between Jesse and me. "Okay, Mischa. We've got two scenarios. The one rolling through town right now is that you were up on that mountain with Jesse, screaming. And then he sped home, and you walked home in tears wearing a torn-up, bloody dress. I'm sure you know what that implies."

My breath leaves me the same way it did an hour ago when Preston slammed me against the stucco wall. I think back to the torn white dress stained in Jesse's blood where he grabbed my waist. That's what Preston was talking about.

"First my brother, and now Jesse."

Only, there's a stark difference between Blake Wilcox and Jesse Alford. One that a town like Grover won't extend the same amount of grace to. To ninety percent of Grover, Jesse will become a monster if that narrative is spun.

I shake my head feverishly. "No, we were just, just—"

"Oh, I know that's not what happened." Sheriff Freeman scoffs. "So that just leaves the second scenario. The one we both know is true."

I frown and bite my lip. I pull my arm from the sheriff's grasp and turn to Jesse. His face is an amalgamation of expressions. He looks confused, frightened, and angry. I did this to him. I damaged this perfect boy. I tried to protect him from Alyssa, but I'm the one who almost ruined him. *Almost.*

I give Jesse a weak smile and nod. I nod because there's so much that I want to say to him, but I'll never get the chance. I'll never see him again. Not because I'll be dead as I hoped, but because I'll be locked away at Beacon Pointe, and he'll leave for college.

All I muster is a weak, "I'm so sorry, Jesse." And then Sheriff Freeman is guiding me out of the door with a soft grasp on my shoulder.

Sheriff Freeman doesn't take me to my house before he drives me to Beacon Pointe. He drives me straight out of town. The entire ride, I stare out of the window with tears silently streaming down my face. Just like last time, I don't get to say goodbye to my Littles. They'll come home and I won't be there. The sheriff will pick them up from school and take them home and tell them I ran away again. Hopefully, Frankie will remember to give Grandpa his meds. Mom probably won't notice I'm gone until she wakes up tomorrow. Joe's still in jail, so that's good, but Mason left town without a word before I met with Jesse last night.

But that's not why I'm crying.

I'm crying because I was so close. Six weeks away from the most important day of my life.

And I slipped up because I fell in love with Jesse Alford.

Chapter Forty-Two

Jesse

Mischa has disappeared, and next week is a game of avoidance. My dad and I avoid each other, and Sheriff Freeman avoids me. I briefly wonder if Mischa's absence from town and my text notifications is another form of avoidance, but after a week of seeing the Littles walk themselves to and from school, I get the sense that she's gone again like last time.

When I probe Trey for information, he just tells me that his dad came home late Thursday night and spent the weekend making calls. Whenever I try to catch the sheriff around town, he dodges me. I go up to our spot and sit near the cliff, hoping that Mischa will show up and we can talk about whatever is going on with us—*with her*—but she never shows.

Dinner at the Alford home now consists of me and my mom eating in front of the TV since my father has been staying at his firm in the city. I'm grateful for this avoidance because I'm not ready to apologize for hitting him, and I know he'll never apologize to me.

Preston's nose is broken, but the Wilcoxes surprisingly didn't press charges against me. Maybe they know that Preston is an asshole, and he deserved it. Maybe they didn't want to go toe-to-toe with my dad in court. Or maybe they didn't need another Wilcox boy tied up in a scandal that involved Mischa Lawrence. Seeing him pressing his finger in her face and making racist remarks. I lost it. I didn't think before I reacted. I just started swinging.

So, I spend my week-long suspension in my room, staring at my phone, trying to will Mischa to answer my texts. I scroll through the selfies we've taken in the past few weeks and the many candid shots. My favorite is one of her sitting on the cliff waiting for me. I took it back in January during a meetup. She sat on the edge of the cliff with one leg dangling off the edge, the other bent with her arms circling around it, and her chin resting on the knee. She was wearing a short dress, similar to the one she was wearing the last time I saw her, but this one was bright pink.

I miss her.

On Saturday night, after a week of missing school and ignoring calls from Alyssa, I'm hanging out with Trey at his house when his dad comes home just before dinner. Trey throws me a look that tells me not to get my hopes up—that his dad isn't giving up any information about Mischa, but I have to ask. We stop in the hallway just before entering the dining room when we hear his parents talking.

"Jesse's here. They're in Trey's room," Mrs. Freeman says to her husband. I hear a chair creak, which I assume is Sheriff Freeman flopping down at the table. He only groans in response.

"You need to tell him something, Moe," Trey's mom continues. "He and Trey both deserve to know."

Know what? I turn toward Trey, who shrugs.

"Yeah, I know... I just..." Sheriff Freeman trails off. I know it has something to do with Mischa and my heart drops in fear of something happening to her.

"Trey! Jesse! Get in here." We both jump at the sheriff's booming voice. We stand there for a few seconds before rounding the corner, so as not to make it obvious that we were eavesdropping.

"Yeah, Dad?" Trey says as we enter the room.

Sheriff Freeman sighs and shakes his head. "Sit down. I need to talk to you two about something."

We both sit across from Sheriff Freeman, while Mrs. Freeman stands in the kitchen with a pensive face. Whatever this is about, it's bad. I've never seen Mrs. Freeman show anything less than a smile. Sheriff Freeman looks tired, his beard looks fuller than usual, and I can tell something has been bothering him ever since that day he escorted Mischa out of the school. His eyes land on mine, and I can't read the look he's giving me. Sadness? Regret?

"After Jesse described his interaction with Mischa, I immediately knew what was going on. I knew it was risky letting you two get so close, but I thought maybe it was a good sign. I don't—" He drops his hand and rubs his temple. I'm still confused. Nothing he just said makes any sense.

"Moe..." Mrs. Freeman encourages him to just get whatever is on his chest out. She walks over and rubs his back.

He sighs and looks at us again. "Remember when I told you that Mischa's father and I were friends?" We both nod immediately. "He'd made me promise to take care of Mischa because she's..." He trails off again and I find myself growing irritated. What could be so hard to say?

"Mischa is... sick," he says through a deep breath. He shakes his head and scratches his beard.

"Like how? Like she's got cancer or something?" I blurt out, because what are the odds that my life is playing out like those young adult bestsellers that Alyssa and Chelsea pass around?

Sheriff Freeman shakes his head. "She's schizophrenic. And bi-polar."

His words hit me in a strange way. I want to say *"That's it? That's what all the mystery is about?"* But then it hits me again that what everyone says about Mischa is true. She's not just some weird girl with too much on her plate. She's actually sick with a condition that labels her as *crazy*. I think back to everything I've witnessed from Mischa Lawrence, not only since she's been in Grover, but especially in the months we've spent together. The way she pulled the knife out on that guy in Archerville, or how she told Alyssa she'd *'gut her.'* The way she'd talk to herself, or swat at things that weren't there. Had I really been dating some Norman Bates-type of girl?

Then, I picture her crying as she carried Teddy's limp body in the rain the night of his asthma attack. She looked so small and vulnerable as we sat in the diner that night. Not the face of a girl who'd kill unsuspecting hotel guests.

"Is that why she's always dressing weird and talking to herself?" Trey asks, and his parents narrow their eyes at him.

"Maybe she just dresses the way she likes," his dad says. "But she is known to have severe mood swings, and that may affect how she dresses. As for the… other part. Yeah, son. Mischa has hallucinations. She'll see and hear things that aren't there."

My mind flashes back to the cliff. *Fergal.*

"Don't they have, like, meds for that?" I ask, finally finding my voice.

Again, Sheriff Freeman sighs. "That's the problem, Jesse. Mischa hasn't been taking her meds. She's been flushing them every morning since she's been back."

"Back from where? Where is she now?" I ask.

"Beacon Pointe Mental Health Facility."

"That's where she goes when she disappears? She's in the crazy house?" I practically shout. I don't mean to be disrespectful, but I'm scared. I'm confused. How didn't I know that Mischa was… like this? I thought she was just weird. I could get past that. I *did* get past that.

"Hey!" Sheriff Freeman points at me sternly. "We don't use that word. Not about Mischa. She's sick, not crazy."

"I—I don't mean it like that. I just…" Now I'm the one with no words for how I feel.

Sheriff Freeman releases a deep breath. "I know, Jesse. And I'm sorry. I should have intervened when I saw that you two were getting close."

Would I have let him intervene? I cared for Mischa. I liked her—loved her. Would I have allowed Sheriff Freeman to keep us from being together?

"How long is she gone for? Will I be able to see her before I leave?" *Before I leave.* Because that's all it took for me to make up my mind about leaving California and leaving Mischa, I guess.

Sheriff Freeman shakes his head. "You boys can't tell your friends about this. You can't tell anyone." Again, Trey and I nod our heads in unison. "Mischa isn't coming home for a long time. When she's not on her meds she…" His voice cracks, and for a moment, I think he's about to cry. Mrs. Freeman massages her husband's shoulders reassuringly. He swallows hard and clears his throat, regaining his composure. "When Mischa's off her meds, she starts a countdown."

"A countdown?" Trey asks looking over at me. I shrug and turn back to his dad with furrowed brows.

"A countdown until she attempts suicide."

My heart falls into my stomach and my breath leaves me. I shake my head. Mischa may be weird, and yeah, her mood swings were off the charts, but she wouldn't do anything to hurt the Littles. She loved them too much to kill herself. She had mentioned multiple times that they didn't have anyone else besides her.

"She wanted to go with me," I blurt out. I don't know why. But I do. Mischa was planning to go away with me, right? Or at least that's what I thought for about four hours. Until she freaked out on me on the cliff. Was this the real reason that she wanted Mason to stick around for the Littles? Because she planned to...

"She's done it before." Sheriff Freeman's voice brings my attention from the faded wooden table back to him. "That's where she was all summer and the beginning of the school year. She was at Beacon Pointe, recovering from a suicide attempt that almost killed Teddy too."

"I thought she ran away." Trey's voice is smaller than I've ever heard it. He's never been friends with Mischa, but I think the realization that everyone's been treating her like shit her entire life over something she can't control is getting to him. It's certainly seeping in through all the shock and confusion I'm feeling.

"No, son. I took her to Beacon Point, just like I did last week. And she has to stay there until we can figure out how to keep her safe."

The Freemans offer to let me stay the night, but I want to be alone, so I go home. Sheriff Freeman tells me that he understands that I'll need to talk to my parents about Mischa's condition and offers to come over and explain it to them. I decline, telling him I don't want to tell my parents about this.

That night I lie in my bed and watch as the movie that is the last four months with Mischa plays out from my subconscious onto the ceiling. I have so many questions. More questions than I'm sure Sheriff Freeman has the answers to.

It wasn't supposed to be like this. I was supposed to be a teenager on the cusp of adulthood experiencing his first serious romance. Our biggest obstacle was supposed to be that she was an outsider. Our version of the classic "geek-to-chic" high school flicks from the 90s. Romeo and Juliet, though Mischa swears our roles were reversed.

When I think about moments like our bridal-style kiss at the winter formal or our first kiss in the Gravity House, it's hard to pair that Mischa with the one that Sheriff Freeman claims is planning to kill herself. Not that I can blame her. Mischa's life has been hell for someone her age. Her mom is a no-show, her stepdad is an asshole, and when she isn't raising her little siblings, she's being bullied all over town. Maybe that's why she wants to die.

Whatever. It doesn't matter anymore. She's gone now, and I'll be leaving in a few months. I decide to push Mischa to the back of my mind. I'll go back to life pre-Mischa and try to finish my school year without any more incidents.

Mischa will be a thing that happened. A small part of my younger years that I can look back on and tell frat boys about in college. Or maybe my therapist. I have a feeling it won't be easy getting over my first heartbreak with a girl I shouldn't have been dating in the first place. A breakup that happened because she got sent to a mental hospital.

I guess it's better than breaking up because she's dead.

Chapter Forty-Three

JESSE

Trey's girlfriend's grandmother died, and the funeral is the same day as prom. Since he's dateless, and I've been dodging Alyssa for weeks, we decide to show up together. I encourage Dillon Scoops to ask Alyssa to prom to ease the stress of having to turn her down for two social events in one school year.

The prom is tonight. It's been six weeks since I've seen Mischa. In those weeks, I haven't spoken to the Littles either. I see them in town after school, Frankie trying her hardest to wrangle Maddie, while Teddy hides in the Old-man's bookstore. I've still never seen their mother in town, and who knows if Grandpa is getting his meds and eating the way Mischa wanted him? Not that any of that is my concern. It wasn't supposed to be Mischa's burden either because we're kids. We should be focused on graduation and college. Not feeding children we didn't birth and caring for ailing grandparents.

I said I would stop thinking about Mischa, but I can't. During the day, I can occupy my brain by hanging out with my friends, but at night I'm scouring Google and WebMD reading everything I can about Mischa's illness. It's called schizoaffective disorder. My search history is an homage to my time with Mischa and all the peculiarities that I thought were just quirks that came along with her offbeat personality.

Does a person with schizoaffective disorder feel cold? 🔍

Does a person with schizoaffective disorder have random violent episodes? 🔍

Does a person with schizoaffective disorder dress weird? 🔍

For a few months, I had allowed myself to see a part of Mischa that no one else had bothered trying to see. The girl who smiled and cracked jokes. Who loved her siblings like a mother. Who kissed with passion and listened to me recant cheesy stories about Gramps and my childhood.

But Mischa had a secret. This disorder that no one else knows about, but that isn't much of a secret, since its effects are the only thing people can see about Mischa. That she's weird.

Different.

Crazy.

They don't know that she's sick. That she can't help it. That the things she sees and hears are real to her, just like they're real to all the other people I watch and read about in online videos and articles as I research.

I give Dillion Scoops a head nod as he passes me with Alyssa on his arm. They're heading to the dance floor. The pink dress shirt under his tuxedo jacket matches her sparkly dress. I'm wearing the same tux I wore to the winter formal because why not? Ideally, I would have been here with the girl I'd been dating for the past few months, but she's not here. Trey and I took pictures for the sake of our parents having memories of us, but neither one of us was feeling the event. We dance with a few girls but really we just stand around awkwardly waiting for the night to end. Even Neil is here with his girlfriend.

"Where's your date?" he asks me, looking around for Mischa. "She run away again?"

My gut reaction is to grab him by his collar, but I know he means no harm. For a month of weekends, he had experienced the same Mischa I had. He was the first one to admit it. *"You're actually not that bad."* He's making a joke, and he doesn't know the truth. So, I just shrug, and he goes on his way with his girl.

Later, at the mill, Preston keeps his distance from me. He's been avoiding me ever since the fight. The rest of our friends don't have to choose sides because I only hang out with Trey and sometimes Nick. Mischa entered my life like a hurricane, and the aftermath has been category five. I'm just doing what I can to coast until graduation.

Zoey finds me sitting on one of the conveyor belts. Nick is behind her, both of them dressed in black and gold.

"You're really not going to tell me where Mischa is?" she asks me for the hundredth time. She's been asking me about Mischa's whereabouts ever since she transferred back to Grover a week ago during Spring Break.

I shrug. "I don't know where she is, Zoey. We had a fight. We broke up, or whatever."

Zoey sucks her teeth. I'm not sure if she doesn't believe me or if she's just frustrated with the lack of information regarding Mischa. I understand that feeling. The week I spent not knowing where she was before Sheriff Freeman filled us in on the real Mischa Lawrence was hell.

Is that the real Mischa Lawerence? Is she really just oversized mismatched clothes and weird antics? If so, who was that with me on the cliff all those nights? Who did I make love to after the formal? Who was the girl at Winterval? The girl who was mischievously crawling through my window all winter? The girl who looked at me with so much love in her eyes at the bottom of the snow tubing hill?

Zoey is probably Mischa's only real friend besides me. Still, I don't feel comfortable telling her about Mischa's condition. Sheriff Freeman made it clear that his request to keep that information to ourselves wasn't a suggestion. She turns to Nick and pouts. I make out the words *"I'm worried about her"* over the base of the music. Nick nods his head at her, rubbing her shoulders and guiding her toward the exit of the mill. A few minutes later, Alyssa and Chelsea approach us.

"Jesse, it feels like it's been forever! We never see you anymore." Chelsea's drunk. Her straight blonde hair is falling out of its updo, and her words slur as she wraps her arms around my shoulders.

"What's up, Chels?" I chuckle and shift her body so that she's sitting next to me on the belt.

"Guess we didn't think you'd actually ditch us for... *her*..." Alyssa says. She's standing a few feet away from me, fidgeting with her nails.

I don't want to talk about Mischa with them. I don't want to even think about Mischa right now. I just want things to be normal. Everything is so confusing, like for the past four months, I've been hiding in a bubble that someone popped with a pin. I feel exposed and lost at the same time.

I wonder if this is how she felt with me.

"The bullying was never my thing, but whatever." I'm not in a place to defend Mischa, but I won't diss her either.

"Well, hopefully, we can all hang out again for the last few months we're together. We've come this far, right?" Alyssa shrugs. A knowing smile creeps across her face, and I quickly glance around the room for her date. This isn't going to go the way she's hoping. We aren't going to make up, get back together, and ride off into the sunset now that Mischa's gone. Mischa showed me that there's more to life than the fabricated one girls like Alyssa have to offer.

I'm more than Jesse Alford, the Black kid with the cool car and the football scholarship. I'm still not sure what type of person Jesse Alford is, but I know that for tonight I can enjoy a normal high school event with my closest friends—sans Preston, who is hanging with some of the other guys from school.

Tonight, I'll briefly allow myself to go back to the old way. If only for some peace of mind.

Chapter Forty-Four

There are a lot of things I fear. Mountain lions, home invasions, spiders, bats, snakes, semi-trucks as they barrel down the highway when I'm trying to hitchhike, and this one gas station attendant with a missing eye in Stockton. He hasn't really done anything to me, but he's just creepy, so I stopped going in there to pee before I'd head back home. The younger guy who works at the Chevron across the street is nicer, even though he thinks I'm a prostitute and always wants to pray for me.

But the one thing that shakes up my anxiety more than any of those things? Vomiting.

The feeling of your heart rate quickening and the clenching of your stomach. The burning in your throat and the way your esophagus restricts. The lurching and heaving. I hate it all.

I had to get over it though, because vomiting was the only way to get those pills out of my system, so that I could pretend to be zonked like the rest of my peers. Today's date kept me going. I saw the small sliver of hope that I could still make it. I just needed to stay present and get out of here. That presented two problems, though.

The first is that I'm now six months without my meds and the hallucinations are getting so intense I can't tell if they're real or not. I haven't seen Fergal in over a month. The more powerful hallucinations have kicked him out. I hate to say it, but I miss him. I have to stay in my room with the pyro girl and not react to the voices I hear or the creatures I see that aren't really there. She caught me heaving up the pill in a napkin and promised not to tell on me if I gave her the undigested pills instead of crushing them up.

The second issue is that I'm not getting out of here anytime soon. I didn't even do anything to get placed in here, besides pass a piss test, which in this case means I failed because there weren't any drugs in my system. They were looking for antipsychotics, but all they found was weed. So that left me with no other choice but to escape. I slipped out of the room after the midnight bed check and used a badge I'd swiped from a newer employee to get to the basement where I knew I could get out from the loading dock.

It's almost four in the morning when I make it to Mt. Grover. It was too risky to walk the highway, so I walked the entire trek home through the mountain woods. The hospital-issued cotton slippers are tattered and muddy, with prickly little stickers stuck to them like hitchhikers to my doom. They remind me of the slippers Jesse brought me the night of Teddy's asthma attack. The night that changed everything.

Jesse...

Beacon Pointe is north of Grover, so walking through the woods means I don't have to walk through town to get home. Instead, I find myself on the mountain trail, the melody of lions roaring as my guide. I pass the clearing, not because I've changed my mind, but because I don't want to jump off of the cliff in a flimsy hospital gown and muddy slippers. I want to look beautiful as I fall. I need to go home first.

The stickers in my house shoes are probably cutting into my heels and bottoms of my feet, but I'm so numb I can't feel anything. There's howling around me. I'm not sure if it's the wind in the trees or wolves. *Who would win out of a mountain lion and a wolf? Probably the lion? Yeah, definitely the lion.*

Further down the trail, I hear a sound that I recognize immediately. Music. It's coming from the mill. Oh yeah, last night was prom night.

I wonder what Jesse is doing? Did he go to prom? Did he take a date? Is he in the upstairs room on top of Alyssa right now?

Wolves hunt in packs, so technically, they could jump the mountain lion.

Without thinking, my body propels me toward the trail that leads to the mill. Before we made it to intake the day Sheriff Freeman took me back to Beacon Pointe, I'd slipped the necklace Jesse had given me for Christmas off my neck and placed it in my mouth. Since Sheriff Freeman had picked me up from school and driven me straight to the facility, they felt comfortable skipping the intense cavity search, so sneaking it in was easy.

Mountain lions can climb trees, so there's the element of surprise...

But when it reaches the ground, then what?

The party hasn't spilled outside of the mill yet, so I can walk over to the GTO undetected. I pull on the handle and it's unlocked, which isn't like Jesse. The interior light comes on, so I quickly slip the necklace from around my neck and drape it over the rearview mirror. It'll fit the next girl better.

The van is gone when I make it to my house. I was ecstatic to find that April 14th was also aligned with Grandpa's appointments in the city. Joe's truck isn't in the driveway, so I'm guessing he's still in jail. That means mom had to take the Littles with her, unless she left them here with Frankie in charge.

I head to the shed and search for the spare key I keep for the house just in case we need it. I pull the cord for the lamp, but nothing happens. The bulb is out. I feel around blindly until I feel something hard and cold hit my bare leg. It's the axe. I pick it up and set it to the side and then continue to feel along the top shelf until I find the little brass key.

I nearly chopped my toes off for nothing because the front door isn't even locked. They won't learn until they come home and find a psychotic intruder in the house.

Oh... wait... haha...

I tiptoe to the room I share with Frankie, but the door is open, and Frankie's bed is unmade and empty. They aren't here.

I go into my closet and pull out the dress I wore to the formal. The dress that made me feel so beautiful. The dress I peeled from my body slowly, the first time I had sex with Jesse Alford. This is what I want to wear when I do it. I want to die in this dress.

After I strip from the hospital clothes and redress into the gown, I cross the room and head to my dresser. I'm surprised to find that my mom or the sheriff hadn't thrown it away. I pull out the marbles and the fishbowl and drop the remaining orbs one by one into the bowl, completing the ritual countdown.

This is it. All that's left is to make the journey back up the trail and to the cliff. It's finally over. I won't leave a note or anything like that. No need to leave the Littles with any physical attachments. Hopefully, they'll get over me quickly, the way I got over my dad when he died. When people die, that's it. No amount of sadness will change things. Mourning doesn't make the future easier. Moving on does. Besides, what would the letter say? There's no explanation for what I'm about to do. They wouldn't understand. They would have to have the brain I was born with in order to understand.

So, I'll be a moment. Here one day, gone the next. I don't want to be remembered. I want to be forgotten more than I want anything.

I slip on a pair of tennis shoes for the walk back. I'll take them off and toss them off the cliff before I go over. They don't go well with this dress.

I'm walking out of the room for the last time when I hear something.

Crying.

Soft sniffles.

It's the hallucinations. This isn't like last time. Teddy isn't home. It's just my brain trying to trick me. I walk into the living room and the muffled crying persists.

It's just a hallucination. It's been months, and I'm finally here at the end and my stupid brain is replaying the day I almost killed Teddy too.

But that was a cough. Not a cry.

Teddy is crying. He's in his room crying.

Nope! No, he is not. Teddy is in San Francisco with Mom.

I walk out of the house and make my way down the porch ramp. I can't hear the crying anymore. Maybe it was real? If it was a hallucination, wouldn't I still hear it? Maybe that's part of the hallucination? Could I be so far gone that my hallucinations are hallucinations, making them... real?

Fuck it, I'll just check. Worst-case scenario, Teddy is in there crying. Doesn't mean he's unsafe. I'm not planning on gassing us both again.

I walk around to the side of the house where the bedroom windows are. There are three on this side. The middle one belongs to the room where Teddy and Maddie sleep. I drag an old bucket to the middle window and stand on it. Maddie and Teddy pulled their curtain off last year, so a thin bedsheet covers the window. As I peer through the dusty window past the dingy Lightning McQueen sheet, I see...

I see Teddy sitting on the bed. And then I see...

Joe... standing in front of him with his...

And then I see black.

And then there's a light. The shed. The bulb is working?

Black

Joe's belt buckle hanging.

Black

Back in the shed. The axe.

Black

Joe's hand holding his...

Darkness. A screeching sound. The screen door.

Teddy's crying.

My arms burn. Swinging.

Teddy screams.

A *thud*.

Whack. Three of them. Five. Eight.

Warm, thick, goo...

Darkness...

A scraping sound. I'm dragging something against the wood floors?

Teddy is screaming. He shouldn't see this.

A dial tone. Freeman.

I sit at the table, still in darkness...

I need to get to the cliff.

I need to...

Chapter Forty-Five

Jesse

I wince at the sunlight peeking over the hills as we all spill out of the mill. We were having so much fun that we decided to make it an all-nighter. The night was filled with music, dancing, and drinking, and when the liquor was gone, we all sat around and threw around embarrassing stories from the last few years we've spent together. I've known these people my entire life, so there were an endless number of stories we could tell.

Alyssa won't admit it, but it was her falling asleep on one of the conveyor belts that made us all realize it was time to go home. I check the time on my phone and see that it's 6:55 a.m. Trey comes stumbling out of the mill behind me, but I can tell it's from sleep deprivation, not alcohol.

"You mind driving?" I ask him, tossing the keys to him because I know he won't say no.

"Jesse!" I hear Alyssa call out to me. When I turn around, she's helping Chelsea climb into Preston's jeep. "Don't be a stranger anymore." Her smile is sweet, and I know she means it.

My gaze shifts to Preston standing outside of his Jeep. There is an indifference in his eyes that matches mine. We've been friends our entire lives. Most of the stories being tossed around tonight were about us. Antics we pulled on the playground. Pranks we'd played around town as preteens. There was a shift along the way, long before this year. Preston's always been an asshole, but he's also always been jealous of me. Then there's the racist remarks. Sometimes people show you who they really are. It's up to you to decide which line is the one that's too far. I take in the sight of Preston, Alyssa, and Chelsea. Grandpa Lawrence's words echo in my mind.

"They always have loved a nigga that could throw a ball."

I nod my head toward him and then slide into the passenger seat of the GTO.

Trey follows the line of cars onto the mountain road toward town. The sun is rising over the hills and shining through the open window past Trey on the driver's side. My body feels heavy from lack of sleep and a lot of liquor, so I lean into the seat and lazily gaze out the window.

Something twinkles in my peripheral, and I turn back to the dash. The sunlight is hitting something metal dangling from the rearview mirror. I reach out and finger the arrow charm attached to the silver chain. It's the necklace I gave Mischa.

How did it...

"What the fuck, man!" Trey growls as he slams on the brakes. "Sorry, man. Ethan is driving dumb. He keeps breaking—Yo, why is everyone stopping?"

I squint my eyes and crane my neck to see around Ethan Telly's truck. The trail of cars heading back into town is slowly trudging forward, and I see police lights in the distance.

"I think I see your dad's patrol car," I tell him in a groggy voice. "I can't tell what's going on, though."

It takes about three minutes for traffic to move again. We coast down the road, and I realize that we're coming up on Mischa's house. The closer we get, the more obvious it becomes that the lights are coming from their property. When the house comes into view, we see that every officer and deputy in Grover is parked on the property. Officers are taping off the house and buzzing around the yard.

"What the hell?" Trey mumbles as he looks past me at the scene.

We're just about to pass by when I see and hear Frankie. She's on her knees, doubled over with her hands gripping her blonde hair, screaming at the top of her lungs, and crying hysterically.

"Pull over!" I yell, but I'm opening the car door and sprinting out of the car before he fully stops. An officer tries to stop me, but Frankie sees me and extends her arms out to me.

"Jesse!"

He releases me, and I run to her. I pull Frankie from the ground, and she wraps her arms around my middle, holding on to me for dear life. She's sobbing. Choking sobs and I can't make out what she's saying.

"I was—I was at my friend's and—Everyone called and said something happened—I left Teddy—Daddy was home, so I thought—and then—"

There's a commotion behind us, and I turn in time to see Mischa's mom breaking through the same police barricade I had. The procession of cars is ending, but I notice my car parked across the street with Trey craning his neck to see what's happening.

"Michelle, you can't go in there." I finally see Sheriff Freeman now. He's coming off the porch as Mischa's mom runs up the ramp.

"Move, Moe. Where are my children?" Mischa's mom tries to push past him, but he grabs her shoulders.

"Teddy's on his way to the hospital, and you just ran past Frankie over there." When he points toward Frankie, he sees me too. His moment of distraction allows Mischa's mom to run past him into the house. Seconds later, we hear an earth-shattering scream.

She's screaming, *"What have you done? Oh my God, what have you done?"* over and over, and Frankie sobs harder, and her legs give out.

"Jesse!" the sheriff barks at me. "I need you to get out of here. Take Frankie with you. Now!"

I don't know what's going on, but I listen to him. I pull Frankie toward the street, and she uses whatever strength she has left to walk slowly alongside me. I look up at Trey, who is coming around the GTO to open the passenger door for us. He stops in his tracks when he gets to the other side of the car and stares behind us as if he's seeing a ghost.

I turn my head to see what he's staring at and freeze at the end of the driveway. An EMT is wheeling a gurney with a red-stained sheet covering a large lump. A body.

Frankie screams, and her legs turn to jelly again as she crumples to the ground. I scoop her into my arms and jog to my car. I lay her across the back seat and cover her with the spare blanket. She trembles and convulses in the fetal position.

"Holy shit," Trey breathes out as I back out of the car's backseat and push the passenger's seat upright. I turn again to follow his vision, and I see her. Handcuffed and cautiously escorted by Sheriff Freeman. She looks like she's in a trance. Her eyes are void of emotion. Her long black hair is matted to her face and shoulders. She is wearing the dress that she wore to the winter formal. Only now it, along with her face and hair, is saturated and splattered with blood.

It's Mischa.

Chapter Forty-Six

JESSE

As I watch my mom cradle a sleeping Frankie in her arms, I wonder why my parents never had any more children. My mom has a soft spot for kids. She's always holding the newest little cousin or sitting at the kids' table during family functions. She volunteers to read to the kindergarteners at the elementary school once a month and always chaperones their field trips.

Now that Frankie has finally given in to her exhaustion and passed out on our couch, nestled across my mom's lap, the news is on the television. Lindsay Madison, a reporter for ABC7, is standing in front of the yellow tape surrounding Mischa's yard.

"We're unsure exactly what motivated the grisly event today that left one man, Joesph Little, dead and an unnamed minor in handcuffs. What we do know is that the tiny community of Grover, California, will never be the same."

ABC7 has never been to Grover before. Well, except during the centennial of August Creek the year I was born. They were covering the story of how the towns split. They show it at school sometimes. But they never cover any stories here, so how would Lindsay Madison know how the death of the town drunk will affect our town?

Frankie stirs, and Mom instinctively strokes her hair and rocks her until she stills again. She looks back at the screen at Mischa's house and shakes her head slowly. I didn't know what else to do after Trey pulled away from Mischa's house. He was panicking, Frankie was screaming, and I couldn't get the image of a blood-soaked Mischa out of my head. They're saying she killed Joe Little.

Hacked him with an axe almost a dozen times. A picture of her chopping wood the day I picked her and the Littles up for Winterval pops into my mind. I quickly shake the thought out.

"Jesse, are you okay?" Mom's voice is tired. Trey drove us to my house and then walked home while I carried Frankie into my house. Without hesitation, my mom took her from me and rocked her like she was her own baby. After about ten minutes, Frankie passed out.

"How come you never had any more kids?" I ask her, nodding toward Frankie.

My mom frowns briefly before a small smile breaks through. "We tried. It just never happened, I guess."

I nod and run my hand through my hair, tugging at the twisted strands. Whatever hangover I left the mill with is no match for the spin this ordeal with Mischa is sending my head in. She was supposed to be in the mental hospital. How was she there? Why would she—

"Do you think she witnessed it?" Mom's question interrupts my thoughts.

I shake my head. "She said something about being in town at a friend's."

"But Teddy..." her voice trails off.

Teddy was there. At least that's what all signs point to, with Frankie being at a friend's house and Maddie in the backseat of the van with Grandpa Lawrence. Sheriff Freeman said Teddy was heading to the hospital.

The front door swings open, and my dad rushes in with a look of concern I haven't seen in a long time. He looks at me, and I see the relief settle in. When his eyes fall on my mother and then to a sleeping Frankie, his frown deepens again.

"That better not be who I think it is."

"Jesse and Trey were coming down the mountain when the police were responding. Francesca was hysterical, and Jesse grabbed her and brought her to me. She was a wreck." The way Mom describes it puts the blame on her.

"She can't be here." There's a serious look in his eyes, a warning, as he looks my mom directly in her eyes.

"She has nowhere else to go. The house is a crime scene, and her mother is most likely at the police station." Mom's voice is stern and calm, slightly above a whisper so she doesn't wake Frankie. I just drop my head, tired of my dad's antics already. He hates Mischa more than anyone in Grover, so the last thing he thinks we should be doing is harboring Frankie.

"Listen, I know I've been... hard on the Lawrence girl—"

"Mischa!" I raise my head and glare at him. "Her name is Mischa."

He nods. "I know I've been hard on... Mischa... but it's not a good idea for anyone from the Little family to be here right now." He shoots a glance at me and then turns back to my mom. "I need to talk to you in the bedroom."

Mom hesitates, looking down at the sleeping eldest Little. Her eyes meet mine, and she sighs before shifting Frankie's head from her lap and standing. She pulls the throw blanket up to Frankie's chin and then follows my father to the bedroom. I try to listen, but their hushed conversation is muffled by the door.

"My friends don't even really like me. All they ever want to talk about is how crazy my sister is."

Frankie's voice startles me. When I look over, she's staring at me with cold blue eyes. She is still bundled under the blanket, and she looks smaller than I've ever noticed. Usually, her confidence and personality make her big. Today's events have reduced her to the kid she really is.

"Last night, that's all anyone wanted to talk about at Emily's sleepover," she continues. Her tone is flat. "How my psycho sister ran away again. The whole time, I just shrugged and tried to change the subject. You know why?"

I don't reply. I just wait for her to keep talking.

"Because I know she's crazy, and I know she can't help being crazy."

I furrow my brows. "You know about her... disorder?"

"After the day with the gas and Teddy, I knew it was more than just a mistake. After they took her away, I found her pills. She had them glued to a calendar. A pill for each day. The empty bottle was at the bottom of her drawer."

"I asked my—*him*, what they were for. He was so drunk. He said, *'Pills for the family pet. That animal they took to the nuthouse.'* Didn't take much to put two and two together."

"You know what, though?" Again, this is another rhetorical question, so I just stare at her. "Even though she's weird, and crazy, and mean... She was a better parent than either of them. Especially, him. And now she's gone. For good."

I drop my head and clasp my hands together. I can hear Frankie shifting on the couch, and when I look up again, she's standing at the front door.

"Teddy wanted to know why you stopped talking to us after Mischa left."

She doesn't wait for an answer. She just walks out the door.

The State of California vs. Mischa Lawrence. The trial date is set for June 1st, the week before graduation. The lead prosecutor had to step down after the defense pointed out a glaring bias. The defendant is his son's ex-girlfriend.

My dad saw it coming. He told us that Sheriff Freeman would make sure the defense lawyers knew about Mischa and me, causing a conflict of interest in the case. My dad is one of the most reputable attorneys at the D.A.'s office, so he's still on the case, but only as an advisor.

My friend group has completely fallen apart since the incident. Preston, Chelsea, and Alyssa stick together, Trey and I stay to ourselves, and the only person Nick ever talks to anymore is Zoey. Alyssa tries to make conversation, but I'm not in the headspace to be the Jesse she once knew.

The Littles follow their same post-Mischa routine, with Frankie stepping in to take the reins. Marching in front of her younger siblings protectively, like their eldest sister once had. I still can't find the courage to speak to them. I can't even explain it. I cared so much for them, but without Mischa here, I don't know where I fit with them.

As for Mischa. I just want to forget her. I want the aching in my chest to go away. The girl I loved wouldn't murder her stepfather. No matter how much of an asshole he was. The Mischa I loved was weird. Unconventional. But I wouldn't have imagined she'd break out of her mental facility and hack her mother's husband with an axe.

When I get home from school, Sheriff Freeman and three other men I don't recognize are arguing with my father in our living room. They're all wearing suits, except the sheriff. When I walk into the house, all eyes are on me. I look around and find my mom in the kitchen. She doesn't notice me. She's stress-cooking, and I'm not sure what it is, but it smells good. I know she's stress-cooking because that's all she's been doing for the past month.

"Michael, this helps both sides. We both need the information from that kid. Your son might be able to help us all." The suit standing next to Sheriff Freeman pleads with my dad. My dad ponders his words as he stares at me. He's not in lawyer mode. He's in father mode. He's protecting me from something. "Jesse is eighteen. We don't need your permission to question him. I can subpoena him for court. But because he's your son, I'm trying to do this the easy way. We can get everything we need without Jesse ever seeing the inside of a courtroom."

I break eye contact with my dad and look at Sheriff Freeman. He's pleading with me to comply with whatever help they need. Wordlessly, but I can see it in his eyes. Whatever they're asking of me is serious, and if Sheriff Freeman is involved, it'll probably help Mischa. I've fought so hard to purge her from my mind that I don't even know if I want to help her.

"The boy is the only witness, and his teacher claims that he's fond of Jesse. He'll talk to him," the suit continues in a murmur.

At the mention of Teddy, my lips move before my brain processes the words. "I'll do it." All eyes turn to me. My mom comes out of the kitchen and eyes me cautiously.

"Jesse..."

I ignore her. "Whatever you need me to do, I'll do it. If it'll help..." I pause and think about my words. I catch my father's frown and swallow hard. "If it'll help Teddy, I'll do it."

The suit nods and takes a step toward me. "Don Hartell. I'm a defense attorney representing Ms. Lawrence. We need you to meet with Teddy Little in the morning. He's our sole witness, and he hasn't spoken to anyone about the events of that day. If we can get him to tell us what happened, then we can get some clarity on this case for both sides. You can come down to the station in the morning." The thing about turning eighteen is people immediately stop talking to you like a kid. They lose the caution and ease. Replace it with declarative statements and demands. I nod my understanding before retreating to my room.

Mom knocks on the door forty-five minutes later with a plate of food, but I pretend to sleep. She sits beside me, rubbing my back, and whispering about how much she loves me. She tells me she's sorry that this is happening to me. Surprisingly, my dad doesn't bother coming in to brief me on tomorrow. Maybe he knows that I already know the drill. Go in, ask the questions he tells me to ask, and don't say anything that may implicate me in... well, there isn't really anything I can say. I don't even know what happened.

So, I spend the evening tossing and turning, wishing I could sleep. Wishing I could close my eyes and see anything except the vivid image of Mischa's stony face covered in her stepfather's blood.

Chapter Forty-Seven

JESSE

Teddy is sitting in an interrogation room talking to Mr. Oldham from the bookstore. Outside of the room, watching through the one-way mirror, are Don Hartell, the other lawyers that were in the living room last light, and Sheriff Freeman.

"Where is your father?" Don Hartell asks. I shrug because I left the house without even speaking to my parents. My dad's car wasn't in the driveway, but it could have been in the garage.

As if summoned, the door opens, and my father walks in dressed casually in a pair of jeans and a golf shirt. He sits his briefcase down on a table in the corner and nods curtly at the woman sitting in the corner that I hadn't noticed before. It's Mischa's mom.

She doesn't notice my dad's gesture because she's staring at the glass, watching Mr. Oldham try in vain to get Teddy to speak to him. Teddy's just sitting there, his round glasses almost as thick as Oldham's. He's staring at a comic book that I'm assuming Mr. Oldham brought to bribe him. Teddy's just staring at the pages, uninterested.

"Not even a word," Don Hartell murmurs. "Hopefully, Jesse can get him to talk."

"The mother says he hasn't spoken in weeks. Not even in school." My dad is talking, and I guess his words are directed to me because he's looking at me, but we haven't spoken in weeks either. "Oldham thought maybe he could pull something out of him."

"What makes them think I can?" I ask my dad. Oldham pats Teddy on the shoulder and motions toward the book before standing and walking out of the room. The older man nods at everyone in the viewing room. He speaks to Hartell, explaining that he tried his best.

"The mother says he trusts you," my dad tells me. I note how informally he addresses Mischa's mom. Does he even know her name? When I think about it, neither do I.

Don Hartell and my dad take turns instructing me on what I should say to Teddy. I'm not supposed to ask him questions that may appear coercive, but I'm their last-ditch effort to get information out of him.

I enter the room and take Mr. Oldham's place at the table. Teddy glances up and then does a double take. For a moment, I think I see a hint of excitement in his eyes, but then, just as quickly, he drops his gaze back to the graphic novel.

I spent the entire winter talking to this kid with ease, all because I was dating his sister. Now, I feel like I'm drowning in guilt for ignoring him these past few months. I knew he looked up to me. I knew he was proud to have me in his corner, and I abandoned him.

"I'm sorry, Teddy," I tell him quietly. I know the room is probably being recorded, and I should probably stick to the script my dad and Don Hartell gave me, but something about this feels personal. I owe Teddy this apology. "I wasn't ignoring you guys on purpose. This whole thing with your sis—with Mischa—it was confusing for me. I didn't mean to freeze you guys out, man."

Teddy pulls his bottom lip between his teeth and blinks rapidly when I mention Mischa's name, and I wonder how long it's been since someone has spoken her name to him. Not just, *"your sister."* She meant the world to him. Now she's gone, and no one is taking into consideration the toll that must have on him. I decide to go at this slow. Their mom is right. Teddy used to trust me, but now I'm not sure if he does anymore. I've got a small window to earn it back. Not for the case. For myself and Teddy.

"I've been watching wrestling a little. I can't believe they unmasked Ultimo." I add a little chuckle at the end, thinking about Teddy's excitement whenever he'd tell me about the latest antics of his favorite masked professional wrestler.

Teddy's eyes widen, and he looks up at me in surprise. *Shit*, I guess he missed that episode.

"My bad, man. I didn't know you'd missed it." I laugh sheepishly. "You can stream the reruns."

"We don't have any of those apps anymore. Mischa was paying for them," Teddy whispers. His voice is so low I have to dip my head closer to hear him.

"Oh. Well, I have them. You'll have to come by and catch up at my house," I tell him nonchalantly. Teddy's magnified eyes are unblinking as he stares at me, trying to gauge my sincerity. "I'm being for real. I have a couple of months before I leave. We can kick it while I'm still here. Maddie and Frankie too."

Teddy shakes his head, and for a moment, I think he's rejecting my truce. But then he rolls his eyes and says, "Not Maddie, she broke my Ultimo action figure."

"We'll get you another one." I laugh.

We talk about the graphic novel Oldham left. Since all the streaming channels Mischa was paying for are cut off, he's had a lot of time to read his comics. The one Oldham brought is the latest collection of his favorite antihero. He's just about to wrap up what he predicts the conclusion of this storyline will be when there's a tap on the window. A warning to get to the point from Hartell or my dad.

Teddy speaks before I can. "They told me not to tell anyone."

"Who did?" I furrow my brow.

He hesitates for a moment and looks over my shoulder at the window. He's not dumb, he knows they're listening. He knows why I'm here.

"Hey, Teddy." His eyes meet mine again, and I regard him with a serious face. "Everything I said today I meant. It wasn't a tactic. I don't really care what those guys want." I nod my head back over my shoulder. "I just want to make sure you're okay. I want you to know you can talk to me."

Teddy nods. "Mischa said that if people knew what happened, they'd '*make my life a fucking hell.*'" I stifle a laugh, thinking about how hard that had to be for Teddy to repeat because he doesn't like cussing. "When Mason called, he said

I needed to keep it to myself. I haven't even told him anything, and he knows. He told me to just forget it happened and be happy *he's* dead."

I frown, but I don't interrupt him.

"But I want to tell someone. I always wanted to, but he said no one would believe me."

I furrow my brow. "Who told you that? What wouldn't we believe? What does Mason know?"

Teddy shakes his head and looks back at the window again. I can see the fear and nervousness in his small body. There's a weight there that I think we all attributed to his introverted personality. Looking at him now and trying to decipher his cryptic words, there is something heavier weighing him down.

"I don't want to say it out loud," Teddy finally tells me.

I look back at the one-way glass and then back at Teddy. "Everyone behind that window wants to help you. They want to help Mischa too." I know part of that is a lie. My dad couldn't give a damn about Mischa. Still, the weight of whatever Teddy is hiding is crushing him, and now I feel like it's crushing me too.

"I'm not big and strong like you are, Jesse," he mumbles. "No one can hurt you like that."

I shake my head. "Everyone can get hurt. Look at your big muscular wrestlers. They always get hurt. But then their friends run out to the ring and help them."

I can tell he's pondering my words. I want to tell him that even a five-foot-five firecracker could hurt me. I don't, though. He nods and reaches for the yellow pencil and notepad sitting in the center of the table. He writes in scratchy handwriting and then tears off the paper and folds it up. He slides it toward me but keeps it covered with his palm while staring at me intensely.

"Can you read it to them after I leave?" he asks me, even though I know there's only one answer that will get him to release the note. I nod and he stands up. "See you later, Jesse."

He doesn't dap me up or hug me like he used to. He walks over to the door with the graphic novel tucked under his arm and knocks. The door opens, and

I hear Teddy ask someone if he's free to go home. I pick up the piece of paper and unfold it, reading it several times before the words register.

Then, I bend over and dry heave toward the floor. Good thing I skipped breakfast.

Chapter Forty-Eight

Not guilty by reason of insanity.

The issue is no longer a matter of jail time, but how long Mischa should be institutionalized. The plea deal offered before the hearing was for a minimum of fifteen years. Don Hartell, apparently, didn't even give it a thought. He's aiming for less than a year.

Both sides are using Teddy's confession in their favor. The defense says that seeing Joe Little forcing Teddy to commit disturbing sexual acts on him caused Mischa to black out because of her condition. Like a switch was flipped. My dad's team claims that Mischa is too unstable to live among the public, that she doesn't perceive right from wrong, and often lies and fabricates injustices. Like she did with Billy Wessel and Blake Wilcox.

I'm attending the sentencing hearing today. Last night, Zoey called me in tears. She's taking the stand as a sentencing witness, and she's so nervous that she spent half an hour begging me to come.

I arrive at the courthouse in Sacramento with minutes to spare. I slide into a booth in the back of the room so fast that I don't notice that I'm seated next to Mr. Brady. He smiles at me and nods curtly before turning to the front. A door opens on the side, and I see Mischa being escorted by a large bald officer. Her hands are bound in front of her, and there are shackles on her feet. She's wearing a jumpsuit, but not one that looks like a jail uniform. Maybe from the institution they're housing her at? Her hair is slicked back into a low bun behind her neck. As I'm straining to get a better look at her, I notice someone staring at me.

Alyssa.

The curious look in her eye tells me she's as surprised to see me here as I am to see her. The person next to her shifts and turns to see what has her attention. It's Preston. I turn my head before my eyes meet Preston's and survey the room for any other familiar faces. I see the back of Mischa's mother's head, as well as Frankie's next to her. Sheriff and Mrs. Freeman are next to them. Nick is a few rows behind Preston and his parents, giant and brooding next to the Hall family. My dad sits with the prosecution.

The judge enters, and I zone out as my attention returns to the back of Mischa's head. She's staring down at the table and every once in a while, Don Hartell leans over and whispers in her ear. She doesn't nod or respond.

A woman named Dr. Zakarian takes the stand, and with a thick foreign accent, explains how years of being the primary caretaker for her younger siblings made Mischa protective of them like a mother would be. She says that the stress of Mischa's home life, combined with her psychosis, led her to the tragic events of that morning. She claims that Mischa believed she was *a lioness protecting her cub,* and ridiculed the adults in Mischa's life for allowing her to stop therapy and self-medicate.

When Zoey is called to the stand, Don Hartell approaches and asks her a series of questions about her friendship with Mischa.

"So, you can tell me in full confidence that Mischa Lawrence is someone you would consider your *best friend*?" Don Hartell asks her.

Zoey nods. "Yes, sir."

"What about your other friends? You're a pretty popular girl in Grover, right? With a popular group of friends? How do you manage a friendship with a girl like Mischa? A girl that the defense says is a liar. An unstable girl with violent tendencies."

This time, Zoey shakes her head. "I've never seen Mischa violent. Maybe a little moody and closed off at times, but she was never violent." She pauses and looks at Mischa with a small smile. "And as far as I know, she's never been a liar. She barely talks to people in town."

"So, by all accounts, you would say that, while maybe a little socially awkward, Mischa Lawrence wasn't a danger to those around her."

"Yes." Zoey nods. Don Hartell rests, and the leading defense lawyer, my father's friend and coworker, David Wright, approaches next.

"You say that Mischa was not a violent person, Ms. Hall. But what about the events of last October, where Mischa Lawrence assaulted a twelve-year-old in the middle of town?"

Zoey stiffens slightly. "I wasn't present for that."

David Wright shrugs. "I'm sure you heard about it. Grover's a small town and, as you say yourself, Mischa's your best friend."

Don Hartell objects and the judge tells David Wright to *"Watch it."* She's a Black woman with rich brown skin and a facial expression that says she's not about the nonsense. If I had to guess, she has to be in her mid-fifties. I overheard my dad telling my mom he was nervous about having her preside over the case.

David Wright puts his hands up and nods an apology.

"Fine. Let's talk about an event you were present for. The night of a party at the local hangout spot, an abandoned factory?"

"I've been to a lot of parties at the mill." It's evident in Zoey's dry response that she knows exactly what night he's talking about.

"How about four years ago? The night of September 22nd? The night police were called to the mill by Mischa Lawrence. She reported an attempted rape?"

Zoey shakes her head. Not a *'no,'* but in annoyance, I think. "What about it?"

"Well, it's heavily speculated that Ms. Lawrence fabricated the details of that night. That she had consensual sex with—"

Don Hartell calls out another objection, and Judge Perry tells David Walker to get to the point.

"I guess I just don't understand how you claim to be so close to Mischa, while the people around you all feel so differently about her. About that night, even."

This time Zoey is shaking her head in disagreement. "They don't know Mischa. They don't even try to know Mischa. And they don't know anything about that night. Nothing about what was about to happen to Mischa was consensual."

"And you know this how?" David Wright gives her a skeptical look.

"Because I saw it happening. I'm the one who called the sheriff that night." Zoey's voice strains as she tries to make this jaw-dropping announcement as confidently as possible, but I see the fear in her eyes. Mr. and Mrs. Wilcox are sitting in the same row as Preston and Alyssa.

Zoey is the one who called the cops on Blake. Not Mischa.

David Wright tilts his head and then walks over to shuffle through papers. My father sits up straighter and on the other side, I see Don Hartell nod at Zoey. Mischa's still staring at the table, but her eyes are wide. I think back to the morning after the formal.

"I don't remember any of it, Jesse. Not even the conversations with the police."

I look over at Preston and his family, all of their jaws set tight, and their skin tinted red. They are pissed.

Zoey's announcement has stumped the defense. They rest and Zoey beelines it out of the courthouse, her parents and Nick shuffle out of the room as well. A commotion of murmurs breaks out.

"All of those years of torment for nothing," Brady mumbles. I'm not sure if he's talking to me or not.

Judge Perry bangs her gavel and calls for order.

"After hearing testimony from health professionals and those closest to Mischa, I think it's clear what needs to happen here today. Ms. Lawrence, please stand."

Don Hartell helps Mischa stand in her cuffs and shackles and then whispers, what I assume is something reassuring, in her ear. She looks so harmless standing there in the oversized jumpsuit.

Judge Perry leans forward and fixes her eyes on Mischa with a hard gaze. "Ms. Lawrence, it has already been determined that the events that occurred on April 14th, while gruesome, were not the fault of your own. Your actions were fueled by a mental illness that has gone unchecked for too long. Long before you voluntarily stopped taking your meds. To summarize Dr. Zakarian's words, a child should have never been left responsible for self-medicating the type of extreme disorder you are living with. By my account, you were failed, Ms. Lawrence. Failed by every single adult in your life. Failed by your community."

Judge Perry pauses and looks around the room at the sea of Grover faces. She fixes her gaze on Sheriff Freeman and Mischa's mother, shaking her head before continuing.

"But I refuse to be another adult who encounters you, sees your needs, and fails you, Mischa Lawrence.

"My concern is not if you'll harm another person on this planet. My concern is that you can't look me in my eyes and tell me right now that as soon as you walk out of this room another countdown won't start. Can you do that, Mischa? Can you tell me you won't try to end your life after today?"

Judge Perry stops talking and stares at Mischa expectantly. Of course, Mischa doesn't respond, but even from my view of her profile, I can see tears welling in her eyes. Judge Perry folds her lips inward and nods slowly.

"Ms. Lawrence, for the next five years, your peers will venture off to college, explore the world as young adults, and appreciate their love of life. You will not. You will spend the next five years in intensive rehabilitation and therapy at an adult behavioral facility, where you will learn to cope with this disorder. You will learn how to safely reintegrate into society."

Judge Perry asks Mischa if she has anything she'd like to say. Her response is low, so low that I have to read her lips to understand what she's saying.

"But they need me."

"That's not your priority, Ms. Lawrence. It never was. Your priority is to get well. You will do that at North Pine Psychiatric Hospital."

Later, after the hearing is over and I've watched Mischa be escorted out of the courtroom, the last time I'll probably ever see her, I google North Pine.

It's eight hundred miles away in Washington state.

Chapter Forty-Nine

I look around the mill, wondering what the hell I'm even doing here. Everyone's drinking, laughing, and dancing like everything is normal. I guess for them it is normal. Another summer night in the mill, partying like we've done every weekend since we were fourteen. Someone was murdered a few miles away from here three months ago. Last month, our classmate was sentenced to five years in a mental institute. No one, except me, feels the weight of Mischa's absence, even though she wouldn't have been here, anyway. No one in town cares because the drunk is finally gone, and the crazy girl they all hated finally proved them right.

The Wessels were on three different news stations, tearfully recounting the day that Mischa Lawrence viciously attacked their sweet, innocent Billy. My mother watched all three interviews and called the Wessels names she'd never repeat in church. My dad sat there indifferently.

I'm sitting on the same conveyor belt that Mischa sat on when she came to the mill to drive Zoey home last fall. The night seemed so long ago. The next day, we went to the Gravity House and kissed for the first time. Trey walks over and sits beside me. The hearing and its aftermath are taking a toll on his family as well. His parents are talking about moving to Sacramento after he's settled into college at Cal State in Long Beach. No football scholarship. He didn't want to play, and his parents respected that.

"Last weekend in Grover. Seems unreal, man." His voice is lower than the blaring music, but I can still hear him. We're both leaving on Thursday. He's headed to Long Beach, and I'm headed across the country to Oklahoma. Life is moving forward, whether we like it or not. I don't respond with words, I just nod.

Zoey walks into the room accompanied by Alyssa and Chelsea. We make eye contact, and she gives me a half-hearted smile. The type of smile that shows we have something in common now. We both miss *her*.

I try not to think about it often, but I do. I miss Mischa. I figure the more distance I put between Grover and myself, the more memories I can shed of us, and the faster I'll get over it. That's why I stopped fighting my dad on leaving for college in Oklahoma. I've lost all my fight. For the last seven months, I have been doing a lot of fighting. Fighting with my dad, fighting with Preston, fighting with Mischa, and fighting with myself, all because of my relationship with Mischa. Maybe a part of me is happy it's all over.

Zoey breaks away from the two girls and walks over to us. Alyssa looks over and waves with a bright smile. I nod my head at her, but that's all I can muster. She drops the smile and follows Chelsea into the small room where the liquor and food are always kept.

"I know you think I'm a terrible friend for not speaking up about Blake sooner," Zoey calls out over the loud music. I don't respond, I just stare. She's right. How could she not say something? How could she not say something *to Mischa*?

As if reading my mind, she says, "The next day, I asked Mischa if she remembered anything. She said she didn't remember being at the party at all. It didn't make sense because she only had one drink that night. I thought maybe she was just lying. That... maybe she wanted to forget what happened. So, I never told her what really happened. It was shitty, I know. But I wanted us to still be friends, and the sheriff promised me that no one would find out."

Zoey looks at me expectantly, and I just stare back. She sucks her teeth and turns on her heels, sulking into the tiny room where Alyssa and Chelsea are pouring drinks into red cups. No sooner does she enter the room I spot Preston barreling down the stairs and into the room behind her.

Trey nudges me. "My dad said that Mischa was having one of those episodes with her disorder or whatever. Said she really doesn't remember a thing. He told Zoey not to press the issue. That he'd handle it."

Well, he did a fine job at that, didn't he? I don't say this out loud to Trey. I don't get a chance to respond because we hear a commotion in the room where our friends are gathered. Trey and I glance at each other and silently nod before hopping off the conveyor belt and going in. The air is thick with confrontation. Zoey spent the last week of school after the hearing avoiding Preston. Her family left for vacation shortly after graduation, so this is the first time they've encountered each other since she testified at the sentencing.

"Preston, relax!" Alyssa yells at him as he advances on Zoey with a slew of accusations and cusswords.

"A fucking liar, just like your bitch of a *best friend*. The fuck was all of that bullshit at the hearing, Zo? You're the one that got Blake arrested?" Preston is in a rage, practically foaming at the mouth as he rushes Zoey.

"Get away from me, Preston!" Zoey's crying now. I step past Chelsea and pull Zoey closer to me.

Preston looks at both of us and scoffs. "Fuck you, Jesse. Both of you are so far up that crazy bitch's ass that you'll turn on your real friends? You almost ruined Blake's life with that lie, Zoey. I'll get you though. Laughing and smiling in my face, and the whole time you're the one—"

He cuts himself off as his anger pushes him to snap and grab at her arm again. I'm about to push him off of her, but a thick fist collides with Preston's cheek, and he's sent spinning against the counter. Bottles clank and fall to the ground as Nick advances on Preston for a second swing. Trey grabs Nick, no easy feat because Nick is enormous. He's playing football for San Diego State in the fall. He and Zoey are moving down there together on Monday.

I move away from Zoey and grab Nick's other shoulder, helping Trey pull the behemoth from Preston's stunned body sprawled against the counter. Nick, never one for many words, doesn't issue a verbal threat. He just pushes us off of him, points down at Preston, and then motions for Zoey to follow him as he leaves the room. She scurries over to him, and he wraps a protective arm around her as they leave.

"What is this? All the Black kids gang up on us in the name of that freak? What the fuck is wrong with you guys? Everyone's lying on my family and you're mad at *me*?" Preston scrambles to his feet, disbelief etched across his face. I'm ready to break his nose again when a voice speaks up.

"Oh, for God's sake, Preston, *shut up*!" Alyssa's voice is strained, and she sounds exasperated. Her face is made up pretty—so pretty that the tears welling in her eyes are almost unnoticeable. She and Chelsea will be roommates together at UC Berkley. I'm sure she'll meet someone there who will fall at her feet the way she always wanted me to.

"Everyone knows Blake was a creep." Alyssa's words stun me. She's sniffling now, and I can tell that she's been holding this declaration in for a long time. We all had eye-rolling moments whenever Preston would bring up Blake during his tangents about Mischa. I thought we were all just tired of hearing it. Judging by the frustration written across Alyssa's face and Chelsea uncomfortably shifting her weight, the girls had deeper issues with the elder Wilcox.

Again, Preston scoffs. "What? You saying he raped you too?" Sarcasm drips from his voice.

Alyssa shakes her head. "No, but he was always pushing up on us younger girls. Always groping us and telling us he couldn't wait until we turned eighteen. I hate Lawrence more than anyone, but I'm not surprised that Blake finally tried to force himself on someone. Even if it was *her*." She spits the last word out as if it tastes unpleasant.

Alyssa makes her way to the doorway with Chelsea on her heels. She stops and gives me a pitiful glance. I can't read the meaning, but I know she's wishing I was consoling her. Alyssa, like all the others, is one of my oldest friends. The thought of Blake harassing her, and me never knowing about it bothers me. If I had known, I would have done something, but back then I only paid attention to Alyssa when it was time for us to be physical or put on the show. The smile I give her is a genuine show of concern, but I can't give her much more. Alyssa is a mean girl. She did and said horrible, sometimes borderline racist, things to Mischa for no reason. She knew firsthand that Mischa was being ridiculed around town for something that quite possibly could have been true. And she did nothing.

After the girls leave, Trey and I throw one last glance at Preston, who is still leaning against the counter, holding his cheek in betrayal. At graduation, it was announced that he'd be playing football for USC. He'll find a new crew to spew his bullshit to. Tell them stories of how important he was in Grover. Looking at the defiance in his eyes now, I know that he'll never really grow up. He'll never get over this obsessive hatred he has for Mischa. He'll be stuck in his grandeur delusions.

Trey and I leave the mill. When we're outside, I look back at the place that held so many memories of my childhood. I'll never come back here and party with my peers. It hits me then. I'm realizing something I should have seen a long time ago.

I never really liked these people. They were never truly my friends.

Chapter Fifty

JESSE

Four Years Later

The house I share with my friends in Norman is the perfect size for an ex-football player and two pre-med students. At the same time, it's too big and likes to hide my belongings.

Mercedes always jokes, *"The house isn't hiding your things. You're just used to your mom keeping track of everything for you."* Four years away from home and I never quite got the hang of keeping up with my own shit. Like now, I'm scrambling to find the stupid tassel that goes on my graduation cap.

The house is brick traditional in a quiet neighborhood about five minutes away from the university. Moving here was a much-needed step up from the sports dorms and student apartments I'd lived in before we all moved in together.

Mercedes stands at the door with her hands on her slender waist. She's in a black robe and crimson stole like me. Only her tassel is yellow, indicating her biology degree. Pre-med. She'll attend OU again in the fall to start their medical program. My tassel is white to represent my B.A. in Psychology.

Halfway through my second season playing football in college, I tore my ACL. It hurt like hell, but it was such a relief because my heart wasn't in it anymore. Not playing football allowed me to take academics more seriously. I started picking up more psychology courses and found the material interesting for reasons I'd never admit to anyone. After my injury healed and I was cleared to return to the field, I broke the news to my parents that I was quitting football.

I could get other scholarships. My dad was pissed. We didn't talk for months and, in another move of defiance against him, I changed my major from political science to psychology. We patched things up eventually, and he was elated to learn that I had applied and been accepted into law school in the fall.

Mercedes saunters into the room, pushing a stack of book aside, and picks up the white tassel. It dangles like a pendulum as she holds it out on her neatly painted acrylic nail; hip jutted out and a smirk playing on her lips.

"What would you do without me?" she taunts. I take the tassel from her and drop a quick peck on her lips as I fasten it to my cap.

"Let's hope I don't find out anytime soon."

I hear footsteps in the hallway, and Brandon appears past Mercedes' shoulder. Black robe, crimson stole, yellow tassel. "We need to leave. Like, now."

"I'll drive," I tell them as I gather my keys and wallet.

I met Mercedes during our sophomore year while studying in the library. She had taken the same difficult professor in a previous semester and could sympathize with my struggle. I wasn't in the market for a girlfriend at the time, so I didn't think much about the conversation that ensued as she sat at the table. However, when she asked me for my number so that we could link up for her to give me her old notes from last semester, I obliged. We remained friends for a few months before we started dating exclusively. Through Mercedes, I met Brandon. Both are Oklahoma natives, Mercedes from Oklahoma City and Brandon from Tulsa. They're both pre-med and have been my closest friends in college. We moved in together last year. Since Mercedes was the only girl in the house, we gave her an automatic claim on the master suite and a space in the two-car garage. Oklahoma is notorious for hail storms, so with my main priority being a covered space for the GTO, I opted to take the smallest bedroom and use the hallway bathroom. Brandon took the second largest bedroom with an ensuite bathroom and the space in the uncovered driveway. Everything was seamless. I needed seamless because I'd struggled to move on from the madness of my hometown.

I drive the short distance to the Lloyd Noble Center with Mercedes in the front seat of the GTO and Brandon in the back. Every time we drive around like this, I'm reminded of the last fall I spent in Grover.

"Are you excited to see the Littles?" Mercedes asks me with a smile.

I'd kept my promise to Teddy and never lost contact with the Littles, even after I left for college. They call me at least once a week to catch me up on everything. The few times I've flown back home to visit, I always carve out time to have ice cream with them. The last time I saw them in person was when I went home last summer for Grandpa Lawrence's funeral.

I'd flown back to pay my respects, but there was also a part of me that hoped that *she* would be there. I hadn't spoken to her since that day in the school hallway when Sheriff Freeman took her away. She wasn't at the funeral, which caused a huge fight between Frankie and their mother. Frankie didn't understand why her mother hadn't fought harder for Mr. Lawrence's only living relative to be at his funeral.

Mercedes knows about the Littles because I had to explain to her why every Friday night three blonde-haired, blue-eyed kids were video-calling me. Of course, I only gave a piece of the story. I didn't feel the need to explain that the Littles were the half-siblings of my institutionalized ex-girlfriend.

I nod my head. "Yeah, they've been texting me nonstop since they arrived this morning."

"I can't wait to meet them." I look over at her briefly and smile. Her finger flicks the arrow pendant hanging around my rearview. She's never asked me about it, and I've never explained it. She follows up her statement with, "It'll be good to see Trey again too."

Trey came out to visit shortly after we moved into the house, and he accompanied us on our last spring break trip. He's in town with his parents to see me graduate, and I'm supposed to fly out to Long Beach next weekend for his graduation.

I broke contact with most of my old friends from Grover. I never run into them when I visit home, and the only ones I follow on social media are Zoey and Nick, who eloped this past New Year's Eve.

Meeting friends like Mercedes and Brandon, and the other people I've met in college, was eye-opening to the small world I was living in back home. To the bullshit I was putting up with and allowing to happen to others. My mom cried when I told her about the culture shock I was experiencing while living outside of my racist little town. I started to wonder if maybe Grover's issue was not a matter of being uncomfortable with a weird girl walking around town. Being Black and imperfect was the real issue. Trey and I could throw a football, solidifying our worth in the town. My father was an esteemed lawyer, and my mother was his trophy. But the Little family had the nerve to not only subscribe to the image of poor white trash, but they also had a crazy Black girl with them. Add that to the accusations against their wannabe golden boy, Blake Wilcox, who wouldn't possibly stoop so low as to want *someone like her*.

It's all speculation, though. I'll never really understand the truth about my hometown, so I stopped caring and started focusing on crafting my own life. One that didn't involve returning to Grover.

From the volume of cheers and foghorns—*which aren't allowed in the cere-mony*—I can tell that the people here to see me graduate are sitting in various locations around the arena. I cross the stage, accepting my fake diploma. The real one will come in the mail in a few weeks. There are cheers and screams, and then I take my seat again and wait for Mercedes to cross. You can tell the students who are locals by the volume of their attendees' cheering. Mercedes' entire family must be here.

After the ceremony, we find Mercedes' family first and snap a few pictures together. I kiss her lightly on the lips and tell her I'm leaving to find my own family. She nods, but her attention is mostly on her grandma, who is pulling at her robe, fussing over the short dress Mercedes is wearing underneath it.

I find my family standing together near the west exit of the arena. My dad's parents still live in Oklahoma in a suburb outside of the major city. My mom's brother and his wife are here from California. They flood me with congrats, hugs, and kisses. My mom wraps her arms around me and whispers, "Gramps would be so proud of you, Jesse."

My paternal grandma pulls at the patch of hair covering my chin and tells me how grown up I am. She compliments the braids that Mercedes styled on top of my head to compliment the freshly faded sides. My grandfather grumbles something about not getting an all-around haircut. He's definitely the man who raised my father. Judgmental and stern.

My dad pulls me into a tight hug and tells me he's proud of me. The distance has worked wonders for our relationship, but I know part of him is still only this happy because I'm following the plan he'd set forth for me. The same plan his father had set for him.

I'm not surprised to see that my other guests aren't standing around with my family. My dad and Sheriff Freeman haven't spoken since the hearing, and the Littles are a given. I look around for them in the immediate area, but I don't see them.

"Where is your girlfriend, Jesse? We want to meet her family," my grandma asks.

"She's over there with her family. You'll probably see her later at the house. I'm not sure what her plans are."

We take pictures and then they discuss plans for dinner, but my attention falls to a thin girl with blonde hair and bright blue eyes; a cell phone perpetually glued to her ear. She looks around for a bit before her eyes meet mine and she smiles. "I found him," she says into the receiver.

Frankie.

She nods her head to the right, signaling that the others are somewhere in that general direction. I nod and turn to excuse myself from my family. "I'll be right back. I need to go say 'hi' to some other people."

My grandparents frown and ask me why I'm leaving. My dad looks past me at Frankie and shakes his head, but doesn't protest.

"Go ahead Jesse, we'll find Mercedes' family and introduce them to Grammy and Pawpaw," my mom says with a smile. It's a knowing smile, which makes me think she talked to Mrs. Freeman about them being here today. At least they're still friends. The fathers are a lost cause. I nod my appreciation and walk toward Frankie.

Frankie puts up a finger and holds her phone up like she wants to take a picture. I put my cap back on and pose for her.

"Congrats, Jesse." She grins and hugs me around the torso. "Everyone is so excited to see you!"

I follow Frankie to the east entrance, where another sea of graduates and their families are posing for pictures. I spot Trey first because he's standing on the stone steps of the entrance talking to a girl. His body is blocking her, but I'm pretty sure it's his newest girlfriend. He wanted me to meet her and asked if she could come. They've been going strong for about a month now, and he swears this one is going to be the one. I think my boy just loves the single life too much to commit, but we'll see.

I hear my name in a squealing voice as Maddie rushes me, crashing into my lower half with as tight of a hug as she can form. I hug her back, lifting her from the ground a little, and spinning. She giggles in delight.

"Maddie!" I mock her as we spin, and Frankie snaps pictures. We stop spinning and Maddie excitedly jumps in place. Frankie scolds her, and I'm not sure why, because Maddie is always overly excited. Teddy runs over next. We exchange hand slaps, and then I wrap him in a hug. No longer the scrawny little kid with the enormous glasses. He turned thirteen earlier this year, and now he reaches my shoulders. Mrs. Little—well, Ms. Townes now—invested in some normal, more fashionable glasses for him. He's in the awkward acne phase now, but he's doing a lot better in the bullying department.

They've all changed so much in the past four years. Maddie's no longer the chubby little girl with the cute speech impediment. At almost ten years old, she's grown taller, and her bright blonde hair has darkened, making her look the most like their mother. Frankie is sixteen and still boy-crazy. Most of our conversations are about her breakups and newest crushes. She's a cheerleader, honor roll student, and the go-to girl in town for all of your hair and makeup needs. Best of all, she's able to be a kid. She doesn't have to raise her younger siblings. She gets to be a regular teenager.

Their mom stands off to the side, smiling at the interaction and nodding at me. We don't speak much when I'm in town or on the phone with her kids, just a greeting and pleasantries. She's still frail and has bags under her eyes, but she gets out of the house more now that she has to work and raise the kids.

Teddy and Maddie take off toward the stairs to Trey's girlfriend. Her head is turned, and she's staring up at the building. Teddy's sitting next to her now. He's talking, but she isn't really listening. A jolt of lightning shoots through my chest because the scene is so familiar.

I don't have much time to ponder it before I'm pulled into a hug by Trey's parents and take pictures with them. The same sentiments and congratulations. Trey walks over and we all take a few pictures.

"Man, we have got to party hard when you get to L.A. next weekend. We did it!" Trey says slapping hands with me and pulling me in for a hug.

"Yeah, except I have three more years," I half-joke.

"Yeah, well, that's the cost of peace of mind, right?" he jokes back, understanding my plight. We text almost daily, making the distance between each other and our families a lot easier. Trey has always been my biggest confidant, even after I met Mercedes and Brandon. He knows I'm not thrilled about going to law school and that the only thing making staying in Oklahoma bearable is more time with Mercedes. She's mentioned me moving into her bedroom and finding a fourth roommate next semester, but I enjoy having my space to study and decompress.

Thinking about Mercedes reminds me that my parents are somewhere around here waiting for me.

"Introduce me before I have to go back and find my family," I tell Trey. He furrows his brow in confusion. "Your girl?" I elaborate.

"Oh, yeah, that didn't work out." He runs his hand over his waves and grins sheepishly.

I shake my head, not really surprised, but amused. I motion to the girl on the steps, but she's gone. "Who was the girl you were talking to over there?"

Trey looks back at the stairs and his head recoils. He looks around the perimeter like he's looking for her as well. "Where'd she go?" he mumbles.

"She walked off with Teddy," Mrs. Freeman calls out with a smile.

I'm about to ask him what's going on, but then I hear Maddie calling out to my mom. My family approaches with Mercedes. I introduce everyone to her, and my dad stands back quietly, avoiding all parts of my surrogate families. I'd prefer he do that than stir up any drama. Teddy returns, but Trey's friend isn't with him. The Littles seem less interested in Mercedes in person than they were the few times they've spoken to her on FaceTime. That's to be expected, I guess. She takes it in stride, commenting on Frankie's makeup and Maddie's dress. Teddy offers her the most conversation.

We chat for another half hour before the arena staff announces that we'll all need to vacate the premises. Everyone is going back to their hotels until dinner time. We haven't decided how we're going to spend dinner, not with the rift between my dad and the Freemans and the Littles. Mercedes and Brandon are going back to the city with their families, so I head to the GTO alone.

The sky is overcast with dark, billowy clouds. The tornado watch from earlier has dropped to a thunderstorm warning, which I'm grateful for, not only because tornados are something I still haven't gotten used to, but because the air has a cool breeze with the incoming rainstorm.

Part of me wants to stay in California for the summer. I've left my life in Grover behind, but I miss hanging out with Trey and my mom's cooking. Hell, I even miss talking football with my dad in person. Seeing the Littles makes me miss them too. The last few weeks before I left Grover was spent playing video games at my house with Teddy and treating them to ice cream at Scoop's. They became an extension of me, and I could see why someone would give up their youth to care for them. A summer celebrating my accomplishments with Mercedes is equally tempting because we get along so well. She's not clingy or obsessive. She has her own life outside of our relationship. If she's going to the city to hang out with her friends and I need to stay home and study, or simply not feeling social, she doesn't get mad or hold it against me. Her life keeps moving, just like mine does. That's why we work. She just... gets it.

I fish my keys out of the pocket of my robe as I approach the area where I remember parking. Mercedes always teases that for someone who is obsessed with his car, I never remember where I parked it, to which I remind her that there weren't too many places to lose your car in a town that's only nine square miles. I chirp the alarm on the car and look around to find it. It's actually pretty easy to spot since most of the graduates have already started leaving. I spot my car and my heart drops to my stomach.

Trey's friend is leaning against the GTO just in front of the driver's side front tire, staring up at the dark clouds. Only, as I get closer to her, I realize she's not some random girl who flew out here with the Freemans to meet her new boyfriend's best friend.

She's wearing a short, lacy white summer dress, similar to the one she was wearing the day we argued on the cliff all of those years ago. Her legs are crossed at the ankle and the dress stops mid-thigh. Like me, she looks like a slightly older version of her teenage self. I didn't recognize her before because her once long, thick hair is now cut inches away from her scalp in rolling curls that frame her forehead and taper around her ears and nape.

I stop walking and stare at her in disbelief. It's only been four years. What is she doing here?

Mischa finally senses my presence and slowly drops her gaze from the sky to me. Our eyes meet and she looks nervous. Her face is made up perfectly, reminding me of the night we went to the formal together. Most likely Frankie's doing.

We stare silently at each other, lost in an awkwardness that we'd left behind in the Gravity House as seventeen-year-olds. The wind blows between us, swaying the hem of the white dress. I'm reminded of the fabric she tied around my bloody knuckles, and how I told her I loved her, and how she screamed at me.

She speaks first.

"A degree in psychology? How cliche, Jesse Alford." A smirk plays at her lips finally, and I release my breath with a chuckle.

I approach her slowly, shaking my head. "I can't believe you're here. I saw you earlier but I—I didn't realize it was you."

She nods. "I got released on good behavior." She pauses and then laughs a little. Her smile is more gorgeous than ever. "I've been dying to use that on someone." Her use of the word *dying* makes me frown, remembering why we're in this awkwardness in the first place. Mischa notices and bites her lip.

"I'm happy to see you," I tell her because it's easier than saying the things I want to say.

"I miss you."

"I haven't stopped thinking about you."

"During every small adventure I've had in the past four years, I would think about how we should have been doing this together."

"I didn't plan on coming, but the terms of my release say that I cannot be left alone for more than two days. The Littles wanted to see you so bad, so I tagged along." Her arms are folded across her chest, and her expression is now one of nonchalance. These are all mannerisms that I've grown to recognize in retrospect. The way she'd cycle through expressions and emotions. I thought she was just being weird.

"You didn't want to see me?" I ask around the lump forming in my throat.

She sighs and looks at me. Nonchalance turns to stone-faced seriousness. "No. Jesse, I didn't."

Her answer stuns me. I feel like an arrow has pierced my chest. I've thought about this girl every day since the day I saw her covered in blood on her lawn like Carrie. I'd pushed her to the furthest corner of my mind, but Mischa was such a huge part of me in such a small amount of time that even in the deepest recesses of the subconscious, she was too large to ignore.

And now I know that she didn't feel the same.

It's that night on the cliff all over again. When she told me to leave without her. When she made me believe she hadn't felt what I was feeling.

"Why not?" I ask her, trying to mask the hurt in my voice, but failing, I'm sure.

Mischa doesn't answer. Her eyes shift to look past me, and her lips press together tightly. When I turn to see what she's looking at, I find Mercedes watching us from afar. There's a look of confusion and suspicion in her eyes. When she sees that we've spotted her, she starts walking to us again. The wind carries her open graduation robe backward, displaying the cream-colored mini dress that looks amazing on her warm brown skin. She's not wearing her cap anymore, so her freshly pressed hair is blowing wildly in the wind.

"Hey, I thought you were riding with your parents. My bad." I know this has to look weird to her. Some random girl in a tiny dress casually leaning against my car that I am so meticulous about while I stand ten feet away.

Mercedes looks at me and then Mischa and back to me again, eyebrows furrowed and frowning slightly. "I left my purse in your car."

"Oh, okay." Now it's my turn to look between her and Mischa, unsure of what to say. We play a game of awkward staring for about ten seconds. Mercedes staring at me, me staring at Mischa, Mischa staring at Mercedes. Once again, it's Mischa who speaks first.

"Mischa Lawrence. Jesse and I went to high school together. I think you met my siblings? The Littles." Mercedes tilts her head and regards Mischa with a questioning look. Mischa chuckles and nods. "Different fathers."

Now Mercedes nods. "Old classmates," she repeats warily. She turns to me and raises a brow. It's scary how calm she is, even though she believes she's caught me engaging in something inappropriate for someone in a relationship. "You've never mentioned the Littles' older sister."

Mischa notices and smiles. "He and my boyfriend were best friends. Trey?"

"You're *Trey's* girlfriend?" Skepticism is heavy in Mercedes' voice. Mischa notices Mercedes isn't buying her bullshit. She grins, never breaking her cool stance against my car.

"Okay, it's either that or I'm Jesse's crazy ex-fling who has spent the last four years in an insane asylum."

Mercedes recoils, and her frown deepens. "That doesn't sound any better."

Mischa laughs, and the smile she gives Mercedes differs from any of the others. It's soft. It's genuine. "Either way, you have nothing to worry about. I was just congratulating Jesse on graduating. You too. I've heard a lot about you from my Littles. You two look good together."

I can see pieces of Mercedes' guard dropping, and she returns a small smile. "Thanks." She turns to me and nods toward the car. I unlock it and reach across the seat to grab her clutch.

"You need a ride?" I ask her, looking down at her calm expression.

She shakes her head. "My parents are waiting for me. I'll see you tomorrow." I nod and instinctually bend down to kiss her on the lips. Mischa is only about three feet away, but kissing Mercedes goodbye has become a routine as natural as breathing.

Mercedes looks over at Mischa and gives a short wave. "Nice meeting you, Mischa." And then she walks away. This is the Mercedes way. No jealousy when she sees me talking to girls at parties or if someone is trying to flirt with me in the quad. If I'm going to cheat on her, then she'll deal with it accordingly. Mercedes' world is forever moving forward, with or without you. That is my favorite thing about her.

When Mercedes is safely on the other side of the parking lot where I know her family is waiting, I turn back to Mischa. She's smirking at me. Not mockingly, but like she's impressed.

"I like her," she tells me.

"Yeah, me too."

"Good." That genuine smile returns and with it, the arrow in my chest.

"Is that why you didn't want to come? Because you heard about Mercedes?"

She doesn't break our eye contact. "Yes, but not for the reason you think."

Mischa pushes away from the GTO and takes the few steps to close the distance between us. She looks up at me, inches from my face, and I can't help but lean in closer. She's so close that I can smell the mint on her breath from the gum she must have been chewing. I can smell her flowery perfume in the wind. I feel droplets of rain tapping on my hands that are straight at my side, but I don't move away from her because I know that Mischa Lawrence is about to kiss me. Mercedes could very well drive past us at any moment, and I don't care, because for as much as I've enjoyed the life I've been building with her, I've missed the feel of Mischa's lips more. As much as I've tried to deny myself thoughts of Mischa, they've never ceased. I try to ration with myself that my first love as a seventeen-year-old kid isn't worth consuming my every waking thought, but it does. She does.

But Mischa doesn't kiss me. She smiles softly and then reaches up and flicks at my tassel. "Thank you, Jesse Alford."

"For what?" My question comes out breathy because if Mischa isn't going to kiss me, I'm going to kiss her. The rain is picking up, but I don't care. A car honks in the distance, but it's not Mercedes.

Mischa can tell I want to kiss her. She bites her bottom lip and looks all over my face, examining the matured features before gazing into my eyes again. Her expression holds so much. Like the dark storm clouds above us, about to burst with emotions. Pity, sadness, happiness, longing.

Love.

I see it there in her dark brown irises.

She cradles my face and runs the pad of her thumb over my cheek. Her touch electrifies me. Floods me with so many memories and feelings that I'm slowly realizing I can never feel again. Because she doesn't want this. She no longer wants *us*. She doesn't even have to say it.

"For making me feel."

Those are her last words to me.

She turns away and walks to the SUV parked a few yards away with her mom and siblings waiting inside.

The rain is beating down heavily, so I get inside the GTO. I don't turn on the engine. I just sit there as the SUV drives away.

And then I start to cry.

Chapter Fifty-One

In group therapy, they put a heavy emphasis on goal setting. I guess the logic is that if I have goals, something I'm looking forward to, then I'm less likely to want to die. The logic checks out, I guess. As a teenager, I had nothing to look forward to. I didn't care about formals, graduation, or college. I didn't even count down the hours until the weekend. I didn't care about birthdays. Nothing. I only had one goal.

But that's the thing. I didn't *want* to die. I *had* to. Everyone has to. I just had control over mine. I couldn't understand why no one understood that. I'd sit in those group and private sessions, explain the same shit over and over again, and all the therapist would say is, *"Mischa. It's not healthy to rush death. Your brain tells you that you have to die. But you do not have to die on any set day."*

And then there was the family session. My mom and the Littles. I watched as Frankie, of all people, sobbed on the leather couch across from me, snot and tears running down her painted face as she pleaded with me.

"I don't want you to die. I need you."

Maddie and Teddy had similar teary, snotty pleas, but Frankie's was my undoing. She'd never looked at me like that. Seeing her break down the way she did in our family session was like a punch to my gut. It was the first time I'd realized how my condition affected them. It had nothing to do with the embarrassment of having me as an older sister. It was about not having me in their lives. I started taking the meds and actually paying attention in sessions.

"What are your goals, Mischa?" my psychologist, Natalie, asked during talk therapy one day during my fourth year. I shrugged, and she flipped through her previous notes. She has a special leather-bound notebook for each patient. She's probably the easiest person to shop for during Secret Santa.

"College?"

I shook my head.

"Starting a business?"

I shook my head.

She looked down and read a few lines and then asked me, "What about seeing Jesse again?"

Not missing a beat, I shook my head.

"Why not? You two obviously had something special."

I turned and looked out of the window. There were a lot of dense trees around the facility, but from Natalie's office, you could see cars zooming by in the distance on the 101. "Jesse has moved on. He has a life now. Apparently, a girlfriend. He graduates in a few months. He's living his life far away from Grover."

"Exactly what you wanted him to do." Natalie smiled at me, but it was a leading smile.

I nodded. That's exactly what I wanted Jesse to do. The same way that I wasn't long for this world, Jesse was better than a life in Grover raising babies with Alyssa Slade, who would have had no idea how to appropriately style their children's hair. I know from experience.

I didn't want to talk about Jesse. I'd spent my entire confinement fighting thoughts of Jesse. Not just thoughts of him as a person, but of him as an instrument of feeling. The day Jesse and I parted ways, the numbness returned.

By the next private session, I'd had a list of goals for her, and she seemed impressed. So impressed that a month later my family was back for a family therapy session in which we discussed triggers upon my release in three weeks. I would go home fifteen months early.

Trigger number one was obvious. I could not live in Grover again. In order for me to return to my family, they would need to move. The best my mom could do was Stockton. She got a job and moved the Littles into an apartment that was smaller than the house in Grover. Teddy and Frankie would share a room, while Maddie bunked with Mom. I'd have the third bedroom to myself.

The first goal on my list was to be with my grandpa again. Natalie almost rescinded my withdrawal because by this time Grandpa had been gone for about eight months. I meant his ashes. I wanted to spread his ashes somewhere special.

It only took me a month of living in the apartment in Stockton to realize my second trigger.

My family.

There had been a shift in dynamics when I was sent to Washington. Upon my return, the power was attempting to shift back. Before I left, the Littles looked at me as a parental figure. When I told them to do something, they did it. When they needed permission to do something, I was the one they asked. When I left, our mom was forced to wake up and parent them. Teddy and Maddie, being the younger of the three, fell in line easily. Frankie, in all of her angsty teenage glory, rebelled.

After my release, I was able to bear witness to the daily shouting matches between Frankie and Mom. She'd lost all of Frankie's respect, and Frankie was growing out of control. My mom didn't know these children. And now that I was back, they were all looking for me to take over. The power struggle was becoming a negative dark hole. A vortex, much too large for the tiny Stockton apartment.

And then one random day in July, about two months after I did the responsible thing by leaving Jesse Alford in that Oklahoma parking lot, I got an email from the Lawrence family lawyer. My dad hadn't squandered his bequeathments on that stupid double-wide in Grover. He'd also left me a trust fund and his house in Monterey. *Our home.* There was also a payout from Grandpa's life insurance. I had an idea, but I needed someone to tell me it was the right one. I called Natalie and told her about my plan. There was no more special place to take my grandpa's ashes than the beach house we'd called home. Our happy place.

Natalie agreed that my current living situation wasn't ideal, but neither was being alone. So, we came up with a plan. We'd have weekly virtual sessions and stick to a strict lifestyle of healthy routines and rituals. I'd keep creating new goals, no matter how small. I just needed to keep something worth looking forward to.

"So, it's been almost a year since you moved to Monterey." Natalie's smile is genuine. I can feel her excitement through the screen of my iPad. "You've got a job. You've started your renovations. Learned to surf. Made some friends."

I don't think the old couple living next door count as *friends*, but whatever.

"What's this week's goal, Mischa?" Her smile is expectant now, always leading me.

I look past the screen, out my open kitchen windows at the ocean in the distance. Being back in my childhood home is refreshing. It's smaller than I remember, but it's comforting, like a hug. The wood creaks and the wind chimes on the neighbors' porch sing constantly, but it's so peaceful. Sometimes I can feel my dad and grandpa walking around. Sometimes I can see them. It doesn't scare me because there will never be a time that I won't see things that aren't there. I watch the waves roll onto the beach and then pull back.

"I'm going to take Grandpa to the Pacific. I think he's ready."

"Are *you* ready?" I think about Natalie's question for a moment and then nod. I don't tell her it doesn't matter, because he's sitting on my porch swing as we speak. He's not in his chair. He's the same Grandpa he was before my dad died. The ashes I'll be dumping in the tide after we hang up this call are just a physical part of him. Not his spirit.

My phone buzzes. It's a phone call from Jesse.

"Is that Jesse?" Natalie asks.

I nod, but I don't answer. I never do. Frankie gave him my number, and he's been calling and texting for the last year. I never answer the calls. I occasionally react with a thumbs-up to the texts. Only the ones that are big deals. The humble brags about grades during his first year of law school, or a birthday text. He had a one-sided conversation with me about how Mercedes suggested they take a break. Apparently, law school and medical school are too chaotic to maintain a relationship. Over the Christmas break, she moved out of the house in Norman so that she could be closer to the medical school campus in Oklahoma City. Jesse stayed in Norman, where the law school was. Feeling ever so manic that particular day, I liked the message. I regretted it when the calls started increasing.

"I'm proud of you, Mischa." Natalie's voice pulls my eyes back to the screen. The phone stops vibrating. "You've come a long way since the day we met five years ago. Almost a year of living alone. Minor incidents, but no emergencies. You're refilling your prescriptions. Indulging in hobbies. Maintaining healthy boundaries." She pauses and smiles in a way I'm not sure a psychologist is supposed to smile at her patient. "You're *living*, Mischa."

A lump forms in my throat, and I tear my eyes away from her.

"Well, I know you've got a big day ahead of you, so you know my last question. I'll need you to look me in the eye when you say it."

I roll my eyes before fixing them on her. "No new rituals. No countdowns."

She smiles, satisfied with my sarcasm. "We'll speak again next week."

We end the call, and I fix my eyes on the bookshelf in my living room. The gold trim on Grandpa's black urn glints in the noon sun. He's ready. Never one to enjoy the confines of small spaces, he's ready to get out of that metal prison.

My phone vibrates with a text. It's Jesse again. Two pictures. The first one is a screenshot of his grades. All As and Bs. The second picture is a screenshot of some kind of job offer email.

> **Jesse Alford**: Passed my first year of law school AND got the internship I was hoping for!

I smile and hold the message for a second until the menu pops up for a reaction emoji. The messages above this one are mostly about the internship and Jesse stressing before and after the interview. No responses from me, of course, except the thumbs up I gave when he asked me to wish him luck as he went into the interview. Our text thread is like a diary for him. He talks about everything, and never once asks me why I'm not responding.

I stand up from my place at the kitchen island and walk down the narrow hallway behind me that leads to the bedrooms. The house has two bedrooms and a study that was large enough to be my room when the three of us lived here. In my renovations, I painted the walls heather gray and put a desk and office chair in the room that I got from a secondhand store in town. Next week I'll tell Natalie about my acceptance to an online college. This room will be my study. For now, it's extra closet space. I dig through the bags of clothes at the bottom of the closet and pull out the bikini Frankie left here when the Littles came to stay for spring break. The bottoms won't make it past my thighs, but the top, while a little snug, fits well enough. I go into the bedroom where I keep most of my clothes and find a pair of cotton shorts to wear. I had a swimsuit but lost it to the sea one night when I went for a midnight swim and somehow ended up stripping the bathing suit off. I woke up naked in my bed the next morning, not really remembering how I ended up in there. I decided to keep that lapse in sanity to myself during our therapy session that week. Back in the living room, I grab Grandpa from the shelf and carry him through the sliding glass door and down the sandy path to the beach.

The gulls squawk above us, circling in the wind. The tide is high, so we head straight into the cold Pacific waters. Grandpa is tucked under my arms, and as I venture deeper into the water, I bring him around to my chest and hug him tight.

Not really him, but what is left of his physical essence. He'd spent the last years of his life confined to a chair in a cramped mobile home living room. He hated it. I knew that and I did the best I could. He deserves so much more than to spend his afterlife collecting dust on my bookshelf. This will be my gift to him. Freeing him in the endless ocean. More space and freedom than he could ever imagine.

I unscrew the lid of the urn and toss it aside. It floats away with the small waves. The breeze picks up the top layer of ashes and there's part of him in the wind now. Even more endless than the sea. The top of the ashes grows dark as speckles of water fall over it. At first, I think maybe it's sprinkling, but the clouds in the sky aren't producing rain.

I'm... crying.

"I—I wish I could have been more," I say to no one in particular. Tears stream down my face.

I can't tell myself that this isn't what Grandpa would have wanted. I can't find solace in the thought of my dad being proud of me, because I know Grandpa wanted more for me, and Dad has been dead for just as long as he'd been in my life. I lived eleven years with him, and now I've lived eleven years without him. Who knows what he would have thought about how I turned out?

Tears blur my vision as I pour the ashes around me. I pour his entire being into the ocean, and then I sit the urn in the water and watch as it floats away. The ashes disintegrate into the sea and before long, Grandpa is one with the ocean. I lay on my back and float. My short hair sticks to my head. Frankie begrudgingly cut it for me again when they visited in April.

"You're not in that place anymore. You can grow your hair out again. It was so long and pretty!"

'*And heavy,*' I'd thought, as she snipped away at the curls that had grown out to my shoulders in the year since I'd been home. The Littles didn't want to leave after their vacation was over. They wanted to live with me. I was their normal, not Mom. I was close to telling them yes, but then I remembered my boundaries. My goal.

I'm trying to be well. I can't get well if I'm caring for the Littles. I have to care for myself. I am not their mother.

If I'm going to get well, I don't want to be well for the Littles, or my mom, or Jesse, or anyone.

That's the realization that hits me as I float on my back and the sun peeks through the clouds and beams down on my exposed stomach. I could float like this for hours. Sometimes I do. Sometimes I float out here until the sun sets and the gulls have gone to bed, and my body is wrinkly and frozen. I don't feel it though. I don't feel the warmth of the sun or the cool of the night. I'm used to it.

In the distance, I hear my name being called. I sit up and turn toward the beach and see Mrs. Pratt, my elderly neighbor, waving me down. I swim and then waddle back to the shore and kick the seaweed off my feet as I walk toward the old woman.

"Mischa..." Her eyebrows are raised, and a mischievous smirk is playing on her lips. "There's a young man on your porch."

I frown and furrow my brow. Aside from the nurse at the clinic where I work as a receptionist, no men in town know where I live. He only knows because he gave me a ride home shortly after I started.

"Barney's vetting him. Handsome guy. Says he's an old friend of yours?" She wiggles her brows suggestively.

Shock overtakes my face, and then a scowl. He's no different from the seventeen-year-old boy who showed up at my house begging me to go to the formal with him. I head to the house to rescue my uninvited guest from the talkative clutches of Barney Pratt. Salty water drips down my forehead and I brush my wet hair back as I enter the sliding door and cross the living room. My iPad is still sitting up on the island as I pass through the kitchen and stand in front of my stained-glass front door. I can hear his laugh as he turns down Barney's invite to wait inside the Pratt house. My heartbeat quickens because I haven't seen him in a year, and I had planned to keep it that way.

"Oh, c'mon Barney. She should be answering the door any minute now. It was nice to meet you, young man," Mrs. Pratt calls out, and I can tell she's pulling her husband across the flowerbed that separates my driveway from theirs.

I take in a deep breath and wring the nerves out of my hands to no avail. I square my shoulders and roll my neck like I'm preparing for a fight. And then I open the door.

He looks different from the last time I saw him. Still handsome, but his facial hair is fuller, and his hair is shorter. No twists or braids. Just faded sides and short dark curls. He's wearing black joggers and a white T-shirt that hugs his toned biceps. He pulls the expensive-looking sunglasses away from his face, and his eyes roam down my wet body and up again with a smirk.

"You were at the beach? Is that why you didn't answer my calls?" His smile is playful, and my nerves ease up slightly.

"Why are you on my doorstep, Jesse Alford?" I ask him, resting my hip against the door jamb and crossing my arms over the wet bikini top.

He shrugs. "I couldn't take it anymore. I needed to see you."

I bite my lip to keep from smiling because no matter how annoying it should be that Jesse Alford is at my door unannounced, I'm happy to see him.

I step aside and tilt my head, signaling for him to come inside. He steps through the entrance, never taking his eyes off of me and never dropping the smirk. The front door opens into the small kitchen. There is no dining room, just a breakfast nook in the space between the kitchen and living room. My dad, Grandpa, and I used to eat breakfast there every morning. I'd take the middle while both men sat on the ends.

Jesse looks around the house. He's almost as tall as the seven-foot-ceilings, reminding me of my dad who used to move through the house with ease despite the fact that he was always inches away from hitting his head on the beams.

"Nice place. It looks... cozy," Jesse says as he looks around the living room.

An integral part of my therapy was building a space where I felt at peace. Since the day my father died and I was forced to leave his house, I'd never felt peace. I'd thought I'd found peace on that hidden cliff on Mt. Grover, but that was my illness and hormones talking. Returning to this place was a much-needed change, but it needed major updates. The home renovations became my hobby. You can learn basically anything on YouTube. I painted the walls, replaced the cabinets, and updated the bathrooms all by myself. Well, me and Barney Pratt when he felt like talking my ear off. There was no furniture, so I filled the space with mismatched pieces of furniture I'd found at a consignment shop in Sand City. The bedroom furniture came from Amazon. It took me two manic days to put it together. I only bought a spare bed for the second bedroom because the Littles would need it when they visited.

"You mean small and tacky?" I tease. I stay in the kitchen near the island, while Jesse examines the bookshelf.

"I mean cozy." He smiles at me and then touches the empty spot on the top shelf where Grandpa's ashes were once sitting. There's a picture of me and him next to the space. I'm sitting on his lap on the steps of the back porch.

"I know I shouldn't have popped up like this. Zoey told me about your boundaries and stuff. I just needed to see you." He says all of this while looking at the old photos and trinkets on the bookshelf. Mostly pictures I found in the garage of my dad and me. When he finishes his statement, he looks at me sheepishly. Zoey's going to throw a fit when she finds out I let Jesse in my house before her.

"I'd give you a hug, but I'm covered in ocean water and Grandpa's ashes." The sound of water dripping onto my red oak floors reminds me that I'm standing in my kitchen, soaked, in a bikini top that consists of two flimsy triangles, and the cotton shorts.

Jesse turns to me with a curious smile and then, as if something has clicked in his brain, he looks at the empty space where the urn once sat, and then out the back door at the ocean. He nods like he understands.

"Make yourself at home. I'm going to take a quick shower and change." His curious smile turns into a warm, appreciative one, and I have to force myself to turn down the hall and not rush across the room to him.

I scrub the salt water from my body and lather my hair with coconut shampoo and conditioner. Part of me is antsy to get back in there with him. He's here, unannounced, probably digging through my secrets.

Wait, what if he's steal—No, stop that, Mischa!

He's here with me. We're finally alone together. The last one doesn't count because I was so new to the world outside. Seeing Jesse was overwhelming then. I could barely handle hearing his name.

Now, nearly a year later, I'm able to process my feelings better. I can handle reliving old memories of Jesse. I can think about what we'd had without thinking about my mental state back then. I may not be fully healed—I'll never be fully healed—but I can talk to Jesse. I want to talk to Jesse.

Then there's the part of me that wants to believe that he's a hallucination. It's been an emotional day giving Grandpa to the ocean. It was the first time in months that I've cried, and then *poof!* Jesse appears. Maybe he's not real. That part of me is the one that wants to hide away in this shower until it runs cold. I won't feel the cold, but I'll know it when I start sneezing and shaking.

I shake the thoughts out of my head and rinse my hair and body. I spend ten minutes running my hands through my hair in the mirror and wondering if I should put makeup on. Maybe a little eyeliner? I've been sleeping better the past few weeks, so the bags under my eyes aren't as prominent as they can be. If Jesse's really out there, I want him to see me at my best. Right?

A thought hits me and I'm out of the bathroom and in the main bedroom in seconds, wrapped in only a towel. I look out the bedroom window, which faces the driveway. Just as I'd suspected. No GTO. Just a black Jeep.

He's either an illusion or an imposter. Of course, he is. Why would Jesse be here? He's got his pretty, smart, on-again-off-again girlfriend who is going to be a doctor. He's got his new life. I can't believe I fell for it.

I pull a white sleeveless dress over my head, messing up the neat curls that I just finger-styled with mousse for ten minutes. I reach under my pillow and grab the pocket knife. There are bigger knives in the kitchen, but that may tip him off if he's an imposter and not a hallucination.

I slowly make my way down the hall. When I peek around the corner, *"Jesse"* is sitting on my loveseat, flipping through the photo album that I keep on the coffee table. I found the album in the garage. Like everything else in there, it's filled with old pictures of me, my dad, and Grandpa. Jesse turns the page with a small smile spreading his lips.

"Where's your car?" I ask cautiously, fully rounding the corner.

Jesse startles and then fixes his smile on me. "I flew in and got a rental."

Oh. Duh.

I slide the knife down the back of my other couch as I stand next to it. "You staying in Monterey?"

Jesse closes the album and sits it back on the coffee table. "I'm staying at a hotel around the corner. The desk clerk has one leg."

"He has a prosthetic. He just doesn't wear it because he likes to mess with people." I wave off his wariness of Clyde, the manager at the Monterey Stay.

Jesse chuckles. "Only you would move to a city where the characters are that eccentric."

I shrug. "It's no Archerville, but it's home." This makes him laugh heartily. I laugh with him. He's not an imposter, but he very well could be a hallucination. "Thirsty? Hungry?"

He shakes his head but stands to follow me into the kitchen. I open the cabinet and pull out two glass cups. I open the fridge and pull out a pitcher of lemonade I made last night.

"Why are there only two of everything in your house?"

So, he *was* snooping around.

I smirk. He must have spotted the two cups, two bowls, two plates, and the two of everything in the fridge.

"It's part of my recovery. I can't keep more than two of most items in the house. Nothing that can be used as a countdown."

Jesse goes silent. I pour him a glass of lemonade, anyway. If he's not real, then eventually I'll realize that the juice is still in the cup after he'd drank it. If he is an imposter, I'll have his DNA on a glass for the cops to find after he kills me.

"How long are you in town for?" I ask him, sliding the glass across the island to him.

He takes the glass and slides it back and forth between his hands. "A couple of days. If everything went well... with us... I was going to stick around for a couple of days and then visit my parents for a few days before I had to head back. My internship starts on the sixteenth."

It's the tenth.

"So?" I ask, leaning back against the counter and sipping from my glass. Jesse quirks a brow, asking me to elaborate. I smirk. "Is it going well... with us?"

He smiles back and nods. "I got through the door. I'd say yes." He brings the cup to his lips and drinks the lemonade, and I decide that I am officially down to one cup. I'm not washing that one. Because if this is the real Jesse, I'll want to cherish that cup for eternity.

"Why are you here, Jesse?"

He sets the glass down. "I told you, I—"

"Yeah, '*you needed to see me,*' but why? Why do you need to see me? Why do you continue to text me and call me even though I never reply? Why haven't you moved on?" I fix him with a stern frown that lets him know I'm serious. He needs to understand that there's so much more to his life than me. I already had one plan ruined, I can't have the other one ruined too. Jesse deserves it all. He can't have that if he can't let me go.

His face is equally serious, and he stares at me from across the island. He stands from his leaning position.

"I got tired of only knowing you through the Littles," he says. "I watched Frankie's Instagram stories and posts for an entire week while they were here visiting you. I could see you guys on the beach, baking cookies, and riding bikes around town. You looked so... happy. And I was happy to see it, but it was all secondhand. I wanted to know firsthand that you were better. I guess... I felt... left out."

I don't respond. I just stare at him. An array of emotions are bubbling inside of me, but I have to focus on the negative ones. Those are the ones that will get Jesse out of Monterey and back to his new life.

"Are you telling me you haven't missed me as well?" The question sounds painful as it leaves his lips. "You haven't wondered how I'm doing?"

I scoff. "I know how you're doing, Jesse. You text me about a hundred times a month." Plus, like him, I have access to his life through the Littles.

He nods, wounded. "Would you like for me to stop?"

"I'm sure Mercedes would." I cross my arms and raise a brow at him.

He doesn't seem phased. "This has nothing to do with Mercedes. We're—"

"Taking a break," I mock him, making air quotes with my fingers. "Which means there's still a chance for your relationship to grow if you'd just get over your high school crush. We were kids, Jesse. It wasn't supposed to last."

My voice raises a few octaves with that last sentence. I'm not sure if it's my pitch or my words that cause Jesse to recoil.

"Mischa, I—" I don't let him finish. I slam my glass on the counter, causing lemonade to slosh out of the side. I storm down the adjacent hall into my bathroom. When I return, I slam the white contraption in my hand in front of Jesse.

"Do you know what this is, Jesse Alford?" He shrugs. I snort. "It's an automatic pill dispenser. It's timed so that it only dispenses the pills at a certain time. I can only open it to refill it, and when I don't refill it, it emails my doctors." I pull the plastic-wrapped sticks out of the pocket of my dress and toss them on the counter. "Those are piss tests to prove that I am taking the cocktail of mood stabilizers and antipsychotics that are housed inside that thing." I point to the dispenser. "I can't go to Sam's and buy in bulk, because keeping multiples of the same items resembles a countdown, like the marbles I kept when I was seventeen and planning to *kill myself*. I have a standing weekly meeting with my psychologist. My entire life revolves around hiding from triggers and sticking to these routines that mean nothing to me, and for the rest of my life, people will look at me like the suicidal girl." I pause and knit my brows together, a pleading look taking over my face. "So yeah, Jesse, this has everything to do with Mercedes. You can have a normal life with someone like Mercedes because this—" I tab my fingernail on the dispenser. "This isn't what you want."

Jesse just stares for a moment, and then he takes a deep breath and walks around the island to stand in front of me. I try to step away, but the kitchen counter behind me traps me. He places both hands on the side of my face and holds me firmly in the palm of his hand. He's forcing me to look him directly in the eye.

"None of that bothers me, Mischa. I've spent years mulling over every detail about us back then. I've fought with myself, trying to figure out why I couldn't get you out of my head. Trying to push you out and focus on other things. Other people. You say it wasn't supposed to last, but it did. It's lasting, because I love you, Mischa." Then he slowly brings his face down to mine. My eyes widen, but I don't fight him. The closer he comes to my face, the lower my eyes drop until finally they're closed.

And Jesse Alford is kissing me.

The last time Jesse Alford kissed me was on his eighteenth birthday as we slid across the base of the snow tubing hill. His lips feel just as soft as they did all those years ago, only now there's the tickle of his mustache and beard. There's more passion in this kiss because Jesse is a man now and I am a woman. We aren't kids sneaking around in the backseat of his car. We're like two lightning rods, bouncing love and need between each other.

I feel him deepening the kiss and I press against him. He lifts me up on the counter, never breaking the kiss. This Jesse Alford is neither an imposter nor a hallucination. I can tell now. This is sensory overload. I can taste the wavering sweetness from the lemonade on his tongue as it bullies mine. I can smell the cologne on his neck, rich and woody. I can see him. Even with my eyes closed, I can see him. I can see him at seventeen, soaked in the rain as he carried a wheezing Teddy into the hospital. I can see him smiling at me from across a tiny stall in the girls' bathroom, laughing silently as people gossiped about us. I can see him an hour ago, standing on my porch with a cocky smile. No, not cocky. Happy. He was happy. I can hear my own moans as I try to breathe and keep up with this kiss simultaneously. And I can...

I break the kiss, turning away and panting with my chin tucked against my shoulder. Jesse pulls his hands away from my waist and places them flat on the counter next to both of my thighs. For a few moments, there's only the sound of our deep breaths as we race to catch them, the gulls, and crashing waves out the open kitchen window. But no words. Not out loud, anyway.

I haven't been kissed in so long it should feel foreign, but suddenly, the snow hills feel like yesterday. So much has happened since the day I walked into class and was paired with Jesse and Neil on that stupid class project. Yet, for some reason, with Jesse, it all feels so blurry. All the parts except the ones with him. Those are clear as day, and just like him, I haven't been able to shake them.

Still, it's not fair to him.

"I won't let you throw your plans away just to be with me. You have an internship, and law school, and..." I won't say her name again. I won't bring her up again.

Jesse takes my chin between his thumb and bent index and lifts my face to meet his smile. A line of perfect white teeth. "I'm not asking you for that."

I frown and furrow my brow, confused.

"I'm not going to drop out of school, abandon my plan, and come here and disrupt your life," he tells me softly. "That's not what this is. I really just needed to see you again. To know that you were okay. I understand you have a life here now, and I have a life there, but that doesn't mean I don't still care about you. Like I said, I'll be in town for a few days, and then I'm going back, and if all I get are these few days with you, then I'm happy to have them. I can go back knowing that you're okay."

I exhale a breath I hadn't meant to hold and nod absently. He drops his hand and steps back. "Who knows, maybe you'll enjoy having me around and I can visit again. It's not like I don't know where you live now."

I don't fight the laugh that spills out of my throat. I hop off of the counter and adjust my dress. "How did you get my address? Frankie?" I ask, softly grabbing his hand as I walk past him and into the living room.

"Mr. Freeman," Jesse responds. Maurice Freeman, former sheriff of Grover, California. Now retired in Sacramento.

I open the sliding door, and Jesse follows me onto the back porch. There's a swing back here. The only piece of furniture that stayed with the house after we left it. It's my favorite part of the house. I sit out here, smoke, and reflect for hours, watching the waves roll in the distance.

I sit on the left side of the swing, and Jesse walks around and sits on the right. He doesn't hesitate to pull me into him, so I oblige. He runs circles on my bare shoulder, causing additional jolts of electricity to fire through my body.

My skin hasn't stopped tingling since Jesse grabbed my face and kissed me in the kitchen because for the first time in years, something is happening to me that only Jesse can make happen.

I'm feeling.

"This is nice. Like *really* nice." He sighs, tightening his embrace. "I can see how this place can be healing for you."

I laugh inwardly, but on the outside, I just nod. The swing gently moves back and forth.

When you're sick the way I am sick, it's not about healing. Healing implies you will one day be healed. That the symptoms will go away. No, this place isn't healing. It's masking.

I tremble as the sky darkens and a breeze sweeps through the porch. Jesse notices and looks down at me.

"Cold?"

I nod. "I'll grab a blanket." I stand and reach through the sliding door, grabbing the quilt that the Littles gifted Grandpa years ago for Christmas from the back of the loveseat. When I return, I motion for Jesse to sit up, and then I wrap the blanket around both of us.

Jesse looks to the left at the white circles lining the porch near the stairs. "Are those sand dollars?"

I'm tucking my feet under the cover and lying against him again. I glance down at the sand dollars and nod. "Maddie found one when they were here for vacation. It was perfectly round and intact. Every time I find a perfect one on the beach, I pick it up and bring it back for her."

"Cool," he says, pulling me into him. He's about to experience the beauty that is rain on Monterey Bay. The sound of rain hitting the sand and the waves on the beach.

Jesse presses his lips to my forehead, and I can feel the smile on his lips as he whispers. "I love you so much. I really hope you love me too."

For a long time, I thought seeing Jesse would be a trigger. How could my own mother be a trigger and not the boy at the heart of one of the darkest times in my illness? But Jesse isn't a trigger. He's a comfort. He doesn't heal. He doesn't mask. He just brings out the raw, unfiltered feelings that are trapped in my body, behind the voices and the hallucinations. He is the eye of the storm. The calm amidst the madness. He is peace.

My illness. That's what that judge, the lawyers, and Natalie call it. An illness. I call it a way of life.

My way of life. Because this will always be me.

I glance down at the pile of sixty-seven sand dollars. The beach is about one thousand feet away. The average perfect sand dollar is about four inches across.

It would take about three thousand perfectly round, unbroken sand dollars to line the path into the ocean on high tide. The thought makes me smile, but I don't revel in that right now. Instead, I bury my head deeper against his firm chest.

I do love him. So much so. But like all things, I tell myself not to get used to this. There's a chance it's only temporary.

So, I relish in the smell of the wet sand, the crashing of the waves on the beach, the taste of his kiss on my tongue, the beating of a heart I adore so very much, and the feeling of Jesse Alford's arms around me.

Author Notes

First, I want to say thank you!

Thank you to all the readers. Thank you to my family and friends who have supported me throughout this journey. Thank you to my amazing editor! It was our first time working together, and you made this experience extraordinary. Thank you for going above and beyond!

I started writing this story in 2017, around the same time I started writing my debut novel, *Please Excuse Our Confusion*. Much like its main male protagonist, it has grown so much since then. What started as a story about a young, bullied girl with a hidden mental disorder, evolved into a story about the boy who needed her more than she needed him. Jesse's character became more than a love interest or an instrument of normalcy to Mischa. I like to think that in the end, Jesse got way more out of his relationship with Mischa, than Mischa got from Jesse. The help Mischa needed was far beyond anything that Jesse could provide her. But with Mischa, Jesse began to find himself. When I decided to flesh out Jesse's character, I found myself writing this story more about him than Mischa. Mischa is, of course, the main character and holds a very special place in my life. Mischa will always be Mischa, and she will have to grow into the person who wants to live. Jesse was the true representation of navigating growth in this story. Together, I hope they can find a beautiful balance in this world.

I want to explain a few things about this story, just to give readers some clarity about the way the story was told, and some of the language used. Mischa was a very complex character. Not only is she dealing with a very real mental disorder, but she is also a sarcastic seventeen-year-old girl with a lot on her plate. Some of the verbiage that she used in the story was not politically correct and may have even teetered along the lines of offensive when talking about mental health disorders. But that's Mischa. I approached Mischa's character as the teenage girl she is, and not many girls with Mischa's personality would explain Schizoaffective Disorder in a textbook way.

My involvement in Mischa and Jesse's story is complete. What happens to them in the future is in their hands now, and I trust that they'll make the best decisions for their futures. In the end, I hope you take a few key things from this story: tolerance, empathy, and the importance of following your path.

I want to provide links and resources to give readers the facts about this disorder and other topics mentioned in the story. The links are great resources for those in crisis or supporting someone in crisis. There are tips on how to properly discuss the topics of suicide and mental health crises.

Thank you so much for taking this journey with me. I'll see you all on the next one!

Resources:

The 988 Lifeline is a 24-hour national network of local crisis centers that provides free and confidential emotional support to people in suicidal crisis or emotional distress in the United States via call or text.

Mayo Clinic – Schizoaffective Disorder

National Alliance on Mental Health (NAMI.org)

American Foundation For Suicide Prevention (afsp.org)

International Association for Suicide Prevention

References :

Quote in Chapter 39:

https://time.com/5042700/inside-new-american-way-of-war/

About the Author

Jasmine Cartwright was born in Oklahoma City. Her family moved to Sacramento, California after she was born, and stayed there during her early adolescent years before moving back to OKC. She is an advocate for mental health, prison reform, and marginalized voices. Combining her dedication to these social issues with her passion for fictional storytelling, Jasmine strives to create a safe space for the voiceless. An avid reader, she always found herself chasing *"that one story."* When she couldn't find that story, she decided she'd write it herself, and that passion turned into an ambition to become an author. Jasmine writes stories about young people who find happiness at the most inconvenient of times. She finds inspiration for her stories through traveling, reading, and personal experiences. She graduated from Southern New Hampshire University with a Bachelor of Arts in Creative Writing and English, specializing in Fiction Writing.

Also by Jasmine Cartwright

*Please Excuse Our Con-
fusion*